The Possessions of Doctor Forrest

Richard T. Kelly is a novelist, screenwriter, biographer and journalist. His debut novel *Crusaders* was published by Faber in 2008. He blogs at http://richard-t-kelly.blogspot.com

www.doctorforrest.co.uk

'Though 21st-century fiction has so far been very attentive to the vampire, there haven't been as many attempts to explore or update its literary parentage: the gloomy, diabolic, doppelganger-strewn terrain of Gothic literature that was so admired by Romantic poets and thrill-seeking readers in the late 18th and early 19th centuries. In his second novel, Richard T. Kelly does just that, paying homage to a genre that he clearly knows intimately and loves dearly.' *The Times*

'Take three respected Scottish doctors, now all living comfortably in suburban London. Make one of their number suddenly disappear and you have the beginnings of a very satisfying thriller . . . It's all marshalled with a real feel for pace, character and that gap where metafiction meets the gothic novel. *The Possessions of Doctor Forrest* is a big departure from the epic sweep of [Kelly's]

debit novel Crusaders, but is no less important in its desire to reshape the genre.' Paul Dale, *The List*

'Drags the gothic novel kicking and screaming into this new century replete with its own horrors and demons.' David Peace

'Not even David Cronenberg, master of body-shock horror, has come up anything as chilling as the tale that unfolds in *The Possessions of Doctor Forrest*. Mr Hyde suddenly seems a quaint and pleasant companion.' Kevin MacDonald

'Kelly doesn't rely on a twist or a stagey reveal, but rather lets his central plot device seep slowly to the surface so that the reader has the pleasure of gradually gathering the story's nasty truths. The author has also adeptly incorporated modern horrors that might well have intrigued Stevenson, Hogg or Bram Stoker: plastic surgery, celebrity rehab, body dysmorphia, psychiatric manipulations. The world he creates is vivid and seductive . . .' *Scotland on Sunday*

'I found it gripping and most unusual. It's fiendishly clever in the way it keeps the reader guessing . . . and it kept me intrigued until the end. It combines the mystery element of a good detective novel with the creepiness of a horror story. And as an added bonus, the author writes good prose: colloquial and vivid.' Charles Palliser, author of *The Quincunx*

'Overreaching scientists whose morals lag behind their professional abilities are as much a staple of gothic horror as asylums, vampirish beauties, graveyards, doppelgängers and dead people who refuse to lie down. *The Possessions of Doctor Forrest* features all of the above and more . . . Richard T. Kelly has put his own original stamp on the genre.' Louise Welsh, *Financial Times*

RICHARD T. KELLY

The Possessions *of* Doctor Forrest

{ *A Novel* }

faber and faber

First published in 2011
by Faber and Faber Limited
Bloomsbury House
74–77 Great Russell Street
London WC1B 3DA
This paperback edition first published in 2011

Typeset by Faber and Faber Limited
Printed and bound by CPI Group (UK) Ltd, Croydon, CR0 4YY

The right of Richard T. Kelly to be identified as author of this work
has been asserted in accordance with Section 77 of the Copyright,
Designs and Patents Act 1988

A CIP record for this book
is available from the British Library

ISBN 978–0–571–24155–2

2 4 6 8 10 9 7 5 3 1

To my dearest
Rachel, Cordelia, Lucy

Wheresoever the hour-glasse is set up and time fixed, unthinkable yet measured time and a fixed end, there we are in the field, there we are in clover . . . Therewith a man can live at rack and manger like a lord and astonish the world as a great nigromancer with much divel's work . . . How will such an one come to think about the point in time when it is become time to give heed to the end! Only the end is ours, at the end he is ours . . .

THOMAS MANN, *Doctor Faustus*
(trans. H. T. Lowe-Porter)

We are going to be reincarnated. Whether we know what our reincarnation will be, I doubt. I expect it will be full of surprises, most unforeseen. Some, given our vanity, are likely to seem outrageously warped.

NORMAN MAILER, *On God*

Contents

IV: THE CONFESSION OF DOCTOR FORREST

311

I

Dr Lochran's Journal
Uneasy dreams

August 22nd

Last night a dead man came to call on me – a friend, thank God, though to my shame I let our friendship fall away in the years before he died. For my defence it had got that we met, even spoke, so very seldom. Everyday life interposed itself, bedevilling every arrangement, thwarting our best intentions – in the usual way of things. Still, for all my regret I can't say I was glad to see my old friend now, risen from the tomb like Lazarus.

Hearing the rap of our old brass surgery-knocker I went down and opened the front door. There stood Edmond, tall and fair-haired and foursquare as was. But this time no customary crushing handshake, no *'Ah, Grey, old boy!'* He was silent, smiling faintly and strangely, waiting for me to bid him over my threshold, which, of course, I did.

On closer inspection he didn't look so different, save for a certain lunar whiteness to his corneas, glinting in the half-light of our living room. He lowered himself into the grasp of Livy's beloved baggy blue sofa. I fetched us the humidor and a dram of the good Glenlivet, which he ignored. He asked after 'Olivia' and Cal. I responded politely, asked likewise of Anna and Peter – for all that I knew the truth, and that these poor exchanges were just as flat as those we would rush through in the desultory late years of our friendship.

It was enough to set me thinking back, pondering how much Ed and I ever really had in common beyond our vocation in surgery. A love of good sirloin, certainly. Our summer places in Dorset, barely a mile apart. And Lions rugby, I suppose, though Ed always professed a pseudo-plebeian fondness for football. In the main, though, he was a man for The Arts; and though I'm no philistine, I can't be doing with high-flown chitter. But as he sat there before me, sphinx-like and unnerving, I suddenly remembered that stormy etching of Livy's he always admired, gilt-framed at the left of the rear reception fireplace. So I glanced back over my shoulder to check on its dependable presence, and, of course, something wholly other hung in its place. Then we were talking about some unfathomable business in which he believed I could be of help to him – some will or matter of probate, the setting of his worldly affairs in order. It all began to seem so sad and fruitless that I felt a catch in my throat.

'But Edmond,' I uttered finally, 'you died already . . .' Spoken like a child, or some tipsy oaf at a party – a long way short of my best bedside manner, at any rate.

Ed merely smiled as if in pity. 'Grey, old boy, that never happened. We don't die. Not us.'

All of a sudden he held a pack of cards in his hand, offered to 'tell my fortune'. I'd no truck with that. It ended up that we walked outdoors awhile, in the general direction of the Heath. But one minute he was at my side and then he was gone, then I was elsewhere entirely – in the

4

usual asinine manner of dreams. The setting dissolved to the first hospital I ever worked, that grim old hole in Norwich, then to some dank and moss-grown shed in dense woodland . . . On waking from this mire of sinister nonsense I wasted no time in getting dressed and downstairs, the kettle on and the day's graft begun. Still, I confess, I found myself brooding about Edmond for much of the morning.

To this day I shudder to think of how cruel and basically bloody *avoidable* was his death. He drowned on holiday in the Florida Keys, trying to rescue Peter, then only nine years old, in waters that had by all accounts turned very suddenly turbulent. The lad was never a strong swimmer but he'd bobbed and breasted a fair way out to sea alone, only to crack his head on a buoy. Edmond saw it too late. Being plenty robust he swam out swift as Leander, managed to get an arm round Peter and make some headway against the blasted current – but only so far, the shore still a way off, and so he headed for the tip of a rocky peninsula, where he managed to push and shove Peter up and onto a low ledge. By now, though, Ed hadn't the strength left to propel himself out of the water, for the waves were fairly pounding on him. Worse, the rocks were coated with razor-sharp shells that slashed his fingers wherever he tried to grab hold. The panic, on top of the physical exertion, must have been catastrophic to his already thickened coronary arteries. With unsettling ease I can imagine myself in Edmond's place, assuming his plight – the shortening breaths, the numbing fingers, the fearful strain on the left ventricle.

At the funeral Peter, quite desolate, told me that he had watched from his ledge on the rocks, groggily semi-conscious, as his father's grip loosened by a little and a little, and then Edmond toppled back and the water roiled over his head.

I do wonder – if Ed's rescue effort had failed utterly, and Peter instead had been carried out to sea – could he possibly have lived on with the loss of his child? I doubt it. And had he a choice, even a devil's choice like that, he would have chosen it to be as it played out. As for Anna – Edmond would have known she would just carry on, because she was a coper and a stoic, and in time she would find some other man to be with her for the rest of her days.

But what nags at me now is that I just don't know if she ever did. Or what became of Peter. We simply drifted out of touch, another form of death. This is what 'Time the Enemy' will do to us, if we allow it.

August 23rd

Evidently I'm not myself at the moment, my head in an unhealthy place. For sure I never dreamt I'd turn into a hopeless scribbler. I'm well aware the whole anxious business of Robert has been preying on me, but I can't stick all the blame for this disquiet onto poor, dear Doctor Forrest – whatever may have befallen him, or wherever the hell he's taken himself.

The fact is, I've had other bad dreams lately, all much as foul as each other. One night just over a week ago –

PART I
ABSENT FRIENDS

Am I hearing myself think? Or is she whispering to me? Sometimes I can see her lips part, feel her breath at my ear, the poison start to pour. Sometimes not. Regardless, her voice is always in my headspace, probing and clinging like a tongue, insistent, irresistible.

Her voice is not mine. I ought to know the difference. And yet hers has grown so entwined with my own. We're alike now in so many ways — like-minded, she and I, this dreadful intimacy of ours. I suppose I have been waiting, all my life, to be so very close to a woman. From no desire of my own, never, but only because 'telepathy', in some form, is what women claimed to want from me — claimed incessantly. They should have been more careful.

So, now, it's her. My sister, my anima. She stands before the darkling surface of the cheval glass, reflective, as though she were made of the mirror. She awaits my decision, as if she didn't know, as if she didn't infest every thought in my mind.

And he, my enemy — the apex of the triangle we form in this room — he's looking from her to me — perplexedly, some veil of concern on his face. If he had a notion of what might be about to befall him, that concern would be unfeigned and very urgent.

His lips are moving, for sure. 'Robert,' *he's saying*, 'this is all wrong, man . . .' *That mask of sympathy he's wearing, is* it for me? He's no friend of mine. And yet, is there still time enough for me to show him some kindness?

For this feeling now rising up my spine and over my skin like some questing rat, some necrotising rot, is richly appalling but replete and commanding as supreme music – foul, monstrous, a heavy-headed beast swaying and stirring to its senses, gestated from my gut or my groin or cracked out of my head like a malformed god-foetus, the Evil infant, a spider-baby hatched from a skull, majestically fat with venom and filth.

And what am I but the worm, the vassal, the guilty man? I will obey all directives. She to whom power is given, I must rise and do her bidding. There is a pulse behind the din in my head, a chime, diamond-hard, vehement, telling me Do It. Take it. Take what you need. From him. 'You are not permitted to dissect living subjects. Not yet . . .' *Doc Laidlaw's old jest in Anatomy lab, back when we were boys. Now we are grown, for all it was worth.*

And this man before me, I am going to cut in half – be the cut from nave to chaps or ear to ear, I can't yet say. But I do know it now, his fate is sealed – his fate, and mine. I cross the threshold, I step inside, and I fall.

the night before Robert's disappearance, an omen? – I lay awake for what must have been an hour, steeped in the kind of unease that comes with all the nocturnal bangs and groans of a big old house. I started listening to the bedside clock tock-tocking, ever louder – before it hit me that we have no such clock anywhere in the room. On cue, the tocking mutated by degrees into a sound like a humanoid growl, first guttural, then full-throated. I lay there, paralysed by alarm, deaf in one ear on the side where Livy slept soundly, that hellish roar building in the other. Then I felt hot breath on my face, though I didn't dare turn my head toward The Presence. *This is insanity*, I thought, as calm as you like. And yet, in the murk of the dream-state it is blasts of lucidity like this that get one through and out the other side.

What should be my remedy, short of a heavy self-prescription of diazepam? Were I to confide in Steven, most eminent headshrinker of my acquaintance, then the good Doctor Hartford would no doubt tell me all this is highly meaningful – the subconscious daemon wreaking mischief at a time when it knows me to be vulnerable, beginning to worry about the bitter end; hopeful, per-haps, that there might yet be some light – soupily warm, unearthly and beckoning – at the end of the tunnel. All that rot.

No, there is no return to this life, nothing and no one ever comes back. And I've yet to stoop so low as to wish the facts were otherwise, even though I watched my mother be quite incapacitated over my father's cof-fin, refusing to let go for those impossibly tough final moments. Maybe I'll be no different if such a day dawns for me. More likely Livy will suffer it first. Maybe sooner than I think. On these darkening mornings, after the ever more uncomfortable ablutions, scraping at my face before the smeared bathroom mirror . . . I do, as they say, see the old man staring back at me.

But, the End is the End, it must be faced, and in doing so we're reminded to be serious and useful and loving to one another. To be brave, above all. What have I said myself to so many small patients and agonised parents, as kindly as I could manage? *'This is hard for you, I know, but I'm afraid you'll have to play this hand.'* I was only imitating old George Garrison, my and Robert's first surgical mentor. I heard his routine so many times: he was just so bloody good at telling people they were going to die. Not for him the semi-autistic, jargon-infested stammering of lesser men in white coats. Garrison made the unlucky ones in his care figure out their fate for themselves: *'Now, you know what we've been doing here, with your treatment. Why do you think we did that? Yes, that's right. And have you felt any better? No? A little worse? I see. So, what conclusion do you draw . . . ?'*

In some profound way George's patients were always grateful for that sense of self-awareness he gifted them. The fact is, old Garrison could make anyone in the room see that it was all basically out of their hands – when your number comes up then *sayonara* cruel world.

I suppose, if I'm honest, I rehearse these familiar matters in my head as some unsteady bulwark against the fear that Robert is really gone – dead – maybe even by his own hand. Christ alive, is that possible? I've been fighting down the thought ever since I got the news. But the plain facts persist. Robert was last seen around 7pm on August 14th, leaving his clinic for the day a shade later than customary. As I told the young sergeant Goddard, I'd spoken to Robert on the phone the night before: nothing out of the ordinary, we shared some shop talk (even mused a little – I shiver to think of it now – about that wee missing girl who's been all over the news). The next morning he failed to show for a 10am appointment, noon went by, and his loyal secretary Fiona raised the alarm – one that resounds to this day, since there's still no trace of him. I have, as they say, begun to dread the phone, and each time it rings I brace myself mentally: *'Why did you let yourself laugh just then? Now you're about to be told something terrible . . .'*

And yet, still, the spirit revolts: I just won't accept the doomsday scenario. No, it's Robert I expect to see on my doorstep, spreading himself rangily across the blue sofa, eyes shining again after all his recent miseries, tumbler of Glenlivet raised in hand.

'Rab,' – I might say – since no one else gets away with calling him that – *'Rab, thank God you're alive, man.'*

'Ach Grey,' – he might reply – *'you fool, you clod, you fucking eejit. We don't die, not us. And "God" has nothing to do with it.'*

To a degree, I do accept – Robert had been gone from us awhile, in spirit if not in body, his mood of late so dark and erratic. Evidently for those who made his acquaintance in the last five months – the months since Malena

9

walked out on him – he left a poor impression. These late-comers got no sense of his usual liveliness, the high gleam around his presence, the assurance with which Rab could lead you off on a scurrilous evening's entertainment.

It's possible my diehard friendship with such a man struck onlookers as just as much of a mystery. Robert and I were always an odd match, on paper: me, I accept, the guy you'd go to for an onerous favour, the fellow you would trust with your wife; Robert defined by his fashionable lateness, his promiscuous openness to any better offer – not to speak of his doctorate in sexual predation, that quite raptor-like pursuit of any female who took his fancy, whatever her marital status. Edmond could never abide Robert for one minute, may even have thought less of me by association – a supposedly sound paediatric surgeon consorting with this disreputably flashy nip 'n' tuck merchant. (Steven too, of course, has had these 'issues' with Rab down the years.)

Not that I cared, or care now. Our life's great friendships are dropped on us in strange little ways but – I really do believe – for providential reasons. We are meant to encounter our opposites in life and be changed by them – transformed, in some manner. For Robert and me – from Kilmuir College through medical school to our professional practices – our lives have been bonded by links of steel, our heartaches and triumphs and secrets all shared. I love him, I always have – even when he's disappointed me, let me and himself down. This is a moral requisite of any true love, is it not? And in the manner of the Irish I am resigned to the belief that our dearest friends will, as a matter of course, be the death of us.

In loving Robert, though, I have to ask myself if I correctly diagnosed the gravity of his recent decline, or the causes of it. Was he authentically depressed, sufficiently sick of life to want death? He'd begun taking those bloody pills, yes, yet somehow – daft of me – I'd ranked it more of a piece with his long, colourful history of pharmaceutical 'experiments'. Of course I'd noticed in him that share of midlife gloom to which we're all now prey, but I daresay it weighed on him – the greying of his coal-black hair, that turn to 'cragginess' in his looks. He spoke gloomily of 'the gravity of time', such that for his 45th birthday back in April I tried to make light by gifting him a walking stick, a handsome piece of good birch with a silver-plated crutch handle – I have one myself, and I felt sure Rab would accept his membership of the Old Boys Club with a broad grin. But you know at once when you've done the wrong thing . . . Within a half-hour we'd mended fences sufficiently to be sipping champagne on the lawn outside his place, but when I expressed the simple wish that he achieve all he hoped for in the coming year, he emitted a sour sort of a laugh.

'The road ahead's got a bleak look, my friend.'

'Ach c'mon,' I chided. 'There's plenty hunger in you yet.'

'Hunger? Oh aye. I'm ravenous. But it's just not satiable, doctor. It's starting to cause me pain . . .' His mouth, I saw, had set in a hard line and in the next instant he tossed his champagne flute into the air like so much rubbish. It landed on the plush grass without a crack; the gesture nonetheless seemed one of worrying indifference.

He had been sickening of his work a while, I know. For a man who not unreasonably rated himself a sort of artist, he clearly found it harder and harder to live with his flighty clientele, forever pestering him with their shopping list of wants, irrespective of the physical materials at their disposal – their body type, weight, height, colouring – even just the basic matter of how their bloody nose ought to look right bang in the middle of their face ('Could you move it a tad to the left . . . ?') Robert had grown to find all that profoundly vacuous, rightly so.

Then there is his 'bad influence' of recent weeks, that Vukovara woman, *la signora nera* . . . But I just can't believe such a shady female truly got hooks into Rab. He saw through her, I'm sure – she was off the scene.

So, I try to relive his and my last encounters, scour our small talk for tiny signs. But one knows, too, in one's heart, that this is forlorn detective work. For starters, if a man commits suicide who would ever really know why? There are ostensible 'reasons', sure, but none get to the nub. Like the wise chap said, 'The worm is in man's heart.'

Malena's leaving him for Killian counts the heaviest, of course. I saw Rab distinctly red-eyed, cut up – a state in which I'd never seen him previous – on the day after Malena and her possessions were finally shifted out of his place in Artemis Park. But there was nothing he could do to stop that: on one level he had plain ceased to deserve her. Malena told me herself she'd come to feel Robert was 'no longer on the side of life'. The remark had struck me as curious, if clearly damning: mentally I filed it along with what I took to be her frustrated wish to start a family. Rab knew Malena would want children, she a full fifteen years younger than him. And yet he persisted in wanting to bring other things than kids into this world. So, in the space he left her . . . ? Malena is herself an artist, drawn to fellow connoisseurs. Without doubt she was smitten first by Robert's aesthetic genius as a surgeon. But her tastes were wide. At a certain point another model caught her eye, and she his, and that was the end of that.

A huge blow, then, to Robert's heart. As to make a man suicidal? I don't discount it, but still I can't believe it. For, much as I hate the thought, he had got himself back in the hunt, was consorting again with women, however second-rate and disreputable. The Vukovara creature . . . My God, I find that just to think of her is to want her expelled from my mind without delay. But the police ought to be made aware of her, I know it – I really must raise the matter.

Certainly I've shared every other scrap of data in my possession with the appointed officer, young Goddard's superior DI Hagen. Thus far he and I have conferred only by phone, and he's a usefully bullshit-free talker, his habitual stress on the third syllable ('fasci*na*ting') betraying him for Northumbrian, i.e. just the wrong side of the border. Naturally I have lobbied as far as I'm able for Robert's to be rated a fully-fledged Missing Persons investigation. Hagen is not unsympathetic, but I know, as he tells me, that hundreds of people vanish every week, most by choice, not wishing to be found, only a fraction of them victims of crime. Until they have significant evidence of wrongdoing they'll not be embarking on a manhunt. For all that, Hagen's knowing tone sometimes shades into offence. 'Dr Forrest's a grown man,' he told me at one point. 'If he fancied buggering off, that would be his own business. Even with some other bugger's wife. Wouldn't be our place to judge – he's got a right to privacy.'

It occurred to me then that I might have said too much to Hagen of Robert's 'Don Juan' side. Still, I pressed him to say if it was indeed the official view that Robert had engineered his own disappearance. Again the detective disconcerted me: 'I've observed, Doctor, that there's many a man takes a fancy to just . . . walking out, on a life that's not fulfilling him, wanting to be new again under a bigger sky. Have you never felt that? I know I have. I'm maybe just not crafty enough. And, y'know, I'd miss the wife . . .'

'Crafty' indeed. The police opinion, then, is of a man who might just have a gift for disappearing. I can't persuade them of the danger that someone might have disappeared him. True, I don't myself accept that Robert had any enemies of sufficient bitterness, for all that he owes money to more than a few people, and has dallied with the wives of some fairly hard-nosed husbands. That nocturnal side of his life, those dubious enthusiasms, had earned him some shadowy acquaintances, yes. But all that carry-on had been fading away the closer he got to 50. The motiveless crime, though, the meaningless act of violence – that some thug could have stabbed him in the face for his wallet, kicked his body into a ditch – *that* I can imagine, in this feral bloody London. But if so, then where's the body? Hagen is most intractable on this point: 'It's not hard to vanish in this world, doctor, so long as you keep breathing. Far, far harder if you die. Because a corpse is a big thing to get shot of . . .' Yes, there would be a body by now: only the wretched of the earth can be made to vanish without trace. Whereas a man of Robert's status – such a man is noticed, always.

There's one more unhappy possibility, I suppose – that I just never really knew or understood the sort of man my friend was, and so cannot conceive now of some venal act he's gone and done. Even were that the case, would Rab have taken off without any kind of goodbye? And had his actions been so much beyond the pale, would I then have turned my back on him? Or, however guiltily, allowed him the same forgiveness of old?

No – when I call all this to mind I feel awfully certain something wrong has happened *to* Robert, something very wrong. As I mull it over, the truth lies out there, somewhere, cold and comfortless as old Craigleith sandstone. I am assured I can be 'useful' to the police by making enquiries of my own, staying in touch with Hagen and Goddard should I uncover anything new. Well, they will find me diligent on this score.

Oh Jesus, Robert, where are you, son? Where the hell have you taken yourself? Go your own way if you have to, but don't leave us lost in the dark.

DI Hagen's Notes
A man of night and day

FORREST, Robert Kyle ('Rab'), Dr
MisPer ref. # 187–2059 (Amber Alert)

Reviewing actions to date in the case of Dr Forrest, this does strike me as one of those unhappily nagging Medium-Risk MisPers.

There are several decent reasons why the man might have taken off; I don't believe he's fallen down a hole, or done himself a mischief. But small things perplex me, there's a hollow in every scenario I build. He packed no bag, indeed I can't see that he took anything with him he could use, beyond keys, wallet, phone – and he's not used them, has made no calls, not withdrawn from his bank or put down his credit cards. On the evidence of our paper-chase Dr Forrest doesn't seem to be doing any of the things he surely would be doing if he was alive.

On the upside we have good info: credit to DS Goddard of the MisPer Unit. Forrest wasn't seen at his apartment building (Artemis Park in Finchley) on the night of August 14, but his car was. Evidently he drove himself home, and we assume the clothes on his back are still those he wore for work that day – black suit, white shirt, scarlet tie. The searches of both apartment and workplace ('The Forrest Clinic', St John's Wood) were impeccable, Dr Forrest's toothbrush was bristling with DNA, two laptop computers were taken in but have offered nothing of interest.

The man's mental state? His long-time PA Ms Fiona Challenor (who reported him missing) worried to Goddard of his recent 'distractedness'. He was taking the strong antidepressant Remeron, prescribed by his close friend Steven Hartford, albeit at low dosage – Hartford hadn't believed he was really in a pit. But evidently he was still glum over the end of a five-year relationship with Ms Malena Absalonsen, since when he's been alone. (Though Ms Challenor, a keen-eyed observer of her boss – also an ex-girlfriend, I would guess – usefully alerted us to a recent dalliance Forrest had with one of his patients, who, interestingly, is currently lodging at the private psychiatric clinic in Berkshire where Dr Hartford is director.)

This Dr Grey Lochran, a surgical consultant in paediatrics, is clearly Forrest's most bosom friend-confidant: he'll be our point of contact and first to be informed as and when the subject is located. Lochran is also the executor of the will: all assets and possessions of Dr Forrest pass to him on death. But as Lochran tells it, this arrangement only expresses Forrest's wish that his godson, Lochran's teenaged son Calder, be the ultimate inheritor.

In any case there'll be nothing to inherit until we have a death certificate. And still there mightn't be much, from what I understand of Forrest's finances – his accumulation of money troubles and legal difficulties, both current and pending.

Lochran painted me an interesting portrait of his friend: 'self-made' insofar as he was adopted young by an uncle and aunt after the death of his parents in a drink-driving smash-up. (The father, Jack, a publican turned slum landlord/'property developer', was considered responsible.) Lochran and Forrest, also Hartford, all met as pupils at Kilmuir school ('the Eton of Scotland') outside Edinburgh, then went on to medical school together before separating to specialise. Originally Forrest's surgical focus was disfigurement and reconstruction, but gradually he swung toward aesthetics, cosmetics. (cf. Lochran: *'Robert liked beautiful things, he wanted to make things beautiful.'*) In his late thirties he left the NHS for pure private practice, founded his own surgical 'boutique' offering all the beauty procedures and so-called non-invasive treatments. The work paid handsomely, though Lochran believes his friend was disillusioned (*'I think it occurred to him he'd rather sold his soul.'*) And not just the practice in itself but Forrest's own sense of what he ought to have done instead.

As Lochran described, Forrest was at one stage highly engrossed in the theory of full-face transplant for patients who had suffered especially terrible traumas or burns – the sort that would take a hundred grafts of skin/muscle just to give them anything remotely like a human face again. Dr Hartford told me Forrest hired him to do some 'profiling' of the sorts of victims who might be suitable, psychologically, for such an extreme procedure. Of course, if we lived in the realms of science fiction then all this might propose a notion of how a man could make himself vanish . . . The point for our purpose, though, is that Forrest had to bankroll all this pricy research from his own pocket, only to jack it all in for pressure of time and money, having come to the dispirited view that too many of his fellow professionals were too far advanced of him in the field.

Then two years ago he took out an eye-watering loan in order to buy out the investors in his Clinic, apparently wishing to be free of their interference. Not long after that, he was sued successfully by a patient claiming to have suffered pain and facial scarring from incompetent injections of collagen. The culprit wasn't Forrest, rather a woman he'd hired who turned out to be not so well trained as she'd presented herself; but Forrest carried the can. The judgement came down in the same week that Ms Absalonsen moved out of his apartment. Such misery could spill the wind from any man's sails.

This man does intrigue me, though, I admit. The photos we obtained show a fellow very presentable for his age, if somewhat saturnine in looks. Physically he was in decent shape though a habitual drinker, and partial to some soft drug use. 'A man of night and day' is how his friend Lochran describes him, albeit fondly, attributing this to what he calls 'a touch of the Jekyll-and-Hyde' inherent in the surgical profession. That is to say, the incredible rigour of the work produces a commensurate need for a private cutting-loose, what in Forrest's case Lochran quaintly calls 'carousing'. (Mr Hyde can take other forms too, I would say: Lochran, initially open and affable, can switch to a very stern and short-tempered force coming down the phone-line.)

And then . . . these are minor matters, but . . . Forrest's identifying marks are distinctive, suggestive of a 'colourful' youth. Lochran mentioned the scar on his chest, a laceration from some boyhood knife-fight. Both he and Ms Absalonsen spoke of the prominent tattoo on Forrest's upper right arm, acquired after some drunken cavort in his medical school years, depicting a great green snake coiled round the earth (the *uroboros*, as it's known in mythology). A further quirk: we found no private diaries or letters at Forrest's apartment, or among his hard drives, but on his writing desk was a French-language book about a Japanese writer, Mishima, who killed himself most gorily at much the same age Forrest is now. There were various pencil scribbles in the margin, but Forrest had underscored – by a precise slash of red – a line from the man's suicide note: *'La vie humaine est limitée, mais je voudrais vivre éternellement.'* That being, 'Human life is limited but I would like to live forever.' Clearly this Mishima went about the 'living forever' part in a queer way. But I daresay we ought to take Dr Forrest's distinctive and offbeat interests as offering some window into his state of mind.

3

Dr Lochran's Journal

Bad for the soul

August 25th

'Ghosts return gently at twilight . . .' Last night I had a
sad call from Robert's uncle Allan Steenson, whom I've
not seen – whom Robert hardly saw – since Kilmuir.
He must be 70-odd now, and he lost Jenny to cancer
five years ago: the most steadfast and God-fearing of
marriages torn asunder. They raised Robert together so
painstakingly, after the tragedy of his real parents. (Not
that Rab ever recognised old Allan as a father – I knew
when we were lads, the bitterness Rab felt over his dad's
boozy recklessness could never quite mask the sneaking
regard he had for the old bastard's 'maverick' character.)
Still, fatherhood was the duty Allan loyally discharged,
and continues to – hence the awful sadness of his falter-
ing voice asking me this and that about the 'investigation', me unable to say one damn thing of consequence
or comfort in respect of his lost middle-aged stepson.

This afternoon I took the family to Jon's for our annual
reunion of St Andrews Class of '83: a supposedly 'fun'
occasion I'd hoped might lift my mood. No spot finer
than Jon's epic roof terrace overlooking the Highgate end
of the Heath, and after this dank, dour, generally *dreich*
summer we were blessed with a crystal day of high sun.

Only by late afternoon could you feel in the air and the shadows that we're now slipping 'between seasons' – always a wistful feeling for me. Another summer fades, a finite number remain, this much achieved, that much unresolved.

The big difference this year, of course: Robert's absence. (Not to speak of Malena's.) But then I was much the closest to Robert. Today it seemed the company just didn't want to speak of him. And I suppose Robert had somewhat estranged himself from said company. Our ranks are depleted anyhow, what with Donald and Kate decamped to Boston, Duncan to Côte d'Ivoire. And poor Edmond, of course. I don't think I let the clouds hang over me, I impersonated my usual self, made conversation. But today lacked that good sociable grease, the easy shift into topics beyond the commonplace. Too much talk of minor ailments, far too much of fucking *golf*. It was Livy I felt for, for all that she managed gracefully.

We have hung together as a bunch, despite the dispersing tendency of the vocation; and, on the whole, we turned out as we expected. Character is destiny, yes? Didn't we know as late adolescents – at first sight in halls of residence – that Jon, with his ponytail and Black Sabbath tee, was earmarked for Pathology? (Today, still, he drew me over to his stack of Denon separates, tried to enthuse me about some dreadful hard-rock racket.) Susan – how soon we understood! – was too kind for her own good, so heading down the pipe marked 'Palliative Care'. And Tony, given his remote engineer-boffin air, his obsessive tinkering with car engines and Jon's hi-fis

– he had been chosen for Orthopaedics, destined to doggedly perfect his plates and screws even as the patient expired on the table. I've never asked but presumably they looked at me and thought, 'There's a big dependable oaf, probably good with kids, kind enough to cut them open carefully . . .'

Look at us now then: older, fatter, richer, with grey or balding heads and weary, worried laughs. More kids around us, too – more, and older. They spoil the day somewhat, with that recalcitrant teenage moodiness, studying the affluent oldsters from a distance, waiting for us to die so they can be free to do as they like, since they bloody well know it all already. I should have nipped that little tendency in the bud far earlier – bringing the kids. I should have laid down the bloody law. (Steven's twins Julian and Jacob, for instance, are as cheery as a broken toe, God bless their glum little faces.) But then I suppose I started it all off when I first brought Cal. What was I thinking . . . ?

Well, I was the first among us to sire; plus I reckoned me and the boy were pals; also that he made me look good. For Cal, though, these occasions were mainly a chance to hang out with his godfather Dr Forrest, to soak up that over-age bad-boy routine of Robert's. Once Cal started to 'pop round' to Rab's place for *mano a mano* soirées I somehow persuaded myself it was only a good *padrino* influence, however many times Cal traipsed home with his breath acrid from the smoky peat of Robert's malts. God knows what they talked about, if not the ins and outs of the automotive engine, or the ins and outs of young girls. But plenty at any rate.

Today, though, I felt rueful seeing Cal, sufficiently mature to join us 'properly', yet no longer wishing to be here. Of course I understand, in his own moody way he's upset about Robert. But when poor Steven, with avuncular fondness, addressed him as 'Young Calder', I thought Cal might punch him in the chops. It's not the Scot thing – Cal still affects an Edinburgh burr – but I suppose he rates 'Calder' a name fit only for a squirt in short trousers, not the gym-enhanced, slightly marked Lothario he now reckons himself – sandy-haired six-foot Flower of Scotland, man-mountain of the rugby pitch and tennis court. (Then again, well he might, based on the longing looks Susan's girl Jennifer kept shooting his way.)

One other thing riled me: the approach I had from this woman, Gerry McKissock's latest squeeze. I was taking my turn at the grill, butterflying the organic leg of lamb, and she admired my bold slices and deft editing of fat. Lara was her name, her curves loosely confined by a top one might wear to a dance class, her hair a bit too blonde, as if compensating for her white-wine-drinker's wrinkles and the tremor of sag at her jaw-line. After some meagre chit-chat she lunged in for the kill. *'So you're a friend of the great Robert Forrest? I hear amazing things about his clinic . . .'*

Yes, she was after a referral – one more wretch wanting a little 'work' done on herself. Quietly I had to explain the present circumstances. For some moments she swilled Sancerre round her glass as if chastened. Then, stunningly, she brightened, wanted to know if I too practised cosmetics? I told her a little of my expertise in treating anorectal malformation in newborns, and watched her interest wane.

'No, I never fancied the aesthetic stuff myself. It's technically easy, but bad for the soul – patient's and doctor's.'

That had her wincing into the sun. 'Gosh. You think?'

Steven was hovering nearby so I called him over, had him explain to this Lara what I meant by 'psychological dysmorphism'. He obliged gladly.

'It's when what a person sees of themselves when they look in the mirror is all hashed. Because they can't see themselves as they really are, or take any natural pride in it, so what's normal looks to them like a terrible aberration. That's a fundamental flaw in a person's character, no amount of "work" will cure it.'

So crestfallen was this lassie by now, I felt I had to give her some comfort, namely that Robert had always claimed 100 per cent patient satisfaction from one procedure: namely, reduction mammoplasty. 'A huge relief on the neck and shoulders, especially once you're past a certain age. No more nasty welts off them bra straps . . .' I glanced in the direction of Lara's bare, blemished shoulder. She pushed off shortly thereafter. I know, I know . . . . Unfriendly of me, and ungallant. There was I, outraged on Robert's behalf, but as well both Steven and I know, had Rab been present he would have drawn Lara aside to a shady spot – without it seeming predatory in the slightest – taken out his moleskin notebook and jotted a few details, spun her a sugar-web of words, so luring her inexorably toward a pricy reservation at the Forrest Clinic of St John's Wood.

I drove by the Clinic last week, actually, a small act of homage, recalling that afternoon Robert led me languidly on a tour of the finished conversion, every plane and surface immaculate, fit to be cleaned with a hose: his theatre, with its top-dollar ceiling canopy, then the prep and anaesthesia and treatment rooms, the day-care centre . . . All that shining white-on-white super-sterility (in such contrast to the rose-and-chartreuse Art Nouveau swank of Robert's home decor). Even then I was wondering who paid for it all, and this even before Rab's 'troubles'.

Heading back from Jon's I put pedal to the metal, since Livy was keen to get back to that rather luminous landscape she's been steeped in for weeks. Cal was keener still to do the driving, but I'd seen him neck several beers. Midway through our disputation I had to take a fretful call from young Dr Malik, and so reverted to my professional alter ego: all parties of my household know better than to mess with Him. Cal sank into the leather, muttering that *he* would never answer a phone at the wheel. Not the point. I have duties. And in thirty years of driving I've not had a single accident. In less than twelve months Cal's had two, yet he acts as though these 'just happened', and to someone else, some callow, outmoded model of himself.

For sure, the scares wrought no discernible change in him. Fair enough, like most lads he couldn't wait to get into the driver's seat. As his instructor I took my role just as seriously as if he were a new surgical resident under my eye. I forbade distraction, wanted to instil in him the process, the technique, even the fundamentals of the engine. I wanted Cal to understand that learning is incremental, true skill developed and refined by the experience of unforeseen tight corners, from which one learns anticipation and adjustment. In driving, one assumes the danger of destroying life, beginning with one's own.

Cal, though, just doesn't get it. Some children inherently fear the unknown, the shadowy threat of a hurt that might prove irreparable. So they're afraid to ever take that first bold step, put their foot down into murky water. It's natural, this fear, and it must be shaken out: one cannot be afraid to act unilaterally. But I must have instilled this lesson in Cal too well. He just charges round the blind corners of life as though he were indestructible. He knows full well the sad tale of Olivia's second 'pregnancy' that wasn't – has known for as long as he could talk that he will be our only child – yet, clearly, believes he will live forever.

'Needs a new skin, boss.' So said the chief grease-monkey at Rawlson's Garage after Cal took my powerful Audi out for a tear, and tore up the left flank. Then, of course, Cal damn near needed a new epidermis of his own after he took that country-lane bend blithely unhindered by a seatbelt. A lucky lad, he, that his godfather is so gifted: bloody hours it was that Rab spent plucking fragments of glass out of Cal's brow and cheekbone, prior to sewing him up very nearly good as new. 'A little scar tissue's desirable in a man, lends character.' Thus Rab's tough-eyed verdict on his handiwork. *Jesus wept,* thought I. But Cal lapped it up. I suppose it was then they became bosom pals.

How Robert loved my son, with what touching fierceness! There was something heartbreaking about the proud, fond look in his eye and the way Cal would return it, their avidity for each other's company. Cal used to look at *me* like that – pre-adolescence at least – the eager boy to whom I taught the finer points of all the sports worth teaching, bright-eyed, treading loyally and trustingly in my wake. But the teenage incarnation of Cal – the rangy, cocky insouciance, the sly smile, the mere nod of greeting – I can see whose spirit he's channelling. He and Rab were blood brothers, of a sort.

They 'are', they 'are', goddamn it. Get a grip, Grey.

❧

Earlier this evening I tidied up the references for my long-delayed paper on the use of Hyalomatrix in deep dermal burns; and in demob spirit I fancied I'd take a stroll out in the last of the light, wondered if my dear ones cared to join me. They were still sat over cold dinner plates, Livy with a novel, though claiming to be returning shortly to her canvas. Young Calder appeared stupefied before his laptop, but to my delight he was navigating round some website devoted to hi-tech renderings of the internal organs. I had thought the internet pandered more to a lower interest in gross anatomy. Do I dare to dream the boy may follow his old man's footsteps? A prospective surgeon must be proud as Lucifer, Cal's got that going for him at least. (Of course my generation did anatomy the old-school way, round a dun-coloured corpse on a slab, its face shrouded, we all breath-bated and queasy. Cal's lot, I expect, will do it by computer-sim, free from the butcher's-shop odour of formalin and rotting tissue, the morphology prof's gags about 'cold cuts'.)

At any rate I never got out of the house, because the phone rang, Cal erupted from his chair to get it, and it was Malena. The boy wasted some moments, trying to sound suave. When I finally got on the line, though, my usual pleasure in hearing Malena's Danish purr was denied me, for tonight she was troubled. I'm sure she's worried over Robert anyway, but this is fresh bother – some disquieting rift in her relations with Killian. I tried to sympathise, ham-fistedly, for I'm no one's idea of a marriage counsellor. My sense was she wanted to see me in person, directly, but I couldn't assent, not with Livy's eyes on me from over her paperback.

It's an awkward position for me in multiple ways. I can never speak to Malena too long without feeling I'm being weirdly 'unfaithful' to Robert. But then Rab and I are brothers under the skin, and – just to start with the surface – I see in Malena exactly what he saw: those crystalline eyes, that sculpted face, the long dark-auburn locks so uncommon in a Dane. Robert himself couldn't have improved her. Only age can do that – you just know she'll look glorious at 40, 50, 60. She has, I concede, a touch of the amoral to her, a discreet loucheness; otherwise she'd never have become Robert's girl. At times she appears too satisfied by her own world's wellbeing. But only to a point. And not tonight.

Malena and I have always been able to talk. If unlikely

confidants on the surface, we have a robustness in common. She's of that Nordic female type – maybe it's the cold that makes them so coolly candid, uninhibited. As a mere girl she was driving a snow plough, ice-fishing, putting cherries in her cheeks, cheerfully tossing back vodka with the boys. Though slender as a wand she has the muscles for winter sports, and several inches in height over Killian, who, for all his roguish good looks, is a squirt. An uncouth squirt to boot: he should cut his fucking hair, for one thing. I doubt he has anything in his wardrobe but tee-shirts and denims, all frayed and stained by repeated wiping of his chisel. And this the guy who cuckolded my pal? But, but . . . I've never had reason to believe he's anything but hugely enamoured of Malena, as he should be. And she does love him. Hence my surprise to hear of their running into choppy waters now.

Killian's muse has gone missing, apparently, or else he's in a blue period. I knew he'd sustained a big work disappointment, the collapse of some commission that looked to have fallen into his lap then was just as swiftly yanked away. Ever since he got the news – a week or so ago, the day before Robert disappeared, in fact – he has, it seems, been comporting himself in a moody-peculiar fashion. As a photographer and veteran of the appalling fashion world, Malena knows all about the flighty types. But the Irishman's strange change of temper has utterly thrown her. He has complained of a few ailments, some old rugby injury that never fixed, but to her annoyance he won't see a doctor.

I grunted, rueful, in recognition. 'Rather like Robert – the physician who refused to heal himself.'

Malena winced. 'Please Grey, don't say that.'

I realised I'd been insensitive in the circumstances. Still I wasn't convinced. All men go through phases of loathing their work. And yet there was Malena talking about booking Killian into Steven's clinic.

'For what?' I asked. '"Exhaustion", like the rock 'n' rollers? Malena, I wouldn't advise you pay the Blakedene rate. Sounds to me like all he needs is a rest, maybe a think . . .'

'Huh. Maybe it's me should check into Blakedene Hall. I'll sit and tell Steven all my troubles . . .'

It alarmed me that she might be serious. I wanted also to tell her that Steven would be no help, since he takes a disapproving attitude, unconsciously or not, toward any woman who's gone to bed with Robert. I suppose I also felt a twinge of envy, however puerile – but some part of me has determined to be Malena's Galahad and admit no challenger, not even the honourable Doc Hartford. Especially so when Killian seems suddenly to have put on the armour of black knight. It does sound like quite a falling-off.

⁂

Was it only ten weeks ago that Livy and I called round and found those two in connubial bliss?

It had been with some unease that I accepted Malena's invitation. I only got my excuse once Robert admitted to me he was dallying with a new girl, some pampered princess whom he'd gifted a new nose. So I told myself we were all moving on (for all that it seemed Rab was backsliding). Livy needed no pretext, she knew of Killian's work, where he'd trained and so forth, and was curious. Still, as we clambered into the Audi that morning I couldn't quite shake the sense that Robert was watching us from the cover of some shady remove, eyes burning . . .

Theirs is a good honest home, not an aesthete's showroom like Robert's. Malena brewed us tea in a cheerful, cluttered kitchen, the walls hung with ill-framed posters of Killian's exhibitions (*Pale Graces*, *Amaterasu*, *Red Earth Demeter*). I brought a bottle of Powers Irish whiskey in tribute to the man of the house, but I read in Malena's eyes that this was tantamount to carrying some effigy of Robert over her new threshold. Still, after a bit she duly led us up to Killian's 'workshop'.

Frankly I was ready to give 'the work' a cool appraisal but I must say I found the studio greatly to my taste. Occupying all of an upper floor, exposed brick and floorboards under high skylights, it had the good dusty odour of a masculine den, the sense of being home to a proper industrial/artisanal process. Strewn across the surfaces were masses of pencil sketches, clusters of tools and chisels upright in old fifteen-litre paint cans, rows of pieces shrouded in sackcloth and lined up on metal bracket shelves. The sheer number and variety of tools and accoutrements I found deeply appealing: goggles, gloves, earmuffs, respirator, polisher, hammer drill and grinder, whole sheaves of diamond blades. In one corner some kind of life-size wire maquette reclined blankly in a tall-backed wooden rocking chair. Neglected in the other corner was a sixty-gallon air-tank, some pneumatic tool trailing from it by a hose, begging to be picked up and blasted.

And there, planted thoughtfully amid it all, the Great Killian MacCabe, clad like a plasterer's mate, nursing in one fist a three-pound hammer and in the other a chipped enamel tea-mug bearing the badge of some rugger side from Dun Laoghaire. He peered most intently at a great lump of alabaster that must have been winched up onto the reinforced bench where it sat formidably on a sandbag. Livy apologised for our disturbance. He grinned, waved a hand. 'Nah, yousens relax. Honestly, Livy, I've no intention of touching this boy, not today. It's just been giving me the eye, y'know? Throwing down the gauntlet.'

I gave him a querying look that he was good enough to address. 'A block of this size, Grey, it's got a world of possibles in it. And it came from somewhere, y'know? It's got its own story. You have to respect that, it asks something of you.'

I could see he had that Irish way of looking at one, as if already amused by the quick-witted thing he was about to say, also by the sadly slug-witted manner of your comeback, since 'you', by definition, take life too seriously. *Never worry about me,* his eyes seemed to say, *I do my real stuff while yousens are in bed.* But he disarmed us, young MacCabe, and not just by his unshaven charm but by the selection of pieces he casually unveiled.

He works mainly in stone or wood, sometimes stuff he's bought or salvaged, but more often he prefers a commissioner to provide their own raw material. He 'likes to be surprised' – chooses to believe that in the course of the graft he will somehow 'fuse' himself with the temperament of the donor – likes to feel, furthermore, that the wood or the stone will, by its intrinsic strangeness, 'open his eyes' and teach him something.

'The raw state of a stone has its own perfection,' he went on. 'You could persuade yourself to leave well alone. Respect to "the better craftsman", y'know? But, you've only got one life, so you crack on. Then once you split it – see, it's really the flaws of the innards that get your juices going? The flaws suggest new things.'

It was high-flown yet I found it made sense. Whereupon we had a nice little chat about our shared interest in cutting: cutting tools, cutting things, people. He had more than the layman's curiosity about the surgical. 'When you've someone lying there before you with their guts laid open,' he marvelled, 'there's power in that, isn't there? You must feel like a warlock with that scalpel . . .'

I had to tell him that on some level I fight with indecision every time I pick up the blade – even if only for a fractional second, but it's there the devil awaits you. At worst you can see yourself from out of body, poised over a child, blade in hand like Father Abraham. For me it's the special onus of operating on infants and children – flawless pink flesh, my cut the first violation. Of course, very often the life is at stake, no one else can stand in my shoes at that moment, so unless I hurry up then things

34

will get immeasurably worse. But every time I cut I'm trying, for a moment, not to think of the patient as a human being: trying to put from my mind the precious detail of skin surface, fine hair, complexion, minor blemish – all those things that Robert was required to obsess over, all of the time.

'It's somewhat Zen,' I offered (imagining Robert's wince), 'knowing the "rightness" of your aim. Then once you're in, it's like the tissue falls away from the blade, and it hardly seems to bleed, funnily enough – as if the body were actively assisting the procedure.'

I had joined him on the highfaluting theoretical plane, and his smile was broad. We stood over one piece of his that had a pleasing finality, an abstracted female nude, some big stone lump he'd somehow managed to endow with a fecund, even carnal aspect. I tried a few clumsy words of appreciation: 'It's amazing, how you've suggested so much of a woman just by the flow of that curve.'

'Yeah, but there's aspects of the feminine we're hard-wired to see, right?' He grinned, glancing back at our girls. 'Us fellas? There's a sort of a code we know means "naked girl". It could be a line in the sand, a piss in the snow, it wouldn't matter . . .'

Malena was certainly smiling as she sallied up to us and slid her arms round his waist. 'Gimme a kiss,' he said, and she made a little pantomime of resisting him. Strange to relate, the spectacle didn't make me want to vomit. They liked each other passing well, that much was clear. No, I found I didn't mind making Killian's acquaintance, much as I'd minded the idea. I never confessed my treachery to Rab, though I suspect he guessed. Did it bother him? Was it rank disloyalty? Damn it, knowing Killian was a function of my friendship with Malena, and for sure she became a friend of mine too, whereupon it was impossible not to care for her. I just can't pretend Killian's some sort of demon, or anything but personable as far as I've seen.

Malena, though, has clearly now seen a side to him she hadn't bargained for. So it goes – romance can be a drug for a certain sort of woman, but it's only the spice of life, not the daily common-clay stuff of it. We have to compromise with our lovers. Moreover, I do suspect – however acrimoniously things finished between Malena and Rab – she must retain some feelings for him, be more worried for him now than she's letting on. And Killian could hardly be blind to that, could he?

4

Malena's Diary

His mere possession

August 26th

Who is sleeping in my bed? Or in whose bed am I sleeping? And does he want what I want, or something else entirely? I'm no longer sure – nothing feels solid or secure any more. My honest and earnest and light-hearted lover has, quite suddenly, changed into one of those dark men who keep secrets. Perhaps I'm imagining, some paranoid fear, 'only a phase', maybe. But all I can see now is difference, someone I don't understand and yet conceivably – my worst fear – recognise all too well. 'Rather like Robert . . .' Grim, grim, the very last thing I needed to hear!

Only hours ago our argument was so bitterly intractable that I struggled for breath, and searching in vain for some mercy or concession in his mean, hard face I actually had to ask: 'Who am I talking to?' I believe the question struck home, at least, for he paused, then was most subdued as he replied, 'I'm your lover who loves you, who's always loved you . . .' But his face as he said it – was not a lover's face, no.

Such professions of 'love'. And yet he has forgotten how it's done. Our 'romantic' dinner last week at the St John, his idea – I thought we would talk, he merely drank. Always we've talked so easily (as I used to imagine

did Robert and I, before I realised he was only extract-
ing data from me, one more proof of his ownership). If
Killian wants to revive the first flush of our love he needs
to remember how it started. It is as though he wishes
to begin our relationship anew but on terms favourable
only to him, all the while expecting I will faithfully delight in the new dispensation.

It's his humour I'm missing above all, the lightness,
the silliness, the true romance of him. Over dinner I
wanted us to share again the story of how we met, at
Susanne's party, both of us having gone in search of a
moment's quiet, only to find each other, miraculously,
in a darkened, empty room – then, somehow, dancing
together, close, to the distant music from the floor below.
The mischief of him as he murmured in my ear, 'I feel
a connection . . .' I'd come to consider myself a married
woman – 'kept', certainly – but I fell for him then. That
is our story, and I recited it happily, expecting his eyes to
shine over the candlelight. He listened, brooded, nodded, as though he'd had no part of it, as though some
little Leporello had slipped into his clothes that night
and worked all that charm on his behalf.

Every day now I watch him from the corner of my
eye, I sneak peeks into his studio, and all I see is evidence
of strange new habits – the undoing of what I took for
his habits of a lifetime. That huge hunk of alabaster for
which he paid a ransom but professed great plans – yes, I
imagined it would sit a little while unattended, not that
he would abuse it as he has done. This newfound zeal for
the air-chisel . . . It gathered dust for months, most cum-

bersome of unwanted gifts, Killian was amused by it but showed no inclination whatever to pick up that pneumatic hammer – swore he hated the noise, the vibration, how the stone chips flew. Well, now it is his favourite toy. And it's me who loathes the noise of it. For sure I knew the day he attacked the alabaster, and without a facial shield – that much I saw when he slouched downstairs with a fresh cut on his cheekbone, one that could have been immeasurably worse.

And not just how he works, but what he works on – chiselling away like a jeweller at some small piece, 'small' in every sense. The Killian I thought I knew has always sculpted in order to explore, to excavate the material. He's never made endless sketches or fussy little maquettes. And he would never EVER do a portrait bust – nothing so 'pretty', so banal as that. His women have been bigger, more mysterious, but more generous too – yes, I am so vain as to glimpse myself within their abstraction. Was I flattered, then, that day I sneaked up to his shoulder and saw his desk strewn with precise pencil sketches of my face? A little, yes. But if I expressed scepticism about his intentions it was only that I've never had the slightest wish to be his model – have only wanted him to be the artist I'd admired from afar. So maybe I stung him, perhaps he felt slighted. If so, he wasted no time in selecting another model. 'Don't worry,' he said, not pleasantly, as he tore up those pages in front of me. 'I'll not make that mistake again . . .' This new face he's making is 'beautiful', yes, but a typical man's fantasy of pristine female beauty, and in virgin white. If he hopes to make me jealous I will not take that bait. I saw enough of that from Robert, albeit late, and after so long taking me for granted, his mere possession, his clockwork doll.

I do not believe Killian has anyone else. For one thing he has become so confined to his quarters. And he is drinking while he works. No appetite was ever improved by such a mix. So, after all his recent and quite insatiable amorousness, he is now failing us in bed. Only a fortnight ago he wanted to make love daily, and in the middle of the day too. I wasn't always so ready, but he wasn't taking 'No' – was at least endearing in his insistence – and I went with the flow, my only surprise that he was not more gentle – the natural psychology, I would have thought, when lovers are waiting to learn if they have been 'blessed'. But tenderness has gone astray in him – so far removed from when we first slept together, and I was so clumsy, all fingers and thumbs, not even sure I knew what to do, whether I could please him, having been for so long and so thoroughly – professionally – used, manipulated, by Robert, my body surrendering inevitably to his attentions.

Killian's drinking, I think, is in part an anaesthetic, for this stupid injury he never got fixed from some stupid game of rugby. Three years ago and now he tells me about it, NOW he says he's in constant pain from it. He has muttered complaints of headaches, too, albeit with less drama. But I see it – I see him wince when he thinks I'm not looking. He'll clap his hand to his eye, or to the wall, or sink his head into his hands. And I ask him to take something or see someone but he won't.

No, instead he closes the door in my face. Am I supposed to do likewise to him? Am I meant to become one of those women who seek a refuge from their partners in work? I have no stomach for that. My whole wish was to step off that conveyor, put my camera bag down, bury my passport, let myself be changed by this love – not that we live in compartment worlds, the way that Robert always wanted. Where we ceased to see anyone, and if I tried I felt invigilated. Where he knew me inside and out, supplanted my gynaecologist, sought to supervise my hair and make-up and wardrobe – his power over me a delusion from which I awoke, my Big Love only a false idol, a god of clay, the brazen serpent.

No, I thought I had left all that behind. The things I let him do, the torpor into which we degenerated. And now it seems like a pit into which I could slide once again. Impossible but true.

Perhaps I am a bad penny, a magnet, do I carry a curse? Since it seems I now give Killian no pleasure, then surely Robert has found a way to curse me. Or am I being punished because I thought ill of Robert, and then something very bad happened to him . . . ? I must not think of such superstition. Robert has no control any more. Robert is in some hole of his own making. It is Killian and I who are together now, we must weather the storm, I must find a way to crack through the glacier that's formed between us.

Or could it be that we need 'a break from each other'? Oh please God, no, that was not ever the plan. This is not the time. Tomorrow I believe I will know for sure.

5

Dr Lochran's Journal
The cure for what ails

August 27th

This morning's *Times* brought an unwelcome shiver, Robert's disappearance a small diary item – only a few snide lines, not a shred of concern, mere innuendo glamorised by a checklist of his fancier clients.

At this time of such unease I'm nearly consoled by the routine of a working day spent in urgent relief of the newly/lately born – all yearning for their mothers' arms, no doubt, but needing first to be stabbed and sliced with razor-edged carbon steel by the 'Great' Dr Lochran. Some day in the none-too-distant future a finical robot may replace me, but until that cold day in hell the onus falls on me. However preoccupied I am – and at scrubs I do detect the Team moving about me with more than usual wariness – it's a fact that I can carry off any piece of business in life so long as the needful rituals are observed. There must be structure: order is the mother of assurance. For me, it's four white walls, hard light from nine angle-poise bulbs, and if the Team are on the pitch and I've moved smoothly into gown and gloves then the aura of 'show-time' commands me to step up.

Today's main business was bloody sticky, though: Mr and Mrs Whitaker's newborn Daisy. All their joys had

42

crashed from the day of ultrasound when they'd gone expecting to have the sex determined, learning instead that the baby's liver seemed to lie in her chest, her stomach on a level with her heart – the entire viscera migrated through one hole into the thorax, leaving the heart fighting for space and the poor left lung terribly strangulated. They are Christians, I think, and termination was never an option. Thus they soldiered on, but they have been through seven shades of hell ever since, and from the moment Daisy first swallowed air she had respiratory distress. ECMO gave her forty-eight hours of stabilisation whereupon she could conceivably tolerate the procedure, and the buck passed to me.

The Whitakers needed no lectures in the gravity of the matter, nor did I spare them the bitter stuff: that Daisy might either fail to tolerate the surgery or else all that would follow. I was asking them, though, to endorse me on a further risk. I am opposed to vinyl patch repair. Pain is coming in any case, but the patch option is liable to separation and repeat procedure: a whole vortex of attendant risk. I approve the wager on native vascularised tissue, I assume the responsibility, and in this the Whitakers trusted me. Under the circumstances they were probably far more stoical than I could have been. But what choice did they have?

As usual I permitted Mrs Whitaker to scrub in and be with Daisy until she was under. The comfort, really, is for the mother, but I believe it's the right course. Then she retreated back into the blue of the sterile field, left me in my blood-red world, in charge of a patient I could hold entirely between my two hands.

I worked without music, in deference to the high stakes for Daisy. Babies often serve to silence the chatter in theatre, and apart from my succinct commands we heard only the familiar ambient noise – the clicking of clamps, the suction's low hum, the machine-breath of the respirator. I went in just below the rib cage of her little scaphoid chest, lifted skin, made my window of opportunity, smelt the same humid musk that comes off an opened chest cavity whatever the patient's age – inspected her unspoiled and birdlike innards, sad to be seeing them so soon. With all the finesse we possess we retrieved tissue and organs, spleen last, released them into the sterile bag – not a butcher's bin-load, rather fruit-like. The hole exposed, I measured the amount of diaphragm tissue available, cut the peritoneum to tease out the posterior leaf and see what we had to play with. Inadequate, sadly. So, Plan B: assistance from the neighbourhood . . . I dissected the ipsilateral latissimus dorsi off the chest wall, divided the thoracodorsal neurovascular bundle, went through the bed of the tenth rib to place the muscle flap on the hemithorax, sutured it safely in place. Even old George Garrison would have nodded his approval. Still, we had booked for the full four hours, and I used them all. Thank God I've always worn sensible shoes.

Stepping into the waiting area one always meets with a plaintive sight: disparate little family units, each wrestling with their individual share of air-conditioned fear, clutching their forlorn bags and big bottles of Evian, all torn between boredom-relief and bracing themselves for the sky to fall in. Whenever I come through the door a sea of faces rises to greet me, but only one group ever gets to their feet. I can only carry one message at a time, sad to say, and it's the law of these things that on certain days I come to bring the sky down with me.

For the Whitakers, of course, I played no game of suspense, just gave them the big beam and the thumbs-up. Mrs Whitaker's face crumpled in joy. I drank that in. I made her joy happen, and without such satisfactions I wouldn't go on. 'Daisy won't be happy,' I warned them. 'Don't take that personally. And there's a way to go yet. I'm not taking leave of her, but the main burden moves to Intensive Care . . .' Already, though, they were trying to see past me, the day's labourer – aching to see and touch their child. Such deeply human moments are a necessary corrective to my very occasional godlike delusions.

ﷺ

Strange, but as the day neared its end I found myself replaying the last of Robert's and Steven's epic disagreements – at least, the last one I witnessed, at that dinner of ours just a few nights after we'd visited Malena and Killian. This daily-mounting concern for Robert has made me hope all the harder that my two oldest friends hadn't become entirely estranged. Back when we were boys at Kilmuir Steven was Robert's pal before mine: at first their tempers were better matched, they had a discerning cleverness, a cultivation in common. But, somehow, down the years the bantering manners of school turned into a tendency to judge each other incredibly harshly. Their quarrels got so routinely incensed that everyone round the table passed from bemusement to seat-squirming well before entrées were served. If they weren't 'in the club' then they couldn't see the tension for what it was: that quintessential non-meeting of minds between surgeon and physician.

I think back to Kilmuir, when the three of us, 'the triumvirate', first began to gad about – supplemented by whichever girl Robert was stringing along, plus her most suggestive mate(s). With the school so temptingly perched on the outskirts of Edinburgh, the city lay open to us, beyond the high walls of the compound. We drank, by God we all drank, as if drink were brewed by and for the angels. But for sure we were sober on the afternoon we decided to call into the Royal College of Surgeons, blundered into the pathology museum – then wandered about in great wonder, past the skeletons in glass cabinets, the gangrenous feet in jars, the array of old amputation knives and saws. Amusing to think of it now, how clear that some life-changing spirit must have suffused each of us that day.

By the time we were junior residents we'd found our vocations. I suppose we began to reveal ourselves the minute we stepped inside Anatomy Lab, that Victorian basement room, that 'rite of passage'. The prospective surgeons declared themselves, for sure – visibly eager to get the saw, separate legs from torsos, crack a sternum in two. That was me, that was Robert. Steven was always passionate about the idea of a career in reconstructive surgery: it would have suited his care for the relief of human misery. But when one got down to the mechanics, even simple dissection was never Steven's forte – much less the infernal tricksiness of knotting two-millimetre blood vessels with tweezers.

No one's ever pretended that psychiatry enjoys the lustre of surgery, even emergency medicine. But there was always a maximum lack of glamour in the conscientious way Steven went about his calling, staunchly resolved to be a therapeutic clinician for people in states of mental torment. He is one of life's instinctive socialists: the world isn't good enough for him, and he's always argued for the grandest, most holistic approach to its ills – if only 'the fabric of society' were more tightly woven, if parents were helped more, teachers better paid . . . This, even after his own career choices put him in the pocket of that ravenous capitalist, Big Pharmaceutical.

For all his training Steven has heard symphonies of condescension from fellow medics, and I know he's a frustrated man, forever managing conditions that, frankly, don't much improve. 'You're always fighting the end results,' he used to lament to me. 'Never confronting the causes.' And yet I know that to this day he remains conflicted about what precisely are those causes: essentially biochemical, or brought on by the big, bad world? It's all so much simpler if you can take a blade to the patient, locate the root cause by way of a scalpel's edge.

Robert never used to go any tougher on psychiatry than all the rest of us who cure by cutting flesh. For sure, he could be withering about the calibre of patient Steven saw – 'head-cases, heroin fiends and hysterical girls' was his favoured formulation – and he liked to tut about 'all *care* and no cure' as if 'care' were a dirty word. But that was only locker-room talk. 'Psychiatry's just a desperately sad profession,' he told me once, albeit sounding genuinely sorry for Steven. 'And we're medical men, you and me, not social workers.'

Still – be it said, latterly Rab turned outright mean and vindictive, a rotten way to behave to a friend of thirty years. But then such has been Robert's mood since Killian supplanted him. Not that Steven couldn't give out too. Once he got stuck into the 'shallowness' of Robert's vocation, anyone overhearing might have decided that it's cosmetic surgery and not religion that is the opium of the people. In the teeth of any such lecture (a 'culture of narcissism' and whatnot) Robert would merely shake his head in feigned wonderment. *'Don't we all like to make a good appearance . . . ?'* was his standard laconic comeback.

That last spat of theirs, though – perhaps most bitter because least important, or so it then seemed. Steven had merely been describing the treatment of certain anxieties in his patients through what he called 'mindfulness training', incorporating elements of Buddhist meditation. But this was the red rag for Robert, by now midway through the second bottle of our good Saint-Emilion, having drained the first one pretty well solo. The Scot in him surged up, the Selkirk tough, as he rocketed off into a tirade against the 'utter fucking shite' of karma, reincarnation and 'a whole load of other equally cretinous beliefs held by certain rich Buddhist pals of my ex-wife'.

Steven didn't bother to defend methods he has clearly found useful. Instead he very coolly expressed surprise that Robert had now 'married' Malena some months after she left him. I must say that in the arctic moments that followed Rab looked very much 'like he could kill a man'. I was startled myself. Yes, Steven can fight his own corner, but usually cedes the field when things turn nasty – decent, diffident, inclined to turn the other cheek, if only to harbour a grudge. That night, though, he got the hard blow in first. At any rate he had said what I knew he felt – that Malena's leaving was Robert's just desserts, that Robert had earned for himself the pain of being 'traded in' for a younger, more gifted lover – his own little karmic redress for a lifetime of treating women cursorily.

Steven and Tessa were the last lingerers at table that night, and so I suggested to Steven that he could show Robert a mite more compassion. (With the redoubtable Professor Tessa at his side I was prevented from adding the obvious point that his own marriage is hardly a model of harmony.)

'You know Rab loves you really,' I ventured, 'would do anything for you in a spot – has done, in the past.'

'I'm doing my best for him,' Steven shot back. 'Who do you suppose is writing his Remeron prescriptions?'

The very idea of Robert taking antidepressants was so outlandish that I was dumbstruck for some moments, a silence into which Steven gloomily injected. 'He's changed, Grey. Really, much for the worse.'

'He's not in a good way,' I agreed. 'Bloody Remeron could change him all over again, to be frank. So now's the time he needs us. Steven, look at the faces we had round this table tonight. These are the friends we've made. I doubt we've got time to make many more . . .' I'd intended to stir him to his senses, but I could see that instead I had burdened him further with my own private gloom. As if he hadn't enough of his own to wade through.

Stevie is a sound man, but one who squats on so much half-suppressed unhappiness. His position at Blakedene Hall pays well, for now, but I'm sure at heart he's still haunted by having followed Robert out of the NHS and into pure-profit private practice. As Steven always tells it, he stepped out of the state system because the recurrent and systemic failures of care were just too depressing and distressing. I know he was greatly shaken by the pointless death of Tom Dole, a patient with whom he'd formed quite a bond. But some part of him must acknowledge: he had a mind to make more money – to impress Tessa, if nothing else. Whereas the Steven of old would sooner have slit his own throat than take that gig.

I'm not even sure quite how well Blakedene's doing these days. When Steven got the Director job the group's business plan clearly envisaged a steady stream of self-paying patients – rich and/or famous drug addicts and their kids – and, for sure, they have a good few of those still, all stumping up their five or six grand a week. But for Blakedene – just as for any other private psychiatric facility, I suppose – the baseline must be met by short-term, high-margin state contracts for the mentally ill. That's where the axe is falling, and so Steven, even in his private fiefdom, is subject to the state's austerity measures. Thus he must sing for his supper, promote Blakedene as an upscale bolthole for posh drunks and waste-of-space cokeheads. There is a price levied on Steven's soul for this. He's not dealing with the conditions that concern him. He treats people for whom he has no respect, he is a dispenser of drugs rather than of counsel and care. He wanted to be a hands-on restorer of sound mental health. Instead he's become the god Hypnos.

On top of it all, late fatherhood has left him looking perpetually knackered. I do wonder, alas, if it's really the twins keeping Steven and Tessa together. I know that six months back they had an unhappy, inconclusive talk about separation. When we were lads he always had such a gallant notion of the feminine, a romantic conception of marriage as the true union of Man & Woman. It sustained him through his thirties and the long relationship with Jessica, flaxen-haired poetess with a fanciful interest in psychotherapy that fooled Steven into thinking he'd found his female ideal. That was a messy ending, whereupon he married on the rebound – wound up hitched to a lassie made out of pins and needles, not a dreamy thought in her head. I daresay it's from such hardy stuff that scholars of medieval history are made – Tessa's doctoral thesis, if I remember right, was much concerned with methods of torture. Though I know Livy finds her perfectly companionable, admirably accomplished and all that.

And to his credit, Steven always maintained he didn't just want a wife who would cradle his tired head on her bosom – or so he said. He wanted an authentic partner, an equal, someone to challenge him. Well, 'challenged' he most certainly has been. Secretly he might feel he would have been happier with one from the delectable parade of Robert's ex-girlfriends – those pliable, decorative dollies Rab used to squire around. Before Malena came along, then broke Rab's heart. Before the Fall.

6

Dr Hartford's Journal
Inmates of Blakedene Hall

August 27th

Pitch-dark and silent outside my window. Since I can't sleep I burn the lights in the office and write. Better than lying awake in bed, watching the ceiling turn to ominous shadowland. I suppose this insomnia means I'm not working hard enough. But I'm jaded, purposeless: the idea of pulling myself together, pitching into the patient load – two dozen inpatients, a handful in day care? – feels futile. A day like today, dominated by our most puzzling 'inmate', is as much as I can handle.

I ought, then, to have more time for my alleged managerial duties. That this in-tray is also near-empty points to the covert diminishing of my authority round this place. Andrew Gillon, our new 'finance director', cuts an increasingly (self-) important figure. The odds of a sell-off/merger seem to shorten daily, in the event of which I fully suspect I'd turn up one morning to find someone else in my chair. This, the paranoia that keeps me key-pushing into the small hours.

I could just switch on the voice-recognition software: mutter away to myself like Richard Nixon, let the room's hidden mics be my witness. Could, in other words, be my own patient. But then should loyal Goran pass my door and overhear, he'd surely think me mental. And that's not really the impression one wants to give, not in my line of work.

Moments ago, in fact, Goran knocked lightly, his witching-hour patrol of grounds and corridors complete. *Watchman, how goeth the night?* He reports that all of Blakedene is sleeping save for me, and him. In his open, smiling face I read mild surprise, perhaps disapproval, at the fact that I was not myself back home and abed in the bosom of my family. Perhaps, too, he sniffed something in the air – the vaguest evanescence of Eloise Keaton's perfume, Ghost or Poison or whatever. Goran knows me better, though – doesn't he? – than to suppose I arrange my end-of-day sessions so as to prey on my younger, blonder female patients.

Still, the hour when I might have made the drive home before Tessa was out cold crept by once again. When I called to tell her she was curt, on Jacob's behalf too. But it's done, the Chesterfield is my mattress tonight. (The temptation to wander over to East Wing, take a room in my own asylum, must be resisted for obvious reasons.) It does feel like my true home, this office – its air of a professorial study, high-ceilinged, book-lined, oak-wain-scoted. I feel stable and centred behind my long desk, a fit perch for a thoughtful man, a fine place to hide out from the hash he's making of his actual life.

This morning, at least, I woke in my own bed. There was a chill in the room, as has been for weeks. Murky light through the louvres, from the en suite the sound of water lapped onto skin. Then Jacob hurtled in, wearing his bunny pyjamas, windmilling his arms. *Get up, Daddy, get up!* Julian traipsed behind, rubbing red eyes. I gave Jules a hug. Jake evaded my embrace, hurtled out the door again. I found Tessa in the tub, her back to me, rinsing her hair. She didn't turn, however long I stood gazing at the wet skin of her shoulders, the gleaming rope of her hair snaking down and round the notches of her spine. No words needed: in the silence between us there is absolute resonant telepathy.

She's displeased that I'm resuming care of Eloise: the minute I told her I felt her tension, the revived resentment of what she reckoned was my excess mental energy on this patient's behalf last time. Frankly it just feels odd to me that Tessa should have so little sympathy for another woman who has been so ill-used, whose abuse as a child was of the sort routinely correlating with a lifetime of adult disorders.

But no, Tessa feels free to lecture me about my business ('You can't help her, Steven, it'll take real people in her real life to get her out of the hole . . .' et cetera).

'I'm well aware she can't recover her childhood,' I riposted. 'But I do believe in adulthood you can be a sort of loving parent to yourself.'

I haven't even had one proper session with Eloise yet – have kept my distance, in a way, out of certain mixed emotions. But earlier today we spoke, and I saw her depression has returned with a vengeance, she complains both of insomnia and of nightmares, has evidently been unable to resolve her ruinous promiscuity, a regrettable outrider to the world of nightclubs and dance music that employs her intermittently (as 'promoter', DJ, host-ess, I never quite understand, but none of it right for a young woman with a decent Oxford degree in French and Italian).

This morning, then – after I'd shaved and brewed cof-fee and the boys came and went from the kitchen table, Tessa made her stomping descent, then roamed restlessly, complaining of the failed floodlights over the driveway. 'It's getting darker every night, Steven, something has to be done. You're at Blakedene all hours, I come home to pitch black.' Her main concern is some snapped catch on a kitchen window. I told her it seemed hardly a high-level risk.

She: *Bad things happen, Steven. Look at your friend Forrest . . .*

Well. I nearly wanted to ask how she'd succeeded where the police have so far failed in determining what's hap-pened to Robert. But of course Tessa never liked Robert, has only seemed faintly bemused by the current crisis.

Then the phone rang. Tessa strode past me to the hall-way. I watched as she lifted the receiver, a terse 'Hello?', then moved into the living room, closing the door over the cord. Truly I've become a pitiful invigilator of my wife's daily doings, such as I see of them. But then, were she really cheating would she still find everything about me so irritating? Wouldn't she be the soul of marital sweetness if only to throw me off the scent?

It was then Julian trailed back into the kitchen, cheeks red and wet, and thrust out the palm of his hand to re-veal weeping beads of scarlet. In an instant I knew. He'd watched me earlier from the bathroom door while I shaved. Alone, he must have been so curious as to pick up my razor, pluck out the blade from its bed . . . I shot out of my chair, swept him up, out into the hallway, hammered at the door. When at last it opened I caught the irritation on Tessa's face, saw it turn to a gape at the state of her distressed child.

'A&E,' I bellowed. '*Now.*'

Mercifully it just needed three small stitches – no tendons harmed, thank God. But this is what happens when two Married Professionals, occupied separately within the Family Firm, start to pass like ghost ships. Setting aside, for the moment, who bears the blame for that larger degeneration – who was responsible here for Julian's mishap and distress? All I can say is that I acted first, and with sufficient conviction as to assume the moral high ground. That accomplishment was nearly worth the misery that settled on me once the two of them had hastened out the front door.

Tessa, how were we reduced to this? Can we not talk about it? Can we not? There's so much I would tell you, if you would only listen.

સ્લ

I'm well aware that, to hostile eyes, Eloise Keaton may seem the worst embodiment of Blakedene's ethos of care: freeloading daughter of Britain's ninety-second-richest man, consummate 'poor little rich girl', husky-voiced and jaded too soon. But I know just how unfortunate she's been, however wealthy and titled her father – a grousing, mirthless sort of multi-millionaire, only amused (from what I've seen) when he has someone at a disadvantage. Her mother Jo was aloof, secretly alcoholic, wracked by her failure to bear Sir James the necessary son-and-heir – an ambition he realised finally with the second Lady Keaton, Nicole, a catwalk model two months younger than Eloise.

Yes, when Eloise first came to us six months ago her presenting problem was substance abuse. I weaned her off the cocaine and insane vodka consumption: a stock fortnight of detox, a standard month of person-centred therapy. She was a model patient, in a way: certainly she seemed like one who had sickened of self-poisoning. Still, she also gave off the aura of one who lived selfishly as a form of retribution – payback now because she'd de-served better then, back in the mists of a lost childhood. Only I didn't yet know just how severe had been the loss.

As we sat together and I tried to fathom her personal history (she irked and dispirited by turns) I couldn't un-derstand how a once-timid child who'd loved poetry, horses and the woodland near her home transformed into one who, aged 15, survived expulsion from her pricy boarding school by dint of daddy's money, having been caught on the grounds after dark with Class-A drugs and two rough local boys. As much as she stonewalled me, at some point she accepted my concern as genuine, for one day I found a wrapped package in my pigeon-hole.

It was a diary, such as a girl would keep – its pale vio-let covers water-marked and ink-blotted, a detail of embroidered flowers crushed lifeless. Flicking a few blue-biro pages I understood this was a bona fide adolescent journal, a secret recess, composed in minute scribble and intermittent schoolgirl-French-like code. I read it in one sitting, and so learned that at the age of 13 Eloise had been abused sexually. 'Raped' is the plain word.

The offender was her father's then business partner Marcus Flint. Their Cotswolds estates were cheek-by-jowl, and Flint kept a big, hardly used stables for his wife, much debilitated by depressions after the births of their sons. At said stables Eloise was deposited every weekend for equestrian lessons. She found Flint a thoughtful in-structor, with a cajoling but kindly manner. He praised her in ways she never heard at school. In fact he was grooming her. It became his custom to take her for twi-light walks in the woods, where he told her of a sadness inside him that caused him pain, was 'exorcised' only by having her near. He told her she was beautiful, and in those cold, dark, silent woods he persuaded her to cling to him for warmth, actually inveigling her into non-mu-tual masturbation. For a while, with snake-like wiles, he persuaded her these encounters were a precious secret, a covenant, since he so 'loved' being with her. That cov-enant broke the day he actually penetrated her, hissing in her ear that it would hurt less if she stopped fight-ing. Still he bullied and shamed her into silence, warning her calmly of who would suffer most if she 'told'. So she never did.

It only ended one night at the family dinner table, when Sir James told Eloise her visits to the Flints would have to cease owing to the upcoming flotation of their company BlueWire. *'Marcus will be too busy for you,'* her father said sternly. She never saw Flint again. Within months some financial irregularities on his part became known – some illicit/illegal use of stockholding – and he fled the UK hastily for boltholes beyond the law, first California, then Guatemala.

Such was the tale of the violet diary; and weighing it in my hand, knowing she had placed it there, broke the ground of a great trust between us. All these years she had needed someone to read her, to relieve her of this grim, punishing secret. She chose me.

Thereafter we worked on some techniques of cognitive processing, but I found her badly 'stuck' in several crucial respects. I'm all too familiar with how women can emerge from such traumas with a drastic sense of themselves as Bad, the psyche coping only by asserting that they are indeed, in some part, fundamentally brazen. Not only did Eloise consider her abuse defining of her, she was consumed by guilt over it. *'I shouldn't have been around'* was her sad refrain. *'Shouldn't have been in his way, moping about . . .'* I managed at least to make her feel her parents' abdication of responsibility, their clear failure to watch over her. Her distress was slow-rising, like a storm drain in a torrent, but what finally came forth was nausea, disgust, rage both at Flint and her parents, but also, still, at her younger self. There was a catharsis in this venting, preferable at least to the cultivated insouciance and fecklessness that had 'protected' her to a limited extent since adolescence.

Still, I didn't feel I had properly guided her to a safer place in her mind at the point where she discharged herself, unwilling to spend any more of her father's money. But her return to Blakedene now – though clearly no cause for celebration – affords us a precious second chance.

August 30th

A day of great commotion, and unhappy revelation. What to make of it?

The morning's drive out to Blakedene was deceptively calm, assisted by the new Blessed CD of *Dido and Aeneas*. As I came up the snaking driveway through the lawns I saw Lawrence engaged in that wistful last mowing of summer. His work has been superb these past months, the grounds have shone, from the rose arbours and pergolas to the gazebos and garden walkways. The begonia is still pink and sweet-smelling, the blue-mauve floribunda roses still copious, the purple-starred clematis dense round the trellises. Even the old woods beyond our walls seem somehow improved by Lawrence's eye. In all, my spirits were good as I climbed the front steps. Then I heard my name called from on high, winced upward past the sun's glare to the veranda, saw Eloise waving a limp, rueful hand at me.

I went directly up the main stairs and out to where she sat, wearing a faded pale-blue tee-shirt, denim skirt and sandals, smoking moodily, her free fingers dancing over the tabletop onto an old Gallimard paperback of Gide's *L'Immoraliste*. 'I'm revisiting my adolescence,' she murmured. 'There was a time I wouldn't touch anything that wasn't by a dead French homosexual . . .' But she seemed to be avoiding my eye. I concede, I've struggled somewhat to see past her 'new look': the regrettable fact in her records (though unacknowledged between us) that after her last admission here she checked into the Forrest Clinic for some 'work'. Only minor refinements, for sure, and yet everything in her face appears somehow more sculpted at the tip – her upper lip a perfect wave, nose newly retroussé, a curved elegance from cheekbone to jaw-line. Even her hair, formerly sunflower-blonde, thick and worn tied, is now a long sleek bob like bottled gold. Her eyes, though, remain the same – small, aqua-green, strangely pained. It's those eyes, that pain, which keep me focused on the care she requires.

We were meant to adjourn to my office, but as she collected her things and I surveyed the view from the veranda I saw a vehicle tearing up the bends of the approach to the building – a white transit van, spraying gravel all about, having somehow negotiated security at the gate. It growled to a halt on the far side of the fountain, by which time Eloise was by me at the balustrade, peering down at the source of the disturbance. A man spilled out of the driver door – tall, black, 30-ish? – made as if to stomp up the front steps, then, spying us, ran back into our full view below. 'Oh God . . .', I heard Eloise exhale.

'Ellie!' he shouted. *'Ellie! Come down, will you?'*

'Leon, what are you *doing*?' As 'Leon' shook a finger at her, so she gesticulated back. Goran was swiftly out of doors and bearing down on him, but the hand he laid on the intruder was shrugged off brusquely, and so I dashed down as fast as I could. Eloise, mercifully, didn't follow.

Yet by the time I was jogging across the gravel this Leon was stood by Goran in a pose of utter cool and affability, even though Goran's own posture was riven by tension from top to toe. As I reached them Leon extended his hand to me, smiling broadly. And I realised how very handsome he was, how deeply winning that smile.

'Yeah, you're the doc, right? The geez looking after my Ellie?'

After a moment's consideration I took the hand, to Goran's clear unease. The fellow introduced himself, 'Leon Worrell' also the name emblazoned on the side of his van, advertising a carpentry and floor-sanding business. He offered me a cigarette, but that I wasn't having. And so he explained – in a manner hopping and hard to follow, polite nonetheless – that he had only come here to check on the wellbeing of his 'girl', the haste and excitation on account of his having come at speed from the main Keaton residence in London, where – after persistent enquiries – he had gleaned from Lady Nicole that Eloise was checked into my clinic.

'Just man to man, I gotta ask, now I'm here' – and he touched my arm – 'can I go say hello? Could you give me that much, doc?' The smile resurfaced, mellow and sweetly warm as Sunday sun. Eloise herself had vanished from the veranda, thus making it simpler for me to give Leon the bad news. He absorbed it philosophically, likewise my assurance that Eloise was in safe hands but needed her privacy at this time. He nodded, told me –

as if I were a pal – that what he would do was write her a letter. His hand was on my arm again, his physicality limber and laconic, muscular yet at ease – for a moment I thought he might lift me onto his lap. Instead he confided in me. 'I understand, she's a funny girl, doc. She's got her sadness. But what's wrong with her, it's just not her fault, yeah . . . ?'

I didn't question his judgement. Truthfully, in short order I'd got the sense he has genuine feelings for her. Then he was clambering back into his semi, waving amiably, driving off. Goran, still primed, jogged over to the golf cart and made to tail him down to the gate. I went back inside and up to her room in West Wing, where I found her sitting on her bed. Seeing me in the doorway she rolled her eyes.

'What a madhouse, right . . . ?

I led her at last to my office, let her spark up her black tobacco, and shortly she confessed that Leon is someone with whom she's had a 'difficult' on–off relationship over the last six months. Old news to my ears: I've gathered it's her habit to reject sexual partners as soon as they breach her defences, her force field. A fear of the particular terrors of true intimacy, I'm sure – though I believe she longs for that closeness.

She characterises Leon as 'troubled', 'volatile' – not the chap I met, for sure, indeed some evil twin. But he has a son by a woman from whom he's separated, of Trinidadian extraction like himself. His brother Lynval deals marijuana, to Leon's despair, though Lynval has, to date, evaded the courts. (And it was through Lynval's good offices that they met.) Among Leon's cousins is a professional footballer, quite successful, though Leon 'doesn't rate him' – not as a man nor as a left-sided winger. Eloise attributes this to envy, though Leon has had his business for five years and is constantly in work. Indeed she sees in him immense psychological problems, starting with the chip he sports on his shoulder concerning their relationship. It wasn't long in our discussion before she confirmed Sir James's vehement disapproval of him.

'Is that any part of his appeal for you, Eloise?'

She threw me a look of asperity, began to fish about for another cigarette, as if despairing of me, or else buying time to come up with a fit response, which she had to hand once she was lit up again.

'His appeal to me is the man he is. He just won't see that. There's no . . . socio-cultural barrier between us, I'll tell you that. Not from my side. Just his – him and his male pride. He says I don't really respect him, don't really want him for himself, I just want – oh, I don't know – some typical white-girl fantasy. Some big dark island man . . .'

'What do you say back to him?'

'I've given up replying to that one, actually. Because I can't see any answer that will satisfy. Other than my agreeing to go to Trini with him and have his babies. Or one more of them.'

'He's put that proposal to you?'

'Not in so many words. But he does seem to think our relationship needs to accelerate to the, uh, patter of little feet.'

'And how do you feel about that?'

She exhaled, with a curl of her lip. 'I wouldn't be a good mummy.'

It was at this juncture, timely or not, that Niamh knocked to tell me the Metropolitan Police were on the phone, an urgent matter – Robert, of course. I ought to have asked Eloise to step outside. For some reason I let her sit, staring wanly through the leaded panes of the long window, while I spoke to the northern-accented Detective Hagen. Oddly he was fishing for more about Robert's abortive work in facial transplant. I could only tell him that the cases I evaluated at Robert's request, all deeply distressing in their own right, obviously came to nothing once Robert abandoned the work, something he and I both regretted. But Hagen clearly wanted to be certain how far that work had gone. Of course, I only know so much.

'I know he did . . . a certain amount of practice, under highly regulated conditions, with cadaveric material.'

'Did he really, doctor?'

'Yes, so, he transplanted the faces of corpses. All donated to medical science, of course . . .'

'Fascinating,' said the detective. And maybe so, to the layman. After I hung up Eloise's eyes were fixed most searchingly on me.

'I'm sorry,' I shrugged. 'There's no escaping this business at the moment.'

She nodded. 'The police spoke to me last week. Rather impertinently, I felt. But you and Dr Forrest are good friends?'

Didn't he say so?, I thought. 'Yes, we were friends at school. And ever since. So you're acquainted with Robert?'

'I had a little procedure, in his clinic.' Her eyes darted aside. 'What do you suppose has happened to him? Something bad?'

'I don't know, Eloise.' I toyed with my fountain pen, conscious of my own conflictedness. 'He's a complicated man, Robert, it's never been easy to account for him. But I do believe he's out there somewhere. I'm sure he'll re-surface.' She nodded, pensive. I felt a slight catch in my throat. 'Are the police interviewing all of his patients, do you know? Or had you been friendly with Robert outside of the clinic?'

Evidently she felt the insinuating edge in my 'casual' enquiry. 'Not quite "friendly", that wouldn't be the word. We . . . had a thing. Slept together, once or twice, after my procedure. Not made to last. Though he was charming, to start with. But actually I'm not sure I met his high standards. And I don't think he was very happy. Not since he'd left his wife.'

'They weren't married,' I heard myself saying. 'And she left him.'

'No kids, though? Figures. *He* certainly didn't want me to have his babies. To the point of wanting to put it just about anywhere other than *mia fica* . . .'

I am inured to her odd, sorry attempts at scandalising me, even in vulgar Italian, and I let her see my disappointment.

'Sorry. It's a dirty world out there, Steven.' She tapped her forehead with one scarlet fingernail. 'And also in here.'

I was not to be distracted, since the subject was on the table, however unwelcome. 'It was Robert who ended your affair? Were you upset?'

She made condescending eyes. 'No, I think it was quite clear what we both wanted. After he dumped me I did drunk-dial him a few times, but he was – aloof. The last time, it was a woman answered. Spanish, I guess, she actually said, "No, *mi hermana*, he is mine now . . ."' She laughed, unconvincingly. 'I told him in the end, I'd started feeling not-well again, and he said to me, "Why don't you just check back into Blakedene Hall, let Steven Hartford look you over?" He didn't mean it nicely. But I decided I would, and fuck *him*.'

Her tone couldn't mask the wound in her, as she sat rubbing her arms through the gauzy sleeves of a cardigan, knees together, toes turned in, a picture of dejection. Behind the mask she is languishing; no proper help is possible with this false self of hers between us. I weighed the moment, thought it ripe, told her I wished us to try a new therapeutic technique. My explanation of the relationship between eye movements and the cognitive pathways didn't quite persuade her, but then I didn't tell her that my most encouraging uses of this treatment so far have been with women who were abused. She chewed a nail warily, finally nodded assent. I rummaged my desk drawer, found a new red-and-black workbook, asked that she begin to write daily on whatever matters occurred to her, past and present – this to be a basis for our sessions.

She sat back, tapping another cigarette on her pack. 'Can I write down my dreams?'

'By all means,' I gestured open-handedly, thinking *Oh Lord, spare me the X-certificate* . . . I'm sure we will take a wider frame of reference once the sessions proper commence. I have to consider, though, that she may wish to say more about Robert. And I must make my own peace on that score.

᎓

I suppose, were he testifying in court, Grey would say of me – without judgement – that I was always somewhat jealous of Robert's way with women, and accordingly a little bitter about my own mixed fortunes in that field.

True, for the one college term that Robert and I were flatmates I had cause to rue the thin wall between our bedrooms, such were the ardent, quickening moans that travelled whenever Robert was 'entertaining'. In that same time-passage I got myself in a foolhardy state of unrequited love for Cleo Glendenning, in the way one only can at that age – and, like in a story, I had to watch while fate turned, against me, and Cleo became Robert's. Fair play, I paid for my passivity – Cleo too, for Robert got her pregnant, then arranged the termination. I don't doubt the experience pained him, if not so much as it did Cleo. The wound I sustained was probably negligible. It hurt, nonetheless.

It did perplex me, though, how a male peer of mine could get away with such conduct toward the most spirited young women – and yet these girls seemed to put up with bloody well everything. Dalliance with Robert, in the end, rarely made a girl feel better about herself – not on what I have observed. But who am I to judge? Robert had something, for sure, his very own burning brand of charm. And perhaps in burning holes through so many girls he acquired an understanding that's been denied me. He must have acquired it somehow, or he couldn't have done what he did in life and with such success.

It was a familiar med-school dilemma – albeit with a shade of taboo, spoken of in winces – but a key consideration for any male student, and unavoidable for those minded toward Ob-Gyn. How can a man truly empathise with a woman – however many lectures and labs he attends, examinations he sits, female patients he palpates – without having felt in his own person the aches of menstruation, the contractions of labour, et cetera? In the brief time Robert teased Grey and me with the notion he would pursue gynaecology, he was wont (smiling slightly) to speak of 'the part of me that is female'. I'm not sure, though, if he could ever have tucked the rest of himself away to the degree the discipline required. ('Before inserting a speculum into any vagina,' I once heard him regale our beer-soaked table, 'always ask the patient to take a deep breath. I recommend the same procedure for anything else one might care to insert up there . . .' This the wit of the man who, as I heard it, never failed to ask his surgical assistants, male or female, to set their clamps '*soixante-neuf* style'.)

A good thing, I suppose, that Robert never had to call on me to be his best man. That would have been Grey's job by right, and he would have made sure the assembled saw all sides of Robert. We were younger then, anyway. I concede that the mature Robert, in company – inspired by fine burgundy rather than fizzy beer – could expound most tenderly about the female form, in a manner befitting his claim to be an artist of skin and tissue. Without wishing to act the sort of bore who buttonholes surgeons at parties, still, I couldn't stop myself asking Robert how he girded himself for bout after bout of labiaplasty, 'the designer vagina', given that the procedure had become a Forrest Clinic signature. 'Has it never made you feel – I don't know – desensitised to women?'

He looked at me keenly as if this were the most profoundly serious matter I'd ever raised with him. 'Not the bodies. No, never. Nothing could change how you touch flesh that attracts you. The female mind, though – that is, of course, a truly appalling vista . . .'

Poor Eloise – one more notch on Robert's scalpel. But in truth she's had a lucky escape.

7

Eloise's Workbook
The knife and the wound

August 30th

Steven, I can't sleep, and I'm glad of that, since the dreams are worse than wakefulness. Shall I tell you what I dreamt last night?

I was in a cottage, a gingerbread stone cottage, marooned in the clearing of a forest – the clearing perfect as a crop circle, hemmed on all sides by tall trees, lilac and purple foxglove. In the sky above was a huge black cloud like a canopy – *un nuage funèbre et gros d'une tempête!* – so even by daylight the cottage was steeped in darkness. And inside I was trapped, stuck in the fireplace – a huge hearth, no fire burning, still I was caged behind the guard, wedged right into the grate among the cinders and ashes, and my parents (they had the faces of my real parents, at least for a time) wouldn't let me out. They jabbed at me with sharp black pokers. I snapped back at them with blackened teeth.

Then came a hammering at the door. My dungeon shook . . . And a man forced his way in somehow, nobody admitted him. I couldn't quite place his face, my rescuer – I'm not certain he had a face. But he swept me up in his arms, bore me on his shoulder as he scaled the inside of the chimney stack, lizard-like, then hefted me up and out and over the roof. When he told me to jump I jumped and, still, he caught me. Then he led me into the forest, and we sat at the foot of a tree until it got darker and darker, and all he did was stare at me.

Then I woke myself up, because it was too ghastly.

ری

I have to tell you, you will understand – I always thought I'd never be able to bear it here at Blakedene – didn't believe it could be the 'therapeutic landscape' your glossy brochure promises – no 'good, safe place' of friends and protectors, not if hemmed on all sides by dark and silent woods: *le bois sombre et les nuits solitaires* . . . However, I now accept: these woods of yours are most pleasant. I think we should be allowed to walk in them more often, all of us sufferers. The darkness and the silence encourage contemplation. They also test the nerve.

I will say, too, that I'm far happier now to be in West Wing with my fellow Depressives, Neurotics & Bipolars. I don't mind the proximity to the Anorexics in Upper Court – they're serious individuals, all of them, I can see that. But the drunks and cokeheads in East Wing – get them behind me, I don't want to go near that particular circle of hell.

Forgive me, though, if I say I'm still a bit troubled to be thought of as the inmate of a boutique asylum. How green would be my girlfriends' eyes at the size of my en suite, my plasma TV, my palatial bed (even more so to know that that pop singer slept in it before me, struggling with her 'exhaustion', even before she'd begun her world tour). But on that first morning I stood before your doors here, tentative, suitcase in hand. I have to say Blakedene Hall just looked to me like some country-house holiday spot for weekending bankers. Even this time I still felt a measure of guilt stepping over the threshold into the foyer. One does expect a porter to take one's bags, a concierge to pocket one's car keys, a maître d' to sketch out what the chef has planned for dinner.

However, I am no inverse snob – that would ill become me. And I would say of the building that it exudes a huge reassurance. Anyone would call it handsome – that Palladian sandstone so grandly high and wide, pleasingly darkened by rain and ivy; the Doric porch and pilasters, the low arcaded wings, the delightful south-facing veranda where a girl can smoke her Gitanes in peace as she writes up her diary . . .

I am a diarist by nature, you know that. Only I used to write so that I could hear my own voice, to cope with the terrible silence in the place where I lived. These days . . . I'm actually rather afraid of what I might be thinking. Do you really expect me to be truthful here on this page? True, when I first made a friend of pen and paper, aged 12, it seemed a needful and acceptable thing to fantasise, succumb to the occasional swoon – since my imagination was innocent, fundamentally chaste. I expect you guessed – that handsome, angular English teacher I penned up a storm about, the one who urged me to read Rimbaud and Baudelaire? He didn't exist. Nor the stable-boy on the neighbouring estate, beautiful but inclined to the spiritual. Such were my daydreams, back then. Before Flint. Before everything got torn and ruined and turned to shit by that fuck-pig, that despicable scum, *ravageur, monstre, corrupteur*.

ಞಲ

Steven – there are things I struggle to tell you – because you will not think well of me. Since last I was here? I made mistakes. I can't help disappointing you, and I fear I will continue to do so. I disappoint myself.

The girls who used to bully me at St Mary's, those viciously bored little queen-bees – yet I can't help thinking they had a point, you know. You told me they were just upper-class English snobs, looking down their long noses because my father made his fortune in cut-price phones and laptops. But maybe they sensed something more: that I was one of life's open wounds, and it would be too much fun for them to pour salt on me. The knife looks for a wound, Steven, the wound for a knife – the old romance of *la plaie et le couteau*.

Can you help me? Even now? And can I still keep my secrets? Without them, you must understand, there's only so much of me that remains.

8

Dr Hartford's Journal

Some devil

August 31st

Thwarted at every turn is how I feel today. My report back to Team on Eloise Keaton's clearly much worsened condition was greeted by . . . a strange, flat scepticism – much as yesterday's management meeting seemed to hum with implicit disapproval of me. Even Margaret Yang tossed a few barbs on how I prioritise my time, to perceptible nods from Andrew Gillon. Then Grey called me at lunch, confirming our run on the Heath tomorrow morning, after so many recent cancellations – only to add it would be a chance for us *to work out what we're going to do about Robert'*. Exactly what does he imagine we can do in the circumstances? Pack torches and spades, form a two-man search party? Trawl the Thames, stake out the airports? I understand his fears, his dismay, I share them. But clearly the police are chasing up every lead.

Of course, it all put me in a less than ideal state of preparedness for two taxing hours with David Tregaskis. I went out to fetch him from the art pavilion, found him sat apart as ever, commanding the space of a whole trestle table, going avidly about a sculpture in creamy water-based clay that he'd perched up on a metal pole. Staring stark-eyed at his work, tugging his long dark locks, his red tongue tapping at his teeth, he looked every inch the Byronic artist. His shirt was open to near the navel, asserting his all-over hairiness.

Evidently the sculpture was a bust, with a rudimentary neck and oval head, but there were intimations of bone structure, the bridge of a nose and full lips had been roughed out. David has talent, no question. How quickly he's taught himself this craft! Little sticks, paperclips and sponges were strewn about, and in his hand he was turning a sharp-pointed divider-calliper that made me a tad uneasy. But Dora Holzman manages the pavilion, it's her call. And I do consider David harmless, even to himself.

He 'greeted' me first by a distracted nod, while he twisted and tugged at the fine silver bracelet he wears always on his wrist – a distressed but clearly precious loop of intricate little knots. Finally he turned those hard orbs of his onto me.

'Yeah. It's blank now but all will become clear. You want to start right, see, at the outset of any piece. You treat the structure respectfully, especially when you're a novice – with kid gloves. But, at some point, you have to jump in. Do violence.'

With that, still pensive, David turned back to his raw clay head, grasped it in both hands and, with his thumbs, inflicted a twin pair of gouges. Then he popped a rolled-up little eyeball of clay into one hole, and began to scratch a 'retina' with one of his unfurled paperclips. Sitting atop scattered papers on the trestle was a charcoal drawing in his skilful hand, some lovely long-haired female. I complimented his draughtsmanship, he merely shoved the sketch under some other pages.

'How are the kids, Steven? Little Julian okay?' (Too often of late I've noticed this unsettling ability of David's, as if guided by queer frequencies, to seemingly intuit whatever's wrong in my household.) 'And how is Tessa? You know there are still a few things I'd really like to discuss with her, if that were possible . . .'

I wish I'd never let on to David that Tessa is a medievalist. He's hinted before as to which aspects of the period preoccupy him – namely the persecution of the Knights Templar by Philip of France on Friday the thirteenth, October 1307; plus the alleged usage of the blood of Christian children in the Passover meal. Intelligent though David undoubtedly is, I find his intellectual interests highly selective. And given his tendency to lead any topic down a rabbit-hole, gesturing wearily or testily if one fails to follow his impossible turns, I don't think a 'discussion' between Tessa and him could satisfy either party.

Margaret Yang, the first of us to treat him here, told me she knew his type: 'the sort of guy who really believes he's Jesus Christ, but the trouble is he's got a very detailed and not completely implausible explanation for it'. When his parents brought him in his poor little mother wept to me, 'Oh doctor, he always had a wild imagination, it's only more recent he's started to *change* . . .' What he had 'more recent' was mental distortion from years of marijuana and amphetamine abuse. He was at art school when they diagnosed him depressed, prescribed him

Seroxat, whereupon a whirlwind was unleashed: turmoil, his asserting that he'd ceased to feel 'real'. That psychosis, at least, is past. His sense of unreality, though, persists. This is David's fourth stay with us. I had believed he improved each time, if I didn't quite understand why. Now I'm less sure. Still, we are committed to people once they've come, we see them through – I've waived certain charges in David's case, not that he will ever thank me for it.

Lately I believe he's finally found something here that he truly responds to – not our cares, alas, rather an aspect of Blakedene's history that appeals to his mystical bent. On the shelves of the ground-floor library, amid a modest collection of titles devoted to local history, David seized on our copy of the privately printed memoir of William Harron, a rightly obscure old fraud of a 'society medium' (from Kirkcaldy, no less) who used to conduct séances here during the 1860s, at the invitation of the then lord of the manor, the disreputable third Marquess of Ravenscourt. Indeed, once David and I were seated in my office he spent fifteen minutes petitioning to be moved from his room, as he believes it to be the very site where Victorian visitors to Blakedene were haunted by the shade of Roisin Slaney, a servant girl reputedly impregnated then killed by the depraved Ravenscourt. Trying to keep us clear of that rabbit-hole, I assured David that in all my time here I'd received no reports of any spectral sightings.

Whereupon things went downhill. I append the transcript, which is, by its oddness, self-explanatory. I should say it was preceded by a silence of maybe thirty seconds wherein David merely glowered at me.

DT: *I'm disturbed, Steven, I'm disappointed by your, your— flat, your dull, your may I say boring, may I say resentful tone of voice?*

SH: *I'm sorry, 'resentful' because—?*

DT: *Because you're so mired in your all-too-human thoughts. Human thoughts have changed a million times since this world began. They'll change a million more before it ends.*

SH: *David, shall we . . . speak of something else, some other—?*

DT: *No, don't make me talk about— banal things, not now when we just got near the essence. Just because you resist it. Have you even thought for one minute about the walls around you? These spirit-ridden walls?*

SH: *Well— I'm a sceptic in this area, David, as are a great many people. I have given it thought, believe me. I do accept there's a vital part of our lives that is 'spiritual', for want of a word with fewer connotations. But I've never been convinced that the spirits of the dead return to us in order to . . . bang on a parlour table. Or upturn a vase of flowers . . .*

DT: *You're talking about Harron? Yes, I agree. The gods don't do magic shows. Harron's methods weren't refined, nor were his peers'. But in their day, for their time, they were pathfinders, Steven. True scientists, with true theory of death. We owe them better than this modern-day, pseudo-sophisticate contempt.*

SH: David, as you know, science proposes a method, standards of evidence—

DT: Of course it does. If spiritualism can't refute any scientific enquiry then it's not true spiritualism. My spiritualism is founded on knowledge, not faith. On spiritual power, Steven. The whole problem is that spiritualism's never been properly applied, properly tested – because of the sceptics, the faint-hearts, dimwits who hear the word 'spirit' and imagine only evil. Roisin Slaney wasn't evil. Never harmed one of the dozens, dozens of people who saw her here—

SH: But you fear she might harm you? Since you want to change your room?

[. . .]

DT: No. My concern would be that Master Ravenscourt might choose to come after her again. 'The satanic Marquess . . .' He was absolutely sure he'd be reborn, you know. Such were his— energies. The spirits want human form, they seek the medium of flesh. To get things done.

[. . .]

SH: Listen, David, I take seriously your interest, I do—

DT: I've been seeing the spirits since I was four years old, Steven. Hearing them. I never asked for that, didn't want it—

SH: I understand that, I know—

DT: But, listen, in itself that means nothing. Every one of us has the faculty, it's only that so few trust in it. All I am is one who's open. The spirits are in the air, Steven, they can come in a dream, they can jump out

81

*of a mirror. They're common that way. What are we,
any of us, but spirits enveloped by flesh . . . ?*

I had thought David was improving . . . and now this.
Might his 'spiritualism' be just an 'encapsulated delusion'
– like his fellow inmate Marcia Fallow, perfectly lucid
but for her belief she has been married, at one time or
another, to a man from each and every country she can
name (Dutch men the most affable, Syrians quite despicable, et cetera)?

No, reviewing those baroque exchanges I realise now
just how much David reminds me of the Spartan types I
used to argue with fruitlessly at draughty socialist meet-
ings, forever thinking they'd 'refuted' me by citing some
neglected footnote to a footnote in Marx. That's David
– he's like the last communist. The problematic friend I
can't bear to dump. But I *am* his friend. No one but me
is going to make the effort with him. At the same time,
I must acknowledge, he's assumed the place in my life
once occupied by Tom Dole. This cannot be good, not
for either of us.

Margaret Yang has long argued that David's only 'top-
ping up', playing the system, manipulating my attention.
Possibly. But the pain in his life is real, even if only an ag-
gravated version of a form we're all familiar with: a frustration with the limits of his own person. The problem is
what do I do about that? Call in a shaman?

'Get back in your fucking cage, you mad cunt.'

This, the sensitive response of the bloke I saw being asked for spare change by the barking beggar outside the mini-market first thing this morning. (I could have spared myself the spectacle, but such was my need for twenty cigarettes.) The bloke wasn't aware he was having an argument until he was stuck in it – the beggar jabbing a finger first at the bloke's face then at his own skull, his charge being that certain thoughts were broadcasting from out the top of his head, and this bloke had been trying to eavesdrop. So vehement were the beggar's curses that the bloke's rejoinder was, I suppose, inevitable, even defensible.

The beggar, still shouting after the bloke's retreating back, shoved a hand down the front of his filthy strides, the hand then becoming visibly agitated. I am quite certain that, had I asked him, he would have told me his hand was 'possessed'. This is the sort of man I should be treating, except he can't afford me. He needs a friend, this man. He was a boy once, and all his cares were as nothing. What happened to him?

Of course, we used to think 'behaviours' such as his were the work of witches and demons. Indeed, I've met Somalian immigrants to this country who remain of that view: still comfortable with the notion that the devil – the Deceiver, the Father of Lies – intervenes in our affairs. They come to our cities, take on dirty jobs, pay a fortune in rent and council tax for some hovel where the neighbours hate them. Their wives leave them for some witch-doctor, and they seek succour from some other witch-doctor, who tells them the author of their misfortune is . . . ? 'The devil, probably.'

Do I have a better idea? My profession long ago dispensed with Satan, of course, but initially advanced no further than to the notion that madness thrived in the sufferer's blood, and could be drawn out by a sensible application of leeches. What are the fruits of wisdom that centuries of enquiry now bestow upon me? *Get some drugs into this man! Dampen down those symptoms!*

I saw another beggar this morning, fifty yards down the street from the ranter, slumped under the cashpoint where I stopped to top up. A girl, sexlessly shaven-headed, wearing a vest and khaki shorts and boots, as if she'd just staggered out of a desert. She looked floppy, inert, no sign of will or initiative, not even of any strong feeling, unlike our ranter friend. I suspect she wouldn't eat much, even if food she had – likewise vis-à-vis her personal hygiene. She's not right, anyone can see. But is she really ill? If so, how so? Type Two Schizophrenia? But if you can't see it under a microscope, is it really illness? Mightn't it be those devils?

Back when I was dissecting the brains of schizophrenics at the Maudsley – what did I hope to find there amid the spongy tissue? Some glaring abnormalities in structure and function? Or the finest, most minute strangeness, the stuff of a life's work? In any event, I was disappointed. Yes, I have felt some upsurge of hope lately when we've scanned the brains of patients by magnetic resonance. If one keeps an eye on the bold fields indicative of metabolic rate and blood-flow – there you can perceive a definite visible correlate of the patient's mental turmoil. That's when it feels meaningful. But MRI costs. The drugs are cheaper, faster – 'more effective in the short term'.

No, in the main I have to go by the evidence of mine own eyes. And what I can actually see is distress: people so immensely pained that everything about them is just inappropriate – every thought, every action. Something has ripped the soul out of them, they live in a thought-world of permanent black.

But then what about those black thoughts that seem to oppress all of us, at times, out here in the community of the sane? Mightn't those thoughts just be a necessary part of the human experience, to a greater or lesser extent? I've treated people for the seeming crime of ceasing to wash and care properly for themselves. These mornings of late I stare into the mirror at a pale unshaven shambles of a man, waiting for my double to say *'What does that make you . . . ?'*

<hr />

A curious coda to the day. I went walking over to West Wing, thinking I might slip Eloise's workbook back under her door, but all was dark and silent and I thought better – was on the point of retreating to make up my bed on the Chesterfield – until I saw a slash of light onto the corridor outside David's room. I wandered down, peeked in, saw him in the swivel chair at his desk, avidly at work on that clay bust. Dora must have let him take materials to his room. I must have words with Dora . . .

He had fashioned some delicate small pieces – nose, lips, ears – and adhered them to the mass of the head. Now he was sculpting some surrounding coils into a mass of hair, taking care to suggest flowing locks. To me it rather had the look of Frankenstein fashioning a bride for himself. For a while I stood there peering over his shoulder. I still feel a sort of childish wonder in seeing how a likeness can be brought to life, how by mimetic art we meet faces we never saw before, yet suddenly seem to know better than our friends. This woman being moulded by David – she had an inchoate loveliness, an Attic refinement, albeit something Medusa-like to those coils. In truth I did feel she resembled some face I'd seen before, but far too vaguely to place.

'You like my work, Steven?'

I must one day get myself fully inured to David's reper- toire of unnerving tricks – in this case, the eyes-in-back- of-head. At least here the illusion was broken instantly upon my catching sight of the compact mirror propped on his desk.

'It's shaping up very well, David. Could I see that sketch of yours again? The one you're working from?'

He shook his head. 'I'm working from in here now,' he said, tapping his skull, homage to his own imaginative powers.

'Do you have a name for her?' I asked, half-expecting, I admit, that he would say 'Roisin'. But he appeared to weigh this very seriously.

'I believe her name's "Dijana". As in the goddess. I

think that's it . . .' He half-shifted in his chair and shot me a squinting grin. 'You maybe recognise her? Or just think you do? That's not peculiar. There's aspects of the feminine we're hard-wired to see. Us fellas . . .' This last bit tumbled out of him in a sort of mangled Irish brogue, before he turned once again to his handiwork. The nag in my head persisted. But I daresay David has a point. I shut his door, left the monster to his bride.

9

Dr Lochran's Journal
A disturbing encounter

August 31st

Tonight a most unpleasant duty somehow devolved onto me, and even sitting here hours later I am still a little shaken by it.

Livy and I were stacking the dishes, polishing off a creamy Montrachet and talking in the vaguest terms about Christmas, when I had a call from Malena, a most uncharacteristic quaver in her voice, asking would I *please* hurry over to hers, without delay, as Killian was 'acting very strangely' and had put her somewhat in fear of her safety. I don't know that Livy was entirely convinced by the entreaty, but she waved me away in the view that I'd been given no choice.

I got there in fifteen minutes. Malena admitted me looking pale, embarrassed, even, but, yes, undeniably spooked and speaking in a hush, as if not to awaken a slumbering Cyclops. Pointing upward she told me Killian was in his studio, drunk. 'He's been drinking all day – a *distillery* smell up there.'

Apparently, quite atypically, he'd got stuck into the Powers whiskey I brought over in the summer. (Relating this, Malena couldn't quite suppress the accusation of her eyes.) Then from upstairs she'd heard rending, smashing noises, and she scampered up there in panic only to be roared at, warned to make herself scarce. He had moved toward her with the three-pound hammer in hand and, though I can't imagine she really feared assault, she didn't dally. But she had time to spot shards of shattered stone around the floor at Killian's feet.

I understood her alarm, yes, though not her sense of these being death-stakes between them. What I could do, I thought, was have a sober word with the man, as if I'd 'just dropped by'. So up I went, cursing the mad-creaking stairs at every step, until I crossed the threshold into the darkened studio.

Some pale blue of the night's full moon bled through the skylight, allowing me to see that wreckage was indeed strewn across the floor. Killian had overturned all those rows of small figures formerly lined up on his shelves. His cans of chisels had been thrown the length of the room, red paint was splattered like an open cut down one long wall. The bull had certainly had his way with the china shop: on all sides, things snapped and torn and crushed as if in spasms of violence.

I heard a creak behind me, spun round and saw a ghost – or rather, Killian's rocking chair, shrouded in an old dust sheet. Then the sheet inched away and fell, so revealing the man himself – first his glaring head, then his slumped body. That chair had looked a folksy affectation to me, but Killian made it seem sinister now as he straightened in the seat, set his hands on the rests, started to rock slowly back and forth. His eyes had a queasy gleam, the line of his mouth jagged. The three-pound hammer sat snug between his thighs. I felt a quickening in my chest, and was angry with myself: it was still only a squirt of an Irishman facing me. And yet, I admit, there was something forcefully unsettling in the very air of the room – a chill, an aura, a current of ill feeling. Finally I found my voice.

'Killian, you've given Malena a scare today.'

'Oh . . . I give myself a scare, Grey. She should see what I see in the mirror every morning.'

'Get on with you. Wait 'til you're my age, then you'll see a sorry sight. You're a fine-looking young man.'

He grunted. 'You wanna suck my rod or something?'

'No, son. No, I'm here because Malena's worried about you.'

'Is that so?'

'It is. You've got her in quite a fret down there. Do you not think you should— try to make things better?'

'Do you not think you should stay out of it? Promise you, captain, you should not interfere.'

'Probably not, but— I'm here now, and Malena is my friend, and I'm finding I don't quite like your tone.'

'Oh no?' he sneered, and rose, came toward me, the hammer hanging from his hand, his brow tilted in the manner of a bull contemplating a charge. 'My tone, y'say? Well, see, I have had intolerable provocation . . .'

I held my ground. 'I'd warn you, Killian, don't let the Powers talk you into trying something daft. You may think you've got youth on your side, but I've fifty pounds of heft on you. That'll count if it comes to a ruck, you can bet on it.'

He stood there, swaying a little, seeming to weigh my argument. Then he looked hard at me, that brow still tilted. The foreshortening distorted his handsome face most unpleasantly – dark pools under his eyes, the eyes themselves narrowed to slots under his arched brows. His mouth could have been grin or grimace.

'Tell me something, Grey. I want you to tell me honestly. Do you suppose your friend Malena was a happier soul when she was with her – what shall we say? – her ex-lover? The eminent doctor?'

'That's not for me to say, Killian.'

'But you'd know, in fact you'd have a preference yourself . . . ?'

'Robert is my oldest, dearest friend,' I shot back, without flinching. 'But Malena wouldn't be with you now if she didn't think her relations with Robert had broken down – irreparably. And if she didn't believe you loved her. So I'd say your speculation's a waste of time. As long as you do love her. And show her as much.'

But he'd ceased to listen, had hung his pickled head. 'Huh. "Irreparably". Poor Doctor Forrest. Poor, dead Doctor Forrest . . .'

I wouldn't accept that, not even as drunken maundering. 'Robert's not dead, Killian, so you shouldn't say it.'

He looked up at me flatly, churlish again – a hiss in the breath coming out of him, mingled with the peat-smoke odour of the whiskey. 'Grey, when the vital functions cease, and the heart stops, and the breath leaves the body – we call that death, do we not?'

'It's a working definition of sorts, but it doesn't apply

to Robert, does it, Killian? Robert's missing.'

'Gone missing, gone astray . . . Wherever will we find him? And if we do then would we know so? Where would the essence of Robert be found . . . ?' He prodded a floorboard with the scuffed toecap of his boot.

'Killian, if you're trying to tell me— you know something, about what's happened to Robert? Then pull yourself together, talk to me in plain words.'

He had turned half of his back to me, and when he spoke again it was a near-whisper. 'I'm as much in the dark as yourself. What could he have done to himself? Or anyone? What would be the worst you could imagine?'

He had laid down the hammer on one of his sandbagged benches, and seemed now to be surveying his own wrecking handiwork round the room. I risked drawing a little nearer, truly wondering what in hell had possessed the man. 'God sakes, Killian. How could you trash your own stuff like this? After all what you told me?'

He spoke without turning. 'What did I tell you? Tell me again.'

'I mean all that about . . . respecting the bloody stone.'

'Aw, the materials were good, Grey, but I made something evil of them. And she deserved it, most eminently. I took it all out on her. But much the better, yeah? Would you have me dissect a living subject . . . ?'

His look at me was almost taunting while I wracked my faulty memory for what he'd stirred up. Then it hit me. 'How did you come by that turn of phrase? It was a little joke of Robert's and mine.'

'I know. Now it's one of Killian's.'

For the first time I wondered how well acquainted Killian and Robert might have got, before Robert realised the younger man had plans to usurp him. I glanced aside to the worktop where the bottle of Powers sat drained down to all but an amber heel. Killian followed my gaze, lifted the bottle and knocked the dregs back with barely a grimace.

'I meant that Powers as a present, Killian, not that you should try killing yourself with it.'

'You're right. We should take care, yes? When we un- leash the Powers on ourselves.' He seemed to slump, the heel of his palm on his forehead. 'Grey, I've had such a lesson. No end of a lesson . . .'

If at first I'd found him menacing, now he looked merely forlorn. 'Killian, you need to get a grip on your- self, man.'

'Yeah, I need to— master these extremities, it's true. It would be simpler, but that I have bad dreams . . .'

'Aye well, I know that feeling. What do you dream about?'

'Things you're not to know, Horatio. There's more to heaven and hell than you ever . . . whatever.' Red-eyed, he waved a hand. 'I'm drunk, Grey, okay? So pay us no mind. I'm drunk, and tomorrow I'll be sober. None of this will matter. We'll forget.'

He managed a grin, as if I should join him in the jape. In the next instant he'd slung an arm around me, and was singing into my face:

One night I came in the bedroom door,
Just as drunk as a fella could be,
To see a young lad lain there in the bed
Where my old bones should be.
I grabbed me wife and yelled for dear life,
'Can you ever explain to me?
Who owns them bones by you in the bed
Where my old bones should be . . . ?'

Then he staggered against me. I gave him the full benefit of my shoulder. 'Right,' I murmured, 'let me help you clear up, you eejit.'

'Leave it be. My mistake. My bloody mess . . .'

And yet he allowed me to support him back to the rocking chair. Then I stooped and collected up one can of chisels, set a couple of figures back upright on a shelf. Whereupon I properly noticed the two pieces of lunar-white alabaster, clearly broken halves, their jagged edges speaking to one another. I suspected the three-pound hammer had done this damage. And so I picked them up and pressed them together, and what formed in my hands was a sort of death mask, a Greek severity about it, with empty sightless eye-sockets and fine-boned female features. Then – I swear – something twisted hard in my chest.

Killian lurched from his chair, snatched what was in my hands, hurled the broken stone across the room where it struck bare brick.

'Get *out*, Grey. Out of my world . . .'

I had seen enough of it, that was for sure. I hit the door, made my way down the stairs. By the second flight

I could hear him coming down behind me, a stumbling sort of tread, and I braced myself to renew hostilities. But then I heard him stagger off aside, into the small guest bedroom that lay off the third floor landing. Boards creaked above my head, as they do when a body crashes down insensate on a mattress. Then all was horrid silence.

Malena was at the foot of the stairs, still worryingly grim. I couldn't tell her what I had seen, since I wasn't sure myself. And I couldn't face climbing those stairs again. So I told her what I believed to be true – that he would be a different man again once he'd slept off the whiskey. But this terrible bitterness he's brought to their relations – in all honesty I'd be less certain that will pass.

September 1st

Some sort of movement in Robert's case this morning – or so I dearly hope. I got a call from DS Goddard on behalf of DI Hagen, who asks that we meet for an hour or so on Friday at Robert's apartment in Artemis Park. I agreed, of course: on paper there's nothing I can't shift that day, work-wise. But since the appointment was made by proxy the mystery is in no way lessened. Perhaps there's been progress. Or perhaps I am to be among the privileged first to be told some bad news.

There are, at least, new things I can tell Hagen – about Killian MacCabe, for one thing. I don't know if they interviewed him during the preliminaries, but they should bloody well speak to him now – because there is something about his new fixation on Robert that I find disturbing, if not downright suspicious.

And then I must try to face up to – just get clear in my own beclouded head – this business of Dijana Vukovara, the 'dark lady', Robert's mystery woman. The trouble is, she has been such an elusive, strangely half-formed figure in my memory – for one thing I had entirely forgotten her face, what she looked like.

But Killian was right: we can recognise a woman by just a pair of smudged lines. If she wore a mask we'd guess by the frame of hair, if she wore a greatcoat we'd know her by the turn of her ankle. I had sight of Dijana just the once, but – no mistake now, no seeming shroud of fog around her, no curtain drawn across my mind – I'm nearly certain I saw her face again, the contours of it, eyeless but unmistakable, when I rejoined those two broken shards of alabaster.

10

Dr Hartford's Journal
Through the trees

September 2nd

More grief last night – my prize for coming home. I was barely through the door when I heard the *tok* of Tessa's heels across the kitchen tiles. Her theme: that the house is no longer big enough for four, needs extension – a cellar dug, perhaps, or an add-on out the back? What has she got in mind, really? A den for the boys? Or a room of her own, somewhere to be free from the sullen men-folk in her life? Frankly I don't see the need, nor do I feel like paying for it, or having to manage an invasion of bricklayers. None of that will solve our actual problems.

At least I have Grey . . . Calder must think the same, as would the rest of the big ebullient brood that Grey and Livy ought by rights to have had, so easily and with such authority does Grey play paterfamilias. But just as Grey was raised not to dwell on misfortune, so he will never have thought twice – whereas I agonise – over whether he's a fit paternal role model. He just knows it and gets on with it.

To this day I'm as obedient and biddable in Grey's company as little boys are with their fathers. Robert, I know, has felt similar, much as it would kill him to admit it. But I've got to be on guard for any outward show of mawkishness. I suppose the simplest remedy is to imagine Grey's face – his mirthful, annihilating riposte – if by some awful Freudian mishap I addressed him as 'Dad'.

Gruff as he is, Grey is a rock in this shifting world, his opinion of a thing the same today as it was yesterday. When we met as lads at Kilmuir – he prefect and Head of House, de rigueur – I thought him too bumptious for his boots, imagined he drew his assurance entirely from being so physically bullish and well made. But time and friendship showed me his was an inner strength. (Otherwise Robert and I, both lean and speedy backs rather than hulking prop forwards, would have left him to the fascists of the First XV, drinking beer from a boot to the delight of the ladies.) Being proportionally larger than the rest of us has only ever made Grey more conscious of the need for delicacy toward others. 'From each according to their ability', indeed. He takes his clout as a duty, not as an excuse to throw his weight about, smack down lesser specimens.

This morning our run was on, so I laced up and jogged away from my doorstep just after 5.30 a.m. Having worked up a head of steam I found him pacing in wait for me on Wildwood Road and, wordlessly, we set off abreast. He didn't look lively, though – wincing at times – and when he pulled up and bent double near the entrance to the Heath I made solicitous, but he only waved me off.

So I headed in and uphill, over the unmown grass, between the sparse cypresses, the Heath seeming deserted. For me a run is always the same punishment: ten minutes of what feels like virtuous purging, then a further half-hour of being stabbed in the chest and beaten round the knees. I was sat nursing my calves on Parliament Hill, oblivious to the city vista under wan sun, by the time Grey finally crested the rise at a trudge.

'Dear me. Shall I fetch your stick?'

'Piss away off. You weren't so far ahead of me.'

'I'd already run a mile before I met you, old timer.'

From his shorts Grey retrieved a book of matches and a crushed pack of red Marlboros. I trust he didn't spot the hungering look in my eye. 'I'm no' a medical man, Steve,' he growled in his cod-Jock manner once he was sparked up, 'but ah reckon somethin' in mah chest just broke. A rib, mebbe? What'd be your diagnosis?'

'Nothing so severe. Though I suspect if we did have a doctor to hand he'd advise you to cut back on the sugar, and the cholesterol. And maybe the tobacco.'

Grey stretched that bass-drum chest of his, exhaling in my direction. 'Pish on that. The Lochrans have never had heart disease.'

'So you're immune.'

'Naw, naw,' he said, pounding a fist on his evidently stiff right shoulder. 'Never said such. In fact, all things considered, I'd not rule out the odds of a total blockage in the left anterior descending. The "widow-maker".' He chuckled. 'But, sure, you cannae stop what's coming down the pipe.'

'I think Livy and Cal would like you to muddle along to at least retirement age, Grey. Maybe a while longer.'

'Retirement, Stevie? I am *needed*. Not long now, but.

Five, six years tops. Anyhow I'm not as bad as the cardiacs, or the micro guys working their fingers arthritic from dawn to midnight.'

'Nonetheless. You work, what, fifty hours a week? Not counting the on-calls? Taking all your factors into account – you might want to look to your lifestyle.'

'Aye, well, come that cold day in hell then I'll do as you ask. For Christ's sake, Steve, you're not even a real Scot, however did you get so bloody Calvinist?'

It does irk me, Grey's occasional wrapping of himself in the saltire, a flag of convenience beneath which I, born of Romney Marsh, may not stand. He does it as and when it suits him – he and Robert both, their accents are usually mere lilts, the posh Scots of London. But this morning he laid it on thick. I was taking it lightly until I saw his genuinely sour face. Since he had plonked himself down on the grass with his fag, I joined him.

'You know, I used to enjoy these wee runs of ours, Steven, but they're getting to be a bloody bore, and I think it's something to do with your womanish bloody fixation on my health. I know you "care" and that, big man, but let a fellow go to hell his own sweet way, eh?'

There was a familiar edge on that word 'care' that I didn't care for. Grey knows full well that I associate his poisonous, clogging tobacco and booze intake with Robert, and the undergraduate manner in which they've so long carried on.

'Sorry. You want to talk about Robert, then?'

And Grey looked to his toecaps then back at me, nodding as to say that, yes, we were as well to get down to the real business. 'I've been asked to go see this Hagen fellow,' he said finally. 'At Robert's place. Find out what they're doing about finding him, I suppose. Or not, as it may be.'

'Right. Yes. Hagen called me the other day.'

Grey's brow furrowed, and he gave me a grilling of his own, clearly assuming I had pumped the detective for information. Since I had not, he seemed peeved at both of us. *I will get to the bottom of this* – so said the set of his chin. He brooded a little, then turned back to me.

'Listen, I've begun to have – oh I don't know – a few doubts, I would say, about Killian MacCabe . . .'

He told me how Malena had summoned him to the aftermath of some marital dispute, where he found Killian heavily drunken and threatening, 'singing shanties to himself'. It did indeed sound like a grim domestic scene, as would make mine look tame, and yet not the worst account I'd heard of a 'creative' temperament.

'Grey,' I said, 'he can't be the first Irishman you've met who's come on all heavy after ten big belts of whiskey.'

'Aye, but this . . . it seemed way out of character.'

'How well do you know MacCabe? From one or two house calls? What are you saying, anyway? You think he knows something about Robert? Did something to Robert? You can't think that, surely? Robert maybe had cause to do *him* an injury. But not vice versa?'

'I don't know. He made . . . innuendoes. Said things I thought were queer. He was drunk, aye, but . . . he just made it sound like he knew for a fact that Robert's six feet under. And that he wasn't too displeased.'

'It's not easy,' I said, soothing. 'The change from part-ner to partner? We all carry baggage into these things. Male pride's a naturally occurring phenomenon, he wouldn't be a man if he didn't wonder. It's the intimacy of rivals. And he could just be disconcerted, given how Malena must be feeling over Robert.'

'She could do without him giving her all else to worry about. I called by again the next day, to check the lay of the land. His nibs wasn't about. But Malena was giving me the brave face, I could tell.'

His diligence surprised me. 'How does Olivia feel about all these gallantries of yours for Malena? All these house calls.'

'Livy's not mad-pleased. But I'm not in the dog-house. Not as you are, Doctor Hartford . . .' I didn't care to discuss my domestic difficulties, but in any case Grey only shook my shoulder. 'Thank God, Stevie, you and me are the marrying kind. Not of the divorcing classes . . .'

We were wandering back along a well-worn track through the West Heath, silently admiring the plains of agreeably unkempt grass and the good rosy morning glow in the treetops, when we saw, at the same time and plain as day, two lithe young men flitting through the trees, near identical in their shaved heads and denims, close together and conspiratorial – thieves of love.

Grey raised one bushy eyebrow. 'The last of the boys of summer, eh? By God, they've had an early start. Or been at it all night.'

'I've a story in that line, actually.' Grey only grunted,

still a little distracted. 'Yes, I was out walking here around dusk a few weeks back.'

'Spying on our homosexual brethren, were you? Or escaping from your family?'

I let that slide. 'I could be wrong, but I was almost sure I saw Robert. With a woman.'

'What bloody woman?' Grey's humour had flown.

'Well, it was back there, I say I can't be sure because it was late, the moon was pretty thin, and I wasn't dallying. But I made out a fellow sat on the bench, and a woman stood behind him, in a black coat – but bent down, with her head to his neck – like she was whispering sweet nothings in his ear. An intimate look to it, anyway. And when she straightened up I thought the chap could have been Robert. But I wasn't going to hang about to find out.'

Grey stared at me. 'You've kept that bloody quiet, Steven.'

'I meant to say, but it slipped my mind . . .' This was the God's honest. 'I don't know why I forgot until just now. Will you believe me?'

He nodded, rather darkly. 'Oh I do. Describe her, the woman.'

I had to risk a chuckle. 'That's the thing of it. I saw her face clearer than the man's, but nothing of it stuck with me. Just that she was a beauty, probably. Dark, I'd say, the hair? Pale skin.' Grey still nodding, still grimly mute. I had to ask. 'You've a notion who she might be?'

He grimaced. 'Ach, who the hell's to say? But you told Hagen, right? About her?'

'Dad' had me bang to rights at last. 'I didn't, no. Really, just because I'd forgotten about it altogether 'til this minute. I know it sounds mad. It was probably to do with being back in this same spot . . .'

I wasn't lying, odd as I know it sounded, but Grey and I scarcely spoke again before we parted ways on Wildwood Road. Still, he embraced me there, we wished each other well as ever.

Back home Tessa was readying the boys for nursery drop, not inclined to caresses. Rather, she picked her moment to tell me that as of tomorrow she'll be away for three nights at some scholarly conference in Cambridge. I was torn between stupefaction and relief, since now it can hardly be argued that I am the sole partner remiss in their duty. She has arranged for her parents to move in and manage the boys. 'You'll be crashing at Blakedene, I expect,' she told me while addressing her compact. As if I would shirk my chores. I know for a fact she will enjoy the nights away from me – the book-chat, shared drinks and meals, all the things we used to enjoy together and now prefer to do separately.

She even frogmarched the boys over to give me compulsory hugs, as if I were the one pissing off in the week before they start Big School. Their matching sweaters and doleful faces tugged at my heart. We're both to blame, we fell into that 'identical' trap – not wanting to favour one, even unconsciously, so tending to buy them similar. (We should have named them better too, why the hell did we fall for that alliterative thing?) They certainly know the difference, otherwise they wouldn't bore and rile one another so. They're still so young, of course, but they seem younger – a sort of toddler clumsiness, forever stepping across or barging into one another. Or maybe it's some muted, inchoate competitiveness, each trying to occupy the exact same space? There are certain traits they share: they're not wholly incapable of playing together. But Julian is so much his brother's shadow. He wouldn't want for friends quite so badly if he only liked me a little better.

I can't just sit and play the wronged party. I must, *must* make proper time for us all, block out the diary in black marker. We'll go to Dungeness. It's mad we let the cottage lie unused. Possibly Tessa and I both know, it reminds us of a moment before children, when we were sufficiently wrapped in each other, capable of being silly, certainly of seeing more things in life as possible, desirable. But in buying a family holiday place where we'd first weekended *à deux* we were guilty of glancing backward. *Nature trails for the kids!* we thought. But the boys haven't warmed to the strange terrain. We might have done better with a caravan in Camber Sands. But then did I make the effort to involve and stimulate them? Did Tessa? These are the things we must reckon. It will all start come their half-term. I'll make the plans tomorrow.

September 3rd

When I walked back into the mayhem tonight Tessa's mother must have seen in my eye I was in no shape to chat. I did manage to read the twins a story, one about a self-pitying goblin who felt himself unjustly maligned for his incumbent need to gobble up little children. I'd begun to feel a tad sorry for the creature myself, when I realised that both boys had turned their heads, sought their pillows instead.

Today's session with Eloise proved distressing for her, but also for me. I will persevere with the optical therapy but it was an inauspicious start. Maybe I should have read the entrails better. When I collected her from the library I found her tense, dressed as for a job interview: pin-stripe shirt with a white collar, a suede skirt, hair brushed, face made up. Worse, David Tregaskis was browbeating her from the leather armchair opposite. They had been 'discussing' world politics, David confiding his ambition to enlist with Al-Qaeda, an organisation he considers insufficiently intrepid on the simple level of physical bravery. (Typical David, not for him a place among the common herd, rather a leadership post ahead of others just as sociopathic as himself.) Eloise, to her credit, was unbothered ('I'd have to take him seriously, he'd need to have half a brain . . .'). But our troubles began up in the office.

She was visibly wary of the rig set up in the middle of the room: the light-bar behind my armchair, the special reclining seat opposite, flat black sensor pads on its hand-rests. Deprived of a cigarette her hands were soon all about her, coiling her hair, picking at the arm-rest. But I had the graceful rise and fall of Beethoven's piano concerto #5 just audible as we prepared for what we would discuss.

Her workbook has testified all too clearly, we had to return to the scene of the crime, her abuse by Marcus Flint. The single most distressing image she retains of the ordeal is a moment when Flint, after his own climax, rammed his fingers into her mouth. This brutally encapsulates her sense of having been dirtied, sullied. And yet still she believes she 'let it happen', can't accept how inescapable were Flint's predatory wiles, the adult's advantage he had on her. When I propose alternative, more positive ways she might conceive of how brave and dreadfully unfortunate she was, she thinks this 'silly, fake, wishful'.

But once it was time to begin we agreed the emergency stop-signal: she would raise her right hand, make a fist. The room was cool, dark, still. I asked her to place her hands on the sensor pads, activated the alternating pulses, turned on the sound: a pulse, a sonic throb, gradually resolving to a note bouncing back and forth between the speakers on the walls. I shifted my chair, gave her full view of the light-bar, asked her to follow the blinking red-green dots as they passed rhythmically from right to left, a set of thirty pulses, two per second. I asked her to be thinking all the while about the distressing image and the positive thought: *'It's not my fault.'* Watching, I was struck as ever by the strangely meditative, hypnotic aura of this treatment: the subject following the lights and yet, gradually, discernibly, starting to drift a little through their own psyche.

After the sets, though, Eloise reported no real change in her feelings. Rather, she returned repeatedly to how hard it was for her *'not to feel dreadful about something*

I knew was wrong and did anyway. I had to refute her assertion I was trying to 'sell' her something. But I was reminded again of the fatalism in her, a black and pessimistic strain.

We resumed the bilateral stimulation. Suddenly Eloise had a sneezing fit. When I told her to relax, asked her to describe her feelings anew, she told me she had got confused: a new memory/feeling had arisen in her. I assured her (albeit warily) that this was natural, that we should follow all byways and try to resolve those too. She began to talk of efforts Flint had made to stimulate her – touches, caresses, whispers in her ear. None of it sounded so different from the story as I knew it. And yet she insisted, she believed he had wanted her 'to feel something too'.

I may have been irritated, felt her being overly opaque – wrongly. What, I demanded, had he wanted her to feel? How had she felt?

But she had stopped, hung her blonde head, and now she raised her right hand, shakily, curled the fingers into a fist. I saw one perfect tear drop on the parquet floor. Her hands went to her face. 'It's rolling over me and I just can't bear it,' she said between gulps.

I considered letting her distress play out, but it had gone beyond the pale, we couldn't continue. I darted over, knelt beside her, put my arms round her – a hug of encouragement, of reassurance. She seemed to recover calm as I looked in her eyes for some moments. I reminded her of her relaxation techniques, comforted her back to an equilibrium.

It is, of course, a painful but unavoidable element in certain experiences of abuse: yes, the victim may have felt extreme discomfort, helplessness, humiliation, fear. But the body, irrespective, can respond to stimulation. These sensations come unbidden, create complexity.

Therapeutically speaking, I confess, I did everything wrong. I reacted too quickly. I am only dabbling in this technique, without qualification, trying tricks I've read in journals, improvising round an established process. But I was concerned for her; and having opened a patient up, one must be able to close the incision successfully rather than inflict some fresh trauma. My behaviour was not quite appropriate. All I can say in mitigation is that it had the right effect.

No, the difficulty arises because of what happened next. I heard the door open, I did flinch, move back from Eloise, but then I only expected Niamh, who knows me better than most. Instead, framed in the door, a look on his face of black relish, was David Tregaskis. Niamh pushed by him then pushed him back out, apologised frantically, said he had simply refused to sit outside waiting his turn a moment longer. I know that's what happened. But I saw – evidently by our faces we all felt – a sort of damage was done.

Dr Lochran's Journal
The looking-glass

September 3rd

Tonight I'm bone-weary and feeling bothersomely, non-specifically 'unwell'. But sleep feels far off. Too much unease.

This afternoon I drove to Robert's apartment to meet Bill Hagen. I'd cried off my supervisions to give him the time he asked for, and by God he took it. Rashly I hoped for some reassurance out of him in return. Instead the effect of our 'chat' has been to stir up snakes in my head.

Of course my mood was affected from the outset by the location. Gunning up the driveway of Artemis Park, past the sycamores and the signage for tennis courts, it struck me anew that some twerp of a banker might just about fool himself he'd bought into desirable luxury. The main building is splendid, yes, those cast stone details and the old Venetian Gothic campanile rising imperious. As I parked I caught myself imagining as ever that the bloody bell was about to start tolling, however long it's hung dormant – the shade of some Quasimodo, summoning the lunatics to vespers. Then I looked up to Robert's windows and had the brief, disconcerting experience of seeing a man standing there behind the sun-spotted glass.

I trudged up the stone stairs to the second floor, down the hall to Robert's door, which stood open. Memory took my hand as I crossed the entrance hall, under the Venetian lanterns, over that fine rosewood floor in Bernese panels. His walking cane – my ill-advised gift – was jammed in the umbrella stand. The big reception was enjoying the light from that floor-to-ceiling bay (whereas Robert tended to keep his crimson drapes closed, bathing the space in uterine gloom). I never had any quarrel with the Victorian handsomeness of the space, the tall proportions, the exquisite mouldings. It was the hi-tech extrusions that made me shake my head – the manufactured mezzanine of bedroom suites overhead, Robert's boudoir; and that Kraut kitchen with its custom cabinetry, temperature-controlled wine storage and other such shiny appliances of Kraut science.

Through the doors to the dining room I found Hagen sitting pensive by the fireplace: 50-ish, lean-faced but solidly made, clearly no tubby desk-man. Unshaven, I couldn't but notice, and the act of shoving his somewhat lank and silvery fringe aside from his eyes was clearly a tic with him, one he might cure by a call on a barber. On the long dinner table before him lay one of Robert's blasted black masks; in his hand he toyed with a scalpel. Seeing me, his greeting was a nod. 'Doctor Lochran. This is a hell of a thing to leave lying about, wouldn't you say?'

I took the blade off him, turned it under the light. 'A number fifteen. Robert's favoured tool. For when the incision wants a very controlled, artful sort of a curve.'

'Artful?'

'As, say, round the aureole of the nipple.'

Hagen nodded keenly. 'Fasci*na*ting. And can you tell me anything of this object here?' He gestured to the mask.

I sighed. 'That is— an invention of Robert's. A piece of product design he took to market. None too successfully, alas.'

'What's the gist of it then?'

'They call it cold therapy. A cold-compress mask, for patients recovering from a procedure on the face – facelift, eyelift.'

Hagen had stood and plucked the mask off the table; now he was fumbling to separate and sort the varied flaps of PVC. Finally he raised it to his face and stood there, mutely black-visaged, for so many silent beats that I was made a touch queasy by the off-key jocularity. At length I realised he was studying his reflection in a mirror behind me. Finally he lowered the mask, bemused.

'Produces something of a sinister aspect, doesn't it?'

'Quite. A touch of the fetish. I'd guess that's partly why the trade failed to embrace it. I told Robert it'd look better on Halloween night than in a recovery suite. But that only tickled him. He wouldn't be told. Not on matters of taste.'

'Dear me. An entrepreneurial stroke, though, by Doctor Forrest?'

I nodded. 'Like most of us Robert looked forward to working less. Finding his pot of gold. On this, though, he wound up losing money. As he'd been losing it left, right and centre. As I've told you already.'

Hagen smiled, thrust his fists into his pockets. In his

suit of black corduroy, quite worn, pockets slack, he could have been a Norwegian cattle farmer come to market for the day. But his eyes had something very patiently quizzical going on in there. 'You'll know this place of his well then, this pad?' he enquired.

'Yup. Robert would entertain here on occasion, he was a fine cook. Not in recent months, though. Not after Malena moved out. After that I came here less too. I was never mad keen on the environs, to be honest.'

'Of course, it was the old psychiatric hospital, this, wasn't it?' Hagen had resumed his seat, resting his chin in his hands.

'Aye. The county asylum before that, back when we had lunatics. Dedicated to the paupers. I daresay a fair few of them are still buried out under the bloody tennis courts. You've talked to my friend Steven Hartford? He was a consultant here in the last years of the hospital.'

'Really? He never said. Why was it shut down?'

'The old story. "Essential cuts".'

'Shame, that.'

'Yes. A big blow to Steven. It was the kind of hospital he was committed to – what it embodied, that tradition of poor man's medicine. To see it all boxed up into prime estate was hard to bear.'

Hagen rose, paced to the window, surveyed the view of the grounds before turning back to me. 'Presumably, then, another sort of a blow when his old pal Robert went and bought the showpiece apartment?'

'That' – I weighed my words – 'was a little insensitive on Robert's part. But something about the whole Gothic

Revival madness of the place just appealed to his . . . temper. Rather a nineteenth-century boy, our Robert.'

Hagen smiled in the style of a wince, as if to say he'd not a clue what I was talking about. Then he gestured for us to move through into the living room, led the way, and I followed. It was with a pang that I saw – on the low marqueterie table between the two facing chaises longues – that lovely oak-and-silver spirit case to which Robert never failed to refer as 'the tantalus', with its crystal decanters of malt and cognac, beside it on a tray his vintage teal-green soda siphon and quartet of heavy crystal tumblers. Hagen and I settled on the chaises longues – less comfortably, perhaps, than he had hoped. I took advantage of that discomfort.

'I assume you or your colleague spoke to Killian MacCabe. The sculptor? Malena's current partner.'

Hagen pursed his lips, as if mildly intrigued. 'We did that. If you're interested, he has an alibi for the night of August 14. He met with a private art collector, off of Harley Street, then he went home to the missus.'

'I've heard that, yes. But you've checked it out?'

He nodded, looking at me most intently. 'Interesting mind you have, doctor. I'd like to have a look at Doctor Forrest's bedroom. Could you show me?'

I was taken aback. 'You need me for that?'

'Bear with me. I'd like your view on something.'

As he stood again, patting his pockets meditatively, I wandered idly to the main bay window – and there my eye was caught by something extraordinary. Down below in the car park I saw, I would swear it, Killian MacCabe's quite unmistakable green Alfa Romeo tearing out through the Artemis gates at speed. And yet, when Hagen asked me 'if anything was the matter', I considered how I might word it, admitted defeat, shrugged and moved past him.

But I remained distracted as I led Hagen up the main stairway, into Robert's master boudoir, the big octagonal chamber, cool and dark with the heavy drapes closed in front of the three tall bay windows. The epic bed was un-slept in, creamy sheets smooth as glass. Hagen stood by its foot awhile, by the antique *cassone* carved in Florentine walnut that I had shipped for Robert from Siena. The detective was staring hard ahead, as if by such means he might peer through the fog into the past.

Finally he gestured to the archway leading into what had been Malena's walk-in closet, and we stepped through together. The two long walls of mirrored closets were fa-miliar, but the space had a new inhabitant – typical Robert in its antique splendour – a big, fancy free-standing mir-ror ('cheval glass', I suppose, is the term), all of eight feet tall, scraping the ceiling, as if scaled for the Palace of Versailles. It was set in a good dark wood surround, fixed by swivel screws to a frame on legs, crested by a garlanded cartouche with a low relief of entwined snakes.

Hagen sauntered up to it, rapped a knuckle on the mirror's lightly mottled surface. 'Peculiar thing to have about, isn't it?'

I shrugged. 'A mirror's a mirror. This one, I grant you, is a baroque specimen. But Robert was a collector.'

'Hardly short of mirrors, but, is it? This little room.' Of course he was right, not that I was any the wiser.

'Would you say Doctor Forrest's an uncommonly vain sort of a fellow?'

I had to smile. 'Always a handsome lad. Of course, by the time you've hit your middle years even the golden lads have sustained some wear and tear. Robert liked to cite that line of Orwell's. How after 40 a man's got the face he deserves.'

'Oh, I'd agree. But the trend these days is otherwise, isn't it? Which is how Dr Forrest earns his keep. So, a little perverse of an attitude on his part perhaps?'

'Well, we never discussed it, but I'm fairly certain his pride would have stopped him from ever going under another man's knife. Anyhow, he remains a fine-looking fellow . . .'

'Yet his fine-looking young wife left him for a fine-looking younger fellow . . .'

'They weren't married. She was his girlfriend.'

'But these past weeks, months – to your knowledge – he was living alone, sleeping alone? No one had taken the place of Ms Absalonsen?'

This was the moment, the prompt I had waited for. And still I couldn't understand why I had forestalled it, what even now – however obscurely – I seemed to be afraid of. Hagen saw as much.

'Please, Doctor Lochran, say what's on your mind. We've not got any time for secrets.'

So I sat down on the foot of Robert's bed, and said what I had long intended. 'Recently – maybe a month ago? – Robert met a woman. From whom I think he became quite inseparable, all of a sudden, though he told me later it had

just been a . . . rush of blood. Her name is Dijana Vukovara.'
I phrased it carefully – *Vu-KO-va-ra* – just as I had heard it,
and for the record, since, for the first time in our interview,
Hagen had taken out a notebook and a stubby pencil. 'I
don't suppose anyone else has mentioned her?'

'No. Ms Absalonsen said nothing.'

'Malena wouldn't have known about her. Nor anyone
else Robert knew, because their relationship was, I think,
conducted entirely covertly – nocturnally, even. I only
met her once myself. But Robert confided in me about
her, one night he came to mine, we drank a fair bit of
whiskey. He said they'd taken up, got very close. I was
glad, I tried to invite them both to dinner, but that wasn't
on, I was told.'

'How had he met this Ms – Vu-KO-va-ra?'

'I'm not sure. I've a notion it might have been at some
cultural evening. She seemed that type.'

'And how do we contact this lady?'

'I've no idea. Not a clue. I don't know where she lives,
what she does, where she comes from . . .'

Hagen closed his little book, bothered. At long last I had
intrigued him. 'Well, now. Can you at least describe her?'

'She rather defies description.'

A gruff half-chuckle. 'How bloody convenient. Quite
a skill, that. Would you have a go for us, doctor?'

I winced. 'She was foreign, for sure, but what extraction . . . First I thought Slavic, the name sounded that.
But her accent was more Italian. Maybe she'd been to
school there. In a certain light she looked rather French,
though. Maybe it was just that she smoked and drank

the way their women do. But her looks, too, I thought there was something French there . . . Slightly imperfect good looks.'

'An attractive woman, then?'

'Oh I'd have to say so. Anyone would say so.'

'No need to qualify it, doctor. I won't tell your wife. "Imperfect" how, but?'

'Well, I'm one to talk. What I'd say is, she made quite a stunning impression – very dark hair, dark eyes, red lips. Good bones, good figure, all fragrant, dressed with flair. I wouldn't have said older than late twenties. But . . . the longer I spent in her company, the more I felt – she seemed *over*-made up, *over*-perfumed. A little older too, maybe. Close up, you saw her skin and teeth weren't the best. At first I'd took her for a woman of some means, but then I started to wonder – was she for sale? You understand me? Like when you see a girl in the street all fine and presentable, heels and bag and make-up and hair . . . but, really, she could be either. Heiress or prostitute . . .' Hagen was studying me curiously, and I was suddenly conscious of having babbled, as if in reaction to the long silence I'd kept over this cursed woman. 'It sounds odd, maybe, but I'm sure anyone else would say the same if they'd met her.'

'And, hang on, you met her where exactly?'

'Here. I paid a call on Robert. Purposely. He'd become so . . . elusive. And I knew it was because he was slipping around with her. So I felt I needed to meet this woman – just to understand for myself, what my pal was getting into. I don't know that Robert was overjoyed to see me at his door. But I came into the living room and she was sat there. Drinks got poured, Robert poured one for me. But there was an atmosphere.'

'How so?'

'Because of her. She struck me as disagreeable. Demure on the surface but there was something— provocative, in her. She had this tinkling laugh that sounded rather pitying. Even her smile was like . . . as if she had some great and awful secret about you. You weren't quite sure you were worthy of her company.'

'But Dr Forrest seemed enamoured of her?'

I shook my head. 'That night? It felt more like he was wary of her. What he'd described to me before was what I suppose you call "romantic love". There'd been something dreamy in his eyes. But that night – I wasn't sure he wanted her there any more than me.'

Hagen was inscrutable now. He had me on his hook. 'Well, doctor. That's quite a nugget of information you've been sitting on.'

'I'm sorry. My own mind hasn't been clear. Clouded, somehow, I don't know why. I've not been sure I wasn't— seeing a death's head in an ink-blot. About her. She was only a woman. You get me?'

'Oh, I think I do. No, for sure, we'll just have to find her. Ms Vu-KO-va-ra.' He chuckled. 'And then we'll see for ourselves.'

September 4th

This morning Livy and I made love for the first time in, I daresay, four months. It's only time and the quotidian

119

round that get in the way, making the merest intimacy take on that burdensome aspect – so it starts to seem a problem. And yet how easily that's all dispelled, in the lightest reminder of familiar and best-loved things – the fragrance of her hair in my hands, the feel in my fingers of that nightdress with the lacy neck, inched off – then pulling her close, the currents flowing again, her into me as I into her, rolling all over the sea of our bed.

Later, as we shared some larky push-and-shove at the bathroom sink, Livy told me I'd been like a schoolboy – not in the tautness of my physique, alas, rather in my (to her) comical hot-bloodedness. Well, she may laugh . . . Precious things, these are, intolerable the loneliness without them – the sense of communion with another, one's share of the elemental, the dearest, warmest feeling. Whatever the state of our fortunes in life we all need this peerless intimacy to keep living. Olivia – so much my comfort, my better half, my strength and solace. The first time I met her I sat up that night and wrote her name in my notebook a hundred times. 'Schoolboy', indeed. Thank God she felt the same for me – or rather, not 'the same', but similar – complementary.

I have never looked at another woman since, not *really*. That is the plain fact of the matter. Because I love her and love her and love her, ad infinitum. I am a lucky man – I only need look at my poor friends to know as much.

Today I tried my intent to play sleuth, making it my business to test Killian MacCabe's alibi for that night before Robert vanished. First, the ticklish business of calling Malena and asking, on Livy's behalf, if she had kept a note of the address Killian had visited to meet with his prospective patron. Not the subtlest effort, yet I could hear her taking down the diary from the kitchen dresser. When she came back on line, though, it was to tell me that the page for that week had been torn out, most likely Killian took it with him as an aide-memoire. Did I want her to ask Killian? No, I fucking did not. Rather, 'not wanting to bother him', I wanted her to try to remember for me. On reflection she did seem to recall his mentioning an Italian name, Ragnari, and a mansion block of apartments, on the corner of Harley Street and— Carrefort? No, Cavendish. I assured her that was all I needed.

Thus come dusk I was striding down the street of dreams, home to medicine's multi-millionaires, that swathe of rich London in impregnable white stucco, its rows of spiked iron railings warding off the penniless poorly. From street level the terrace seemed a row of haunted houses, vacant or darkened, save for an occasional fire burning in the hearth of a reception room, the odd ornate ceiling lit by flickering chandelier.

I found what had to be the building. 'Ragnari' was not inscribed beside any buzzer, but as I peered through the glass doors I saw a bald, flush-faced old boy in shirt and tie shuffle out from behind a recessed counter, down the hallway runner toward me. I was admitted to a high-ceilinged lobby. At my right a grand winding staircase led the way to upper floors. To the porter, though, I seemed an untrustworthy face.

'Who are you seeking today, sir?'

'Ms . . . Ragnari?'

'*Mrs* Ragnari in 6F. Lovely name, isn't it? Foreign. But sweet. Interesting lady, Mrs Ragnari.'

'Really? How long has she lived here?'

Rashly I'd underscored my ignorance. His expression turned bankteller-obstructive. 'Oh, I'm afraid we couldn't give out information of that sort, sir. It's against the law. Our residents are entitled to their privacy.'

His eyes still chastising me, he punched a number on an internal phone, but got no reply. I asked if I might pop a note under Mrs Ragnari's door, in relation to our private matter?

'Of course you may, sir.'

Then I heard a clanking noise emanating from behind the frosted glass of a nearby elevator door. I pulled on the handle. It didn't budge.

'Won't open, sir, until the lift is exactly on the level. For safety, you know.' He chuckled. 'It wasn't built into this place originally and it's always been a tad faulty. The story goes – one old chap used to live here. Came in with his groceries one day, out of breath, calls the lift, opens the door, steps in without thinking. Lift, of course, comes right down on top of him. Can you imagine?'

'That', I said, 'is quite a story.'

'Isn't it? Accidents, sir – only take a moment, don't they?'

'I'll take the stairs, I think.'

Up I went, an arduous ascent, then down a darkened, plush-carpeted corridor. I knocked the door of 6F but there was no response. So I took a card from my wallet, scribbled a message, *Mrs Ragnari, please contact . . .*, then off I went. There was some haste in my step. I felt a little eeriness in the hush, a prickle of hairs on my neck. (The porter's grisly tale hadn't helped.) Back out under the front porch I stopped to check and found RAVENSCOURT the name neatly printed by the 6F buzzer – making nothing one iota less murky.

Hagen is a thoughtful man, a seasoned sort, he'll have heard a million things in his time. I could tell him this. Steven is the best friend I've got, I could tell him *anything*. And yet still I'm limping on alone with my secret. Why can't I spill it and be done? Would it really sound as mad as I fear it? What am I afraid of anyway? Some slip of a girl?

This is it. On that sole evening where I had the dubious pleasure of Dijana Vukovara's company (that clearly unwelcome call at Robert's door), the mood was just as I told Hagen. You know when you've walked in on something – one party amused, the other not. Ten minutes before I dropped by they could have been fighting or fucking like wolves, I don't know. But every glance and remark of theirs seemed to bear on whatever was happening in the room before I stumbled into it.

What did she and I talk about? Nothing that was normal. *'Grey'* – I remember her saying, as if marvelling, rolling my poor honest name round her mouth like it was Russian for something depraved. 'Grey by nature?' she added, gratuitously. Then she sashayed over to the window, surely expecting me to follow, while Robert mixed a drink. There, we discussed . . . ? The moon, I think. How she found it 'thrilling'. Didn't I feel the same? (Her eyes, dark moons of their own, knowing otherwise.) Then I believe she was describing how she loved to 'bathe' in moonlight, hymning 'the mystery of the waters', 'that most curious *con-san-guinity*' between the lunar and menstrual cycles. She beckoned me and I felt her breath in my ear. 'A woman is wounded,' she whispered. 'Periodically, most intimately. But a man is not so different. We all of us carry the wound within . . .'

So, yes, I found her a disturbing creature, whatever her willowy, dark-eyed allure. And having seen her and had my cordial drink, I was ready to leave. It was then she drew me aside and said it to me, whispered, into my ear, something I remember as utterly, sickeningly foul – insane, even.

So why have I told no one else this? Because it sounds deranged. Because I still don't quite believe it happened. Because those same offensive words of hers – even their sense and import – have just evaporated from my memory, like breath off a mirror's surface.

I left Robert's thereafter, I know I did. That was the sum of our interaction that night. And yet, madly, I retain some image in my head – fractured, no relation to anything else – of Vukovara's body, naked – her having exposed herself in some manner. White thighs, dark mound, belly, breast, the sight of them somehow malign.

All of these feelings are weighing on me, oppressing me. What do they amount to, really, but superstition? And still, inside, everything hammers and resonates and tells me – she, Vukovara, is behind all of this. She has to be. *Of course she is.*

PART II

CAUSES OF DEATH

12

Dr Hartford's Journal

The mask

September 5th

Graveyard shift again – silence nested in the grounds and premises, shadows scampering over the walls – I pace the office floor, Goran knocks to find me burning the lamp. Tonight I sent him off more curtly than normal: it's just I so badly need these hours to pick over the bones of my near-grotesque session with Eloise. For the first time, I have to wonder – what she has truly felt previously, what she feels now, whether it's beyond my reach – or just contrary to my wishes.

I played by the rule-book, conscious that last time I had carried on like a blundering amateur. Yet we began the session by revisiting the end of the last: we had to try to process this business of her imagined response to Flint's attention, this shame she harbours over what she sees as the treacherous nature of her body. I wanted her to see the degree to which she'd been robbed of control, urged her toward the positive thought: *'I wasn't passive, I did my best.'* But Eloise was not happy with that. It was if she was being animated by some rebellious spirit.

EK: Why should I stop feeling how I feel because you try to wave a wand? After all these years . . . what if

I'm right to have 'negative feelings'?

SH: Eloise, I only ask you to think about it. That not
everything happened just as you believe you see it
now. Don't endow the child you were with adult
consciousness, adult freedom of choice. You went with
Flint because you had no reason but to trust him. Not
because you anticipated what would happen. You
didn't want to be there, you didn't want to do those
things, Flint knew that, it's why he took you there,
isolated you from your bearings. How else could he
have possibly pretended it was normal or right?

EK: Maybe it was the wrongness of it that I— embraced .
. .

[. . .]

SH: Eloise?

EK: Sorry, I'm thinking of something else.

SH: From the woods?

EK: No. Yes. Different woods. This was a few years ago.
A traveller guy, in his caravan. In Epping Forest.
There was a free party and I was— procuring some
'entertainment' for some friends of mine. His place, it
was just squalor, and he talked to me like I was this
posh tart he'd lured back to his den of iniquity. He
was loving it. And I had— an odd moment. It was
like the clocks stopped. And I thought, if I had to, if
I was forced to— I could move in here, yeah, we'd
manage, him and me. We'd be travellers together. I
could let loose of who I am. There was something in
my stomach. Like butterflies in a hollow.

SH: Butterflies like excitement? Or nausea? Fear?

EK: What it was . . . The way he spoke to me, it was like
	he wanted to lead me down, into another world. And
	I do think part of me did want to go there. It was like
	standing over a deep, dark hole – made my head spin,
	but still – part of me did want to step off and just fall.
SH: But you didn't.
EK: Shack up with the crusty? No. I bought his drugs, got
	the hell out of there. I couldn't see a future for us . . .
SH: Why do you think you thought of that now?
EK: Because of the base wrongness of something. It has an
	allure. Pulling me in. Do you understand? Like your
	friend Doctor Forrest.
[. . .]
SH: I'm sorry, do you want to talk to me about Robert?
EK: Can I? Is that okay? Because there's a dark man for
	you. A man with a black hole inside. Kept it well
	masked, I should say. Not 'the doctor', no, he was
	sweet reason personified. Sort of man you'd let take a
	knife to your face . . . I remember my stay-over night
	at his clinic, the recovery suite – I woke up the next
	morning in all that whiteness and I thought it was
	the pearly gates. He was sitting by my bed. Those
	eyes of his, his little half-smile. And he quoted some
	Baudelaire. 'Comme les anges à l'œil fauve, je
	reviendrai dans ton alcôve . . .' How could I fall for
	that? But he did just strike me as romantic, somehow,
	in a brooding sort of a way. And brilliant, obviously.
	I just had this feeling he might be a new kind of man
	for me. Older and wiser. Improving, maybe. That was
	a joke as it turned out. You'd have to say I can pick

them . . . Should I go on? Tell you when I met the real
Forrest?

[. . .]

EK: *Okay. He called me a week after I checked out.*
'Aftercare', right? I said, sure, come over. I was
nervous, so I rolled a grass joint. And when he turned
up, I offered him a toke. Thought it might give me
the upper hand. Well, he burnt through that without
a flinch, and I got wasted . . . Then he just lifted me
and carried me upstairs . . . Sent me flowers the next
day. Never called, though. Days went by, he didn't
call, so I gave in and called him. He told me to drive
over to Artemis Park. I didn't really think twice. That
was a . . . nasty little transaction.

SH: *Nasty how?*

EK: *I got there, his door was open, lights off. So I tiptoed*
in, called hello, no answer. I reached his dining room
and he was just sitting there, silent, in the dark,
wearing this black mask – he uses them at his clinic,
they're leather—

SH: *I know what you mean.*

EK: *Right. So you can imagine. Then he stands up, walks*
toward me with his hand out like he's going to seize
my throat, and I— freaked, I ran, but he came after
me, cornered me, forced me up the stairs backwards—
and I still couldn't say if it was a game or if I— really
had to get away from him, you know? When we did
it he had his hands round my throat. Intense. But it
didn't hurt.

[. . .]

EK: *After that it went by steps, really. Steps leading down. I'd call him. He'd tell me to drive over to his. Dracula's castle . . .*

SH: *Did you never feel like saying no?*

EK: *Sometimes – if I could tell he'd been drinking his whiskey. But I'd go. I knew I'd rather see him than not. He made me feel like leaving the house, not just sitting there crying. Sometimes I'd stand at the foot of his stairs and think, 'Should I go up?' But I did. Kept going, until he told me not to come back.*

[. . .]

SH: *I'm sorry, Eloise, I hadn't thought you were quite so besotted by Robert.*

EK: *Was I? I don't know. You have to understand, he was such a mix – kindness and cruelty, any given day I never knew who I'd meet. It's true, I bought him a bracelet – a token. He bought me scads of things, beautiful clothes, an amazing Jil Sander dress – which he then tore. But he would instruct me, what to wear, how I should do my hair. This bob, it was his idea. He liked to watch me dress in this closet room he's got. Sometimes he'd bathe me, just sit there lathering my hair while I wittered on about my boring day or whatever. In bed he would – tie me up, wrists and ankles. I was usually too aroused to care. He was very talented. And I did as I was told.*

[. . .]

EK: *So, do you understand? I have to ask myself, Steven, if this is not my nature.*

SH: *Eloise, please listen, I have to ask you how long you're going to punish yourself for something you didn't do.*

EK: How am I doing that?

*SH: By this . . . painful submissive behaviour. I wish I
could make you see just how desperately, desperately
sorry it makes me feel. How long are you going to keep
on warding off the people in life who actually want to
care for you?*

EK: And who are they?

[. . .]

*EK: Steven, I can't just 'accentuate the positive'. It's not
enough for me to just think it, I'd have to be someone
other than who I am.*

SH: You think 'who you are' is so set in stone?

*EK: Well, what have I ever done with my life? How have I
carried on? Same old, always.*

SH: Has how you've 'carried on' made you happy?

*EK: No. So I'm here, in this room. But who's happy
anyway? The few times I've thought I felt it were just
moments. And they flew away so fast I felt sick.*

*SH: Can you consider— that you're choosing to be cursed?
Fulfilling your own prophecy? Isn't it that you actually
might just need to learn something new in your life?
Be responsible for your situation, take responsibility
for yourself . . . ?*

I realise I had grown somewhat irate, but her story had
been a hard thing to sit through, for all that elements of
it were clearly 'performance'. The insight she offered into
Robert was, of course, dismal – but then one could have
suspected as much without knowing. And the greater her

insistence on her own depravity, the more plaintive her insecurity.

With the session derailed and clearly unsalvageable, I had to get us back to some place of good order. A solution came to me hurriedly. I told her to forget writing up her workbook that night; asked her to write something else – a letter, addressed to her 13-year-old self, authoress of the 'violet diary'. She groaned, bashed the chair, asked what on earth would be the point of that? Quietly, trying to make each word resonate, I told her I would have thought a girl of that age, so lonely and confused, would be in need of a friend, someone to comfort her and reassure her, show her that somebody understood.

'You could say how sorry you are for what she was subjected to. That it's all right to feel scared, hurt. But she's not alone, doesn't have to bear it alone. Because she'll get through it. Because she has a friend . . .'

Eloise was looking fixedly downward now, tugging at the hem of her skirt with gathering agitation.

'You can tell her who you are now, the woman you've become, all that you're trying to do. To help her.'

'Oh Christ. What would she think of me . . . ?'

She looked up, her face wet. This time I stayed seated, let her cry until she was cried out. A vital emotion, this pity – vital for her to feel it fully, what the girl she was deserves. What the woman she is now must be reminded of. I am her friend, yes. She must also be a friend to herself.

September 6th

I will head home tonight: I expect Tessa to be back, and thus I can say I have thwarted Tregaskis's prophecy.

However poorly I may be functioning at present, whatever anyone may say, I know I controlled my temper with David today. And I was sorely pushed. But I resisted. Of course he now believes he has something on me, and so wasted the start of our session goading me about Eloise.

DT: Come on, Steven. Wouldn't you say she's as shallow as a puddle? Spoiled? Annoying? Bit of a dumb blonde object?

SH: No. And I don't know why you would. People come here with serious problems, people like yourself, who need help.

DT: She needs something, yes. A bit of self-improvement . . .

I managed to shift onto the front foot, get him on the defensive, by turning the topic to his own recidivism in respect of Blakedene – how many more stays here he believed would be right and proper for him. Did he not feel the pull to have a normal life? He was rattled.

DT: Steven, whatever you think, I've no desire or intention to be turned into some salary-man, some cunt with a mortgage and a new car and a meaningless job.

SH: David . . . all I want is that you at least think about doing something with your life – that would make you feel usefully engaged with other people.

DT: *Maybe I don't fit in that way. Some 'useful' idiot. Maybe it's my job to preach, pave the way for something greater, whatever this world says. Be a vassal that way, for truth and revelation. Not a walking poster for this tenth-rate world and its values. You don't get it, do you? What you think you see out there – is not real. Little children can see that. I told you, I knew when I was 4. You see it in people, their eyes, doesn't matter how old they are. They know. They just know. Your secretary, Niamh?*

SH: *Ms Dwyer. What about her?*

DT: *She has a daughter.*

SH: *How do you know?*

DT: *I saw her this morning. I was on the terrace, I saw Niamh's husband dropping her off, her little girl climbed out of the car to kiss her goodbye. Then she saw me, the girl, she looked up and right at me. For a long time, Steven. She knows, I can tell.*

SH: *I'm sorry? Knows what?*

DT: *Come on . . . How many more times? That 'this' isn't this, 'that' isn't that, 'you' aren't you, or me or they.*

SH: *I see. The issue you're raising is, of course, one of the core questions of philosophy.*

DT: *Yep. From when we were all in caves.*

SH: *And little Kate Dwyer, you feel she shares your view on this matter?*

DT: *We don't 'share' anything. Not yet. That's the problem. How do you suppose me and little Kate could truly commune?*

The wilful flicker of menace in his eyes at that point, I found objectionable. But it wasn't his hostility so much as the creeping clock that had me on my feet, proposing we adjourn. David didn't want to leave.

DT: *Steven, you know I value your company. My room, I've told you, I'm— wary, of being alone there. The presence, it can be very strong.*

SH: *The presence being – Roisin Slaney? Master Ravenscourt?*

DT: *No, no, that's not it, you know. You must feel some of it, the aura that's settled on this place, even more in just these last weeks? Don't tell me you can't feel it when you're sleeping alone in this office damn near every night.*

SH: *David – I sleep in my bed, at home.*

DT: *Don't lie. Not tonight. Tonight you're sleeping right here where I'm sitting. 'Your bed at home' will be cold as the grave. That's not a home, Steven. What do your children think? Your wife?*

At this point the transcribing software could not adequately render the noise that burst forth from Tregaskis: a loud, harsh, feigned laughter, whereupon he broke into song – lustily, a prodigious sound from out of his chest, and as he sang his eyes twinkled, eyebrows vaulted in mischief. I, at least, understood every word.

> *O! Che caro galantuomo!*
> *Vuol star dentro colla bella!*

Had we time, were I not so put out of patience, I could have asked Tregaskis if he'd ever seen – even performed in – *Don Giovanni*. As it was, he now strolled from the room as if in peace.

September 7th

The house is quiet again. Tessa, having swept in last night, relieving/debriefing her ragged parents, has now whipped the boys away for the afternoon. Nothing to do with my wishes, but presumably a consequence of our having argued vituperatively last night. The inciting incident seems trivial now, if only because of the bizarre way it all came to an end.

Large glasses of wine didn't dissolve the tension between us. She wasn't happy with the reports she'd had of my absence from the house, for all she must have expected as much. She had no interest in or sympathy for my work stories – considers me blind to my professional obsessions. I told her I might say the same of her. The same old rewind of the tape.

Under questioning she told me nothing of the conference proceedings, only, with a prideful look, of how much she'd enjoyed a student production of *Don Giovanni* some of the delegates had attended. The coincidence was freakish, I admit, but what really flabbergasted me was this sudden interest of hers in a passion of mine she's previously viewed with indifference.

'Would you have gone to that with me?', I demanded.

'Oh you'd never have asked, Steven. Opera for you is what you play in your car. Alone, in your own universe.'

My eyes were drawn to her hand as it twitched on the kitchen worktop, fingers tracing the edge of the heavy glass ashtray, as if she might suddenly lift and swing it at me. The silence was intolerably fraught. But then the telephone rang, four rings, we glancing from each other's hard eyes to the black handset, until the cut-off and Tessa's familiar discouraging message. Then the crackle of the other end, heavy breath and clunking fumbles, the clear semaphore of someone all at sea on a tide of booze.

'Ah Tessa – sweet Tessa, Tessa babes. It's so late and I'm so lonely.' An Irish voice, young, clotted by whiskey. *'But I just had a powerful need to hear a friendly voice – from the old country. So please, would you ever get on the end of this fucken line?'*

'Pick it up,' I gestured to Tessa.

'Are you mad? *You* pick it up. It's scaring me.'

'You don't know who that is?'

'No, I don't!'

'Tessa. I send you my love. All my love. Kill sends all his love all the way from Dun Laoghaire . . .'

I continued to stare calmly at Tessa, my accusation implicit.

'Steven, I'm telling you, I don't know who that is . . .'

I could believe her, I did, except I felt no need to let her off the hook. And then the voice began to sing. *'Ah, you're drunk, you're drunk, you silly old fool . . .'* And I remembered what Grey had told me of Killian

140

MacCabe's recently soused behaviour, his bawling of drunken 'shanties'.

'Yes, I am drunk, on the spirits, and it's bad, Tessa. But where's that man of yours? Where's Dr Steve?' (Now Tessa stared at me, the tables turned.) *'And will you ask him, does he remember the time we had that time, down by the water with your man Tom Dole? Has he heard from that fella since . . . ?'*

For a moment I couldn't believe my ears – a crucial moment, as it happened, for I snatched up the receiver and barked 'Hello' only to hear the other handset replaced – dropped? – with equivalent force.

Tessa's eyes were narrow. 'So, a friend of yours then?'

I suppose I was punch-drunk, since I murmured distractedly, 'Dr Forrest, I presume.'

'Don't be stupid. That wasn't Robert's voice.'

'No. No, it wasn't. Perhaps he has an emissary . . .'

'Steven, what are you talking about?'

But I had not been speaking for her or for anyone else to hear or understand, otherwise I wouldn't have said it. I am hoping still that I didn't hear what I thought I heard. But I will have to wait – for the next move, the next communiqué, from beyond the grave.

13

Dr Lochran's Journal

Like a monster

September 7th

Tonight I'm sick of this bloody world, unutterably depressed about the depths to which it drives us.

The working day had been largely predictable, I was done and headed for the door – when the tannoy called out for a surgeon, *any* surgeon. A callow boy, Jamaican origin, 11 years old, had taken a gunshot wound in the chest, was sinking fast. No time for nicety, directly to theatre. The bullet – a 9mm pistol round – went in just under the left ribcage and followed a crazy course, ricocheting internally off bone, ruinous damage to the internals. I found it in the thorax, removed it, then stood, blood-boltered, as they pronounced the lad dead. Beyond my control, or anybody's. So will I be forgiven if I say my deepest regret is that I wasn't already long gone through the door before the summons went out?

I had a right to think the day could get no worse, and yet I switched on my phone to a message from Malena, wretched, saying she had been 'hurt', 'attacked', was in the Royal Free. For some shameful reason the first thought in my head: *'Rab, what have you done?'* I managed to get hold of her and, of course, the culprit was MacCabe.

They had quarrelled, he struck her – knocked her unconscious. When she came to, she called an ambulance. It had taken a nurse at the hospital to summon the police. Killian's whereabouts were – still are – unknown. In the moment, in my outrage, I couldn't pretend I cared a damn for him, though Malena clearly and unhappily does.

I drove to the Free directly, all the while weighing two warring thoughts in my head: my usual grim satisfaction in being her champion, but a nagging guilt that I should have foreseen this. Then when I saw her, pale and propped up on a bed, blackened under both eyes, bottom lip lacerated – I was seized by so harsh a delayed urge to get the Irishman in my hands that I had to clench and unclench my fingers, pace out a circle in the cramped little private room. Malena was composed, not in pain, but she'd lost something of herself in this horrible experience, that is clear. Worse, as I feared, she seemed unduly preoccupied by Killian's 'plight' and present whereabouts, as if more concerned for her attacker than for her own condition. I know that some call this love. Dr Hartford would have another word for it, I'm sure. I tried to question her circumspectly.

'Malena, I hate to say it, because I feel responsible, but this was coming. From that night you called me to your house. Surely you must have . . . feared it?'

She shook her head sadly. 'Not "feared". I've been worried, yes. But only for him. He was not the sort of man to do this.'

'But Malena, he *did*.'

'Yes, but it's not— explicable, Grey. To do this . . . Only a weak man, a bitter man would stoop to it. Killian was never that.'

I do believe I groaned. 'Malena, do you know how many women say this sort of thing right after their men have damn near killed them?' She met my gaze, shrugged, as though such humdrum statistics were neither here nor there in this exceptional instance. 'Have you told me everything? About before? Has he hit you before? Before that night I came to yours? Or since then?'

'Grey, no, never. That night – was the great aberration. Killian never drank to be drunk, never lost his head on purpose or lashed out. Not like Robert.'

I don't think I was truly surprised by this new information, but certainly dismayed. She saw as much, and was silent.

'Well, possibly you and I have never talked – properly – about any temper of Robert's?'

'We wouldn't, Grey. That is between a man and a woman.'

'But you asked me to intervene with Killian.'

'Robert was not . . . changeable. *You* could not have changed him, you've been allies for too long. But Killian, I thought, he and you could maybe talk . . .'

I chewed my lip. 'Malena, I have to know now, did Robert ever hurt you?'

'No, or I would have left him.' (I didn't interject, *You mean 'left him sooner'.*) 'There was never real violence. But his temper made a mood in the house. A climate, a threat. Never that way with Killian, never. That is what I *mean*, Grey.'

144

I didn't make the obvious point about how relatively little she and MacCabe knew of each other over – what? – nine months of an affair conducted illicitly, amid the unreality of the art world, and a mere five months of co-habitation. Instead I sat and asked as gently as I could if she would go back through what she had told the police. She sighed.

'I hadn't seen much of him today, this is how our days had gotten to be. But I'd asked my friend Susanne for dinner, we needed to decide what to prepare. I went up to the studio, found him clutching his stomach, staring at the floor. He agreed to come talk to me in the bedroom while I dressed. Then I asked him to fasten a necklace for me, and . . . I guess he saw, in a drawer of my jewellery box I had my old keys to Robert's apartment.'

'Wait, you still have keys to Artemis Park?'

She winced. 'That's what Killian said. I didn't remember to put them in Robert's hand that day I left, there were other things on our minds. And after that . . . it never seemed the time, I just forgot. So, they were there. Killian went silent. I knew, he was tense. He stomped out of the room. I couldn't believe he was jealous, not for that, but it felt so . . . I went down to the kitchen but then I heard him banging around above, he came down the stairs in his old coat, said he had to go out, see someone, straight away, wouldn't tell me who . . .'

'Did you believe him? That there was somebody?'

'I had a— a little suspicion . . . I didn't really believe, but I did think, about that night he went to see the woman who'd wanted to commission him, then "changed her mind". Thinking how different he was after that night, I had wondered, was he keeping a big secret? But then to look at him . . . He was a man in pain, that was what frightened me, I was sure something was badly wrong with him. He looked sick, not in control of himself. Hunched all the time, roiling his head and shoulders, like an ape.'

That I could picture all too easily from our last encounter.

'In any case, he wouldn't listen to me. So I got in his way, barred his path to the hallway. He seized me by the shoulders and just . . . *hoisted* me aside, I was shocked, I hadn't imagined such strength in his hands. Then he was stomping off, down the hall, so I flung my arms round his neck, and he twisted and *roared* at me but I just clung to him, and he began to crash us both into the hallway walls, side to side . . . I begged him to stop, then I fell, right in front of the door. And I put my whole body against it, thinking this was so absurd, so awful, it had to stop, it just had to. Then I saw the sole of his boot coming at my face. The last thing I knew. For a while . . .'

My hands had gone over my eyes, reflexively. When I looked at her again she saw my horror. 'That is monstrous, Malena.'

She nodded. 'A monster, yes, he was like that – utterly maddened, berserk. In the grip of something.'

'Of what? I mean, what you're describing is junkie behaviour. Craving a fix, a hit.'

'No, no. I would have known it for that if it was. No, something has happened, Grey. He is not the same man.

146

It is simple as that. And my fear now is . . . he will do something to himself.'

'Malena, you are far kinder than I or anyone else would be. Or the authorities. You told the police all of this?'

Her eyes fell. 'What I didn't tell them, the doctor who examined me did. You should know too, Grey. I'm pregnant.'

I felt a sick surge in my innards. 'Is the baby okay?' She nodded. 'How many weeks gone?'

'Maybe a month, if you take from my last period . . .'

'And Killian, he was aware?'

Another mournful nod. 'We planned this together. We'd been trying, on my dates, we'd talked about it even before I left Robert.'

I was quietly going spare. 'Malena, this makes it so much worse. When did you tell MacCabe the news?'

'Straight away, after my test, a week or so ago.'

'So he already knew, that night I came over?' I groaned. 'You tell me this now. How had he reacted when you told him?'

Again she avoided my eye. 'A mix of emotion, you might say. I ran to show him the little cross, on the test, and he . . . he disputed it, said it was too faint. I said I'd done two and the first was the same. He just looked at me . . . like this was some ironic thing, someone else's small misfortune. Then he asked if I would leave him be, said he just had to work. I had counted on at least a little euphoria. That's how people feel in love, isn't it?' It was my turn to nod. 'How could I have misunderstood him so much?'

147

'But Malena,' I insisted, 'do you understand, how outrageous it is, that he raised a hand to you in your condition?'

I wasn't sure she was listening, or wanting to hear me, nor was I at all convinced she had given the police the account she ought to, in all its gravity. For sure I knew they ought to be seeking his arrest, while Malena sat there consumed by the pity of it all.

'Malena, listen, I'm sorry but I need you to tell me – anything else you can remember about how Killian changed, acted different, after that night he came back from seeing the Ragnari woman. The night Robert disappeared.'

Her eyes clouded. 'No, it wasn't until the next day we knew Robert was gone.'

'When *we* knew, yes.'

She still looked wary. I knew I had to modify my bedside manner, for something of the implacable Hagen seemed to have overtaken me. So I changed tack. 'What did you know about her, this Ragnari?'

'Just some rich patron, collector. He met her at some viewing, she said she was a fan, contacted him after. I didn't see why they had to meet at night – as if to make me jealous. But he joked about that before he left.'

'Tell me how he was when he came home, that night.'

She shot me another suspicious look – then laughed softly, as though this were indeed a tale of which she had wished to unburden herself. 'I remember I heard the key, came down the stairs and he was standing in the hall, in the dark – he'd stolen in so softly, like a thief, you know?

Seemed thoughtful. Not crestfallen, though. I asked him how it had gone. He smiled, said it just 'hadn't happened'. But he came toward me and – embraced me, so hard, his face in my neck and his nose in my hair like we'd been apart for days, weeks, not a few hours. That night, the next few days were very happy. He was hugely attentive. It was sort of a second honeymoon . . .'

She smiled, but in a wistful, broken way, then put a hand to her face, and for some moments she composed herself behind there.

'This is what pains me. He was being so dear. It was funny, I thought he should be working. But he was amorous, like a schoolboy, like boyfriends I had when I was fourteen.'

I winced, reminded of what Olivia said to me postcoitus the other night, thinking I didn't care to be identified with this thug.

'He was like, "Oh I don't need to work right now." I thought perhaps he was hiding his disappointment for me, like a man does. But he'd had other plans before. They just fell away. Then, well, you know, you saw. He changed – again.' She looked bitter. 'We began to argue, like we'd never done before, about who we were, what sort of people we were. And it had just seemed to me that we had known something about each other the first time we set *eyes* on each other, but now all of that was— illusion.'

'It's possible. People can become strangers again. They hide parts of themselves.'

'He hid this *exceptionally* well. This animus, against

me, against the world. A bitterness I had never seen in him, never imagined existed . . .'

She was tiring, the lure of sleep was strong. I assume she will discharge herself tomorrow. What is for sure is that she can't go home until Killian's whereabouts are established. After that, who knows? I asked her to come and stay with us, told her Livy could collect her tomorrow. She agreed to consider it. Then I left, deeply upset. I drove by their house, all dark – not to say that Killian wasn't up in his lair, crawled into a bottle or rocking in his blasted chair, contemplating his handiwork that day. But, somehow, in my mind, I saw him running – running scared.

ৎৣ

Halfway home I remembered to call Olivia, acknowledged her upset and my dereliction of duty. Something worse was rattling her, though – Cal had taken off after dinner without telling her. Hardly a surprise, and it was hardly late. She had done the ring-around, Susan reporting that her Jennifer had snuck out too . . . So I had a theory. But I had to take her worry seriously, put a lid on the bleak story I had to tell, focus instead on stroking some ruffled feathers. In truth, I worry too, about our connection to our boy. I have no faith in his telling us honestly where he goes out to at night. He's heard our admonitions, but only grown more covert in his ways.

At home I went up and admired her impressively moody rendering of the sea at Thorpeness, then we came down and slumped together into the 'baggy blue', she in jeans and the loose paint-spattered shirt she considers her 'smock'. Incompetently I tried to roll her a cigarette, but she stayed my hand with a sigh and took over. I fetched myself a Montecristo and we sat there in our shared funk of smoke and nagging worry. At length I explained about Malena. Livy was appalled, and instinctively sympathetic, of course. Thus my contrition. After a period's reflection she sighed, smiled forgivingly.

'It's not easy for me, Grey. The two of you bulls crashing around this place, always going your own bloody way.'

'I know,' I groaned, fingertips to my temples. 'I know, darling. Do you think we ought to have had a daughter? Would you have liked that?'

'No, no, it was better we sorted out your son and heir . . .' She smiled, a funny mime of female forbearance. 'If we could have had a second, maybe. I don't know. If ifs and ands were pots and pans . . .'

'We'd all be tinkers. Aye.'

'But since it was the one – no, I think difference is a better experience in life. It was more interesting, I think, that this shouty boy-child came out of my body. All ruddy and big-headed, with his little bits and bobs.' She was suddenly animated, smoking expressively in the way I love to see, as when extolling her beloved Dutch painters or explaining why Jackson Pollock is just wallpaper. 'Plus, I'm glad you got stuck with the job of role model and not me. The talkings-to, the instructions? Cal's never really wanted me to talk to him that much. And I'm fine with that. A daughter – we'd have been intense together, I'd imagine. I know I exasperated my mother. And she me. I'm sure I'd have been more anxious with a girl, loading her with my stuff, seeing myself in her – wrongly. Trying to live again through her, basically.' She settled back in the blue. 'No, it's been an education, with Cal, I've learned from him, about the male of the species. I get to look at my big hand-some boy and marvel at him. I can see how Jennifer must feel. But, I know too – it's all show and bluster. Deep down he's a sensitive soul. Like you, big man.'

I think, finally, I understood. Her worry tonight had not been so real and pressing as the need that we talk just a little in this manner. Soon afterward we heard the key in the door and sat ourselves up in unison. I had to let the boy know we were vexed. Yes, he'd been to see Jennifer. Yes, he is feeling life-pressures, remains tense about Robert. 'Jenny calms me' is how he phrased it. Lucky girl, landed with such a job, for Cal's moodiness could clear a room.

'Come here,' I said, and pulled him into a bear-hug. He struggled, the little bastard, but I was quite insistent, needing to feel him, needing him to feel me. There is no time for unwarranted anxiety now, not in this house. We are going through too radically disturbed a time in our lives, and we must ride it out with care for each other.

I ought now to try and preserve that so precious and dearly bought peace, by switching out the light, climbing into my bloody bed, curling up behind my dear girl. For all what dreams may come.

14

Dr Hartford's Journal
Intruder

Grey would not say over the phone what was the matter, but I knew by the hard-bitten tone of his few terse words – he was deep in his own stoical version of anxiety. He said he had to see me, and clearly I had to get moving, since he was so awake and so fraught at not-quite-5am. No time to query him, much less be irked, so strange was it to hear the big man sound this troubled.

I pounded up to Parliament Hill and there he stood with Calder, both in jogging sweats. I suppose he'd per-suaded the lad to join him on a sprint. Still, they were sucking fretfully on cigarettes, Grey's usual parental rein relaxed – I nearly laughed, so clear was the evidence of how much his agitation must have wanted company. I'd have liked a few words with Cal, but some prearrange-ment between father and son was wordlessly invoked and the boy wheeled round, jogged off down the hill. Grey tossed his fag-end to the breeze.

'So what's the mystery, old fella?'

'Ach. Wanted to tell you in person, instead of you hearing it on the news.'

'What? You're retiring?'

My friend's sorry look knocked back my try for levity.

'No, Steve, no. It's Killian MacCabe. He's dead.'

I never met the man but still I was shocked, and I assumed Grey must have felt all the worse for his closeness to Malena. I soon sensed, though, that for all the gloom around him he had already moved into a mode of obsessive analysis, and as I listened to him tell the full story I realised he would expect from me some astute, up-to-speed opinions on the sorry turn of events.

'I had a call just after 4am from DI Hagen, who's had, I should say, quite a night of it. They found MacCabe's body just after 11pm, in the aisle of an overground train headed north out of London. Now – mark you this one – at that same hour Hagen was attending Robert's apartment in Artemis Park, there'd been a break-in, albeit done without damage to the locks. A break-in for which Killian MacCabe is the chief suspect – or at least he was as soon as I'd told Hagen that Killian had access to Robert's bloody keys.'

How was I meant to compute all of that? I put my hand on Grey's shoulder, as if I could, for once, be the rock in this relationship. 'Grey, wait, listen, start again. With Killian, what was the cause of death?'

'Undetermined as yet. Foul play not suspected. Hagen said the view from the pathologist is something to the effect that' – and he grimaced – 'it looks like one of those weird ones where the heart just stopped. Some defect, like Eisenmenger's. Not really explicable in one so young, but. One for the procurator fiscal, as Hagen puts it.'

'Weren't there any witnesses?'

'Nope. Train was near-empty, it chugged on a wee

while before someone found him lying there on the floor. No CCTV in the carriage. They're looking at the cameras at the station stops, but it's not a well-covered line. Me, my first thought was suicide. Overdose, based on what I've seen and heard lately. But, there were no external injuries, no signs of toxicity.'

'You've spoken to Malena?'

He nodded slowly. 'She's just . . . destroyed. The poor girl. God knows how she comes back from this.'

Whereupon Grey informed me that Killian had beaten Malena badly prior to his absconding – the grim culmination of his recent manias, I suppose. I was almost relieved to have something of my own to relate on this score, and told Grey I was more or less sure it had been MacCabe who rang my house drunkenly the night before last. Grey appeared to like my input not one bit.

'Killian called *you*? Why the blazes would he do that?'

'God knows. He was pished, for sure, or off his head on something. But it was like you'd said about him – almost a sort of a threat, in every word out of his mouth.'

Grey nodded. 'Right. You need to tell that to Hagen, Steve.'

The idea oppressed me somehow. 'But what does it mean? It's not like there's a crime here. Just a man who came off the rails – drastically, yes, assaulted his wife, yes – but now the bugger's gone and died. It's all ghastly but . . . I mean, what does it amount to, Grey?'

His eye on me had a critical caste. '"Off the rails", you say. What does that behaviour say to you, Stevie? About MacCabe's state of mind?'

I could only shrug. 'I'd need the real story, but . . . the point, the tragedy is it's all too late now. Isn't it?'

'What was Killian playing at, breaking into Robert's apartment?'

'Hang on, do they *know* it was Killian? I mean, God, could it not have been *Robert*? Is nobody working on that possibility?'

'Robert wouldn't be an intruder in his own home, wouldn't creep in like a thief. This man came stealthily, and left the same way – only after putting young Sergeant Goddard in hospital, mind.'

I was beginning to feel an ache between my eyes. 'Grey, you'll have to explain . . .'

'Hagen's had Goddard watching Robert's apartment the last week or so – not round the clock, just checking in. He was parked outside last night, spotted a face he didn't recognise scurrying in the main door, and when he sees a light in Robert's window he goes up. Gets in there, checks around, sees some things disturbed in Robert's office. But no one in sight. So he goes upstairs, *then* hears a noise below, hares back down and there's his fella making a bolt for the door. So Goddard reckons he's got the boy good and cornered, right? But I expect his bloody heart stopped when he got a better look, because the guy's only got on his face one of those hellish black masks of Robert's – the cold therapy things?'

I nodded, swallowed, aware as I am now of Robert's ugly 'recreational' uses for same.

'He's not so big, but, the intruder. So Goddard reckons he'll take him. Only Robert's umbrella stand is by the door. And Killian pulls out that cane I gave Rab on his birthday, whacks the lad with it, knocks him down and thrashes away at him where he's lying on the floor. Until the bloody stick snaps.'

The violence sounded so horrendous, Grey's contempt for it so palpable, that I needed a moment to remember what had stirred in my mind. 'You're saying "Killian", though, like it's a certainty.'

'The guy's got Killian's height and build, and it's Killian who's stormed out of his own house with Robert's keys a few hours previous. So, aye, that's our man, Stevie.'

'Was anything actually taken from Robert's?'

'Odds and sods. Some leather carry-on bag got swiped from the office. Some papers, pages ripped out of a file of patients' details. No, I've no bloody clue what Killian wanted with them. Nor the scalpel he swiped off of Rab's dining table, it had been sitting with the mask – they were both there that day I met Hagen. But who's to say we're not missing something else? They're going to need the light of day in there.'

Mentally I was still wading through a mire. 'Hold it, surely – whatever items got taken were found on Killian's body?'

'Nope. Not the bag or the paper, not the mask, the blade – nothing. He'd been pickpocketed clean. Scavenged.'

I glimpsed a light of sorts. 'Could Killian have stolen those items so as to pass them on to someone else? Who was it actually found his body?'

'A passenger who got on, probably the second stop down the line from when it would have happened. Found him just sprawled there in the aisle, like a broken doll.'

'Grey, I do defer to the pathologist but . . . it *is* hard to believe he just stopped breathing and that's it.'

It was Grey's turn to shrug. 'Malena had thought he seemed very sick, suddenly, at the end. It's just not reflected in the pathology. Not yet. Like you say, he's gone, that's it, he's in the morgue. The stuff he nicked is God knows where. But Hagen's not unreasonably formed the view that anyone whose details are in those pages could know something – or else be in danger. So he's contacting them all as a precaution.'

We sat awhile. I wanted badly to say something that could help dispel the murk. What occurred was this: 'It would be useful, wouldn't it, if Robert picked this moment to resurface? At a police station, ideally.' Grey stared as if to say he didn't follow, or didn't care to. I held up my hands. 'Grey, I know you don't like to hear this, and I didn't know MacCabe, or his friends or his enemies, but I do have to say again – if one were writing a list of people who might wish him harm, then surely Robert would be on it. Prominently.'

Grey scowled. 'Steven, this is a stinking mess, but you tell me what part of it suggests Rab did any harm to Killian. It's Killian who's been the aggressor. Unless you're telling me Rab managed to stick some mind-altering drug into his tea. Something to account for what twisted the man. No, you ask me? I'm still not convinced Killian's hands are clean about Robert's going missing but whatever's happened to him now – you and I, we know Robert had no part in it.'

'Do we?'

I meant to lodge my point, but Grey's eyes had acquired the flintiness I recognised from past occasions when he was minded to 'persuade' by force. 'If Robert "resurfaces", Stevie, then you and I, his best pals, we'll know about it. Don't you think? Right now, though, he remains missing. And it's not looking good. Jesus Christ, I'm more inclined to worry if someone *did* do for Killian – *if* – then maybe they did for Robert as well.'

Rare it was for me to feel like the sober, grounded individual among the two of us. 'Grey, just think about it. There's nothing here but a tenuous connection, no real motive for anything, no circumstance to make it plausible. The link's only poor Malena, I suppose.' I did feel an urge, not unreasonable, surely unforgivable, to remark on the seeming propensity of her lovers to come to harm. I held back, knowing Grey's feeling for her, in which he did look rather immersed.

'Aye, I know, it's true,' he said after a long pondering while. 'Malena's the link. But there's got to be something else. Somebody. Who is it, Stevie?'

He looked at me very searchingly but I had said my piece as best I could, and no answer was going to fall on us from the pale-rose of the morning sky. I asked Grey for one of his red Marlboros, he obliged wordlessly, without surprise, and we smoked in silence.

ৎฐৎ

I was late out to Blakedene, cursing myself, for I'd had an important session scheduled with Eloise, had hoped also to grab a serious word with Gillon beforehand. But that chance evaded me again.

Eloise I found in pensive mood. Niamh had knocked on her door first thing this morning, as a call had come from Hagen's team. Turns out the pages torn by 'the intruder' from Robert's files last night contained personal details for all his recent patients with surnames beginning J–L . . . So, for the sake of form she had reprised for the police the details of her treatment at the Clinic, described (in tersest fashion) her brief entanglement with Robert, asserted she had never met Killian MacCabe, was herself in no one's debt, and did not believe that anyone had grounds to blackmail or otherwise injure her. As we sat, though, she seemed to want to fathom the same mystery over which Grey and I had been ineffectually troubling our heads.

'What do you think it means, Steven?'

I threw up my hands. 'It's a riddle . . . All I see is a man's dead, Robert's still missing, neither event is quite explicable.' I wanted to stay focused on her. 'I do have some worries, though. With Robert. Given what you've told me . . . what he's capable of. If he is still roaming around with something on his mind – understand, I don't mean to alarm you, Eloise, any more than—'

'I'm not afraid of Robert,' she said simply, her frown suggesting only that I was the one with comprehension problems. 'He always knew where to find me. But he never cared. And I do think he's gone – for good, I'm afraid. I'm sorry if that sounds . . .'

I have no idea how she's arrived at this view, but what she said next so gratified me that I ceased to worry.

'Anyhow, I've never felt as safe – "looked out for" – as I do here . . .' She stood, hugged herself as if chilly, took a little turn around the room. I sat, thinking that our aborted session could hardly have delivered a more gratifying outcome.

♪

David Tregaskis was unhinged today, there is no other word for it. I may have to admit defeat with him: anything less might be dangerous to us both. As we began I was no doubt preoccupied, and David too wore a subdued air, an unusual meekness about him. It wasn't long before he flared, though. I had suggested, given the skill in his hands, he might consider turning this to an occupation – carpentry, say. But he resents this, loathes the very thought of earning his keep in life.

DT: . . . *The true worth of a man is not work or money. It's his soul, how he suffers what the world throws at him. No one suffers like the poor, Steven. You're too pampered, insulated, to see it. Do you know what it means to have nothing, to be junked on the street, turned away from every door? Spat at, despised, rejected, beaten, burnt?*

SH: *I don't claim direct experience, David. But most of my work as a hospital consultant was with the unwaged, the long-term homeless, the—*

DT: *'Your work', yes, not your experience, no. I tell you this – if there is a God, a true master, then I know He's* been among us, He's lived as a despised man. Nothing human could be alien to Him. Any great force contains multitudes. Also humility. He is everybody. And, in that, He teaches us not to be narrow or defined. God should know how to feel as a man feels. Or an insect. His power should be that He changes his form, is capable of that great corporeal sympathy. By being embodied. From the great heights down to the lower depths.

SH: Well . . . yes, David, you will know, legend has it, that God so loved the world he gave his only begotten son. 'Who was pierced for our transgressions.'

DT: Don't give me 'Jesus'. Jesus was a cross-maker, a rat, an informer . . .

For all the sneer in his voice there was a low excitement on David's face, and he was jogging up and down restlessly in his seat, twisting that silver bangle of his to and fro like a combination lock. I thought I would hazard a friendly enquiry.

SH: David, are you aware just how often you worry at that bracelet of yours?

DT: Yes. I am. It's just— tight. It chafes.

SH: Why not loosen it? Or slip it off awhile?

DT: Never. It's too dear to me. It has power, see.

SH: What kind of power?

DT: To ward away evil.

SH: What sort of evil?

DT: How many sorts do you know of?

SH: Forgive me, I was thinking of your spirits. Master
Ravenscourt? The Slaney girl.

DT: No. I was mistaken there – about the spirit-ridden
nature of my room. In fact I now think it's Miss
Keaton's room that is the locus of that— disturbance.
Maybe I should loan her this bracelet . . . When I
pass her door, I swear, I get a very precise pricking
sensation in my fingers and toes. Which is a sign.

SH: 'By the pricking of my thumbs—'

DT: 'Something wicked'? No. But wondrous, perhaps.

[. . .]

DT: Forget it, Steven, I'm having sport with you . . . No,
the truth? I was led at point of sale to believe my
bracelet had transformative powers. I don't know,
but . . . I think it could possibly be some sort of an
agent in that line. I could believe it might have those
properties. I've seen it happen.

SH: 'Transformation'?

DT: In my mind. Sometimes I don't want to be myself.
This body, this . . . envelope of flesh? It's distasteful,
Steven. I get sick of these hands of mine, big thick
woolly wrists. I have hands like a burglar. Like a
strangler. You want to try my bracelet on? I'll let you.

SH: You said you wouldn't take it off.

DT: I lied. No, it's just I notice your wrists are quite
slender. To be honest, it would suit you better than
me. And then you could transform.

SH: I'm content as I am, David.

DT: Oh you are?

SH: What do you transform into, David? In your mind?

DT: A bird, mostly, Steven. They're so obvious, aren't they?
Human dreams. Wanting to take flight from the
ground, free of gravity's pull. Sometimes I'm a spider,
scuttling into your mouth at night . . .

I was already gazing past David, out through the window, at the hues of twilight, the ink and the fire in the sky. I knew it was time for home and that, tonight, I would leave. Tregaskis was visibly irked to sense my withdrawal, but I also wanted to catch Gillon before he left for the day. So I sent David back to his room, muttering all the way.

I found Gillon in his office, asked him for an update on the sale/merger situation. Regrettably what I'd thought would be an awkward exchange turned into a full-scale quarrel. I had believed matters were moving sluggishly – in fact they seem to be flying – the point is that I am excluded from the loop, and Gillon doesn't seem to care how I feel about that. I had to ask him outright if he believed he'd been hired to help me or, rather, undermine me at every turn. He threw me a disbelieving scowl, said we 'should both stick to what we do best'.

Back behind my office door I felt rattled and – almost without thinking – took the Remeron bottle from my desk drawer, popped a capsule. Whereupon my phone rang and I jumped, like a guilty child nabbed in the act by Father. It was Grey, of course, commandingly sure I'd want to brood with him over some details he'd received from Bill Hagen about Killian MacCabe's autopsy. 'Natural Causes', definitely, for all that Grey seems to wish otherwise. Transport Police and crime-scene technicians were all over that carriage, dusting and tweezering up all the prints and micro-fibres they could want, but they found not a speck of Killian's blood. The SGM guys combed his corpse, found the obvious traces of Malena – hair, skin, also blood – plus DNA of at least one unknown person, but nothing matching the database. So be it. Tonight I had nothing to give Grey for his pains. The Remeron was washing over me, I only heard myself assuring my newly superstitious friend that we do well not to make a mystery where the facts are plain.

As I dandered to the window, phone in hand, I saw that Tregaskis had inexplicably left his precious bracelet behind on the sill. I picked it up as I talked to Grey and, absently, slipped it round my wrist. There was something pleasing in its cool silver clasp. I was staring out of the darkening window as I listened, and – just for a fraction of a second – I felt a little current of shock as the features of my reflection swam and seemed not quite my own. It was, as I say, the briefest blurring, then I relocated my familiar frown. But for a moment I was sure the face in the half-light was slighter, softer, more sculpted, even somehow female . . . The lesson, no question: Remeron is never to be toyed with.

Driving home in the heart-sore company of *Katya Kabanova*, I found myself chuckling at the memory of a more high-spirited soirée at Grey's, where Robert nonetheless contrived a bit of a row in relation to something I said about a patient of mine, a 50-ish Glaswegian guy whom I was mentoring through the needful steps in advance of gender realignment surgery – 'the unkindest cut', as Grey cheerfully called it. Whereupon Robert weighed in, sourly: 'Jesus wept, those creatures depress me when I see them. The pre-ops? That straggly hair down their backs, and the wee totter they do like they're practising to manage with heels and a handbag . . .'

'They're in pain, Robert,' I said with my customary patience.

'They soon will be,' he snorted. 'They have no *idea* of the pain that's coming down the pipe. Come on, Stevo, that whole nonsense is such a sorry delusion. "Born in the wrong body." Pish. What they *are* is the body they are. There is no *person* apart from a body.'

'Such an essentialist, Robert,' I murmured, meaning to deflate his bluster, but The Man From Selkirk was off and away.

'I don't deny the fantasy's got a hold of them, right in its fist, I'm just saying, let's call dysmorphism for what it is. Let's admit we allow them these procedures, massively complex, hideously expensive, all to gratify a whim. Not a *need*. These fucking guys, they just want to play with dollies. They want to play at a version of "being a girl", like they've seen in the magazines. Because it takes their fancy.'

At Robert's side Malena had been studying him with the ghost of amusement round her lips, and now she laid a hand on his arm. 'Oh but darling – don't you think we all do that, now and again? "Play"? *I* play at being a girl sometimes, you know. It's fun. You play at being the great surgeon. What you do when you close the door behind you . . .' She twinkled. 'For all I know, you get out your dollies.'

Malena had delighted the table, less so her angry lover, since, as I recall, we heard little more from him that night.

15

Dr Lochran's Journal
The Burnt Man

September 9th

This morning I attended MacCabe's funeral at the Church of the Transfiguration in Kensal Rise. Malena asked me, and it wasn't my place to refuse, despite my ill feeling for the deceased. The marks he left on Malena are still too wincingly visible. But she needed support, no question. She had told me he was on poor terms with his family, apparently a fractured (and fractious) mob in any case. His mother was there, plus a sister and a male cousin, all of Killian's reduced stature, all stony-eyed and tight-lipped: some suppressed anger/recrimination at the ready. The clans kept apart, at any rate. I spoke only briefly to Malena, flanked stolidly by her parents, who will be taking her back to the family estate near Odense for the foreseeable.

I was a tad late to the door, hearing the strains of a hymn from within, and was admitted discreetly by a kind verger who handed me a service booklet, then scooted past to deal with some black-clad wraith of a beggar who was loitering at the gate. Inside I tiptoed down the left aisle of the nave, the odour of old stone and wood polish in my nostrils. The strangeness of this funeral was compounded by it being an 'art world' occasion of sorts, quite a few notably dandified characters in the pews. But several of MacCabe's peers spoke interestingly, and the religious service I found moving in spite of the flummery. I am a Protestant man, I suppose. Prayer and ritual always seem to me ineffectual, redolent of the dour school chapel at Kilmuir. But the handsomeness of this church, the soul of the organ music, the frozen grief of the statuary . . . these have a power, beyond the all-too-human straining, even if it's mere human 'artistry' to which we respond.

As we all trooped out I saw that Bill Hagen had attended, an honourable gesture on his part. He drew me aside, confided that someone has come forward with new information about the night of Killian's death: a woman who boarded the train with her boyfriend around 2230 – twenty or so minutes after Killian abandoned his car and got on at Oakleigh Park, twenty minutes or so before he 'dropped dead'. The couple can't say they saw Killian, but were sure there was at least one other in the carriage save for themselves and a fellow sat opposite them. (In fact they changed carriages, somewhat to their shame, because this fellow's face was awfully burnt and they were made uneasy by him: Robert's old saw, sad to say – the stigma borne by the disfigured.)

The crux of it, though: there is (and Hagen relayed this in clear dissatisfaction at the world's annoying imprecision) some shadowy CCTV evidence of someone seeming to flee the train in haste at a station stop, five minutes or so before Killian was found. The 'figure' leaves the frame in such a direction as to permit no exit from the station other than back down the tracks from whence the train had come.

What are we to make of that? How make it fit with all the other baffling facts? I don't know where to begin, nor, I think, does the wily Hagen, who seemed vexed. I asked him if he had got anywhere in trying to locate Vukovara, and he indicated that had I been more bloody useful at the start then his task would be proving less bloody forlorn now.

I thanked him for the 'briefing', phoned Steven from the car to keep him abreast, and hastened to the hospital. What awaited me was a Syme amputation on three-year-old Jessie Waugh for her congenital pseudarthrosis of the tibia. In this we were finally conceding the defeat of three previous failed efforts at bone-graft and limb-lengthening. Her mother was very much crushed, I must say. Even I find it harder to brace myself for this procedure when the life itself is not at stake – the crossing of the line is so profound, the amputation blade so fearsome when applied to a child, the stump so raw and piteous when it's done – perfect white bone, red muscle, pink skin.

I suppose I've always derived my satisfaction from the manner in which I can repair what the body itself cannot renew. Thus, when I am the one who taketh away . . . Perhaps today was just not a day on which I was fully girded to perform that function. But there's no time for self-pity. Or else how could I face the mother and her child, having demanded all that fortitude of them?

I begin to believe in premonition, and to forgive myself for it, because last night, once again, I dreamt of my late friend Edmond.

Lying in bed it was as if I heard an entreating voice in my ear. I rose, belted my robe, padded downstairs. The rooms were dark and still. But I crossed to the rear reception window and there he stood in the garden below, sombre and silent. I couldn't see his eyes, yet I knew he was staring fixedly at me. I went out and we set off together, trod the earth in silence, past what was real and familiar until we were deep in some blasted wood, where I had to take his arm.

'Edmond, old man, I'm glad to see you. But you make me worried, my friend. Do you understand?'

'Grey, believe me, I feel the same seeing you. But your concern, there's nothing I can do for it. You're right to be concerned.'

The lucidity of the conversation was striking to me, even the convincing feel of soft earth under bare feet. I had released my hold on him, but then he took hold of me.

'Do you see? Through the trees . . . ?'

I looked to where he was motioning, fifty or so feet away, glimpsed two obscured white faces, picked up faintly on two murmuring voices. I was starting to feel an unsavoury voyeurism when the two faces merged into one, and white hands clutched a broad black-clad back. I knew then that Edmond had gone, left me, but in that same moment I felt hot breath in my ear, and I spun round in fright, so crashing my forehead into the pillow . . .

The clock read 4.17, and within minutes I knew I wouldn't be getting back to sleep. I rose, quiet as a thief, pulled on soft clothes. At the front door I was minded to take my cane – I wonder now what clairvoyance possessed me? I stepped out, past the sober façades of the street, through a little morning mist. Ten minutes later I was at the Heath, wending up to Parliament Hill.

I saw him at a point when to turn back or detour would have felt— unacceptably cowardly, somehow, whatever alarm bells were clanging inside me. A 'street person', a vagrant, clearly – slumped on a bench, in old black jeans and boots and a long black hooded anorak – his head propped on his fists, duffel bag at his feet, a piece of human wreckage, a picture of despond. It was solitude I'd wanted, not to be solicited, and for that reason, too, I could have simply turned heel. What is it in my nature, this denial of fear, this insistence on facing down every dark possibility? Who do I fool, since I don't fool myself?

It was only when I stole another glance at him, sat there like a man made of stone, back hunched, black hood thrown up, that I felt I recognised the posture and the garb – felt nearly sure this was the same character the verger had dealt with for lurking outside Killian's funeral.

Then I was past him. He did not look up. I pressed on, up to the crest of the hill, there surveyed the panorama, the hazy imprint of London's grandeur, the dim rose-coloured promise of day. I chose then to look back over my shoulder, back toward the bench, saw that it was empty. And now I was afraid.

In that same moment I heard the footfalls over grass, swivelled to see him trudging up the incline, out of the silence and the mist, head bowed, hands thrust in his pockets, monk-like. My skin prickled as he drew nearer, whereupon it was clear – something was very wrong under that hood of his. Ten feet away he stopped, raised his face, I saw only sleek shiny contours of black; realised I was staring at a mask – Robert's mask – its leather straps and flaps hugging and hiding every inch of the face save for the eyes and nostrils, like the visor of some Corinthian warrior, or a baleful unbidden guest at a Venetian masquerade.

'Robert . . . ?' I murmured. A reflex, I couldn't help it.

His hands came out of his pockets and straight away I saw the left was scarred by burning, missing two fingers. He threw back his hood, exposing some scant hair disarrayed in curls and horns around a reddened scalp. Then he gripped and un-strapped the sides of the black mask, lowering it to reveal a truly terrible sight. Half the face was as sorely disfigured as the hand – third-degree burns, skin livid and crusted by hard eschars, the thin lines of his mouth and eyelids cruelly distorted. And yet he gave me a piteous excuse for a grin, baring some poor teeth. Now I remembered the evidence of Hagen's witnesses from the train – the stranger they couldn't bear to face – and I felt danger much increased. Still, I had my cane in hand. I kept my composure.

'You've an honest face, captain,' he said, the words

struggling out of that tortured mouth, with a slight escaping hiss.

'Thank you. How did you come by that mask, my friend?'

'This?' Again, the nerve-straining hiss. 'Found it in the street, boss. S'amazing, things you find . . .'

'I'm afraid I don't believe that. Was it not maybe given to you? Or did you maybe take it from someone?'

'You calling me a thief? Thief and a liar? And here's you and me just met?'

'No. No, but— I need a better explanation. Because that mask isn't a thing you buy over a counter. It's unique. It belongs to a friend of mine.'

'Ahh. No good to him now, but. Right? And some comfort to me.'

'So, you admit, you stole it?'

'I do not.' He stood there, swaying slightly, exuding what seemed the most unlikely insolence in light of his condition. I sensed he had a secret, one he was sure I could use – indeed the purpose of this confrontation. So I tried my luck.

'Tell me, would you happen to know, where I might find that friend of mine? Robert Forrest?'

'Robert Forrest . . . What would you pay, for that information?'

'Not a penny. But if you know you'd better say so or else—'

'Or what? You'll summon the law?' He came a couple of steps closer, cocked that disturbingly raw, skull-like head at me. 'Don't you think I might be glad of that?

Police cell, bone-dry, four walls . . . I'd not turn up my nose. The body is prison enough, captain – I suffer that way.'

His odd croaking eloquence, the sad hash that his slit-like mouth made of the word 'suffer' was enough to disarm me momentarily.

'I'm sorry for you,' I said quietly.

'Huh. Yes. Wretched, aren't I? But, as low as I sink – the blood moves the body, drives me on. Life clings to life. But you know that. I'm not telling you anything, am I, Doctor Lochran?'

That went straight to the hairs on my neck. I felt my fists clenching. 'You know me, then, do you? And do I know you?'

That lizard-skin gaze of his looked me over again. 'No, no, kind sir, apologies . . . This is a new game to me. All I was hoping was that you could spare me a coin? Or two.'

My hand went to my pocket but my eyes stayed on him, for I was weighing up how best to make a citizen's arrest. He was still five good strides away from me. I had to be sure, if I got hold of him, that he would stay got. I pulled out a fistful of change.

'Here you go then. Take it.'

But his eyes hadn't left mine. 'No, that'll never get me a room for the night. Four walls. That's what I'm after, captain.'

I shook my head. 'There's not a hostel in the land charges money. Why don't you say what you really want?'

'*You* wanted some information? Concerning Robert Forrest? I can tell you – he is incarcerated.'

'Where?'

The Burnt Man didn't answer, merely rubbed the rough pads of his fingers together like Fagin. It had gone beyond the pale. I squared up, hefted the cane in my hand. 'No, you're mistaken, my friend. Now stop fucking me around, or you'll regret it, I promise.'

With a painful slowness his mouth made the shape of a sneer. 'Dear, dear. I had hoped for a better reception – "my friend". I'll not forget this.'

The eyes in his ruined face narrowed as he lifted the dangling black mask and refastened it in place. As he did so, past his shoulder I could see another figure coming over the heath, indeed two – some dog-walker with a Staffy frisking about at his side. My enemy glanced backward to where I was looking, and in that instant I resolved myself, rushed at him, grasping his sleeve. But he reacted, struck away my hand with a rising arc of a clout that caught my chin, rattled my teeth. For some moments I saw only fractals before me. The next I knew, he was haring away down the hill, a shambolic sort of a run but far too fast for me. The dog-walker looked to me in some alarm. His Staffy gave chase, only for the owner to call him back from what he evidently rated a bad scene. I thanked them both between gritted teeth, then hobbled off homeward as swift as I was able. En route I left messages for Hagen and Steven. The detective was a damn sight quicker in getting back to me, took my account commendably seriously, sent the patched-up DS Goddard round to ours.

If this bizarre chain of events still fails to conform to

any logic, nonetheless we know now what became of the goods Killian stole from Robert's apartment. Hagen accepted my contention that the Burnt Man's demand for money had been no simple act of beggary, not even a would-be mugging. Rather it felt like something more sinister, some kind of botched attempt at claiming a ransom.

It wasn't until tonight that Steven called, sounding not entirely healthy. And he didn't like my story one bit – in fact, seemed so rattled that one might have thought it was he who'd suffered the disturbing encounter rather than me. Soon I almost felt myself slipping into my default position of trying to reassure, in this case that I'd just been so unlucky as to run across one more spot of feral London street-level nastiness.

'But it was money he wanted from you, right?' Steve's voice crackled, riled. 'How much, do you think?'

'Ach, I don't know if it was money or what he really wanted was to get under my skin. For whatever godforsaken reason. To earn my pity, even. Anyhow, it's a police matter now, this guy's wanted and he won't find it easy just to melt into air. Not looking like he does. *Le fantôme* . . .'

'That's a rather sensational way to put it, Grey.'

It was my turn to get riled, by his censuring tone. 'Well, it was a bit of a fucking "sensational" experience, Steve, and it happened to me, so I'll call the guy what I bloody well want.'

'I hear you, I'm sorry. I just think it's important neither of us . . . go entirely mental over this.'

'"Mental" is not a word I thought you used, doctor. But I agree. I prefer a reasonable line on things. At the moment, but, it's hard.'

I heard Steven's long sigh. 'I know, Grey, I know . . .'

'It does make me wonder, Stevie, wonder again – whether Robert's not been, y'know – done away with.'

This, however depressing, was my genuine sentiment. And yet Steven's reply stunned me. 'No, Robert's alive, Grey, I'll bet on it. Maybe closer than we think.'

'Steven, are you drunk? Or have you got some fresh evidence? Anything you want to tell me?'

The line crackled back at me again, that uneasy breathing. 'No, of course not. I'm just like you, old man. Putting things together that don't add up. Maybe it'll look better in the morning. Let's get some sleep, eh? We both need it.'

I was bothered, stood awhile over the dead phone. True, we are old friends, we deceive one another habitually, without malice. But I suspect Steven well knows – a joke to think otherwise – that neither of us will be drifting off easily tonight.

16

Dr Hartford's Journal

A tempest

September 10th

I know what I will do, what I have to do. Stupid of me to dream for one second that I had any choice.

Lying to Grey might even be the worst of it, since I've no better friend on this earth. But then I've lied before in this matter, haven't I? Isn't my whole predicament just the latest in an iron succession of one lie by another? Grey can't come and pull me out of the mire now – the damage was done a long time ago, in an hour of dire need, when I chose the wrong friend. Ever since, I've only been waiting for the karmic payload to drop. Yes, I was a coward for not telling Grey tonight, but I was a coward before, and even now I fear exposure – disgrace – as much as the next man. So my cowardice will persist.

I read the look in Tessa's eye instantly on my return last night: it had to be a security issue, but this time not the floodlight, nor the broken lock. As she told it, she hadn't been long home, was changing bed-sheets upstairs when through the window she saw a gaunt figure hobble up the darkened driveway to our door – a long, lean individual clad from head to toe in shabby black. He disappeared under the porch and Tessa stood there, disconcerted, until she saw him hobble off again.

'You're sure you've not seen him around before?'

'I wouldn't have known, he was wearing a hood . . .'

Downstairs she found he had shoved a small envelope through the letterbox, and I saw '*Dr Hartford*' scrawled across it in a jagged hand as she passed it to me. The unease on her face convinced me, astutely, to shove it into my back pocket.

'Aren't you going to open it?'

'I've other correspondence, Tessa. I doubt this one's terribly urgent. But I'll let you know . . .'

And off I stomped up to the office, the bills and circulars brought by regular mail pressed piously to my chest. With the door shut behind me it was, of course, the grimy hand-delivery I tore open first, a letter composed over several note-cards, almost gentlemanly. Then, in an instant, came a crushing, vice-like sensation to my head on all sides.

Dear Dr Steven:

A friend of mine has bequeathed me a most disturbing story, as a result of which I know what you did – or shall we say failed to do? – in the sad case of Mr Tom Dole.

Poor Tom. However could you have left him out in the cold and the dark, there to fall into a hole yet colder and darker? The coroner, I understand, adjudged it a cerebral haemorrhage. Would it not then distress his loved ones (also, your employer) to learn that the true cause of his death was You? That you let him die, and arranged for the disposal of his body – like so much garbage – just to save your skin?

If I'm not to make this information more widely known, then it seems to me you must make reparation of sorts. For your convenience I will be the collector of dues.

What you must do is place £10,000 in notes inside a plain carrier bag and get to Bishop's Wood for 8pm tomorrow night. Enter the wood by the gate on Temple Fortune Hill. Walk 60–70 yards in, until the paths diverge. Take the left fork, until you see a red-painted bench under an oak. Take such time as you need to ensure that no one has sight of you, then walk into the woods directly beyond the oak for fifty or so paces: you will see a cherry tree into which a pentangle is cut. The tree-stump has a hollow near its foot. Place the carrier therein, leave it, exit the Wood directly, do not look back or return. I will be watching.

Do all this exactly. Do not attempt to inform any other party of our arrangement. What I know in respect of yourself and Mr Dole has been written out, sealed and lodged with a notary, and will be made known in the event that anything should befall me. In which case, you know what will follow. But said document will be destroyed following your compliance with my instructions as above, whereupon, you have my word, you will not hear from me again . . .

Didn't I always know this would rise again, that the bones wouldn't stay sunk? Five, six years vanish that way, cease to matter – my heart is back in my boots, just like the night Tom died on my kitchen floor where I'd left him. I lived a lie from that moment, went through the motions, commiserated with his family, loathsome to myself. In keeping my secret from Grey I clung to his approval of me and, I suppose, assured myself I would never tell another soul. And I never did. But my accomplice, my rescuer that night, the man who shook me hard, told me, '*You weren't the cause of this, Stevo, you can't let it ruin you . . .*' No, my old friend Dr Forrest never took any vow of silence.

Could anyone else but Robert know what he and I did? I can all too easily believe we were witnessed in some part of the act, I always feared as much. But that the witness should have kept quiet all this time? Or else – might Robert have kept some written account, now fallen into other hands? (The break-in at his apartment!)

If this is Robert himself – then it's insanity, because he's running the risk of damning himself alongside me, if I chose to call his bluff, tough it out. Robert knows that the truth indicts him too: our 'plan' that night, it was his idea. I stumbled along with it, yes, but I didn't conceive it. (This I tell myself, knowing full well the counter – that I was desperate, couldn't face taking the honest course of responsibility for my actions, or inactions.) Could Robert be so desperate for money? Does he imagine he's become invisible? Maybe he has, God knows.

The letter is not in his handwriting, so he can only have an accomplice, an 'emissary', in this 'Burnt Man', *le fantôme*, who tried to hustle Grey for the coins in his pocket but wants ten grand out of me. How could Robert have made such a partner in crime? He writes just as fancily as Robert: possibly he was taking dictation. And yet the letter speaks of the 'friend of mine', who 'bequeathed' . . .

No, out of all the mad scenarios only one seems to pass all tests of credence, if barely so: Robert must be in hock to somebody, heavily, some serious extortionist. Any one of his many debts or misadventures could have put him in the hole to someone so remorseless. I think Grey has it right – we are dealing with a kidnap, or a kind of forcible identity theft, or some sort of warped ransom situation. Someone's got him, is holding him, bleeding him for cash. That's why the raid on his place, that's why this blackmail.

A police matter, no question. Except that I'm no more ready to face them now than I was then. The truth will put me in a place where I can no longer face myself. If I came clean to Grey . . . he'd forgive me, I do believe that, but it wouldn't hold him back from doing his blasted duty. The 'Burnt Man' is a suspect in this obscure 'investigation': I'd have to surrender his letter to forensics.

All these thoughts ran round my head, the deceptively logical processes we use to persuade ourselves we are in control, and it's all really okay, and the worst will never happen . . . But really I knew what I would do the moment the shock receded. The rest was only a making peace with that, a ritual burning of each pretend option. My reputation, my livelihood, the life I've made, all are at stake here. In going along with it – I'm not so stupid as to imagine that will be an end to it. But there's no other hope.

Thereafter my actions were fast and precise. I fed the note-cards into the shredder. I logged on to our current account, booked a withdrawal from the branch on Haverstock Hill tomorrow. Then I came down and made dinner, whistling tunelessly as I sliced pearly scallops in two. Tessa wandered in, poured herself some wine.

'So what did your little note say . . . ?'

'Just some poor itinerant sod, looking for work. "Odd jobs." I don't think he's the handyman we're looking for, do you?'

I segued by telling her the tickets I'd ordered for *Idomeneo* at the ENO had arrived. She dipped a finger in my *sauce vierge*, tasted, made an approving face, even kissed the nape of my neck on her way out. Any other day I would have thought this progress. Tonight I flinched.

September 11th

It's done, despatched. Nothing for it now but pray to God another call never comes. Even as I went through the prescribed motions, my mind was wrenched two ways. I am bargaining with – taking the word of – an individual probably dangerous, possibly deranged. Grey's tale of his clash with the Burnt Man on Parliament Hill was alive in my mind, had me feeling hollow-legged as I picked my way into Bishop's Wood at dusk. Stepping between the sycamores and over the breaking twigs I kept fighting back the skin-crawling premonition I was about to catch sight of him suddenly, studying me through the trees, crouched as if to spring . . . His instructions, at least, were exact: all was as I found it, and I hastened back out of those mournful woods as fast as I could.

My day at Blakedene, between the collection and drop-off of blood money, was one for which I doubted I'd be capable. I was so sure my fraudulence was rolling off me like a stink. And yet, I showed myself again that I can pack away anxiety as if in chambers round my person – just as I did in the days after Tom's death. I can create a sort of doppelgänger, an efficient second self – breathe life into him, fill him with sufficient reality to carry out my chief functions. Still, as I moved from room to room there was a devil on my shoulder deriding me: *Behold the good man, the kind clinician. Shall I tell you the terrible thing he did . . . ?*

I sat in on all the morning groups, joined in Marcia Fallow's team conference, found myself genuinely engaged and moved by the account of her good progress. I considered cancelling Eloise, fearing (absurdly) that with her perhaps I'd fail to hold it together. But then our previous session had been lost. More than that, it's through her, above all – the thought of helping her – that I can see some route back to the mooring of my 'good' self.

So see her I did, and something quite unexpected passed between us in the room – whereupon it became blindingly clear to me what I must do, for her sake.

There was an odd moment, though, after I'd been told by Nurse Gardner that she was out on the veranda. I found her sleeping in the tall-backed wicker chair, a little slumped, head to one side and cradled in one hand. The air was warm, I could see perspiration on her brow, wondered if she was unwell, heat-struck. But as I stepped closer, I understood her condition was languid rather than awkward. She sighed and shifted, her breathing easy. There was a sweet breeze, a small holly-blue butterfly flitted by. Studying her face I was forced, reluctantly, to admire Robert's skill, her skin having retained its honey tone and fine down without one blot of that taut, marbled collagen-iridescence you often see in the 'worked-upon'. On the table before her were two elegant calla lilies, purple as our clematis in the gardens, their long stems wrapped in cellophane. Also an embroidery hoop and pincushion: a small needlepoint in progress, of an emerald snake coiled within larger spirals of hexagonal black and white. I thought it commendable work until I was uncomfortably reminded of that leering serpent tattoo Robert had etched onto himself while a student at the Bute.

Then I had a sixth sense, turned to see David Tregaskis standing close to the wall a few yards behind me, only seeming to stare through me. He was breathing strangely, his eyes blank, flickering upward, his body in a curious trance-like posture. I shouted at him, grabbed his shoulders, and he came back to us. But I had to summon Brian from the orderly team to lead him back to West Wing. Was it genuinely 'an episode'? Once he revived he was so much his familiar self I can't be sure he wasn't feigning it, to unsettle me, like so much of what he does.

Yet, up in my office it was Eloise who truly knocked me for six by presenting me with those two lilies. '*Les fleurs du mal . . .*', she murmured. A strange moment – I had to wonder quite what she was offering. In fact there was a sweet explanation: these were just two blooms out of a heaving bouquet delivered to her this morning, sent by Leon Worrell.

'I do want to thank you, Steven,' she said, eyeing the floor. 'For being a friend. I'd buy you a drink if I could . . .'

She half-smiled, yet the look in her eye was so earnest I felt something tighten in my chest. I almost didn't want to sink us back into the routine of the therapy. Still, we sat and strapped in, 'ran the numbers' for her target traumas, and I could see she had been reflecting on things, however ruefully. I can't pretend to see any uplift in her, any obvious indicator that her depression is 'shifting'. But I sense that the disturbing force of the memory of her abuse has been dislodged, is fading. Her 'disturbance-level' she rated as one/zero. When I asked her why, though, her answer troubled me.

'It was just a thing that happened to somebody . . .'

'It happened to *you*, Eloise.'

She only shrugged, scrutinised her fingers spread out on her knee. Yes, she accepts that what Flint did to her was 'not her fault'. But what I must do now is turn her focus from past problems to future solutions, to end the self-sabotage, the death-drive, build instead on the things that make her feel capable. Here, though, she is so worryingly passive. 'I can't alter what happened, or what followed. I just feel . . . used up, Steven. Past my sell-by date. How can I change the given now? How can I redeem myself? I so want to, but it just seems . . . hopeless.'

That earnest wish, though – to redeem herself! – God, but it resonated with me. Could we get to that place together, even if it need be by different doors? She has been brave enough to begin to face what's oppressed her. In that, she has a lesson for me.

The answer, I was sure, lay in those flowers from Leon. I gathered they'd been accompanied by a letter – 'a lovely letter', she said grudgingly, as if that only complicated matters. Her feelings for this man are nothing but complicated. They have circled each other, their relationship 'off and on', hostage to these alleged 'barriers' between them. The positives – their mutual physical attraction and basic compatibility – we have established. His worthiness as a suitor appears self-evident. Yet Eloise resists paying him the compliments she knows he merits. Still I believe that what glimmers through the murk of her insouciance is some trapped desire to come through for him, be the partner he wants her to be.

I dragged her round to describing for me how their relations had proceeded, after his brother Lynval had effected the introduction:

EK: I was promoting this club night, but I had twelve points on my licence and Leon offered to drive me around, deliver flyers and posters, carry gear. Then he sanded a floor in my place – that's his business, he can do anything with wood. He was sweet, but, you know, the motive was clear. He got what he wanted.
SH: After you slept together, did you begin a relationship proper? Dating?

EK: No, I wasn't doing that. We just took it as a one-night thing. Or two or three nights, probably, at the start . . . As it has continued.

SH: But he stuck around. Even after it was clear you weren't 'an item'?

EK: Yes. I . . . I got sick, it was a bacterial pneumonia and I was pole-axed for a few weeks. He came over, looked after me. Cooked me breadfruit casserole. His mama's good buljol . . . What?

SH: He cooks too? I'm waiting for the downside, Eloise.

[. . .]

SH: I mean, he's never stopped helping you, has he?

EK: He was a friend and I needed that, I still do – that doesn't mean it should be a relationship. He can turn, his temper, so quick. Don't be fooled by the smile . . .

SH: What makes him angry?

EK: Ha. Once I asked him how he could have left the mother of his son, and he went ballistic, said 'It's right I break with a woman when there can't be no peace.' I thought that lacked commitment. Then again, I met her, she's a piece of work . . .

SH: But you've met other people in his life? You get on okay?

EK: Oh yeah, that's all cool. I mean, I remember a night in this club he likes, a girl he knows hissed at me as I went past, but that's just— urgh, predictable . . . That same night, though, he told me off for 'faking', as he calls it, I'd gelled my fringe and he hated it. It's important to him that 'people be what they be'. Like he's always himself . . .

SH: How does Leon mix with your friends? You've
introduced him?

EK: He's not . . . wildly comfortable. He tries but he knows
he doesn't slot into the rest of my life. My background.
People with daddy's money, degrees . . .

SH: Does it matter you and he can't talk about French
poetry?

EK: Oh but Leon speaks French. Oh yeah. His dad was a
teacher. Leon rebelled, wanted a trade, to work with
his hands. But his French is good . . . No, you know
what I'm talking about, it's what formal education
means. Embodies.

SH: And do you feel so comfortable – in the rest of your
life, with your 'background'? Is it something you'd be
sorry to let loose of?

[. . .]

EK: It's just hard – relinquishing who you are. Whatever
that is.

SH: When Leon is angry with you, do you argue back?

EK: Yes. I tell him not to be silly. To grow up. He hates that
too . . .

SH: I'm not surprised. No one cares to be condescended
to. Do you not think you might be trying to make
him surly? Just to confirm your thesis? Clearly he's no
monster.

EK: Hmm. Maybe you and Leon should get together,
Steven. Since you think he's the man of my dreams . . .
Don't let me get in the way.

SH: No, we know the man of your dreams. Who steals you
away into slavery, submission. I don't want us to deal

in your dreams, Eloise, I want to know why you push
away someone who's trying to care for you.

EK: *Look, it's not my dream to be— dragged off to hell.*
But I don't want to be rowing all the time about
bullshit either – details, inane things, who owns who,
or owes what to whatever.

SH: *You mean growing up? I'm sorry Eloise, that's what it*
is. What it means to have a partner in life.

EK: *Right. Barefoot and pregnant . . .*

SH: *You've said that before. Has Leon done anything more*
than say he'd like children? And are you so opposed .
. . ? You know, I do think it was a good thing for us
as a species that sexuality was split out of procreation.
But you can't make the two wholly incompatible. Does
it scare you so much?

EK: *You've got children, right? Is that joy all the time?*

SH: *No. No, it can be quite 'inane'. Marriage, too. Love is*
compromise, surrender. But it's still the dearest feeling.
The warmest of all, Eloise.

[. . .]

SH: *Are you all right?*

EK: *Yes, no . . . Sorry . . . I hear you, I do . . . It's just . . . I*
ask myself, could I ever come through for Leon? Screw-
up that I am? In the end what would he want with
me? What would I teach our children? How to mix a
Cosmopolitan?

SH: *You could teach them French and Italian . . . Leon*
cares for you, Ellie. You push him away because you
fear the closeness. You distrust real intimacy, the
banality, the baby-making . . . What?

EK: You. Your theories are amusing, Steven. Did Leon put
    you up to this? Did he write you a letter too? Did you
    get flowers?
SH: No . . . But I'm not sure I should let you out of there
    until you promise to give him a chance. If not him,
    look . . . what I want you to just consider is that you
    can't do it alone. When you've felt yourself in that pit
    . . . you need someone's hand – not to drag you off but
    to lift you out, lift you up.

Was she persuaded by me, or rubbing along with what
I wanted to hear? I was wheedling at her, for sure, keen
– maybe too keen – to encourage what I take to be her
finer feelings. I don't dismiss out of hand her insistence
on Leon's volatile machismo – I have seen too much disturbing evidence of that in others lately. And love can't
be brewed like a potion in a bottle. But love and trust,
letting oneself be vulnerable in the right circumstances,
with the right person – this is what she must learn for
her own future well-being. And the idea of love, this love
above all, overcoming the odds . . . it would be a fine
thing.

When we were done and I showed her to the door, she
embraced me, to my surprise. I let it happen, knew I was
in control, put an avuncular hand on the crown of her
blonde head. 'You're one of the good guys, Steven,' she
murmured, and I shook my head, knowing better. Then
she was gone, leaving me to my appointment in Bishop's
Wood. The daylight was dwindling, I had to get on my
way.

John Teacher from the next-door farm happened to be rolling by in his big Deere tractor as I waited for the electronic gates to open fully, and he pulled over for a word. Turned out the tractor ride was a treat for his little girl Emily, who sat very quietly at his side – he was running her to see mummy at the shop in the village. Apparently Emily had suffered a fright out in the fields, believed she'd seen a 'nasty man' – John had to assure her she'd been spooked by Mr Mandrake, the carefully tailored scarecrow he propped up just this morning to brood over his runner beans. Really I think he was made for Emily's enjoyment, but that's backfired – she seems quite sure that Mr Mandrake walks and talks. And, looking in her eyes, I believed I'd felt just as she had, her fear – that slow-creeping cold flush over the skin. I clambered back into my car and drove off, scarcely any more hardy in myself than little Emily, with only Schubert's *Winterreise* for solace.

Fear is a ghost, and I live with one now, he's at my side always. I realise that I have for some years been carrying myself – even if only unconsciously – as a condemned man. But I swear, I truly swear, if there's still some redemption to be had for me here, then I will do better, I will work harder – I will be a better man.

September 12th

Once more I'm confined to Blakedene overnight, but this time not the fault of my bad timekeeping, rather because of the quite cataclysmic weather that befell us late this afternoon. It has caused trouble all round the place. For one, regrettably, my night at the opera with Tessa has gone to the wall. The sudden tempest, the near-alien strangeness and fierceness of the elements, made a disturbing atmosphere for our 'inmates'. But, nothing we could do about it. I'm concerned, nonetheless, by the highly irresponsible behaviour of Eloise and David. Whatever they thought they were doing out of house tonight it was at best heedless, and, for me, unsettling.

Lawrence, to his credit, had the measure of the day first thing this morning. I should have heeded him. As I went in he was attending to the beds at the front, and he frowned at my casual remark about the 'pleasant skies', said he fancied we might have an autumn gale on the way and should batten down the hatches. Blithely I said it seemed far too soon, what with our Indian summer and these mild southwesterlies. He shook his head with the indulgence of a veteran sky-watcher. 'New moon, see, tides run heavier. And you've got the mare's tails up there too, look.' He gestured to the long finger-like clouds streaked across the sky's turquoise.

'Fingers crossed they'll blow over,' I chirped – suddenly reminded that Lawrence had spent perhaps too much of his twenties and thirties imbibing noxious teas in the Peruvian Amazon, and, so I hear, has passed the odd hour with David Tregaskis in his shed at the rear of the grounds, chatting about the *kalachakra*. A pensive fellow, at any rate, and he wasn't going to let me away with any glibness.

'Oh no, you watch, there'll be some black old wrath come in from the north, before the day's end. You watch . . .'

After doing the diary with Niamh I strolled over to collect David from the art pavilion. It was earnestly on my mind that we needed a more productive session than our fractious tos and fros of late. Yet I found him standing in the middle of the back lawn, eyes closed, swaying slightly, challenging me with his oddness as ever. Perhaps he was channelling Lawrence – for then I noticed a light wind shaking our blossoms, stirring the treetops, especially the tall pines at the far end of the property. Even those windows of the house that had been thrown open to the morning air now rattled a little behind me.

Once I'd shepherded him upstairs he confounded me again. I am used to his oscillations of mood, and what I got today was a kind of serene indifference. Indeed he was glowing, freshly bathed, clad in a loose white shirt like a smock, his hair braided – resembling a supplicant monk, albeit with a dash of Rasputin. I returned his beloved silver bracelet to him, imagining he had missed it. He sat tranquil, hands on his knees, smiling affably, told me I should keep it, for he had another, indeed he showed it me – a black leather cord holding a silver figure of Asclepius, the snake round the staff.

'Interesting,' I told him. 'The symbol of the healer.'

'Is that so?' He seemed pleased. But I assured him I couldn't accept his old one, and he remained adamant it was of no further use to him. Thus it sat on the table between us, and the tone was set for our 'discussion'.

DT: *Steven, I see how anxious you are. A child could see it. But I want you to understand, things have got better for me now. Radiant. Amazingly so. My sun is rising, Steven.*

SH: *David, it's hard for me to accept what you say, when your experiences and moods are so— solitary, and inward – when you remain so much apart from the rest of us.*

DT: *Steven, of course I'm apart. I'm here, you're there. We are apart. I wish that were different, I do. But I'm saying, don't think about it. In my case it was meant to be. There is a change coming on, I feel it. Whether it's what you want, whether that's 'progress'... I can't say, wouldn't dare to. But now I know the master is at hand – the sense is so rich I can touch it, taste it.*

SH: *David... What 'master'? Not still Master Ravenscourt?*

DT: *No, don't be a fool, Steven, I've told you. I'm talking about the god of high and low, god of multitudes, king of the spiders, master of all vermin... call him what you want, he has called me. I will not say no...*

I have a serious decision to make in respect of David now: whether to keep revolving him between the houses of Depressive and Bipolar here, or whether he needs to be taking a more radical mood-stabiliser, and trying to forge a new therapeutic alliance. Because I am floundering, to be honest.

After our session I wandered back out into the grounds,

thinking only that I might smoke a cigarette, but on the lawn I saw Gillon, wearing the linen suit he likes for 'business', gesturing extravagantly round a standing circle of smart-suited Asian gentlemen. I didn't hesitate to press myself into the gathering, and it was with poorly veiled irritation that Gillon introduced me to Mr Heng and party – clearly the 'Malaysian interest' mentioned in Gillon's group emails these last few months, now on site and 'getting the tour'. No need, of course, for them to meet the director of the facility . . . Once I realised no meaningful conversation would be had for as long as I stood there, I decided to retreat. Whereupon all hell broke loose.

I had been conscious, from the moment I stepped outdoors again, of the disturbing white-nacre shade of the sky, the wind in the treetops now a shuddering hiss. Autumn is here, for sure. But as I marched across the lawn away from Gillon and his Malaysians, it seemed the air was full of moaning sounds, behind these a dull but rising roar. Then the storm broke. A wind gusted over the lawn with one great sweep that had my trouser-legs flapping hard against my skin. The next moment, Lawrence's high piles of leaves and shrubbery were being tossed up through the air. I got hit in the face by one thorny branch, and through my hands I saw the Malaysians fleeing in ungainly fashion back to the house. The air was all flying debris and jet-engine drone. Then came the rain.

I ran to the art pavilion, told Dora to bring everyone there inside the main building too, while they still could. And yet after herding them out, watching them dart through the side fire-door – I stayed. By now the gusts were sweeping down at what had to be sixty, seventy miles an hour. I saw the lids plucked from the black bins, the bins themselves tumble and skitter away. The metal garden chairs and tables all went over and away. The clematis was wrenched off the covered walkway, its arches buckled. A roof slate plummeted and smashed on the patio, five feet from the door through which I'd sent Dora. From my safety behind glass, I admit, there was an awesomeness to these elements, akin to my own black mood. But moment by moment the damage was mounting. I heard one bone-grinding sound of shearing and torsion, later discovered to be the old apple tree, first planted for the birth of HRH Princess Elizabeth, now crashing to the earth.

I'm not sure how long I stood there, transfixed, before making my own dash to the house. Inside was a lot of understandable fuss. My only concern was that everyone stay together, properly supervised within the common spaces. I found Lawrence in the kitchens, drenched, silently surveying the 'black wrath' through the window while rolling a cigarette. I was nearly minded to ask him for one. 'You were right,' I told him, patting his shoulder.

But he kept his impenetrable look. 'No, I was wrong. Wasn't from the north that came out of. Queer.'

The local news was reporting that drivers were warned off the roads, with fallen branches and other debris lying and the hazards for high-sided vehicles so obvious. Thus, heavy-hearted, I made the call to Tessa. No such weather havoc in Primrose Hill, and she failed to sound as if I hadn't fixed everything to fall out like so.

It stayed squally and blustery until past 9pm and supper was all squared away. An hour or so later I was actually dozing in the office when Goran roused me to say Eloise Keaton and David Tregaskis were both out of their rooms and nowhere to be found in the building, not as far as he could determine. Panicked, I leapt up, said we would go outside together to check the grounds.

He and I headed out with torches, padding down the lawn beyond the pools of the floodlights. The ground was wet underfoot but there was a sense of the air cleared: also a distinctive mix of odours, flower fragrance and damp, fungal autumn. As we trod down the paved side-paths, flicking our torch-beams about, I found myself distracted by the colours of the blooms by night – somehow artificial, some quite evil-looking in their structure – cascades and curls, furls and pyramids, intense purples and fuchsias, blues seeming to feed on darkness and moonlight. At the back of the grounds we had still found nothing. But I was peering just as hard at the trunks of the tall pines, like limbs twisted and fused, straining up and clawing for the air of the upper reaches.

I followed a half-notion, up the path under the pines parallel to our back-wall perimeter with the woods, toward the furthest corner of the grounds, shrouded somewhat by the heavy-scented lilac bushes, their sprays of clustered star-like heads. Then I heard a groan, a woman's, throaty and uneasy. And I made out a white face, a white nightdress – a figure reclining on the black aluminium bench-seat, also some dark heap hunkered or crouched at her feet. When I turned my torch-beam that way the light picked out two eyes like sharp, shining red dots. David Tregaskis, wrapped up in his black velvet frock coat, got up off his knees onto his feet. My eyes darted past him to where Eloise sprawled on the bench.

'David, what the hell are you doing? How did you get out?'

'The back door combination? I have studied it, Steven . . . My apologies. I needed some air, some good night air, as did my friend.'

His sanguine expression was maddening, but I simply moved round him, sat by Eloise and tried to revive her. For all that she appeared near-waxen, her throat and hands were warm to the touch, and she swayed her head languidly before turning her face to me, eyes snapping open. I really wasn't sure whether to be angered or concerned.

'Eloise, are you all right? What were you thinking of?'

'Leave her alone, let her get her bearings.' Tregaskis, over my shoulder.

'Shut up, David,' I admit I snapped. Then I saw Goran's torch, heard his tread. I asked him to help me escort Mr Tregaskis back to the building while I assisted Ms Keaton. I took her hand, helped her to her feet, but when I put my arm round her shoulder she gently slipped free.

'Thank you, but . . . there's no need.'

I couldn't quite shake the sense that her faint smile accused me of something. But I had resolved to consider my response rather than start a row, so Goran and I only led the miscreants back indoors – Eloise, for all her professed assurance, stepping most unsteadily, Tregaskis striding forth like General Fairfax at Naseby. Back in West Wing I gave them both the same stern admonition at their doors – that on this night, more than usual, it was vital for their own good that they followed house rules. David's triumphalism gave me no reassurance whatsoever: grinning, he advised I should change all the door codes round the building if I was so concerned. Then he wandered back into his lair, there perhaps to toy with his clay woman, who sat gazing out blankly from his desk.

Eloise, for her part, fell down onto the edge of her bed like the soul of soft compliance. 'I won't be going anywhere Steven. Not now. You can be sure of it.'

With doors shut and lights out I instructed Goran that we say nothing of this incident to anyone else, since it was clearly an aberration that reflected poorly on all parties but which was unlikely to occur again, so long as we took our lesson, made a discreet review of our freedom-of-movement policy, and kept vigilant. Those codes, too, will all be changed before sunrise.

September 13th

I'm making a hell for myself, yes, but I've no other choice under the circumstances, I'll just have to make right whatever I've done wrong whenever there's some let-up in the turbulence. Tonight I seem to have offended Tessa beyond all forgiveness by failing to be home in time for some parents' night at the boys' new school. I just cannot see how it was so vital, couldn't be made up by other means. But the air is utterly frozen – *'Why are you doing this to our family?'* she said, hardly able to look at me – and so I will take the living room couch tonight.

Earlier I did something possibly foolish, and dangerous, but I couldn't fight the impulse, and what I learned was bewildering. I went back to Bishop's Wood to ascertain if my 'dead-drop' had been collected. I pushed my way through the gloom, found the pentangle tree, felt in the hollow and, incredibly, the bag was still there. I looked about me, then retrieved it, brushed off insects and twigs, unfastened the knot, saw the crop of innocent rubber-banded banknotes. Then I thought twice, and twice again, replaced the hoard, and hastened out of the wood.

I don't imagine my blackmailer has changed his mind, can't believe he is so busy that he simply forgot. I've done as was asked. Yet nothing has ensued. It maddens me to think of that pot of gold stashed away there under dry leaves – but I have to steel myself, watch and wait, keep my nerve for the moment, even if by any chance the extorter has lost his. I let myself fantasise that he has met some sort of misfortune – so much the better . . .

This morning saw more torrential rain: the freakish weather had one thing more to say, it seemed. The wreckage caused by the storm was visible all round the Blakedene grounds – early in the gloomy light you could believe we'd been assailed by a hurricane. Still, the day brightened, and veritable armies set to work making repairs all round the premises.

Eloise had been sleeping late, 'feeling unwell'. I had a strong urge to speak to her, but I let it go. Then it transpired she had asked Nurse Gardner to ask Niamh if she could see me. I made time, she came in, didn't sit, inspected my bookshelves for some moments, then turned and asked if I could possibly give her loan of a speculum kit? Yes, she wanted to perform an internal examination on herself.

I was— surprised, for sure. I'm aware this is something that some women choose to do these days, and a useful skill, no doubt. I had just never thought for one moment that Eloise would be interested in or capable of such a personal care.

'Are you worried about something?' I had to ask. It was the low fear, I admit, that something might have passed between her and David last night. But the smiling shake of her head was entirely blithe.

'Not specifically, no. I just . . . let's say it's something I want to do for myself. Part of being a well woman, if you like.'

That much made sense to me – the notion of empowerment, I suppose, which I fully endorse. 'And, you've done this before?'

She nodded, almost indulgently. 'Oh, I'm experienced, Steven. I know how to proceed with care.'

I did assure her that Margaret Yang would happily attend to this matter, but she was quite resolute in her request. And so it seemed only right and proper that I grant her this. In fact I fetched the goods myself from Nurse Gardner. I passed Eloise downstairs after lunch, said 'Are you okay?' Again that beatific nod. In the next moment I felt a twinge of oddness for having asked, but

Eloise showed absolutely no self-consciousness to speak of. And I suppose she and I know each other well enough by now.

PART III

DIABLERIE

17

Dr Lochran's Journal
Conspiracies

September 14th

I begin to fear my boy wants me in an early grave – not from any malice, no, only because I've started to cramp his style, forfeit his respect. In all previous father–son spats I've had faith in the power of my 'clunking fist' to come down hard and quash the pipsqueak revolt, while avoiding any lasting sense of hurt. I thought I could freeze the air with a cold glare – and I believed, more fondly, that the kid actually hated the thought of my disapproval. Well, tonight marked a decisive farewell to all that. Moreover, not content with making me feel like a relic, Cal has also contrived to unnerve me.

I was late back from the hospital, not greatly receptive to Livy's insistence that we needed, once again, to confront this issue of Cal's 'nights out'. He was in tonight, all right. And my understanding was that when he was out he was mostly with young Jennifer, doing what young men should, so long as they can. But . . . Livy tells me Susan has been calling her in consternation, saying Jennifer is near-confined to her bedroom in tears, initially over the cursory way Cal was treating her, then over his curtly delivered decision to 'drop' her. Since Olivia rates herself incapable of intervening directly in what she calls her son's 'love affairs' (if only . . .) it fell to me to climb those stairs, rap that door.

His bedroom was dark and he lounged across the bed, watching a DVD on his laptop: *The Exorcist*, amusingly – the first X-rated movie I bluffed my way into. Thankfully he paused it and I cut to the chase, though I have to say I hated the sound of my own voice, all fussy and mimsy ('Susan Wills has been talking to your mother and I . . .'), and I fully expected to see the same venom in Cal's gaze that got turned on Steven at Jon's barbecue. He was adamant he 'didn't want to discuss it'. What bothered me the longer I stood was that the boy didn't look quite on top of his game – a dazedness there, an enervation. Not narcotic, I'm sure, the pupils are right-sized. But seeing his tennis racket neglected in the corner, his rugby shirt crumpled on the floor – it did occur to me that my young champion has hit an early slump.

'Cal, since I'm told you're not with Jennifer, I need to know where you go at night.'

'Dad, I just get out to clear my head. Some air, some good night air. Just get into the car and drive . . .'

'Where to, son?'

'Depends. Sometimes down to Regent's Canal. Or the old Saint Pancras church. Anywhere there's peace. Sometimes I follow the canal route on to Little Venice, St John's Wood. As far as Robert's clinic.'

'Nothing to see there, but. All locked up, right?' He shrugged. 'And you do these wee wanders on your lonesome?' A nod. I suppose I should have been grateful for that much data. Still, we lapsed into silence awhile, sat on his bed, me gazing blankly at his dark and cryptic wall-posters – 'Down', 'Muse', 'NIN', 'Garbage' – while he picked at the caps of his Dunlops.

'You know, you've got your mother and I a bit perplexed.' I anticipated his wince, put my hand on his shoulder. 'I understand you've your own life going on in your head, Cal, I really do. Just remember mum and I have lives too, we all have our anxieties. We worry about your godfather, you know that. Every day seems to make it worse.'

Whereupon Cal turned on me the sort of gaze I'm sure he reserves for the dullest, least able lad in his form. 'But that's all just a ruse, Dad. Rab's gone off with his woman. Bet you any money.'

I met his eye, hard. 'What woman's that, son?'

'Dijana. You know about her, right? She knows you . . .'

Abruptly I could hear myself breathing, felt that slight, unaccountable roil in my gut. By his grin he knew he'd got me, for sure.

'Robert told you about her?'

'I met her. One night at Rab's.'

Again, that internal stab. 'You didn't feel like telling me?'

'I don't report back to you, dad. Right? You know I go there, you know Rab. And you met Dijana, didn't you? So you know the score. Tell you what – *I'd* go off with her. Like a shot.'

'What do you mean, but, "gone off"?'

He sprawled back on his bed, arms behind his head, a lazy posture I didn't care for. 'I just think they've escaped, you know? Taken off. Rab's got that spirit in him, hasn't he? And she'd be the kind of woman would drive you to it. To do infamous things . . .' He rolled his eyes. 'I envy them, frankly. I do.'

'Cal, when you met Dijana – what happened? What did she say to you?'

A would-be rakish chuckle. 'You know what? I don't remember. It was only one drink, then I was out of there. But it's her, uh . . . *presence* that stuck with me, I have to say. I'd doubt it's the conversation Rab keeps her around for. She looks like she knows a thing or two, what she's after. The way she looked at *me* I thought Rab would prefer I got offside. Didn't want to be causin' no ructions . . .'

For all that I was hating this teenaged affectation of the Man of the World, it seemed wisest to let him run his mouth off completely, now I'd got him talking. But a loud yawn indicated he thought we were done. 'Anyhow. That's how I see it. He's found a soul-mate, and they're off together, on a party. When he gets bored he'll be back . . .'

I gave him a long, withering look. 'Uh-huh. So, you reckon a man of Rab's age can do that, Cal? Eh? Skip off like some college backpacker? Abandon his livelihood, his home, his responsibilities?'

'I know he'd want to, Dad. Don't you?'

With that Cal rose, stretched his rangy frame and sauntered over to his window, there perhaps to contemplate the moon or some shite. So he didn't take kindly to my announcement that he was grounded until further notice. Finally I got the basilisk stare off him, and he barked that I 'couldn't stop him'. But whatever the diminishing of my paternal authority – or of his filial piety – I'm bloody sure that once I stood up and planted myself then the boy couldn't see a way past me. And that's how we'll be doing things for a while around here.

September 15th

House chilly, silent. Cal, I know, is abed, and if by any chance he tried to 'escape' I'd catch him by the tail. I long, I truly long to join Livy in the warmth of our bed, because some moments ago I had what the old dears call 'an episode'. The length of this grisly day must have told. A stunning, imperious fatigue fell over me, like a cloak heavy as tarpaulin – the strange, sudden weakness all but pressed me down by my shoulders into a chair. I felt leaden from head to foot, my breath seemed to be coming drastically slow, and I needed some moments to regain my good proper pulse. I could have been my father in his autumn years.

Steven's long given out that if my workload doesn't do for me first then the smokes will put the nails in my coffin-lid. Right enough, I'd be glad of my heart serviced, my blood renewed, organs cleansed, spirits lifted. But I can cope. It's just events, dear boy, events – the unexpected. I'm just not sure how much of it one's meant to withstand.

The work I'm drifting through, have been on autopilot for weeks. This morning, gastrochisis on two-hour-old

Annabel Leigh, the simplest task to resettle her bowel. Then a hypospadias I might have done in my sleep, had it not been for the hysteria of the boy's father (infancy the only time when dads want to be bothered by the state of their sons' genitals). But I was in a form of productive drift, the artist levitating serenely above his own handiwork, idly paring his nails . . .

Then, Steven's incredible message: 'Your *fantôme*, Grey, your Burnt Man. He's here, I think, at Blakedene. In the woods behind the estate.'

The area had suffered freak storm conditions at the weekend, and those woods were part-impenetrable, but apparently a dog-walker's hound had snuffled its way through the fallen branches and found the dead man – 'some young tramp' the initial report. Man and dog hastened round to the gate-lodge at Blakedene having called the police, and when Steven emboldened himself to pick a way out into the woods he found, slumped at the foot of a tree, a man in filthy black clothes, face badly burnt, ring and pinkie fingers missing from the left hand.

'Was he wearing Robert's mask?' I asked Steven instantly.

'No, no,' Steven muttered, 'I searched him, nothing.'

'You did *what*, Steve . . . ?'

This, only the first sign of Steven's current confusion, his worrying drift from the port of good sense. I called Hagen, left a message saying I was headed directly into Berkshire, my intention to see this body with my own eyes, and that if he hadn't heard the news then he'd do well to get onto Thames Valley police . . . Presumptuous of me. Once I got clear of the London orbital the drive felt like no time, but as I came down under the tree-lined lane toward the Blakedene gates I saw Hagen had beaten me, his unmarked Passat lined up alongside the big chequered police wagons, behind forty yards of roadside cones and fluorescent orange DO NOT CROSS tape.

A brisk WPC escorted me on foot from the 'outer circle' cordon to the lodge, whereupon an affable moon-faced security guard named Goran (from Dubrovnik, he told me) drove me by golf cart through the grounds to a heavy-bolted door in the back wall. We came out onto a scene of considerable police activity in a clearing of twenty yards or so. Thick tufted grass led to the shade of the path into the woods, this also cut off by a cordon of tape.

Steven stood in conference with a couple of constables and a burly bloke I took for CID. Shoulders hunched, arms folded in spite of the afternoon's warmth, Steve threw me a plaintive look. Bill Hagen hovered nearby, hands thrust into his black mackintosh, flanked by young Goddard. He came over to me, *sotto voce*. 'We're treading lightly here, doctor. Another force, their patch, some diplomacy needed. Not really an all-guns-blazing matter for them if some rough sleeper beds down in a wood and doesn't wake up.'

The burly CID, Franklin by name, sheared away from Steven's group toward Hagen, and my presence was negotiated – I heard myself introduced, 'like Dr Hartford' as 'a close associate of Dr Robert Forrest, missing from home this past month'. Indeed, by Franklin's sceptical scowl one could tell there was no pressing sense that the human wreckage in the woods was any kind of criminal genius.

With a nod Hagen lifted the cordon and motioned me to follow him down a trail of duckboards, under the wood's canopy and into the dark shrouded hush. The tent was set up about seventy yards in, at the foot of a willow tree. A good deal of white-coated industry went on around it – a thoughtful photographer selecting angles, ponderous shufflers bagging and tagging soil, a frowning woman stooped over a plaster casting. Hagen held the flap of the tent for me. The pathologist was still bent over the dead man, attended by some crazed kamikaze flies. The corpse's contorted pose spoke of rigor mortis, his mutilated hand visible on the end of an arm thrown out stiffly to one side. That ruined face was drained of colour – its ridged pallor putting me oddly in mind of a snake's shed skin – but the hard eschars of his burns were only the more pronounced. No peace in death, for sure, after a life of evident hardship, marked on the body. A pitiful end. And seeing him now – some mother's son – my feelings were uneasy, conflicted. Had I really imagined him to be so menacing, a phantom? *What was your business with me, my friend?*

Finally I nodded to Hagen, we exited, were silent for a while as we picked our way back to the daylight.

'No question that's the fellow confronted you?'

'No. Now he's dead, forty miles away. Do you have a theory?'

'Well, one could be tempted to say he came in search of your associate . . .'

We were of the same mind, but now rejoined the group of Thames Valley coppers round Steven, who was pulling on a cigarette. Clearly in all this turmoil tobacco has got him by the lungs again. 'Is it him?' Steve demanded of me with surprising vehemence.

'Dr Lochran', Hagen announced to the party, 'recognises our man as the same fellow who assaulted him in London four days ago.'

'Right,' said DI Franklin, visibly none the wiser. 'How's he got himself out here? And why?'

One of the constables spoke up. 'If we find out who he is then maybe this is his neck of the woods, as you'd say.'

Franklin fixed on Steven. 'Doctor Hartford, who'd have the use of these woods ordinarily?'

'Very few. Lawrence here, for one.'

The group had been joined by Steven's 'head of gardens', Lawrence Banner, a man with unkempt dark hair and pensive hooded eyes. Worriedly he confirmed Steven's assessment. 'Your people are gonna find traces of me all over the patch, my old boots and that . . .'

'As I understand,' Steven added, 'you'll get the odd group of bird-watchers now and then. John Teacher, the farmer, he's in there for wood once in a while. Then the occasional guest from John's holiday cottage across the fields. But I've never thought of these woods as populated. Unvisited, rather.'

'You don't see much human traffic yourself?'

'There's no decent view of the woods from our premises. You see the height of our pine trees, the seclusion they give . . .'

'Right. Not an accessible spot. We found that out from having to get our vehicles round through Mr Teacher's property.'

Steven nodded. 'Worse because of the storm, I imagine.'

'Hairy for you too, that, was it?'

'We took some damage, and it alarmed some of the patients, so I had the place on lockdown, effectively, through the evening and overnight. The grounds were off limits. And have remained so, while we've been repairing . . .'

Steven tailed off as the pathologist Seymour-Ure was stalking toward us, peeling off his gloves. He didn't look like one who wished to be detained further. 'He's movable now. Body temperature and the eyes tell us he died within the last thirty-six hours. There's no blood, no defence wounds to suggest he fought anybody off. From head to toe he's a veritable canvas of historical drug use. Track marks, the sort of cuts and scratches you'll get if you're living rough and not keeping the very best company. Whole universes under his fingernails . . .'

'So what did for him?' DI Franklin ventured.

'Oh, hard to see past hypothermia. We'll see what's in his blood but I strongly doubt he was leading an abstemious lifestyle. The weather's been extreme, obviously, cold overnight, he'd been soaked, his clothes are still damp . . .'

Hagen frowned. 'The woods wouldn't have given him some shelter? Is he lying where he fell, do you suppose?'

'Oh I'd say so, detective. Not dragged, anyway. And you'd struggle to get him over your shoulder . . .'

As Seymour-Ure hastened away Franklin fixed on Steven again. 'Is *anybody* else in your building acquainted with these woods, doctor?'

'As I say, you're looking at them,' Steven gestured as to include himself, Banner and the loyally silent Goran. 'And we'll cooperate in any way you see fit. I'm happy to make a room available for you on our premises.'

Hagen, having been sunk in thought, looked up. 'Thank you, doctor. I'll want to speak again to Miss—Keaton? Who was Doctor Forrest's patient?'

Everything in Steven's expression tightened vividly. 'I will need to be present for that, I'm afraid. Miss Keaton has only just emerged from a very demanding, very draining course of therapy for a serious depression, I'd have to ask that you respect my concern for her welfare.'

This might have daunted a lesser individual, but I can't say Hagen looked convinced. 'Let's see how she's feeling, shall we?'

Steven, unhappy, tramped off with his staff and the local constabulary, back across the ragged grass through the gate into Blakedene. Hagen had stepped aside, muttering into his phone. Now he drifted back to me, albeit peering still at his screen. I found my voice.

'Something else I wanted to make you aware of.'

'Oh aye?'

'The other night I learned from my son, Calder, that he'd also met the Vukovara woman – at Robert's, prior to the disappearance.'

'Uh-huh. Naturally. And?'

'I think he formed the same impression as me, that

217

she was a dubious character. Who could easily have had something to do with Robert's vanishing.'

'Other than enticing him to run off with her?'

'Well, what are you thinking at this point, detective? About this chain of events we've got?'

'My problem, doctor, is seeking the linkage from one to t'other. Can you make one out?'

'You said it yourself. Steven and I are Robert's closest "associates". I think anyone could consider it plausible to say we're both of us being . . . targeted, somehow.'

'Evidentially, Doctor Lochran, we've still got just the one felony in all this. That's the break-in to Dr Forrest's home, plus the assault made on DS Goddard. And we would believe that perpetrator's no longer with us. Whatever else . . . right now you can only call it coincidence.'

'But the sort you'd have to call meaningful. Come on, you know that. "Coincidence"? It has more the look of conspiracy.'

He laughed softly, shook his head. 'Conspiracy to what? I take your concern, believe me; Doctor Forrest has been gone for twenty-eight days now, the chief inspector will have to review the file to date.'

Hagen's gaze had strayed over my shoulder. I turned to see Steven, a study in unease, framed by the doorway into Blakedene, its surrounding walls dense with crimson-flowered Virginia creeper. The sun was behind the clouds again. I asked Hagen for a moment, joined Steven, rummaged for my red Marlboros, offered him one that he seized upon.

'Ghastly business . . .', he shuddered.

'Aye. You have any feeling about it, Steve? Any sense of what went on?'

He shrugged, drew on the smoke. 'I'm as much in the dark as you. As if I didn't have enough to contend with.'

'The Keaton girl. Has she any possible part in this, you think?'

'Oh Christ, no. It's grossly unfair she's even being brought into it. Pointless, interfering . . .'

'Steven,' I pressed quietly, 'another man is dead. Something is happening here. It came to my door, now it's at yours.'

'I'm not blind, Grey. We've all had some nasty surprises. But, there you have it. It's done now, over. Dead.'

I found his language perturbing. 'You say that. I've begun to wonder – whether what dies might not return, somehow. Or not leave us, at any rate.'

Steven flinched – in annoyance. 'Ach Grey, for crying out loud. Get a grip. We should just look to get over this, move on – we all of us need to *move on*.'

A striking volte-face in our relations, I suppose – Steve now the would-be hard-nosed man of conviction, me seeming to thrash about in two-minded disarray. But I know I've got my feet on the ground, no question. It's Steven who's floundering – not quite stable – 'not the same man'.

219

18

Dr Hartford's Journal
Dispossession

September 17th

His name was Darren Carver. He was 25. His last known address was the Hoddesdon home of his mother and stepfather, which he left in angry circumstances four years ago, thereafter finding work and lodging through the construction industry. It was by medical and police records that he was traced. Two years ago the burns unit at Chelsea and Westminster treated him after an accident at a squatter-dwelling, the butane canister of a portable stove having exploded in his face. Last year he was arrested and spent a night in a Paddington Green cell on suspicion of 'aggressive begging', charges subsequently dropped. A week ago, it now seems clear, he witnessed Killian MacCabe die.

I can only assume he stole from the dead man some scraps of information, themselves stolen, that he believed he could turn into money. In doing so he exhibited a level of initiative evident nowhere else in his unhappy CV. All I can say is I wanted him gone, and from the moment his body was bagged and removed from our woods, God help me, I began to breathe easier.

Goran, alas, looks disquieted for having been party to a minor deception, since he kept his silence with the police over last week's nocturnal 'episode'. I have reiterated, there was no need for our rare lapse, our atypical ill discipline, to be dragged into this, or that two difficult patients be disturbed any further. It is an internal matter. Still, Goran respects me just a little less, I think. But for me it's worth everything to feel that a danger has passed.

Last night I went to Bishop's Wood, found all as I had left it, took back what was mine.

September 18th

If I have overprotected her, shielded her too closely, I thought it was my duty. And I will do it a while longer, for her own good, whatever her newly minted views on the matter. My concern – as must be hers, unless I've been blind – is this unwelcome new zeal of David Tregaskis.

Despite the virulence he sometimes exudes, David has never posed me any problems in his behaviour toward women, whether staff or fellow patients. But now he is dogging Eloise's steps, really – at mealtimes, before and after group sessions, about the common parts, the veranda and the grounds, art room and canteen . . . I had only just persuaded Eloise to participate more in the shared life of Blakedene; now, for her pains, she's being stalked. Still, when I raised it with her, she only laughed softly. 'He's harmless. To me, at any rate.'

She has given me worries of her own over recent days. Her interactions in those group sessions to which I reintroduced her have been fitful. Having broken her 'frozen sea within', I thought group could allow Eloise to express herself in a safe environment, including other survivors, familiar with the tumult of emotion, there to let her know she's not alone. Listening to the others I heard so much that I felt sure Eloise would recognise and respond to. Yet she appeared bored, remote.

My problem is that her mind feels closed to me, there is a new opacity there. For sure she is improved, and I take such credit as I'm entitled to. But I hoped, intended, that the past cease to have its throttling hold on her; not that she should now present this rather odd, quasi-repressive avoidance of all we went through together in my office.

Today's was a curious session. The tone of her voice sounds a little different, also the range of her reference. She seems to have matured, somehow, the slight jadedness no longer so affected, rather more 'earned': she has grown into that rasp in her voice. There is the strangest poise about her, a self-command behind her eyes, in the way she stands. And she sits upright, posture open, hands on her thighs, rather casual, as though 'dealing' with me.

'Am I done here, would you say?' she asked, quite abruptly.

It was she, originally, who had wanted another week's stay beyond the end of the optical therapy, and I had been happy to concur. Now all of a sudden she is itchy to move on.

'I would be glad if you feel so. But I think, to be honest, I'd like you to remain an outpatient for this week.'

'Shouldn't you trust your clinical judgement more than that? Why hesitate? Go with it.'

'I'm not one to be hurried.' I felt I had to say it another way. 'I am your friend in this, Ellie.'

'I know,' she said. 'I have been less of a friend in return.'

I was startled by wherever that came from. I can't even attribute it to nicotine withdrawal, as she seems to have ditched that habit with an extraordinary despatch.

'Can I trust you', I ventured, 'not to slip back to your hard-living ways? On the outside?'

'You have my word,' she said airily. 'I intend to treat this septum more kindly . . .' Beautiful women are accomplished liars, if they can be bothered, though of course they benefit from your wanting to believe them. Eloise, though, exuded the glow of candour. 'I *would* like a good glass of wine . . . Maybe a taste of Mary-Jane. You know what Picasso said about the intelligence of cannabis. That princely high.'

I didn't intend to be over-censorious, but I may have looked so, whereupon she leaned forward. 'Steven, trust me, you don't need to worry. Life is precious – I've got that, I understand. I'm not going to waste another moment. I've no interest in artificial stimulants. Just to be able-bodied, vigorous. While the blood runs warm in my veins.'

Her avidity had me speechless for a short while. 'Well, yes, you've only got one life,' I managed, and she smiled a little wearily at my cliché. 'I suppose you're anxious to have your phone back?'

'I can wait. I wondered, though, if you would make a call for me? I'd like to ask Leon for a visit. Would you do that for me?'

The freakish episode of Leon's previous 'visit', tearing up the driveway, shouting the place down – not a scene we cared to repeat, and Eloise's behaviour at the time spoke volumes for her state. But today, she was lucid, composed, clear-headed. A new Eloise seems to have emerged: a young woman newly appreciative of the world and its possibilities.

'Of course,' I said. 'Gladly. He'll be pleased, he's asked us before.'

If, then, I am some sort of relationship counsellor *manqué* . . . Wasn't that what I had intended here? To encourage, enable her acceptance of love? To join her hand, after a fashion, with a man who cares for her and for whom she will care? I do assert that I'm a romantic, whether or not anybody believes me. Eloise's progress does my heart good, restores my battered spirits. I don't pretend this is momentous work on my part, nonetheless a young life appears to have been salvaged, set back upright and on course.

As such, I feel myself free of what, I can see, was probably a slightly obsessive concern with her. We have to live the life that's in front of us, not in some figment of an overheated brain. With Eloise returned to the community I will make better use of time, review my priorities, get properly focused on my fractured relationship with Andrew Gillon. My position here must be defended: I must show a strong hand to any prospective new owner.

September 19th

These, the reflections of a voyeur . . . acutely aware of the ironies in his position, only 'doing his job'.

Today was surprisingly exquisite outdoors, the garden pleasant with daisies and butterflies, the air bearing a languid, spiced sort of aroma more appropriate to July. Leon arrived at the given hour, submitted affably to Goran's swift pat-down – 'Oh, I've been handled worse,' he said with a coolness that showed he meant it – and handed over his car keys compliantly. The waiting Eloise also seemed calm, content, all fragrant and hair-brushed, lips lightly painted. She wore some jade-coloured cotton summer dress, strappy and full-skirted, under a denim jacket – she 'looked like someone's girlfriend', as the song goes. Leon's gaze was warm with appreciation.

I put them together in the reading room, 'alone' as such, but observable from the foyer. Jana was manning the desk, Dr Yang was flipping the index files, so I was quite assured they were under watch. Their conversation looked to be hushed and serious. I was due to call Marcia Fallow's mother concerning her unfortunate lapse, the agreed hour clear in my mind. Still, I dithered and dallied, wound up making the call from the front desk a little ahead of schedule. By now Eloise and Leon had joined their hands over the table, he stroking her knuckles with his thumb.

Then Eloise came out to me. A problem? No, the pair of them wanted to take a walk in the back of the grounds. It felt silly not to permit this on such a fine day, everything going so well. But twenty minutes, tops, I told her. I wanted to see her in group at 11am.

They crunched off across the gravel, toward the side-path. Our new communications woman was showing a

Swedish journalist the lawns, Goran and Lawrence were stood in conference by the art pavilion. Again, my need for surveillance was striking me as officious. I left the lovers to it, went back up the steps and through the door.

Why, then, did I choose to wend my way through the ground floor and out the back, surreptitious? I suppose – I considered myself their 'sponsor', wanted to be sure my instincts were right. I could see they were still dawdling down the paved walkway between the beds to my right, headed to the furthest corner of the grounds, the perimeter boundary by Lawrence's shed. I felt the absurdity of my half-walk, half-dash across the lawn, glancing behind me to check if any eyes followed me from the building. Realising these two had a destination in mind and would be checking behind them too, I broke off left to the opposite path, took the counter-route to the back of the grounds, treading lightly, managing my breath.

Moving up behind the lilac bushes I first heard the rustle and the low, urgent exchanges from the vicinity of the tree by the dry-stone wall. Then her low, throaty laughter. And I saw them, or parts of them – her sandals kicked loose at a distance, she pressed up yet supported against a pine trunk, his faded jeans loose at his knees, her thighs hugging his hips – enough to see they had wasted not a moment of 'precious time'. I stole away as fast as I could manage.

From the kitchen window I watched, checked the time, saw them re-emerge, hand in hand and beaming, swinging down the lawn. Leave them alone and they'll come home . . . It's good, natural, my part in this is precisely what I should be doing. I had time to shake Leon's hand, be briskly pleasant to them both. While I retrieved Leon's keys they stood close and spoke to each other with an obvious fondness, indeed a distinct intensity. It seemed a golden thing to observe, this closeness.

Eventually I squired Eloise to group. She wandered along at my shoulder, a little dazedly, dreamily. I was treading a thin line, silly of me to expect that everything should thereafter run smooth. Tregaskis's odd behaviour manifested itself, he caused a minor disturbance. As requested, everyone had brought along a Shakespeare soliloquy or sonnet of their choice: Eloise gave a charmingly brief rendition of Caliban's *'Be not afeard; the isle is full of noises'*. But Tregaskis made a quite lunatic Puck: *'My mistress with a monster is in love.'* It was directed shamelessly at Eloise, and I could feel my nails digging my palms in annoyance.

September 20th

This morning I had to confront Tregaskis. I was stung, seething.

SH: *David, why are you so interested in Eloise all of a sudden?*
DT: *Hello Mister Pot. My name's Kettle.*
[. . .]
DT: *I'm not 'interested' in Eloise. Never have been, you know that. But didn't I always say she was in need of something? A bit of self-improvement? Well, she's had it. Oh yes.*

SH: We're certainly happy here about how she's responded to treatment.

DT: Oh, I see. You think you've 'saved' her?

SH: No, she has done everything for herself, with our help. That is what we do here, David. Or we try to.

DT: Huh. Yes. In her case, though, your treatment came a little late, I fear . . . Anyhow, it's ceased to matter. Eloise in essence? Pah. A mere bagatelle. Eloise as a vessel? Now that is of interest. I wouldn't have wanted to waste a moment with a girl of her – what should we say? – profile? But she's not the same girl any more. And that's all to the good. She's part of something immeasurably greater. Extraordinary. I couldn't believe it at first, of course, one wouldn't – you certainly wouldn't. When she began to speak to me. Speak to me and her lips weren't moving, see? I've waited all my life, Steven, to achieve telepathy with a woman, I hadn't thought it was possible, not neurally, physiologically, biochemically. And then, wham, out of the blue . . . Wasn't her, of course. Men and women, we'll remain different, not the slightest natural communion there. No, she was already gone. Away with the fairies, sweet Eloise. The bond we were negotiating was . . . stranger. And yet more familiar. I should have seen it far quicker – took me a few beats to accept it – the master's hand in all of this.

SH: The master? Oh David . . .

DT: Call it what you want. There's a higher power, Steven. I know we can't imagine beyond ourselves without it being . . . hopelessly infected, by our own sorry limits.

But isn't it absurd to imagine that this, this . . .
physical morass, is the sum of our being? That nothing
could fly free of the body? It's a stretch, I know, and I
needed proof, but I got it. With mine own eyes.
SH: *What proof? What did you see?*
[. . .]
DT: *I don't really want to talk to you any more, Steven. I*
mean, not to say that won't change, in time, once I
understand more about this journey I'm on. Once I'm
out of here. But not for now. You're a negligible figure,
in my context, our context.
SH: *David – I can't say at this precise moment that I'm*
comfortable with the thought of you going anywhere.
DT: *Oh I'm not leaving yet. Not for the minute. When*
things are at this pitch . . .

There is a striking level of instability, a clear undercurrent of threat. The lithium is not doing its job, not in light of this mania. An atypical antipsychotic needs to be considered – Seroquel, I think. And I am going to need to keep David away from Eloise.

September 21st

A good and frank discussion with Ellie today, she wants to get going and I won't stop her now. I felt I could ask her if she was feeling fully committed to her relationship with Leon. Her answer did hint at an ongoing effort to convince herself.

'Yes. Yeah. I can make this work, I know.'

'You're sure? All the doubts of the past? Your different stations in life, that temper of his . . . ?'

'My own temper's not so *placido* . . . No, it has to work, Steven, it just has to. I have a chance here. I'm not sure I get another. So I'm going to try, God help me.'

That sounded a little more fraught than I would have wished. 'Ellie, I— I know I've encouraged you, to reach out this way. I don't mean for you to plunge into something just as a— test of strength. I want you to build your confidence, as gradually as you have to.'

'Steven, like you said, I've only got one life. Understand, I'm aware of the consequences – I won't do anything just for the hell of it.'

I knew then, I was more than happy to sign this woman out of my care. She saw as much; asked if I would call Leon to come and collect her. This, though, posed a fresh dilemma, and an acute one. The formidable Sir James, her real sponsor here, was entitled to be advised first of her intended departure. But Eloise was adamant.

'I'd like to . . . make good my escape.'

'Ellie, am I meant to be helping the two of you elope? Is it the Gretna Green option? Because if you were to get hitched, I'd expect an invitation to the ceremony, you know.'

She didn't disdain my lame segue into humour. 'No, no, I just need to get my bearings. I think I deserve that now. Don't you?'

I nodded. 'But you'll head back to Holland Park?'

'I suppose . . .'

'You think Leon can bear it?'

'It'll be good for him. I've had to adapt to altered circumstances, he ought to . . . shift a little too. Actually I've been thinking we might have a night away before we head for London. On the road. Just as respite.'

'Anywhere in mind?'

She nodded. 'I know a little hideaway hotel close to Blenheim.'

'Not the Cadogan?'

'You know it?'

'I took my wife there, before kids. It was a haunt of Robert Forrest's, actually, he recommended it to a friend of ours. Used to whisk his own, uh, partners up there . . .'

On reflection it was of course tactless for me to have blurted out any of that. Eloise's expression had indeed turned a shade doleful. But I wasn't expecting what followed.

'Do you know how Malena is . . . ? That was his—partner, wasn't it? Do you happen to know?'

'I hear she's quite broken, by events. She's suffered the most terrible misfortune.'

Eloise looked downcast now, the energy of moments ago all drained from her. I really didn't wish for her to be dwelling on this. 'Ellie, I have to tell you, it would worry me, if I felt somehow that Robert still had any sort of—hold, over you.'

'Why so?'

'Well, you know. Because of the nature of your relationship. How he treated you. It was wrong. Unhealthy. You knew as much.'

She looked up at me, her gaze rather penetrative. 'Did

you actually like him? Your "old friend" Robert?'

'I loved him.' This I surprised myself by shooting back, yet more by feeling so suddenly that I meant it. 'But he did become . . . well, over time he just lost the things about him I was fondest of.'

'And are you just the same good soul you were as a boy? Or do you maybe judge him too harshly?'

This came snapping out of Eloise with such bite that for a moment I had no response. But she calmed, visibly, seemed to see she had overstepped the mark. When she spoke again her voice was husky.

'We were neither of us "healthy". But both grown-ups. We're all grown-ups, Steven. Some of us get married, some even for love. Some have children, some don't. Some stick together, others fall apart. But it's all done by consenting adults. For better, for worse . . .'

I didn't quite accept this coming from her – a shade too much of her former feigned world-weariness. But it's too late now for me to reopen the workbook. And Robert, at least, is out of her life.

September 22nd

A day so well starred has wound up shrouded in misfortune. On some level I blame myself. At a suitable point I will have to step back and assess properly my own conduct throughout this whole episode.

I was planning my afternoon on the basis of being free to wave Eloise off, when Niamh told me that Tregaskis had requested – indeed demanded – an audience with me. In the first place I don't know why I imagined I could cruise through that confrontation. Yet I went to his room directly, albeit ensuring Brian, our sturdiest nurse, was posted outside the door. There were dark circles under Tregaskis's eyes, he gazed sorely at me from seated.

'She's leaving?'

'Eloise? She's checking out, yes.'

'You decided that . . .'

I shrugged. 'She and I both. Her treatment is done. Didn't you know? Since you and her have such a bond . . .'

That is the moment I regret: the quite needless barb. Yet I'm not sure it struck home. Tregaskis was in the depth of such dolour. 'I just don't hear her in my mind any more,' he muttered. 'But I can see, how wrong it is – wrong, wrong, wrong.'

'David, I'm sorry, we do need to look more seriously and honestly at this whole business of who you think is talking to you.'

He jabbed a finger at his sculpture, his clay woman.

'Where do you think *that* came from, Steven?'

I was going to say I thought it was cracked out of his very own head, when suddenly he grabbed my hand.

'She's not human, do you understand me, Steven? She's a *vessel*, for a *spirit*. And the spirit is nothing but pure, brutal essence of self-seeking. Thinks of nothing but its own safety, its own advantage, how it can live and feed off others –'

I got up, he tried to bar me, began to shout. *I'm talk-*

ing to you, one sane man to another. You mustn't let her go.'
Then he lost it, was howling, jerking around, his hands
up in my face. Brian barrelled through the door, David
kicked and windmilled but was soon neutralised, face
to the floor, Brian holding both arms. I didn't want to
break out the haloperidol, but then nor was it lost on me
that David has always feared and hated restraints – had a
horrible experience of them once when sectioned. I only
wanted to go as far here as was necessary, while carrying
out my duty to preserve the peace.

'This is not acceptable, David,' I stooped and told him
calmly as I could. 'I have to ask you to spend the rest of
the afternoon in the seclusion room. Unrestrained, but
on your own. Until you're calm and I can trust you in
that.'

He nodded assent between hard breaths. I went to
the door, Brian helped him to his feet. 'On your head,
Steven,' I thought he said, and I turned to him. 'When
what will happen, happens – may it fall . . . let it fall
on your head. Because you'll know I tried to warn you.'
Then he fell into silence, sat on the edge of his bed resignedly, looked into space with lacklustre eyes. It was
a sorry sight. But not one that led me to anticipate violence, not of any kind.

I collected myself, went down the corridor to Eloise,
knocked on the door and waited. Having had no response I turned the handle, walked on in – yes, again, inappropriate, a mark of my disordered thought processes.
Still, I was glad I did so, for I learned something.

I could hear water running into the sink. The wardrobe lay open and cleared out, bedcovers smoothed. Some clothes, goods and chattels were stacked neatly on the bed next to her two matching monogrammed Vuitton holdalls. I looked through the door of the en suite where Eloise stood over the basin in an azure-blue bra and skirt, brushing her teeth. Thankfully she didn't see me and I turned away, abashed, intending to redo my entrance, rap harder this time. But then my attention was snared by what was poking out of the top of the packed Vuitton bag. I wouldn't have pried: other eyes might have seen the tangle of black padded PVC and Velcro and imagined some sort of fetish item. But I pulled it free knowing it had a wholly different function. From memory I folded up the various straps and flaps and panels in the proper manner, and so assembled the infamous Forrest cold-therapy mask®.

I looked up to see Eloise gazing at me curiously. Without obvious self-consciousness she joined me at the bedside, shook a cabled roll-neck jersey from one of her stacks and pulled it on over her head.

'You like that?'

'Sorry . . . I'm just surprised you have it with you. It's not usable in this way, is it? You don't still have discomfort, do you, from when Robert operated?'

She shook her head. 'It's a souvenir. A relic.'

'But you've kept it since Robert . . . worked on you?'

'That would be right.'

She began to pack up her second bag. Unpleasant as I knew it would be, I had to raise the matter. 'Ellie, this may sound difficult – but when that man's body was found in our woods last week . . . Well, there was reason to believe he might have one of these masks about his person.' Her eyes met mine now, patiently. 'Now I didn't think it at all right that you be dragged into that just because of some circumstantial . . . whatever.'

She smiled slightly. 'But you think perhaps I robbed this? From a corpse?' She rode over my wince. 'It's mine, Steven. For better or worse.' She reached and took it from my hand, I relinquished it. She had succeeded in turning the tables, from her peculiarity to my impoliteness. 'Now, do you have my telephone, inspector?' Dumbly I handed it over.

By 3pm she had said her goodbyes to the staff and those few patients with whom she was on first-name terms. I stood with her a while on the steps. The small talk was dwindling – I think I was on the point of offering her a cigarette – when we saw an old silver Jaguar XJ coming up the long winding drive. Such a difference from Leon's first appearance weeks ago . . . He parked with a flourish and got out, his amusement mirrored by Eloise. I followed her like a dutiful retainer, they kissed, Leon loaded her bags in the back. He told me his 'boy' Curtis, a car enthusiast, had loaned him this vintage 'ride' just for the occasion. Leon is cool, for sure, but today he was boyish – 'proud as Lucifer'. I shook his hand, kissed Eloise's cheek, feeling for all the world as if I were giving her away. They got into the Jag, Leon started the engine . . .

Then I heard the shouts above and behind me from the common veranda – angry, alarmed cries. I turned, and then – truly it seemed in slow motion, as they always say – David Tregaskis was jumping up onto the stone

236

balustrade, wild-eyed, staring at us – and before any on-rushing staff could get a hand on him he had leapt off the edge. He plummeted the full thirty feet, hit the ground, I looked away, but from so close I heard – felt – the sickening crack of bone.

I ran to him, howling at the orderlies to get all the patients off the veranda. The adrenalin from the drop, the shock of his landing, those endorphins may have cushioned him – but the pain signals were headed for the brain. Everyone was swinging into action around me, Leon at my side first. What I saw was a tibial fracture, jaggedly through the skin, a grisly sight. The left ankle was done by the impact, turned all of ninety degrees to the right. I shouted for ice, codeine, blankets. Then David started raving in agony.

Leon, I must say, was a rock. He wanted to help, was all for loading David up and driving him. I assured him the patient could only be shifted by paramedics, that we had all the means for the best possible comfort, that he and Eloise should get on their way and not linger at this awful scene. I was only sorry that such a pall had been cast over the day. I'm sure Leon won't forget what he saw.

Eloise stood at a remove. Her expression – I can't say it was appalled, even shocked – grim for sure, but her chin was in the air, as if to say, *How could he have done this?* In that, she would be right. But there was an economy of pity, in that look: proof, if nothing else, that David's sudden recent imagining of their profound bond had been written entirely on the wind. In any event, she and Leon waited for the ambulance before departing.

Then I gathered up the pieces of the story: how David had tricked his way out of the seclusion room, asking for water then attacking Brian with considerable force. It is an ugly, sorry end to our relationship: we have seen the last of David here, that is for sure.

The remainder of the day I have spent on the telephone. I called the chairman, and Eileen Tregaskis. 'A regrettable incident . . .' I told both that my investigation was under way. Later I spoke to the orthopaedic consultant at the hospital: severe compound fracture of right tibia and fibula, a steel nail inserted; left ankle dislocated, ligaments separated, needing a screw. David will have a long time inside his own mind to weigh up the cost of his actions.

These, though, were far easier calls than the one I then made to Sir James Keaton, the special anxiety compounded by his PA keeping me on hold for what stretched to several long minutes. I have no fear of this 'powerful' man, and I feel the barest modicum is owed to him in terms of courtesy. Where has he been for all of Eloise's life? What great business was he engaged in? I had bought the lovers just about enough time, and I could feel his rage, the lack of preamble before his threats began. But I knew where I stood.

'What you've gone and done, Hartford,' he said with what seemed to me a pantomime of controlling his anger, 'understand, that's not okay with me. And you'd better watch out for what's gonna follow.'

'I'm fulfilling my duty of care to Eloise,' I maintained calmly. 'Exercising my professional judgement.'

'Yeah, well – we will see, won't we, precisely what the fuck *that* amounts to.'

A perfect end to the day . . . It's nearing 8pm now, but of course I can get home and I will. I want to see Tessa, God, I so do. The slightest solace she can offer, I will seize with open arms.

September 23rd

I am in the largest spare bedroom at Grey's, the room that 'would have been', for the second child they never had.

'Family man' – what a sham. This life I made was not the one I intended. But we rubbed along, Tess and I, said to one another that this was adulthood, these our shared responsibilities. Even now it's anathema to me that I should relinquish them.

But just how mistaken have I been? Is it possible I'm as much the guilty party as she contends? Already last night feels like it took place years ago, a judgement passed down in some other life. Returning to the house, stepping over the threshold – nothing felt different to how we'd muddled along yesterday. I was chasing sympathy, yes, but I also felt I had an ace in hand, that my duties with Eloise were now discharged.

Did I spend too long in the quiet hallway, shrugging off coat and scarf, turning out my pockets, rifling the mail, scanning the paper – forestalling our first conversation? We have not communicated in any manner but this for so long now. I found her in the kitchen, standing over the empty sink, her back to me – not upstairs by the tub, or sat on the stepladder to the twins' bunk.

'Where are the boys?'

'At mum and dad's.'

I admit, I went to the cooler, poured a glass, thinking only that it was good we had this evening to ourselves. I had taken a swallow, allowed other thoughts in, before I realised Tessa was staring at me, her eyes tragic, the line of her mouth tense and foreboding.

'Steven, I dropped the boys off because I didn't want them to be here. For what I want to say.'

'Which is what?'

'You've been making life unbearable for us. And you just don't seem to care. You're not a husband to me any more. Hardly a father. You know it, I know you do. And you're just not sorry for it, and you won't do anything to change it. So . . . I want you to leave.'

'"Leave."' Time had slowed, drastically. 'Now?'

'I'd prefer it, yes. I'd think it kind of you, if you packed a bag tonight and went somewhere else. You could drive back to Blakedene. I mean, it's got so you might as well have your mail forwarded.'

I was still reeling. 'And then what?'

'I don't know. We should take some time apart, and if there's something to talk about at the end of it, then we talk. But things can't just continue. Not like this.'

There were so many things I could have said, things I should have said many times before. What I said was: 'Tessa, please. This has been, just a dreadful day. You've really pulled the rug from under me.'

'How can you be so self-pitying? How do you think my day was? What do you think our life *is*, Steven?'

'I'm not under any illusion—'

'No, you just want to be free of what your life *actually* is, or have some spare compartment in it you can retreat to. We don't have that luxury, Steven, I didn't marry you dreaming we would.'

'We all have separate sides, marriage has to accommodate that—'

'No, you just want me to put up with it from you. I'm tired of you having no interest in my side, my mind. Resenting it.'

That charge was so hard I began to feel a perishing hopelessness in the discussion. In my mind I was, indeed, now packing my bag . . . Then the awful skittering bleep of the phone, its echoing double in the living room. Part of me expected Killian. *The dead man speaks.* A male voice came on the machine, yes, but irate.

'Tessa? Tessa, it's me. I don't care, just pick up. If he's with you pick up and put him on.'

She was unabashed. I tried to mimic him. 'Pick it up Tessa. Say what you have to.'

She shook her head, let the machine click off. 'He's not . . . we're not. Before you jump to conclusions. He's a colleague, he's been a friend to me. Listens, respects me for who I am, all the things you stopped doing.'

'Ah, good of him . . .'

'I've never been unfaithful to you, Steven. Don't console yourself with that one.'

'And I never cheated on you. Don't just look at me, I haven't.'

'I can't read your mind but I know when you're not with me. I'm sorry I'm not your dream woman. Sorry for you. But I'm not going to be made to feel shit about it one more second.' Whatever fight I had in me was gone. She saw as much. 'As I say, I'd take it as a kindness if you would pack a bag.'

'Can I not just take the sofa? Just for tonight?'

'Do what you want, Steven, I know you will.'

She walked out and up the stairs. I walked out and into the hall, saw the boys' coats, their bikes side by side. At that, truly I felt a gnawing in the heart, felt weak, thought that I could weep. The boys favour their mother – I, just a restive stranger round the house.

Upstairs in my office I found our bank statement open on the dresser: the cash debit of ten thousand pounds, its re-credit three days later. Of course, she's not wrong, I have too many recesses.

I was considering a hotel. Finally I called Grey, fell on his considerable mercies.

The devastation feels complete. In my heart I'm quite sure things were meant to go this low.

But another sort of certitude comes along, the one that braces itself for things to bottom out so that one can resume the climb, albeit from the foot. I wasn't made to collapse in a crisis. Where I have landed has a barren feel, a very circumscribed space, and my current resources aren't even adequate to fill it. But that will change. Now I have work to do.

This is abysmal, this is hell – I've been put here on purpose.

It could never have been foreseen, not this – no one by what they'd seen could have believed this could happen. I looked in Leon's eyes, I saw his care for her, read his happiness, his hopefulness, it was all of a piece with hers. Yes, she spoke of his temper, but this linked to all the things he believed she couldn't or wouldn't be for him. *Now they were going to be together, it was all agreed.* It was entirely well starred.

What's going to happen to me? Pitiful, but I have to think this, now, quickly. Even Niamh is looking at me differently. This is a tragedy we're all experiencing right now, but the staff are looking to me and how I handled this patient, who now lies on a mortuary slab, killed, allegedly, by the man into whose hands I entrusted her.

As of 2pm the phone just rang and rang. I had been expecting the latest on David Tregaskis. Then I saw from my window, the Thames Valley police coming up the drive, the dread procession. Niamh ushered them in, Detective Franklin and his sergeant Parker, he carrying one of Eloise's Vuitton bags. Had I released from my care a Miss Eloise Keaton, did I know a Mr Leon Worrell? The XJ Jaguar, found ablaze down a bank in some woodland . . . Woman inside, 'too terribly burnt for a positive ID'. My chest was full of knives, intolerable pain, I needed some moments for composure. At a certain point

I switched on the transcriber. I will need to be clear on my legal position.

DF: . . . Ten o'clock this morning, sir, we got a call to the site of what appeared to be a car crash, vehicle ablaze, it had come off a track and down a steep drop in the Warrendale Forest, off the A40. The fire brigade were already attending, it was them called us. And once the blaze was out they confirmed what they'd thought, which is there was a body in the passenger seat, female. The investigating officer had one look and rated it suspicious. So we got in there, traced the vehicle registration to a Mr Curtis James of Wood Green, London. Mr James told us he'd loaned the car to his friend Mr Worrell a couple of days ago – in order that Mr Worrell come and collect Miss Keaton from your premises?

SH: Yes. That's right. That's correct.

DF: Miss Keaton had been staying with you how long, sir?

SH: I treated her for depression these last five weeks. It had been – a success.

DF: So in your opinion she was in a good fit mental state?

SH: The treatment was successful. She was ready to go home.

SP: And with Mr Worrell?

SH: They were in a relationship, she asked that I send for him to get her.

DF: Did you have a notion where she and Mr Worrell were headed once they left?

SH: Yes, Eloise told me they were planning to spend a night in a hotel in Oxfordshire. Then carry on down

to London in the morning, to Miss Keaton's flat in
Holland Park.

SP: Well, that would make sense, wouldn't it?

SH: I'm sorry, the body in the car, there's no question, is
there, that it mightn't be Miss Keaton . . . ?

DF: As I said, sir, we can't try to make any formal
identification 'til the post-mortem, that'll happen
tomorrow. Like as not it'll have to be on dental
records. But, considering the luggage in the boot, and
we have a description from an eyewitness that puts
a blonde woman in the car half an hour before the
incident – and the pathologist on the scene reckoned
this was a woman in her mid-twenties . . . We feel it's
very likely, I'm afraid. However, we took the view not
to contact her next of kin until we'd spoken to yourself.

SH: And what about Leon Worrell? Where is he?

DF: As I say, there are circumstances here we consider
suspicious, sir. There's clearly a need for an
investigation.

SH: Can you tell me, what you think happened? With the
car?

DF: First we knew of this business was from a member of
the public driving on the A40 – concerned citizen,
a doctor, as it happens. He'd been sitting behind the
Jag for a few miles, had been admiring it, I think.
Then it started looking to him all of a sudden like the
vehicle was being driven a bit – 'erratically', he said.
Weaving. And as he went to overtake, he saw some
sort of altercation going on between the gentleman
driving and the woman beside him – he said it looked

245

to him like a struggle for the wheel, the woman very
agitated. He drove on, our witness, but he saw in his
rear-view that they turned off the motorway, onto the
road to Warrendale Forest. He was bothered by it, got
off at the next slip road, came back round. And he
followed the road into the woods, to the point where
there's no access but by this rutted old track that runs
along the top of a ridge. There's a steep drop off to the
left, down a bank into a ravine. Our chap, since he
hasn't seen a soul he parks, gets out, has a stroll, and
then he sees smoke, hears the crackle of fire and some
bangs like shots, and sure enough he sees the Jag's
there, about fifty feet down this slope, smacked into a
tree and burning. At which point he gets on his phone
to the fire brigade. Fire brigade get there, put out the
fire and they call Police Homicide.
SH: On what grounds?
DF: Evidently the car left the track, travelled down the
slope until the trees broke its path. The question is
why the car was burning. Whether it was burning
before or after the impact. Whether it was forced off
the track, or driven off the track, or propelled off it –
whether we're looking at an accident or a felony. The
fire brigade's investigating officer didn't read it as an
accident. He smelled petrol in the car interior, the
clothes, the upholstery. We're not liking the look of the
ground on the track – the pattern of footprints.
SH: As would suggest?
SP: That the car was propelled down the slope. From
stationary.

246

SH: *You're seriously proposing Leon Worrell would have done this deliberately?*

DF: *Oh at this stage, sir, we're not advancing anything. But Mr Worrell's departure from the scene, it— poses questions. Doesn't particularly speak up for him, you might say. Under the circumstances. Which have the look of a concerted effort to destroy a vehicle and a body . . . Are you all right, sir?*

SH: *I'm sorry, it's— it's very hard for me, to take in, to accept what you're proposing. Leon and Eloise, they were in a relationship.*

SP: *Mr James told us the same thing, sir. But he gave us the impression that it was a— quite a turbulent one? As relationships go . . . ?*

From here, things deteriorated sharply. A set of suspicions is already hardening into a bed of nails. I was asked who else would wish Eloise ill, and since I had no alternative suggestions their silence seemed to conclude that Leon certainly did.

They wanted to see Eloise's room. I had Brian show them up. Eloise's bag remained on my table, a lapse on their part. I couldn't help myself, I opened it up, released her scent, her folded things inside unsullied by the smoke damage. I took a swathe of that green dress of hers between my fingertips, but by tugging it I saw the black Forrest mask fall free of its folds, and I snatched the fucking thing, confiscated it – since it had no place there, never did, and ought now to be destroyed, eradicated, made to disappear like its maker.

247

19

Dr Lochran's Journal
The shape of a man

September 24th

Our poor houseguest is in a simply horrendous state, such that I've put him on the same Remeron he once prescribed for Robert. By his own admission it's a huge undertaking for him to hold himself together through a day's shift of work. For myself – well, I might have helped pull Steven out of some troughs in the past but this time I wonder if I've really got it in me to be the shoulder for his grief: this procession of stunning losses, unsupportable, unanswerable.

I have spoken to Tessa in confidence: she is not unsympathetic, but quite resolute, claims (albeit in sorrow) to have seen all this coming, the premonition itself a part of their marital fracture. It's plain how deep is the gulf between them, one that Steven, clearly, allowed to worsen. He concedes as much. But then, right now he is so miserable I believe he would confess to any unsolved crime going. I've heard the slight stammer, noticed the unsteady hand, seen the strain in his smile. The weight on his shoulders is driving him down into the dirt: my guess is that at every turn he's seeing just how total could be the ruin of his life.

Above all, that unannounced, annihilating call paid on

him at Blakedene by James Keaton has left him very, very shaky. I don't suppose one recovers easily from looking down the barrels of such a hatred. I've long held a dim view of Keaton based on what I've read in the papers, and Steven's grim account of the man's personal/familial failings only stack up the prosecution. But – the plain fact is he's lost a daughter in odious circumstances, Steven stands accused of clinical negligence, and there is nothing he could say to Keaton's face that will make a blind bit of difference.

Of course Keaton's express threat to make Steven's life 'hell', framed in the language of some Sicilian thug, shows the ugly streak in the man, and can't be dismissed. But, again, I can imagine all too easily Steven offering his neck to the blade. The worst pain for him as far as I can see is that he has no proper outlet for his own misery, is simply not permitted. He had real feelings for that girl, I think – for better or worse, the poor bastard. So he's already in hell.

The Blakedene board are circling him – he ought to mount a defence of some sort. I have suggested he talk to Christine Rainey at Cruikshank Kearns, who worked so deftly for McKissock's wife over her unfair dismissal. Steven nods, but he doesn't hear me, screwed into some fatalistic frame of his own making.

I can't always see a case for him leaving our house in the morning, but he does, and he will have to run the gauntlet for the foreseeable. Even Tessa was doorstepped and besieged yesterday at 7am, this while dressing the twins for their first day at school. One can't be sure who sang to the media: I wouldn't put it past one of the underpaid RMOs of Blakedene. But Steven has muttered about 'old friends' of Eloise Keaton's who could hardly be thought friendly; also some associates of the wretched Leon Worrell, including his own brother. In any case it's painfully clear that when the svelte blonde daughter of Britain's ninety-second-richest man dies in violent circumstances, that is a story, a horribly interesting story.

So, raincoated figures loiter outside the Blakedene gates, tramping the perimeter, assailing the dry-stone walls, not far from the spot where Darren Carver's body was found just over a week ago. The local press have never had such an imbroglio to feast on, and Blakedene, accordingly, is assuming 'a sinister aspect'. The long-lens news photos are in the classic manner: deserted grounds, blind windows, silently speaking of guilt. I try to keep this stuff away from Steven, not least because they are recycling the same college-era photo of the Keaton girl, her down-in-the-mouth prettiness exacerbating the morbid glamour, the distasteful sideshow, the all-round exploitation of misery.

Naturally the papers are soiling themselves in glee over the 'star-crossed lovers' angle, trying to read psychopathic rage in the eyes of Leon Worrell from the one innocuous holiday snap they managed to steal. I admit, were Steven not so dogged in the man's defence then I would probably draw the same glum conclusion – that this was a lovers' quarrel, over deep-seated differences, which tipped over into something terrible. (It seems Worrell and the Keaton girl were overheard arguing loudly at dinner in the Cadogan hotel, evidently 'a domestic', with overtones of jealousy.)

'Leon didn't do this, he couldn't, he wouldn't, he loved her . . .' Steven's lament. I have tried to tilt the lens this way and that, pushed him to interrogate the basis for his view – which is really no more than his own good nature's reading of what Eloise Keaton told him in the course of her treatment; and I'm just not certain Steven had his head screwed on and facing straight throughout that process.

But do I know any better? The media version is a hash of innuendo, yes, but I can't say the hacks are doing much worse with what they've got than I or the authorities. I could tell the papers a tale or two, for sure, throw them fresh meat. A former patient of the missing Dr Forrest – also, it seems, an ex-lover – dead, murdered, her name on a list stolen from Robert's apartment . . . ?

I have a theory, it's true. Eloise Keaton was killed by the curse of Robert Forrest. Those are the mad fingers playing on my strings. It makes no sense, obviously. Yet the connections are real: what remains obscured is any kind of design.

When I spoke again to Hagen I could hear his own struggle with this latest escalation of morbidity. It's be-devilling him just as it is me, I know it. But Hagen has other matters to occupy his time, whereas more and more I can think of nothing else.

Eloise links Robert to Leon – she was lover to them both within the same window of months. Could Leon's rage have been a fit of sexual jealousy? Might he have first taken this out on his rival? Made accomplices, some-how, of Darren Carver, Killian MacCabe . . . ? But the tower just falls, always, at any attempt to add a second tier. Steven is the only sounding board I have, but in his fixed and self-abnegating mindset he is absolutely no use to me.

It *is* a curse – a plague on both our houses. Steven can't see it, refuses to see it. And yet now he's being bedevilled far worse than any of us.

September 25th

Late yesterday Steven got the invitation to his own beheading, and this morning he drove out to face the Blakedene board. Precisely the verdict one expected – 'in light of recent unfortunate events', blah, 'deeply con-cerned about the standard of his judgement', blah-blah. With a calculating thrust they do not demand his resig-nation, but invite him to 'reflect on his position'. In his diminished state it was only human that he nod mutely, accept their derisory offer of a week or so to 'reflect'.

This evening we consoled him as best we could. Cal, who's been a reformed character since his grounding, made me proud by drawing Steven into a conversation over something he'd read about 'the psychology of being left- or right-wing', and Steven began to expound some-what like his old self. I was glad to slip out of conversa-tional duties, frankly, for we have had some more bad news. The great George Garrison, my mentor, is dying. He was poorly a while without diagnosis, at first they thought gallstones, then obstructive jaundice. But nothing was right. The endoscopist went in and all looked murky, so the Ca 19-9 was ordered and the results are horrific: the pancreas a stone, tissues hopelessly fibrotic, pancreatic head a frightening forest, nothing resectable. At 70 years old and Stage 4, George has no truck with radiation, accepts it will be months if not weeks – admits he should have heeded the abdominal pain, the loss of appetite. Muriel is devastated. I must visit them in Harley Street, and do it this week.

I hate to think how shaky I am at the moment, worse that it's compounded by the goddamned dreams. Last night Edmond called on me once again . . . and it drained me as much as any lived experience. I seemed to wake and find him stood at our bedroom door, mouth twisted in a sad smile, his eyes dun-coloured and unreadable. I took him downstairs . . . but soon, sure enough, we were wandering down the strip-lit corridors of the Spire Hospital, then he led me down to the banks of the River Yare at dusk.

'Death by water,' he said after a while. 'So strange, complete, to be swallowed that way. Stolen. Or lost.'

'But you died so bravely, Edmond.' I said it and meant it, vehemently. The ghost, however, seemed not to hear me.

'I wasn't prepared, Grey, when the moment came. Culpably unprepared. I let myself believe it couldn't happen. My fault, for so much sadness.'

'Ed – these accidents, tragedies . . . they're not foreseeable.'

'There are no accidents, Grey.' He turned toward me fully. 'The hourglass is turned, the sand runs. We fight it in vain, for the most part. There is a slim chance, though, to change the given – I think – if one is alert. But I couldn't save Peter.'

'But you *did*. Edmond, you saved his life. You were a hero. Peter's alive.'

He shook his head decidedly. 'No, Grey, that's not what happened. I learned, too late. There was something I did, you see. Or something I failed to do. For that I was judged, found guilty, and my son was taken. I had to surrender him, it was . . . decreed.'

The sheer self-cruelty of his incomprehension was driving me to tears, in the dream – but my eyes were still wet when I forced myself awake, and evidently I'd been groaning in my sleep too, for Olivia was bent over me, with a deeply worried mien. God love her, she pulled my head into her chest, stroked my hair as if I were her boy. And I was too much unmanned to act the stoic. So I told her, about this dream and all the ones before it.

September 26th

I was afraid this day might never end, but it's 2am now and Steven has limped away to his bed. We had little left to say to each other by then. I don't know which of us has been more – reduced? – by the events of the day. I feel strain all across my chest muscles, pointed pains in my shoulder-blades as if tightened by a screwdriver. But Steven has the look of one who's been broken, finally, by what we went through tonight, and the grim, grim confession he made to me.

At first light I must try to reach Hagen, as I ought to have done far earlier today. How much do I tell him? The urge to defend my friend is a massive pull. Yet the outcome for Steven might not be as grave as he fears. Clinical negligence, yes, compounded by an awful error of judgement, and that ought to be faced. I'm saddened, by his deceit. But I've allowed him to drag me into it too. And I can't but feel, however obscurely, that I will have to pay. Superstition, dread, these have started to feel like the only fit responses to the hole we're in. I believe now that nothing will ever surprise me again.

Late in the afternoon Steven rang me, greatly agitated, insisting we meet to talk. He had been rattling round our house, so wrapped up in gloom that I was mistakenly encouraged, rushed to meet him at the earliest feasible moment. His news? Leon Worrell had called his mobile – a nerve-straining occurrence, I assumed. But the man had hotly protested his innocence, asserted the Keaton girl's death to be murder, some sort of a frame-up into which he'd been fitted, a conspiracy – he used the expression 'honour killing'. According to him the borrowed Jaguar was run off the road by parties in the employ of 'the Keaton family'. The police, he insisted, were also in James Keaton's pocket, and so the investigation would be wilfully blind.

I found this grotesque, told Steven as much. People just don't do such things, even the likes of Keaton, for all his Little Caesar affectation. And yet Steven remained adamant about Worrell's absolute integrity. With his bloodshot eyes levelled at me, he insisted 'we both know' the police to be inherently prejudiced in these matters. I rated that neither here nor there, rated Steven much too overwrought to make a judgment. Whereupon he threw the thunderbolt: Worrell had urged – begged – Steven to meet with him secretly, in some old cemetery north of Muswell Hill, to fetch him clean clothes, money . . . A summons, from a fugitive – and Steven had already resolved to comply. His ask of me was not advice but that I be his wingman: he was begging me to go with him. *'Help me do some good tonight,'* he pleaded. Good grief . . . I couldn't have made my disapproval clearer: 'Steven, how can you ask me this? Can you not see the wrongness of it?' But he saw no such thing.

I interrogated him again on what he'd gleaned from Thames Valley police, what we could expect of Worrell. The facts combined against the man, no question. But all I could hear in Steven's replies was a febrile certainty, his clinging to a new and miraculous faith in a proof that could absolve Leon – and, of course, himself. In that faith he had set doubt aside. Yet still he felt the need of back-up . . . I found myself wondering if I had the right to refuse, much less accept. Finally the debt to friendship forced my hand. But the argument between us was strenuous – I felt the afternoon pass away, and I only wish now that we'd argued all night.

The rendezvous was set for dusk, 7pm. I drove us, parked at a distance. The sky had been overcast, darkness now closed in fast. Steven led the way unerringly, we passed the locked gates and at a shaded spot he gave me a footer over the cemetery wall, then clambered over himself. Two overgrown schoolboys, playing a hazardous game.

It was a ghastly old place, Victorian Gothic, grey and dismal, hemmed by juniper and cypress, clearly unmanaged and in disrepair, certainly a setting made for illicit/illegal activity. The graves had long been overgrown around the tombs and old stone crosses – those that hadn't already crumbled or keeled over. In great disquiet we picked our way past the resting places of dissenting priests, dearly beloved husbands, wives and children, some of the fallen of the Napoleonic Wars. One tomb, I saw, bore an inscription from the Psalms: *'My flesh also shall rest in hope.'*

Through the trees Steven led us, as instructed, to a derelict chapel at the rear of the grounds. Its stone walls were solid but the roof was staved in by two fallen trees. Rogue branches had long ago invaded the window frames, picked clean of glass. We peered into the near-pitch-black depths: the wooden font was intact, all else shattered, dilapidated. In the stillness we were alone. Steven asked that I hide myself, per our plan, so as to do nothing to 'alarm' Worrell. I picked a spot in the trees twenty yards back, hunkered down at the foot of a yew, watching Steven retreat into the chapel. It was a sombre vigil: the murk, the wind in the grass and the boughs. I was cold, anxious, my conscience bad.

Some clock tower chimed seven. Steven's face re-emerged in the shade of the chapel door, looking about as if to locate me. Then I heard the swishing approach, we both did, Steven visibly stiffened, and I sensed movement between the trees to my right – the figure of a man, making haste, but with a prowl in his stride. This, my first sight of Leon Worrell in the flesh, and he was in shabby condition, visibly a man sleeping rough, wearing a hooded jersey like a boxer. But his eyes were like thunder in his head, and he was a strapping great creature, no question.

Into the chapel he ducked, whereupon I broke cover, scuttled my way to a spot by the door. There, unsighted, I could only hear Worrell's harsh breathing, so I decided to hazard a look. Steven and Leon were embracing, I heard sobs, saw Steven's hand consoling on Leon's broad back – a pitiful pose, held for some moments in the half-light. At last they separated.

'It wasn't me. They think it's me, don't they? It wasn't. On my boy's life.'

'Leon, no one thinks anything yet, they don't know. You have to tell them. Tell *me*, exactly what happened.'

'We got run off the road, doc. They followed us from that hotel, just sat behind us. Soon as I knew I tried to lose them but they got right onto us, ran us into a ravine.'

'Help me understand, Leon. Who was following you?'

'Keaton's mob. His stooges. Two, in a black Beamer. She'd called him, see, I said she shouldn't but she told him she was finished with him, he was no father of hers. And he flipped, I mean, you don't know what he's like—'

'I do, Leon, trust me.'

'Cos I've had the stooges round before, yeah? Passing on his messages. How I got no business with his little girl.'

'You were threatened before?'

'Me and her both.'

'And Eloise, she was sure too, this car was her father's men?'

'Oh yeah. First I hadn't wanted to panic her, I just floored it a bit, did some overtaking, but they stuck on us, man. She saw something was up, I couldn't keep it from her.'

'There's a witness, says the two of you struggled, in the car?'

'You kidding me? She was scared, man – freaked, said we had to get away. But that old Jag didn't have it. So I pulled off, soon as I could, followed a trail into these woods – we lost them, I thought. I got us hidden on a dirt track, killed the engine, just sat. But then we heard them, the Beamer nosed onto the top of the track and right down on top of us. And this track was hairy, man, all I could do was reverse and reverse, and they revved and revved, then we were sliding . . . Ellie, she was desperate, they bumped us, she swung the wheel and I lost control, we went over – through this nothing barrier, down the ravine – forty-five degrees and we must have gone fifty feet, clipping all trees 'til we hit one dead on. It was so fast, you know, branches thumping the screen, being thrown around – I didn't know anything 'til I opened my eyes. My chest was right on the wheel, felt broken. Then I saw Ellie. She wasn't moving, her head was just blood, like a crack in it, and I put my ear to her heart and it was – gone . . .'

He hung his head. Steven embraced him again. High drama, yes. I wasn't remotely sold. It seemed to me a performance, a soliloquy.

'How did you manage to get away, Leon?'

'I was fighting just to get out my door, then I saw them, coming down the slope, grabbing on branches to keep from slipping, but one's got a tool in his hand. I just hacked my way down that slope to the foot of the ravine, then I ran. But I heard the car go up. I'd smelt petrol, the tank had leaked. I dunno – could have stood my ground.' He buried his face in his hands. 'I was a coward.'

Steven took his shoulders. 'Leon, you have to come in with me. To the police.'

Worrell's proud head shook. 'No chance, man. No chance.'

'It's the *only* chance, Leon, you have to tell them this story.'

'Bullshit, no one'll ever believe it.'

'I believe it. I believe it.'

'Then you tell them. I'm keeping free, as long as I have to.'

'You won't be able to run for long, believe me.'

'Watch me. You just watch me, Steven.' He had turned resolute with a knife-edge rapidity. 'Now listen, have you got something for me? Like what I asked?'

'That's no good. It won't help.'

'No, c'mon, tell me you brung me something.' In the silence I clearly heard a sharp sucking of teeth. 'You want

260

to help me or not, boy? I've begged you. Can you not do one simple thing I ask? I need *money*, Steven. Give me some fucken *money*.'

That was game up to me. I stepped from cover, strode toward them, a little shaky, seeing anew Leon's big six-foot frame and club hands. Moreover, he had taken a hold of Steven's lapels.

'Leon, this is my friend Grey,' Steven blurted, still blind, it seemed. 'He's a doctor, you can trust him.'

Leon released his grip on Steven, turned his gaze on me, stepping slightly onto his back foot. I saw his left hand clench into a fist, his right plunge into his jersey pocket. Was he palming something there?

'*You* got something for me then? Doctor Grey?'

'Just advice. Steven's right, Mr Worrell, if your story's true and you're innocent, you need to stop acting so guilty.'

He was looking from one to the other of us. 'Fool, I was . . .,' I think he heard him mutter, the tenor of the voice altered. And then . . . his frame seemed to relax, and it was as though a puppeteer had let go of the strings, stepped out from behind the velvet curtain. He looked up and around him at the darkened treetops, the night sky, and I thought for a moment he would laugh.

'*Voici le soir charmant, ami du criminel . . .,*' he proclaimed, then grinned in the face of our stupefaction. 'I'm sorry, how things went for you, Steven. Must feel like the end of the world. But you have to know for me it's far worse.'

I butted forward. 'You did it, didn't you? Killed the girl?'

His gaze hardened. 'I had no choice, Grey. You couldn't understand – or care, I'm sure – how I've suffered. But in here, you see, it is very dark . . .'

His presence had become disturbingly quiet, nested into his imposing bulk. At my side I felt Steven twitching, breathing shortly. But his apprehension, clearly, was gone, replaced by fire.

'You are despicable,' he snarled. 'The worst.'

'No. You haven't lived, Steven. Don't know you're born. Is it my fault all your love was in vain?'

Every word from Leon's mouth emerged mockingly, on the edge of a breath – quite some composure from a murderer on the run. I stepped to close the distance between us. 'Don't waste your time goading us, you're in a world of trouble, friend. It's about to get worse, I promise you that.'

'Not possible. Don't you be threatening me, boss. I got height and weight on you, if it comes to a ruck . . .' Hearing that I was dumbfounded, and he saw as much. 'Listen, I'll not confess again. I done it just for you, friends. Because it brings closure. Now you should take Steven's confession, Grey. The two of you would be closer still.'

I glanced to Steven, who only stared, newly wary, at Worrell. 'I never meant to drag you both into this,' he breathed. 'Not even you, Steven – my ungrateful old friend, who despises me. I've borne it all from you, haven't I? And are you so stalwart, always? Were you such a friend to Tom Dole?'

'Shut your mouth,' muttered Steven.

'The hell are you talking about, Worrell?' I exclaimed.

'Ask him,' Leon replied coolly.

Steven looked deathly. 'Did Robert Forrest tell you that?'

'"Tell me"? No. But certain *effects* of Doctor Forrest have come into my possession . . .'

I saw bitter relish in Leon's stare, knew I'd seen that look before. But then he thrust the heel of his palm to his brow, winced as if in pain, staggered slightly. I didn't hesitate, rushed right at him. He shoved me aside and I swung my right, but he feigned, hit me a club of a blow to the jaw and I fell. Then his boot was stamping on my legs and torso, and I feared the worst – until Steven threw himself at Leon, heavy as a sack of coal, and brought him down. Briefly they grappled beside me in the damp leaves, before Steven rolled aside, choking grievously, clutching his throat. Worrell gave him a swift kicking too. Then he was away, hurtling through the trees and the gloom, with uncommon speed.

We lay there for some long moments, battered and winded and coughing. Finally I took out my phone, punched 999, but Steven seized my wrist. In the warning on his face, I did weigh up my own greatly compromised position.

We limped away from the scene. I drove us home in silence. At the kitchen table we made up bags of ice, I examined Steven's neck, he checked my vision. Livy was at Susan's, thank God, but Cal did saunter down the stairs, curious. I told him we'd been mugged and the boy, incensed, was all for roaming the streets with a baseball bat. I calmed him down, asked him to fetch Glenlivet and help us lick our wounds. Eventually I led Steven up to the attic room, taking the bottle. And there he made his confession, much of it with his eyes closed and fingertips pressed to the lids, as if everything behind there was burning.

It was six years ago, he still an NHS psychiatrist, pre-Tessa, but at the death-knell of his relationship with Jessica, over which – he said, and I remembered – he'd become very morose. He had been treating Tom Dole, a troubled young man raised alone and in straitened circumstances by his mother, herself an erratic character. Dole had displayed some flair for poetry, also a passion for leftish political groupings and causes – also a tendency to aggressive, ungovernable behaviour and near-self-annihilation by strong drink and hallucinatory marijuana. Steven diagnosed a rapid-cycling bipolar disorder. But he also developed real affection for the lad, invested much time and care in him, won his trust and admiration by turn, went to some lengths to keep him out of psychiatric hospital. They were pals, spent some social time together. But in this way Steven lapsed into an uneasy tolerance of Dole's drug use, and came to find his excesses alarming. Dole in turn saw this as his most precious friendship, wouldn't let Steven free of it. This much I was familiar with. I'd never guessed what he told me next.

On the day in December when Jessica moved out – for all that the relationship had been moribund for months – she sensitively chose to tell Steven his indulgence of Tom had been 'part of the problem'. A broken heart can make a man incapable, sink him in a sort of insensate self-pity. Late that same night Dole rocked up at Steven's back door, as was his wont, utterly incapable. Steven let him stagger inside, but that night (having drunk a little himself) he had no patience to play nurse. 'I'd had enough of Tom,' he told me now. 'I thought someone else could bear his shoulder . . .' When Dole groped for the kitchen phone, barely able to form words, Steven took it out of his reach. Dole tumbled to his knees. Steven shut the door, locked it and left him there, 'to stew'. He went upstairs to his small study. An hour or so later he returned with a pillow and a duvet, found then that Dole hadn't been drunk or high – rather, at the onset of a massive cerebral haemorrhage, which had now completed its work.

'Well,' I said quietly, struggling for words, 'you couldn't have stopped the vessels in his head from rupturing.'

'He could have been saved. You know that. I knew it.' He flinched. 'It's— that's not the worst, Grey.'

Panicked, afraid, Steven called Robert. In not so many words he was asking for a solution, a get-out, release from what would follow if he called an ambulance. Robert, of the ice-cool head, drove over immediately, parked in the garage, assessed the scene and Steven's state – and, quite calmly, said the body had to be removed, deposited in water, before lividity was fully established. They shouldered the dead man into the back of Robert's Lexus, Steven propped him there as Robert drove to a park in Hackney, a mile or so from Dole's home, they smuggled him in and together toppled his body into the shallow water of the lake.

Steven later spoke at the inquest, in a manner that Dole's mother found comforting. A toxicology report had found traces of drugs and alcohol in the body. The park was known to be a haunt of his. The coroner spoke of 'a tragic end to a blighted life'.

And me, I sat there staring at Steven as though he had been body-snatched and a stranger was occupying his clothes and my armchair, spilling out these impossible lies about my two dearest friends.

'I know you can only think less of me, Grey,' he said into his chest. 'I swear there's not a day I don't live with it.'

I did pity him, I did, for the deep, pointless injury he'd done to himself, through deception after deception. But by now the night had deepened round us, silences weighed heavy.

'I know you'll feel the police have to know – what happened tonight – I know they do.'

'Yes, Steve. Christ alive, what else are we meant to do?'

'I know that. But I have to ask you . . . to please keep me out of it. I can't face where it could lead . . . Please don't incriminate me.'

It was awful cowardice, I couldn't stop the expression that crossed my face, one he saw and that hit home, I know. My foundations had taken too hard a shaking, by this ghastly vision of my friends, reputable medical men, creeping about like Burke and Hare.

But, but . . . what was done was done. The truth today is of no help to anyone. At this time in our lives – all friendships entail heavily accrued debts, on all sides. If I'm now less sure my friends were the men I believed

266

them to be . . . Was I wilfully blind? At any rate, in every respect, it is just too late in the day.

I told Steven I would lie for him – where I could, where necessary. Mutely he accepted the censure of my tone. I told him I had to have something from him in turn. 'I've heard your confession, I need you to hear mine.' Misery loves company, he might even have hoped to find me suddenly guilty of some past indiscretion. No, what I wanted from him was help with some inductive reasoning.

'Back when this business began. My first feeling – strongest feeling, if I'd had to bet my life – was that Robert had been 'taken', somehow – kidnapped, abducted. I'd a nagging suspicion, about a woman, you may recall. But I . . . I couldn't quite trust my own head. Then when Killian MacCabe went crazy . . . I definitely believed, for a while, that he'd taken out some unfinished business on Robert, done something to him out of jealousy, envy, whatever. And that theory survived Killian's death, for me. But then Darren Carver came into our lives. What do we make of that poor critter? What I thought – or went back to thinking – was that there was some kind of ransom on Robert, and maybe we were about to learn what it would cost to get him back. But no. All Carver ever asked for was a bit of spare change . . .'

Steven, studying the floorboards until now, flicked his haunted eyes up at me. I asked if he had a different view to mine. He shook his head. I continued. 'No, so, the trail goes cold. Then along comes Leon Worrell – this caring, hard-working man – he and Robert linked by a woman, just as Robert and Killian were. Then, just like Killian, Leon shows himself as a monster – kills the woman he loved, who loved him. Why? Is it because he's jealous of what Robert had with Eloise Keaton? That'll be what the newspapers will say.'

Steven nodded slightly. 'I think it's . . . very probably a motive . . .'

'And how do you suppose Leon Worrell knew all about you and Robert and Tom Dole?'

'What he said about having "effects" of Robert's – I did wonder, if Robert had written down some of – what we did – in a diary, a letter.'

'Or could he have prised the information out of Robert in person? Are we back to my grand theory? If we accept Leon's "jealousy". Did he abduct Robert, hold him? Has he been the man behind all this, the great vendetta?'

Steven's head had slumped again, voice distant. 'It's maybe the one explanation that fits . . .'

'You think? A cabal, against Robert and his loved ones, organised by a carpenter, in league with a beggar, abetted by a sculptor . . . If the facts take us that far down a hole, Steven, why stop?'

Steve was spent, finished, aching for his bed. But I stood, paced the space before him, if myself uncertain where I was headed next.

'Y'know, a little boy I operated on once told me he'd been watching me – while I did the procedure. Gave me not a bad account of what my hands had done to him while he was out cold. Six years old, he couldn't have read it in a book . . . So was his mind hovering over me that day? There's no person apart from a body, right?'

'I don't— can't follow you, Grey . . .'

'I've met Leon Worrell. Met Darren Carver. Met Killian MacCabe, thought I knew the man. Robert Forrest? Thought I knew him of old. But now I wonder. And one thing about all these men – I hear them in my head, and it's like what I hear – is one man. Behind it all.'

Steven muttered something that I had to ask him to repeat, louder. 'Vessels for a spirit' were his words. He was smiling thinly, exhausted, I knew, but I looked at him keenly now.

'Steven, do you give any credence to the idea of reincarnation?'

He rubbed at his face. 'You mean, like the "cretinous Buddhists"? No, Grey, no. I sometimes wish, though. Just please don't say you're thinking—'

'Indulge me. If we were thinking, what would you say? Give me your professional opinion, on reincarnation. Psychiatry's view.'

I had given him no choice. He sighed, looked limply aside. 'You mean parapsychology. Nothing that's reputable. Some cases that could suggest some sort of "life before life" – little kids recalling former lives in some detail, realities they couldn't have been aware of . . . who they were, where they lived, what they did. But it's voodoo, Grey. Voodoo. And only ever kids – people taking seriously the jabberings of kids. No, what you have in mind, if I read you right, is "possession".'

'All right. Possession, then. Do we consider a man could be "possessed" by another?'

'A spirit.'

'Call it a consciousness. We believe that when the body dies, consciousness dies, with the brain – evaporates. Right? But could it relocate? Migrate, into the air? Or into some other host?'

'By what process, Grey?'

'If we say – consciousness lives in sub-atomic levels of our brain, in quantum processes? That data could . . . persist, after the body's death, couldn't it? Be dispersed, but seek a home, get itself tangled up into some other organism. That's not out of this world, is it?'

Steven, head in hand, let me suffer a long silence. 'What I think is we're both very, very tired. What I think is, Leon has— got Robert. Got him or had him. That's what makes sense, with the facts. You're right, Grey, you've been right all along . . .'

He hadn't satisfied me, I let him see that. 'Then the police should be told as much, yes? As much as they need of what links Leon and Robert. If not the whole truth . . .'

Steven nodded, red-eyed, resignedly. I lowered my voice.

'You needn't be afraid of me, Steven, what I might do. You're afraid of enough as it is. There'll be a reckoning, in time, for what you and Robert did. Not tomorrow, though.'

'Tomorrow's today,' he murmured, gesturing to the clock on the wall. On that note we were done with each other.

September 27th

A few hours ago I woke with a start, went out to the half-landing of the upper stairway. Edmond awaited me, standing stiff like a valet.

'He's coming,' Edmond whispered, then stepped aside, gesturing behind him – to where an intruder stood on the half-landing below, staring up at us, teeth gleaming through the moonlit gloom.

Livy was at my shoulder. Edmond was gone.

'Do you see him?' I muttered, my heart thumping.

'Of course I see him!' Livy cried.

The intruder began to mount the stairs. I lashed out but couldn't lay a finger on him. I am used to the sluggish wading sensation of dreams, but here I was drastically woozy, listing, giving this ghoul free rein to destroy my life, rape and kill my wife. Only then came the blood-freezing thought – was Cal already done for, down the stairs? Then I managed to wake myself.

Nothing looks right to me today, sounds right or feels right. I've just read Steven's note. Livy called to alert me he had gone – must simply have packed and slipped out of the house while she was shifting about in the eyrie room for an hour or so. He claims to need 'some time apart, room to breathe away from the madness'; asks that I 'please leave him to it, and please keep my word' – a needless, offensive, demoralised request. He pledges to return within a week. He is unable to stop himself suggesting that I, too, 'need to order my thoughts and reflect how this business has distracted me'.

There is no order to be made from my thoughts – though Steven in his own sorry way has contributed to the obfuscation, its strain on me, plus all the strain I have taken for him.

In the early hours, finally, I called Hagen, who in turn alerted Thames Valley, and a sergeant was at my door by first light. Steven sat by me as I'd instructed, and we gave together our fanciful tale of how some anonymous man had telephoned me, claiming to have information about Robert, asking for money, to meet me in secret – a meeting to which I brought Steven, who there recognised Leon Worrell, who in turn made what we both felt was a confession to the killing of Eloise Keaton.

In fact, the investigation already knew for sure that Worrell had returned to London, while physical evidence has established to the team's satisfaction that the Jaguar XJ with Ms Keaton inside was set alight and pushed down that woodland slope by Worrell. Moreover, their own suspicions in respect of motive are indeed related to Robert. Still, they were grateful for my and Steven's time and information.

They can make of it what they will. I no longer know what I believe. Livy tells me I'm driving myself and all of us to perdition. She's not wrong. Out of respect to beloved others, I must put this business behind me. Above all, *I want nothing more to happen.*

September 29th

Home again, released to the bosom of my family – amazing, this medical science of ours. The widow-to-be and my son together put their shoulders to the task of helping me walk from Outpatients, my steps being so tentative. Calder, God love him, had brought 'the Forrest cane', but I was disinclined. We made it home, I made it as far as the baggy blue, felt I could have slept there for years. The house is cold, really time to resuscitate the boiler. Will it feel like home again? Can anywhere? *'The world is not my home,'* my father used to sing. Suddenly it's like the ground under my feet is barely there. I have had a shock, the sort from which I'm not sure I'll recover. Not completely. No end of a lesson . . . I will have to be careful now, so careful.

'A wake-up call', the cardiac specialist called it as he held forth by my bed. Yes. In fact I felt it knocking, its intimations, days, weeks ago. Yet I thought myself hardier, believed it was a reckoning for tomorrow, and tomorrow . . . And I refuse to believe it was meant to happen this way. It wouldn't, had I not seen and heard things no one should.

None of that within the specialist's remit, of course. With his consummate grave blandness, talk of 'ruptured cholesterol plaque', 'stenosis in the left anterior descending', 'sudden and near complete occlusion' . . . I feared he might take up a pointer, show me the chart. Instead I waved an enervated hand. "The "widow-maker"?'

'Not quite,' he smiled. 'Or you'd be dead.'

Certainly the emergency team found me dying. I owe my life to that porter. I was in UCH four and a half minutes later, a minute more would have counted hard against me. My heart stopped but I was revived, catheter inserted, the artery unblocked by a stent.

Such wonder I knew on waking! And how many people wished most urgently to speak with me . . . I struggled to explain to Livy and Cal the circumstances by which a stranger had summoned an ambulance for me, also police, from a mansion block in Fitzrovia. I promised a better story as soon as I had the time to construct it. And then DI Hagen was there, quite beatific, surprisingly unquestioning – serene, even. From Detective Franklin, I understand, it is Case Closed now, the zipper right up the middle of the body-bag. But Hagen, he must be more curious about what's been uncovered – that mirror, the stains, the unexplained absence of 'Mrs Ragnari' – how any of this came to be in that apartment, which, it turns out, is owned (but has long since been left unused) by the sixth Marquess of Ravenscourt, a dissolute character by reputation, resident in Manhattan. Apparently Ravenscourt denies he ever gave Mrs Ragnari keys or permission to lodge. The porter is equally certain they spoke and it had been arranged. They can't both be right.

And me? I just can't tell them everything I saw, saw and heard, because I wouldn't have believed it on any other testimony. They would tell me I was still seeing that warm light, unearthly and beckoning, at the end of the tunnel . . . Or else plain out of my mind. But I am sane. I must also be accurate, for my sanity's sake.

Two nights ago, a thousand years ago – I called on George and Muriel Garrison as arranged, 7pm in the flat on Weymouth Street. 'I still feel human,' he told me.

But he looked dreadfully jaundiced. I didn't believe we would have a drink. Of course we had several brandies, he urged me to smoke. We listened to the music Muriel plays for his spirits: Beethoven's 3rd and 5th, plus a little Jacques Brel. In the repose of the armchair it even felt good to talk – to remember someone before they are gone. Then he asked about Robert: 'I remember him well.'

'Me too,' I said, feeling a certain emotional crumbling. But it turned out George knew nothing of recent events. And I chose not to enlighten him. A couple of hours passed, by which time the rain was pelting down heavily outside, foul stuff to contemplate heading into. I shook George's hand, thanked him, wished him a good night's rest, knowing I'd not see him again.

I wrapped up, stepped out, thought I would flag a cab, considered on what corner of the street I should set myself. Then, fifty yards ahead through the wet mist and the blear of lamps, I saw a figure hastening over the road en route to Queen Anne Street. And my pulse leapt, because I had seen this man, seen him move – prowl – just so purposefully nights before.

I shifted myself with such speed as I could, after the vanished figure, rounding one corner in time to see him turning the next. I kept up the pursuit, Leon never looked back, was in an almighty hurry. By now, after this street and that street, my steps were sure – I knew where I was headed – the logic of the Conspiracy, no?

I was stood under a street lamp in time to see him pound up the stone steps, through the double doors of the mansion block. As soon as he was in I dashed across, intending to hit every buzzer on the intercom if I had to. Instead a couple in evening dress were trooping across the foyer, enjoyably immersed in each other. I held the door for them, accepted their smiling thanks, wished them a pleasant evening.

I mounted the stairs to the sixth floor, crept down the corridor to the familiar door of apartment 6F, turned the doorknob – the door swung open. Then I trod on tiptoe into the gloom of an entrance hall. All inside was silent, shadowy, as if deserted. I flared up my Zippo, throwing shadows onto the wall, stepped to my left into a darkened reception room.

The place felt aged, decrepit, every inch the pied-à-terre of an aristocrat bachelor careless by nature or else on his uppers: off-white walls, high ceilings, tall damask velvet curtains, an odour of dust and moth-eaten fabric. Covers were drawn over all over the furniture. I spotted a curious black stain eating one corner of the ceiling. In the fireplace much matter was reduced to cinder.

It was while crouched at the hearth that I heard fleeting footfalls in the hall, and the creak of the door. I moved as fast as I could, but it was a lost cause, my shouts echoed down an empty corridor. I lumbered all the way back to the stairwell but heard only the faintest click of heels across the marble floor below, then the clunking slam of the main door. Again I shouted, a useless echo.

My heart was thumping in its cavity now. I took out my phone, called Hagen's mobile, left a message. As I turned back to the Ragnari apartment I thought I could hear the porter's voice calling up from ground, but I pressed on into 6F.

This time I took an alternative doorway through which Mrs Ragnari, presumably, had slipped in order to flee; found a bedroom with a bare mattress, no curtains, ancient wardrobe. I flung it open, and the door came off its hinge. Empty inside. Drawers, empty. Next door the kitchen held nothing but one plate and one cup in a cupboard. Desertion, no life, indeed nothing lived in. I peered into a white-tiled bathroom: a claw-foot tub stained high with a ring of scum gave off a powerful sulphuric reek. My suspicions prickled, my stomach felt hollow.

I retraced my steps, entered the rear reception room through double doors in the partition wall. This room was identical to its twin but for two significant items. Robert's antique mirror – unmistakably that same one, eight-foot high, free-standing, ornate surround – lorded over the dark space. And at the mirror's foot lay the sprawled body of a man, motionless, a slick of black blood emanating from about the head.

With care I turned him over by his shoulders, waved my Zippo close, identified Leon Worrell, somehow more lifeless than even his injury would have suggested. A scalpel was rolled up in his fist, the right external carotid had been sliced open exactly. But the arrangement of the body was all wrong to my eye – I didn't accept the wound as self-inflicted.

From my crouch I looked again at the mirror, marvelling still at how it could have been transported from

Robert's closet. I went closer to examine the frame, couldn't avoid peering into the glass – saw my flushed, fearful face behind the stain of my breath – a crimson glow behind me on the ceiling . . .

And then in a piercing instant I saw it – I know I did – the reflection of someone, something, in the corner of the room behind me, deep in the grasp of an armchair, indescribably foul.

I turned and it was gone. Only shadows, an empty chair. But a terror had reared up in me – suddenly vertiginous, physically disabling, a cold flush right across my skin. And with it, I heard slurred, evil, discordant noise strike up between my ears – first dimly, then rising to a din, like the mood music of all my recent nightmares. My hands were frigid, shaking, the extremities no longer obeying orders. I felt a grip like ice on my neck; I could hardly swallow.

Then there was a voice amid that din, and in my panic I couldn't understand if it was in my head or emanating from the walls, which seemed to pulse outward. Numbness invaded my left forearm, climbed up it. A spasm gripped my oesophagus so strong it was as if a fist were being forced down the windpipe. I felt myself topple, my head hit the hard floor.

And from recumbent I watched those shadows in the corner of the room resolve once again into the shape of a man, a shape that slunk head first to the floor and padded to my side, like some jackal, until it was breathing hot in my ear – a humanoid growl, first guttural, then full-throated.

What the Presence said: *'Poor little big strong man, get on your knees, on your belly, bow your head, little fool, we have business with you. Die now, die later, but you will die, and sooner than you think, fool. Get up and run now, run if you can, your house is cursed, the child is gone, all that you love is on fire . . .'*

I didn't wake again until the lights were ablaze all around me. 'A wake-up call', yes. I was awakened. To what?

20

Dr Hartford's Journal

A mermaid's tail

September 29th

They tend to call it 'stark' and 'bleak' out here at the edge
of England, a disturbed place, a desert, wasteland even.
But I find it sits well with me. A place where a man might
vanish – a commonplace yearning, I've come to believe.

This morning's sunrise was of the purest pastels. I'd
long believed that aloneness encouraged 'night-thoughts',
but my sleep was dreamless, as it's been since I came.
Autumn has faded in, and I needed logs for the stove
from day one, so I got up and out as early as was feasible,
made the trek along the coast to the nearest general store
at Greatstone. There, a worryingly birdlike lady pressed
the parish newsletter on me, urgently commending a
short essay therein on passages in Paul's Epistle to the
Romans – an essay of which, it transpired, she was the
author, and began to quote verbatim. *'For the woman
which hath a husband is bound by the law to her husband
so long as he liveth,'* she cried unto me, as if she'd written
that part too. *'But if the husband be* dead*, she is loosed from
the law . . .'* Liking this not one bit, I managed to escape.

Either I'm a lightning rod for the local eccentrics, or everyone here is strange. Or else the strange one is me – that
stranger, out by the shore. Last night, as the fire ebbed,

somewhat the worse for red wine I went and fetched the mask, strapped it onto my face, stared at my black, blank reflection in the mirror awhile, feeling myself a little demented, or at least imagining how that could feel.

The morbidity of it finally brought me to my senses. Knowing I needed air I decided to hazard a drink at The Ship, and there misjudged a friendly loan of a bloke's newspaper, whereupon I got his life story and philosophy rather than the headlines I'd wanted. He works at the nature reserve, came to Dungeness expressly in order to catch many and varied species of moth in light-traps, and keep detailed logs of his discoveries. Much did I learn as I sat there, of the Death's-Head Hawk and Pale-Shouldered Cloud, the Flame Brocade and Marbled Grey, the Beautiful Gothic and Brimstone.

On returning from the store I got out tools, replaced the rain-rotted boards on the side of the shed, painted them sea-green to match the main bungalow. The elements must not be allowed to take a hold. And this place is going to have to be sold shortly. To Tessa it will seem more redundant than ever. For me it's proving a valuable bolthole, but I can't let the respite fool me. I am taking the holiday we were meant to have, or never meant to, but there must be an end to it, and soon.

Dungeness has barely changed since my boyhood. The Magnox power stations rose up, of course – symbols of an ominous future, it seemed, but now history looks to be turning the page on them. There are one or two hyper-modern beach houses, but the overriding mood is still that of the reserve, the mini-railway, the St George pub. As today turned into a bright, chilly day I took a walk down the long shingle beach. It wasn't long before I was reminded how tiring is the trudge on foot over stone. My mouth was dry, I'd brought no water. I saw a raven perched on one of the plant's pylons, as if surveying his terrain, which no one would call picture-pretty. There was a sunlit eeriness to the shimmer from the miles of pebbles, amplified by the pulse of the nuclear reactor.

But once I was over the ridge and onto the grass-way it felt good and reviving to be rambling through ragwort and thistle, rosebay and foxglove. I spotted a wading curlew, a flock of sooty shearwaters flew east above me. My head must have been with the birds because I was startled by the distant crack of gunfire: I'd strayed a good deal nearer to the MoD range than I'd planned. Still, I don't hold with the incomer's view that barbed wire and angry KEEP OUT signage spoil the views. Like everything else here, they suit my mood, keep secrets just like me, assert there are recesses and forbidden zones in this life, and these should be left undisturbed.

It was past 3 when I came back round by the sea: some desultory fishing going on from the shore, a few boats out. The wind seemed light, until it bit at the skin. But all sea air is good air, and it dispelled from my nostrils the slight lingering odour of marsh rot. For some time I stood and stared at the slow-turbid, steely grey-green seething of the sea – its formidable chill. Then sunlight cut through the overcast canopy, making the clouds into an aureole, giving the water a silvery green-blue aspect, like the fleeting shade of a mermaid's tail. Above us now was a fine English fire-in-the-heavens sky. I was lifted by it. This place is medicine to me as it mightn't be to others.

Nothing can erase or redeem the dreadfulness of recent weeks. But removing myself, taking this air, is proving some sort of cure. Out here I had thought I might review my case-notes and journal, seek some perspective. Today, though, I feel better to be free of them. Just to be sleeping at night, in a bed – I bless that peace. Not to feel that Grey's newest gnawing theory is about to bite me.

The sea says 'Afresh, afresh' . . . Wasn't that what Larkin wrote? For me the notion of retraining, starting over, has begun to exert quite a hold. I will be gone from here before the week is out, yes – but I have learned something: I can get by, as a single man, a poor man if needs be. Though an ex-husband, I will be a father still. And from this staging post I'll move forward. The failed life behind me was, arguably, not meant to be. The road ahead will be difficult, but I intend to find a new way of living.

September 30th

Extraordinary to say, I have a guest – I've made a friend. This morning I half-expected to find her gone, but I just snuck a look into the room and she is still bound up in sheets, sleeping soundlessly. Strange, how things work . . . Elsewhere, hugely to my relief, my other (unwanted) visitors of last night have vanished entirely from the boys' room – scattered by the light, I suppose.

It began at nightfall when I felt the pull of the pub but, unable to face the thought of my Moth-Man again, decided to try another hole, The Staff up in Lydd. I put on my greatcoat, stepped out. The moon was full, radiant, sliced by a swift-moving cloud, the night sky splendid with stars – there was something awesome about those black fathoms, the cold darkness felt somehow luxurious to me, full of promise. I tramped over unlit grassland for a stretch, had no torch, and of course one gets started by the merest sound: rabbits thumping their hind legs, the rending cries of a fox. Yet the speed with which my eyes adjusted made me feel pleasingly nocturnal, capable.

Fifty paces from the pub door I saw the young woman was suffering unwanted attention from a drunken, boorish bloke. 'All I want is a goodnight kiss,' was his refrain, but there was no playfulness in how he was pawing at her, or her stung cries. I am not a physically courageous man. But there was something in me tonight, I felt a powerful irritation, and it carried me straight into the fray. All I did, in fact, was impersonate Grey – plant my feet as if to knit my height and girth into something implacable. 'You're mistaken,' I actually said, this in reply to his assertion that he'd rip my fucking head off. But it worked. He kept swearing murder at me, but that was from ten yards away, then twenty. I felt a flush of success: the man with nothing to lose.

The girl was shivering all over, as if she might perish, even though she wore a long black riding coat buttoned to the neck and a scarf like a cowl. But she thanked me profusely – dark-eyed, Slavic accent, said her name was Senka. I offered her a brandy, she accepted but said she didn't want to re-enter the bar. So we sat out at a trestle.

She picked cigarettes gladly from my pack, drank her brandy like a guy, in short swigs. I admit I looked her over as we broke the ice. Late twenties, I'd say. Very black unkempt hair, her hands always in it. Lips like bruised fruit. Her nails need care.

I asked her a few concerned questions, she confessed to being in dire straits. She came over from Kosovo, where her family were poor, their lives perilous. 'I wanted— better life. But is not . . .'

'You have regrets?' I asked her.

'You would not believe . . .' Her laughter had a certain music, her smile wise for her years. Clearly she's educated, her English only slightly broken. She emigrated in the company of a boyfriend, whose idea it had been, but who 'let her down' once they reached London. Her presence illegal, she struggled for meaningful paid work, the migrant's plight. The cost of London living appalled her; people seemed mean and distrustful. ('I see in your face, you know this,' she said, noting my nods. 'Because you are a good man . . .') Alone she had struck out in the rough direction of Dover. A job in a meat-processing factory near here has been paying her £130 a week. Her real wish is to care for the elderly, but even there she can't get a break. Meantime she is too poor, and I sense, too ashamed (by 'failure') to return home, though she misses it. 'I have done nothing,' is how she puts it. There's a sadness about her: a wounded sort of a girl, for sure. I asked if she missed her boyfriend. She shrugged. 'Everybody wants someone to care for them . . . To me you don't look so happy. You are alone?' I nodded.

'A pity, to be alone. Is not a life.'

'It may be my natural state,' I replied, rising to get us refills.

The crux we came to is that she can no longer afford to pay her rent, and is actively afraid of her vindictive-sounding landlord. Her loitering in the cold and dark had been over the question of whether she should even try to get readmission to her digs. I'm old enough to know when I'm being played, and this wasn't such a moment. I told her I had a spare room at the cottage. She accepted in a pained way that spoke well of her. We must have been *simpatico*, at any rate, for when the barmaid came out to collect glasses she chivvied us, 'Move along, lovebirds . . .' I gave my weariest smile; Senka appeared mortified. So I was reminded to behave, confirmed in my Samaritan impulse.

Back at the cottage I offered coffee but she was happy I open some wine. I put on Schoenberg's *Verklärte Nacht*, Boulez's version, which, to my delight, she identified. When I apologised for the darker shades of the piece, she shrugged. 'You have dark in you, I have dark. Is how we are. Like the turning of the earth . . .'

She curled back into the sofa, her animal-like enjoyment of the fire's warmth fully evident. And we talked for some hours into the night – or at least, I did. After several drinks I felt the effect – I was sliding somewhat, I suppose my tongue got loosened on the topic of Tessa and the divorce. But it was so good to offload. I sensed an intuitive sympathy for my troubles, real fellow-feeling in her dark-eyed gaze. No doubt I pontificated, even selfexculpated a bit, but I'm sure I was honest about my own failings too.

I never lost my manners – the coffee table between us, on which, in due course, I set down coffee. I suppose it would have been easy, uncontroversial, to sit beside her. But I wasn't going there. I wanted to preserve our fragile connection. Finally she dropped off to sleep. I stared awhile, fascinated by this enigmatic thing on my couch. Then I got up, squared round the boys' room, changed one narrow bed, drew the curtains, opened a window, folded one of Tessa's plain cotton nightdresses. Gently I shook her awake, showed her through, left her to it, dead-locked front and back doors. I must say I fell asleep swiftly and soundly. But I was awakened by sharp cries before 2am, and I hurtled from the bed into next door.

The kids' old nightlight was on, bathing one corner of the room in ultraviolet blue, colouring the shadows. I could see Senka's alarm but couldn't understand it. Then her eyes darted upward and I followed. The ceiling was dense with dark blotches – then the blotches twitched, flitted – then the whole effect appeared to crumble, and the air was full of small darting shapes, the paper-like flit of wings. My cheek was brushed, I felt a furred touch on my neck, loathsome. Moths! I grabbed Senka's hand and fairly wrenched her from the room.

I offered to take the sofa but she shook her head. So we slept together, but chastely apart, in mine. For a while I lay uncomfortably awake, unsettled as much by the squat belching of frogs outside, increasingly loud and aggressive. Even after dropping off, I stirred at one point, saw

287

her sat at the end of the bed, her shoulders twitching, but I thought it wisest to play dead. At last, before dawn, came that profound sleep I've rediscovered out here, just like an old friend.

ల

Curious. Senka disappeared late this morning, resurfaced for a time, but has now gone off again without warning. This time, at least, I saw her picking a way into the distance across the shingle. But I believe she'll be back. This morning she gobbled porridge, gulped hot coffee, Tessa's ecru dressing gown pulled close. She seemed to appreciate a hot shower. But I only turned my back to find myself alone again.

I washed up, read awhile, glanced for the first time in years at Lacan's *Ecrits* (a scratch in my mind about our 'ineffable stupid existence'), then flicked through some Princeton tome of Tessa's on magic in medieval Europe. I successfully fought the urge to switch on the Blackberry. Then, around 2pm I looked out and saw her sitting on the deck outside the French doors to my bedroom, smoking one of my Gitanes. I asked where she'd been. 'Wandering,' said she (!). She seems sincerely not to want to 'put me out'. And yet there she was. There remains no obvious solution to her housing problem, save for me.

In the silence I suggested a drive, a foray, since she's seen nothing of the regional sights. She was unenthused by Snargate Church or the Martello towers at Dymchurch but seemed persuaded by the ancient woods at Blean. She wanted to drive us, though, and I let her, thus had to watch a little uneasily as she took a remarkable glee in gunning the old Mazda up to 80–90mph. I tried, though, not to watch her too closely.

At Blean we took a walk of several miles. It was sunny on the open acid grassland. I pointed out a nuthatch and a song thrush. Senka told me most keenly of how she thought my living conditions ideal. 'What you have is so good, a place apart, to hide away, be free.' I had to make her aware, as vaguely as I could, that I can't hide from my problems, will be leaving by Friday and, sadly, cannot entrust her with the keys. Still, I did try to engage her in my various inchoate plans of 'starting over' in London, also to suggest that for her, too, this might prove easier second time round. But it just didn't seem to pique her interest.

After a while she drifted ahead of me, between the veteran oaks and silver birches, picked her way over a felled tree and wandered down a narrow path, out of the sunshine into the dark shadow of the woodland canopy. Here and there were lingering patches of *anemone japonica*, an occasional purple orchid. But the leaves were peeling away, horse chestnuts all round, livid fungi on dead wood. All of a sudden I'd lost sight of Senka. Whereupon the muffled, enclosed hush was unnerving to me. With only thin shafts of light piercing the gloom of the wood, those towering trees took on rather more 'character' than I cared for. I turned and Senka was right behind me. A jape, I guess, though her expression was scarcely cheery. Reflexively I touched her face. She lowered and closed her eyes. I knew I'd gone too far. We got back on the path and wandered back to the car in silence, her head still worryingly low, I felt.

I know you think you have nobody, I wanted to say to her. *But it won't always be that way.*

October 1st

Last night there was a fog across the moon, this morning I felt there's been a fog in my head this past forty-eight hours. I woke in a state of sickened realisation, as if I'd dreamt it. She had gone. Last night when she'd climbed into her side I'd dared to curl up behind her, but felt her tense. She murmured that she was still thinking, was troubled, about what we'd discussed this evening, our past mistakes, how they've lived with us. I had mentioned, briefly and partially, an ex-patient for whose death I considered myself half-responsible. I edited my account, for obvious reasons – edited out even that patient's name. And yet I heard her say, over her shoulder: *'I am sorry for your Tom Dole.'* In the moment I was merely irritated, thwarted. This morning I am frightened.

Other things have flooded in, unbidden. Her face – where I think, in fact, I've seen it before. It's crazy. But I have – a sense, a suspicion – of whom I may be dealing with here.

I tried to reach Grey, tried Livy too, no success – inexplicable. I even walked outside, actively searched for her, really wanting to pre-empt, and by daylight, what seems an inevitable confrontation – wanting it at least on my terms. But there was nothing and no one in sight along the shore, save for a catharacta skua feasting on some unfortunate gull, its black cap and long bill dipping voraciously into the mess between its claws. Hating the harshness of the bird's gloating cry, I hastened back across the stones. Now I wait.

𝓮𝓵

She's in there now. Whoever she is. Whatever.

I sat in The Ship tonight until kick-out, just for human company, one last time. On re-entering the cottage I found her at the living room table in front of my glowing laptop, my folders and files opened – my archive, will and testament. It seemed she had lifted the spare keys; seemed she'd done much I was unaware of. Her hair was washed and shining, her lips reddened, she'd made free use of Tessa's closet, raided the long black jersey dress I bought for her fortieth. The Forrest mask lay in a coil at the corner of the table.

'What are you doing?' I said.

'I have been reading,' she answered, brazen.

'So I see.'

Ignoring my computer screen she picked up the church pamphlet foisted on me in Greatstone the other day, and she read aloud:

'For I was alive without the law once: but when the commandment came, sin revived, and I died. And the commandment, which was ordained to life, I found to be unto

death. For sin, taking occasion by the commandment, de-ceived me, and by it slew me . . .'

'Sad,' she said, setting down the pamphlet. 'But I am glad to see you.'

'I've seen you before, Senka, you know that? Not in the flesh, I don't think. But . . . a patient of mine, he made a bust, a clay bust, of a woman's face. His name is David Tregaskis. Do you know him?'

She tilted her head, nodded. 'I knew him once. Another life.'

'Tell me something else. Were you ever – did you ever go walking on Hampstead Heath, with my friend Robert Forrest?'

'Oh . . . I don't know that I did. But I may have done. It's not impossible . . .' Her English, if still accented, was now flawless.

'Where is he now? Robert, where is he? I think you know, don't you?'

She studied me. 'How badly do you want to know? How great would be your need? As great as mine?'

'Understand, I've not got anything here. I'm broke, there's nothing you can . . . extort from me, it's gone.'

'All I want from you, Steven, is this shelter. Not for-ever. Just a while longer. I have nowhere else to go.'

'Then tell me where Robert Forrest is.'

'Haven't you guessed?'

'He's alive?'

A long low exhalation came out of her, she shrugged with closed eyes, as to say the question was somehow – ambiguous. I felt my anger, so long suppressed, rising.

'For Christ's sake, don't play games. Just tell me, or get out. *Tell me.* You'll get nothing more from me but I'll have the truth. If I have to shake it out of you.'

I did not feel in control of myself. And I was sure I saw real apprehension in her eyes. The silence lasted. The room seemed to have become unpleasantly clammy. She was toying with the top button of her dress. Feeling my nails in my palms I unclenched my fists.

'It feels close,' I muttered finally.

'Closer than you think.'

Rain had begun to fall audibly on the roof, visible on the streaked glass of the French doors. I went, closed the curtains, feeling a tumult inside that was making my legs weak. When I turned back she was unbuttoning the dress, not adeptly, trying to keep her eyes on mine, tight as the purse of her lips.

'What now?' I said, shaking my head.

'The effect of this can be – quite striking? – I've found.' She smiled to herself, drew a little nearer. 'I know you think you have nobody, Steven. But perhaps you never did.'

I believe I would have laughed aloud had her presumption struck me sooner. I wanted to be very clear, word for word, and yet my voice still sounded to me like someone else's. 'If this is— an attempt at seduction? I can't tell you how deluded you are. I mean, *mad.*'

She paused, tilted her head again – grim 'Little me?' coquetry – then peeled the dress from her shoulders, unclasped her brassiere, inserted a hand like a scoop and cupped the bell of her left breast. Its milk-softness seemed to slip between her fingers, as if she were weighing a mere bag of jellified matter, a useless, grotesque appendage.

'I carry the weight of the world on my shoulders,' she murmured. 'Who will free me from the body of this death?'

The situation was insufferable, as was the strange heat. I touched my brow, found it clammy. She walked past me, toward the arch leading to the bedroom.

'Think before you answer,' she said with clarity. 'It will be done as you decide.'

Then she disappeared. I stood for some moments waiting to recover my breath, my resolve. Then I followed her. And so put an end to it, to all hopes, such as they were.

She had lain down, made herself ready. The sight of her . . . In my head I saw monkshood, oleander, lathyrus cicera. I had been lured, tugged in by a thread, and I felt myself the injured party – yet, there were moments, our faces so close, her eyes opaque, mouth all hurt, when it seemed she had surrendered whatever power she'd exercised, and I wondered if in fact I was guilty of ravishment, committing some awful act. There is a power in doing anything for the last time. But even before we were done I could feel myself fogged by remorse, a poison-cloud of the world's worst intentions. Beneath me she was plainly disturbed – softly crying, softly laughing, I couldn't tell. But was she whispering to me or was the voice in my head, or did it come through the walls? It seemed for the longest time that I couldn't hear it clearly – or hadn't heard it properly.

'Look close. Do you not know me?'

Yes. Hell is here. I know it, I'm buried in it. Close the lid now, shut out the light.

21

Olivia's Correspondence
Lost in the dark

To Tessa Hartford
October 2nd

Dear Tessa:

I wanted to write and tell you that our conversation today affected me deeply, also to say again that you and your boys are so much in our thoughts at this time. Forgive me for reiterating – these are the moments in life when one wishes suddenly one had said more before, more and sooner. I dearly hope we'll talk again soon, and often, and that you will always regard Grey and I as trusted friends to you and the twins. We have all of us in our own ways been harrowed lately, it's as if some ungodly pall fell over our 'circle' these last six weeks, to the utter exclusion of the light. But Steven's taking his own life is by far the worst of all.

Let me say quickly that we totally sympathise with your wish to be rid of the Dungeness cottage as swiftly as possible in the wake of this tragedy. It's an onerous business, we know, and if I can be of any practical assistance then please don't hesitate to call on me.

Similarly the funeral arrangements. I hope you haven't spent one more moment worrying over whether you should attend. Everybody there will want to see you and the boys, for all the sorrow. Whatever your fears I really don't believe Julian or Jacob will ever hold you to blame for their father's suicide – I am sure of it – nor will anyone else. You are a strong person, Tessa, your boys have the benefit of that and will continue to. I saw Steven in his decline, as did others, and while I wish to God we could have done more to arrest it, he was in the grip of something that moved him past the reaches of our care.

The unhappy roles of Divorcee and Widow have been foisted on you, Tessa. But you must allow yourself the right to grieve too. Ever since I put down the phone I have been thinking about what you told me, how the pain was worse than it would have been had you and Steven stayed together. I think you *have been* grieving – for the loss of him, the man he used to be, the marriage you wanted it to be. And it would only be human if you had been thinking more than usual about the happier times. But we know the breach was real – that anger, that sadness. Steven was changed by this Byzantine business that has dogged Robert's disappearance. We have all been changed. As I said, Grey holds himself responsible, for not seeing sooner, acting sooner – and nothing you or I could say would assuage him, because he's always been a man who wants to act as if our fate is in our hands – fights the idea that some things are beyond our control.

He does truly appreciate your kind concern for his health, and be assured I do too. I fear that at the funeral you'll see all too clearly what this ordeal has done to him, the appalling stress. With his usual steadfastness he's set about the prescribed rehabilitation: a sort of speed-walk three times weekly (which he hates, is drained by), the regimen of half-a-dozen bottles of pills . . . But if I am honest, Tessa – after the tumult of events, I see a sort of dead-calmness in him, a sense of futility I never thought I'd see, as if his core faith in life had been blasted away. I get tearful, I worry over his silences, wish he would talk. 'What can I say?' he tells me. I suppose it is depression – or more simply, heartache. (He wouldn't accept the first label.) Of course he assures me, 'I'll buck myself up . . .' I have told him he must, must abandon any further thoughts of Robert and that 'investigation', since no good comes of it, and the conclusion must be that Robert, if not dead and gone, is 'lost'. He accepts this, I believe – knows he's been living a forlorn obsession. But now I think he has a new matter to fixate on – the fear he'll have another coronary. There's no medical reason to expect it, but then Grey is not quite in a medical frame of mind any more. It's as if he's begun superstitiously to fear something living in the shadows. And no medicine, no plan of exercise will ward that away.

But just as I have instructed him, I must myself not dwell on it – and I wish for you too, Tessa, that you will start to find some peace, see some light, in the days, weeks, months ahead. We are here for you.

With much love to you and the boys,

Livy

To Malena Absalonsen
October 3rd

Dear Malena:

Thank you so much for your call and kind concern. I'm only sorry we weren't around to pick up. I must tell you Grey's mobile is 'confiscated' for the time being. You did hear correctly, alas – he suffered a cardiac episode and will have to take some time in recuperation. I have been put in the improbable job of managing his affairs for however long will be his extended leave from work. A falling-off for 'the big man', as you can imagine. But he takes it seriously, as do I. He sends to you his fondest regards as always.

Malena, I do want you to know that, while I'm aware you and I have never been so close as you are to my husband, perhaps even to my son, I do admire you and consider you a friend. So I hope this finds you well and in some peace after what you were subjected to, and that you are keeping comfortable and looking forward (with whatever trepidation!) to the great adventure ahead. Forgive me for over-sentiment, but I really feel your pregnancy has been the one hopeful, uplifting occurrence among 'our circle' of late, while we have been subjected to some kind of cosmic vendetta. I'm certain you will have a fine boy, a commingling of the best of the two of you. I know nothing can obviate the sadness of what befell his father, but clearly the conception was a product of your love for one another, your shared wish. There's no reason the child's life should be overshadowed by what then followed.

Will you forgive me if I turn again to some matters of great sadness? I have very bad news to relate. Steven Hartford took his own life two days ago, an overdose of antidepressants. He and Tessa had decided to separate, he'd taken himself off to their cottage out at Dungeness, had been there a week or so, and that's where he was found, by a cleaning firm he'd hired to come in. That's the saddest thing: he had planned to return to London, and to leave a property ready to be put on the market. Yet overnight he evidently made a fateful decision. There's evidence he had some dalliance with a local woman in his last days, but nothing to suggest he met his end by any hand but his own. It is a dreadful loss for all of us, I know you will feel it too.

My second piece of news concerns Robert. You will understand I am sorry to be the bearer, but Grey has asked me to make you aware of a new and unwelcome development in what has been a fitful investigation. It was relayed to us by Hagen, the detective, who called to our house late this afternoon. I admit I wasn't sure Grey was 'up to' this visit, I kept a proprietor-like grip on his arm, insisted whatever was said got said before myself and Cal too. Thus Hagen told us the clothes Robert was believed to have worn at the time of his disappearance – a black suit, white shirt, red tie, all with the Armani label – have been found draped around a scarecrow on an allotment in north London. The owner called the police: Robert's wallet was in the coat, albeit stripped of cash and cards. As evidence the materials are hopelessly compromised after all this time and weather. But Grey took this news heavily, believes it is confirmation that Robert is dead. Hagen seems to agree. Calder, too, was very cut up, as of course was I, and I appreciate it will come as upsetting news to you above all.

I wish I could tell you more clearly what is the police view, Malena, but this Hagen's manner was perplexing. Grey had certain questions, concerning Steven, and a woman he believes Robert was associating with before he disappeared. Hagen seemed to shrug all this aside, make out as if Grey has a screw loose, 'chasing shadows'. His language was inappropriate, insensitive, as if he didn't mind causing upset, which he certainly did. Grey was angered too, and baffled, for he'd formed a better opinion of this man. I must say, he even seemed almost amused by Grey's obvious ill health. 'You need a rest from your labours,' he said, 'a new lease on life.' Grey assured him, between gritted teeth, that he intended to take every conceivable care and then return to his work, to which Hagen replied – somehow coldly, I thought – 'Of course, Doctor Lochran, it will be done as you decide . . .' Most odd.

Cal was really bridling on his father's behalf, and after Hagen was gone he was most zealous to impress on Grey that his Uncle Rab couldn't be given up for dead just on this evidence. But I was very struck by Grey's reply, which issued very heavily from him. 'I just wonder now,' he said, 'did I really know your uncle? He seems more like a stranger to me. If he were to reappear now? I'm not sure I wouldn't bar the door.' I have to say, Malena, that Grey's perception of Robert has shifted somewhat of late, in a way that you would no doubt recognise, though Cal very much retains a godson's faith in the man he knew.

You will be gratified to know that Cal has shown a huge maturity throughout these trying recent weeks. We know you have always followed his progress with interest, and he sends you his regards. Grey and I feel we owe him our closest attention and care right now. He has been through some curious stages, as befits his time of life, but we've been reminded of his true character, and we're doubly mindful of this important year ahead for him and his future plans.

Please keep in touch, write and tell me how you are feeling and coping. We will want to know, and send our best wishes. You are in our thoughts.

Yours ever,

Olivia

To Tessa Hartford
October 5th

Dear Tessa:

I am so sorry your calls have gone unanswered, Grey and I have been in a terrible way for the last forty-eight hours. A catastrophe has been averted, but we have gone through hell and had no rest since. Two nights ago Calder tried to take his own life while Grey and I slept, attempted to hang himself, in his bedroom, with a belt round his neck. By some heaven-sent stroke Grey woke up and managed to intervene, undoubtedly saving Cal's life. The wait for emergency services was an agony, and we had further panic in the intensive therapy unit – the painful-looking intubation and ventilation, fears about cardiac arrest, about brain damage. But Cal has now stabilised.

Yesterday morning I saw the spots of colour amid his pallor, the slow rise of heart and pulse. By the afternoon he'd regained an imperfect sort of consciousness, very drowsy, mentally sluggish, with a few clearly confused notions in his head. With a thick tongue he complained of pains all over. His short-term memory is impaired, for how long I don't know. We know he will require psychiatric consultation.

Now, though, we are just living with the despair, asking ourselves how it could have happened, how our boy sank so low and we failed to see it. The growing-pain troubles we've had with him in the past just seem as nothing now – yes he has been feckless, at times introspective, but lately he had responded with maturity to our troubles. Now this.

We have been replaying and replaying the events of the last few days, weeks, looking for some clue, some explanation. In truth, he had seemed sombre. We wonder if he was especially upset by Steven's funeral. Of course they were never especially close, not as Cal was to Robert, say, but there was an affection, for sure, and the funeral was a deeply mournful occasion. Cal was visibly moved as we all were by Grey's eulogy, knowing it was a deeply felt observance on his father's part, and having some share in the sense of what we have lost both in Steven and, so it sadly seems, Robert. That added, I think, to the gloom around us, certainly around Cal.

There was also an episode, a disagreement, the night before, which we obviously regret. Cal 'relapsed' to a habit with which we'd become worryingly familiar: going AWOL, leaving the house without announcement and being gone for most of the night, no answer from his phone. Grey drove out to some spots he believed possible, forlornly. He got back, quite beside himself, and we were down in the kitchen talking seriously about contacting the police, when I looked to the back porch and saw Cal's unmistakable shadow through the door's opaque glass. Once he was in, though, he seemed glazed, dull, lethargic. He told us he'd been by the canal, Grey refused to believe him, after having driven there, Cal only shrugged. Grey wanted to talk, nearly wanted to shake him, I think, just because we've been through this before – told him he was putting us through needless worry, 'being a bastard'.

'I'm much, much worse,' he said. 'You should have barred the door.' This a reference to something Grey had said the other day in relation to Robert. I found it strange, unsettling, this identification with Robert. But evidence of the inner turmoil he's carried.

The night it happened – we'd all retired unhappily to our bedrooms. God help us, we might never have known until it was too late. But Grey has suffered from disturbing dreams lately, and he awoke from another in the startled manner I've become familiar with. This time, though, he surged out of the bedcovers, ran from the room and I was so alarmed I followed. He was beating on Cal's locked door, getting no answer, he ran and fetched a club hammer and just smashed the latch. We were met by the most dreadful sight I have ever seen, Cal up by his neck from a belt he'd fastened round the beam, chair kicked away under him. I froze in the horror of it, but I heard a sound from Grey as if he'd been gored, then he lunged into action, frantic, tearful, getting the chair up, freeing Cal, hefting his weight down to the floor, cradling his head and neck. All I could see were Cal's eyes, prominent, glassy, pupils wide and fixed, his lips so livid, skin so ashen, a depression like an oblique slash on his neck. I screamed then, but Grey told me to just hurry and get the ambulance, because there was a pulse. Then he started breathing into Cal's mouth, I did as I was told. The next minutes were hellish, but the ambulance was very fast – Grey was dealing with the paramedic questions, I felt he had control and somehow the worst of all worlds was receding. As we rode together to the hospital he told me the 'drop' had been short, and Cal couldn't have been suspended long. Our real salvation was the nightmare that woke Grey. He told me it had involved his old friend Edmond Warner, who died some years back.

We are thankful, so thankful – because for an agonising stretch I know we had both been thinking the same – what would we do, what would Grey and I be, without our boy? Keep us in your good thoughts.

With all our love,

Livy

To Malena Absalonsen
October 8th

Dear Malena:
We are distraught. Two days ago, at some point unbeknownst to us, Calder slipped out of the house and he has yet to return. We discovered in due course that he had packed a bag, gone on to withdraw money from a bank, acted, in other words, with intent. But given the condition he's in both physically and mentally we didn't hesitate to call the police.

Malena, if by any chance he should make any sort of contact with you, if anything should reach you from him or concerning him – please, please pick up the phone to us straight away. I know you'll understand the despair we are in. All the worst feelings are rushing back. The small positives we had to hold onto are gone. We are in fear all the time – Grey is heartbroken, heartbroken. Neither of us can understand why Cal would do this unless he was in the gravest confusion, why he would put us through it. My worst fear is for his mental state, the chance he might come to harm.

After we brought him home from hospital, still very subdued and unwell, confused and struggling with memory, yet responsive to us – I was so hopeful, felt we'd had a blessing. We began to rebuild brick by brick, as we were advised. But then there was a deterioration. That first night back at home I'd left him sleeping, but I heard him sobbing, went to him, he was inconsolable, desolate. I asked him, 'Are you remembering things, Cal? Have you remembered why you tried to hurt yourself?'

'I remember everything now,' he said, but would say no more. We just sat in grievous silence. Grey hobbled in but it was as if Cal couldn't stand to be in his presence, recoiled from his gaze. And still he kept saying, 'I'm sorry, Grey, so sorry . . .' He'd never called his father by his first name before – that was so much the stranger to us. But Grey hugged him, pulled him into such a fervent embrace, talked to him in a way that made me cry: 'I know you can't see it, Cal, but your life is a precious thing, the world's out there waiting for you – you have it all going for you, son, you really do.' Cal, though – he just looked so broken down, inert, bereft.

'It wasn't enough, Grey,' he said. 'Just not enough. I'll explain.'

And we sat there, and he looked at us hauntingly – we were waiting for him to speak but he didn't.

What he did instead was begin to write, alone at his laptop, behind a closed door, for hours and hours. He shunned our company, really, hardly spoke. We've had the computer professionally scanned, on the hard disk is a large hidden file, password-protected, but we hope to get it somehow decoded – it must be what he was at work on so feverishly, the contents must be meaningful somehow, we're convinced.

Grey himself had been writing a diary every day for some weeks, since Robert disappeared – I had come to see it as a morbid symptom. But he'd dropped that, he'd been vowing to me that everything henceforward would be Cal and I, family first from now on. 'I'll make things right, spend whatever time it takes,' he said. Now we're left sick with the feeling we were too late.

Last night when we ate – when Grey insisted I ate something, was prepared himself to prepare it – he also set a place for Cal, lifted a glass to him, his voice awfully strained. 'Where have you taken yourself to, son?' were his words. 'Don't leave us lost in the dark.' This morning he told me with surprising vehemence that if Cal doesn't reappear then he will go out and find him, cross land and sea, 'whatever it takes'. But even if we had any realistic hope in that – Grey hasn't the strength. All we can do is wait, pray for news to come.

Keep us in your thoughts, Malena. We are support to one another, Grey and I, strong together always, but . . . really, we have to ask the sky whatever did we do to deserve this? Who decided that we – all of us – should have to suffer so much?

Yours, always,

Olivia

PART IV

THE CONFESSION OF
DOCTOR FORREST

How to begin? *'I, Robert Forrest, being of sound mind and body . . .'*

I have my wits about me still, however badly I wish otherwise – no, for me it is reason right down to the end. And yet, who will believe me? Or imagine anything but that I've lived a dream?

As for my body – well, that has had no 'soundness' about it for quite some time. I have been, in the words of the prophet, that creature void of form.

Where I'm bound for now I cannot imagine. I no longer have Her as my guide, counsel, scourge. But when last we spoke I demanded that She tell me what 'Hell' is. This was for Her a glorious, exultant moment, I'm sure. Her incisors gleamed in Her red mouth.

'The lower depths, place of the dead – how you say, Hades? Pandemonium? Pokol, Sheol, Abaddon, Gehenna, Tophet . . . Daydreams of mankind, most admirable fancies! The doctrine of endless punishment – lake of fire, infinitely slow-grinding rack – these, for sure, are splendid notions. But Hell is only what befits the guilty man, doctor. For some, who lived in gross excess of their meagre selves – a term of solitary confinement, utter deprivation, that will suffice. To be tortured by tedium alone, by nullity. Others will have been so unfeeling in their former lives that – yes – they re-

quire a physical shock, prolonged, a rending. But then there is a certain ingrate breed, who saw not what they had, or knew but would not act – they must come back, suffer it all again – the punishment of return, which is yours.'

I asked Her then what had never before occurred. 'How many others are like me?' She looked at me as a mother would.

'Oh, no one is quite like you, doctor. And yet, be it said, "Hades" is full of your sort. You are more gifted than most, a prize in that way. And yet, finally, no better than the strop is to the blade. No, it would be against nature, the right way of all things, if one such as you did not come onto us.'

'And the ones I— whose deaths I caused?'

'That you killed? Your victims?'

'What happened to them?'

'You are hoping perhaps you delivered them, at least, to their maker. Well, they are consoled, some of them, perhaps. Perhaps not. But that is no business of yours or mine. Did you imagine I knew better? I am only the most mediocre familiar – minion, common doppelgänger – just as low a sort as was needed in your case . . .'

Such relish for Her in my disgrace. How fatuous was I, to revel in the seeming proof of my theory that the Devil is a woman? The woman was only the instrument, the knife that fitted the wound, fashioned bespoke for use on me alone. Why didn't I see? In my foolishness, in my fear, again I hear that false, evil, musical laugh, sonorous between my ears.

It happened this way: I reached my middle years in life and, somehow, felt the urge to protest my lot. The risible folly of it strikes me now like a boot in the gut. God no, my life had been lucky, charmed, if any orphan can be counted so.

My sober-sided aunt and uncle gave me all they had. I was cared for, reared, educated to an enviable standard, while they scrimped and sacrificed. I straightened up just because Allan and Jenny, so solemnly, asked me to – I saw a door was open but would very shortly close, and I hared through it.

Yes, there was anger planted in me, having witnessed my father's depredations. Always I will see my 7-year-old self, trailing home early from backstreet football to find him in the living room, ruddily naked, odiously drunk, that woman spread beneath him. Then, not satisfied with stealing my innocence, he stole my mother too. Always I felt infected by his blood in me. And yet while still a schoolboy I came to learn – it hit me with the force of revelation – we are not our forebears, we can fly free of that. Why, then, did I fail?

It was at Kilmuir that I formally became Myself – where, however much I felt I was Many, I resolved to be seen as One. The school uniform proved helpful: I put it on and liked the look of myself. Grey, amusingly, took me at first for one as posh as him. But I could carry it off, that role. Street fights had taught me to be quick to rile, impervious to pain – I had only to polish these virtues by a certain tone of voice. This I recognised as the fellow my friends saw when they looked at me; my greatest sham posture, or so it seemed then.

I grew up able-bodied and vigorous, a 'quick study', my wits about me, better than pleasant to look at. Moreover I had inside what a vital human creature needs: something that wanted expression. The world didn't scare me, it was a field where I intended to roam at large, hungry for knowledge and attainment, also to make a good show. Laughter came easily to me. I found that I liked a lot of people, and that, on the whole, they liked me back, at least when I wished them to – women above all, since I had the means. Such enemies as I made, I was comfortable enough in my own skin to shrug them aside.

So, for as long as I remain I will have to ask myself – why this secret wound inside? A shadow dogged me, always. Was it put there at the kirk where I was dragged by honest Allan and Jenny? For sure I was cursed with old Calvin's sense of the body as the prison-house of the soul. All through my youth I was fighting dual urges: the pull to excel, to make something of myself – and a warring desire, to run all my energies to waste, down that same hole in the ground into which all life tends, the great endlessly spiralling vortex. That second desire, impossible to assuage, felt like a wound at the core of my being.

But in that wound I seemed to find something essential to me, essential if not eternal, there was no shifting it, and it was my friend if not always my helper – that is to say, it never let me down. This was 'I', me, mine: I could not deny it, nor say I hadn't tried it and liked it. It was in my blood, perennial, an ever-combustible agent, forever setting me on fire. Years failed to put it out, always I felt myself burning.

Yes, I had enough discipline and willpower, enough of the sense I was born with, to pull clear of the vortex, carve out a fine career, the least my hungry ego demanded. I felt the call of money, the nag of material wants. So I made a success of myself, made something of my name. With time, though, I came to wonder what they would say of me once I was gone. Most likely, that I hadn't done the work I could have. True, I was less than the man I'd believed I would be. My vocation failed me, I disappointed myself above all . . . It's no excuse, I know, only the commonest woe. The cure is to buck up, count your blessings, *get on with you, son*. But we won't always be told, will we?

It was too sharp in my breast, this want of something that life couldn't requite – because 'human life is limited but I would like to live forever'. Since one life couldn't be enough, for what reason had I ever existed? That was the distress call She heard and answered, heard it for the despicable vanity it was. And now I have had such a lesson, oh yes, no end of a lesson.

I believed I could soar. Rather, I have had my face rubbed in the filth of my lowest fears, jealousies, prejudices – one after another. I was given treats, yes, but they were only the sugar of the fly-trap, sweet enough that I be drawn back, there to have my wings picked anew by the wanton girl. I was tricked by the trickster, but I let it be so – I let evil suffuse me, so I could carry on, just one more life, one more . . . I could even fool myself there was something fit, fated, in each of my victims. Until the last.

Ꝯℓ

The subterranean plot against me ground its mills slowly. I was on the cusp of a crisis, had built a reputation to the point where I could imagine nothing more gratifying than to toss it away. Gloom had settled on me. 'Career' had made me a slave to money, to work I despised. That streak in me, that urge to test my luck – because luck is magic! – had proved to be a failed gamble. Really, what I had needed was some of Grey's good steadfastness. But I was tired of old and worn-out friends, the staidness of their lives nailed in place by children and attendant chores.

Then I woke up at 45 years of age, looked hard at the mirror, saw that my future faced cancellation. My body was revolting against me. How badly I needed some colour to my complexion, some white in my eye, a lift in the slackness and heaviness of the flesh envelope.

At least, I consoled myself, *I had Malena* . . . Whatever the differences in our habits, the coincidence of our moods was always extraordinary. We were co-conspirators. We knew what was fraudulent about the world and what it cost us to live in it. She understood my need for privacy, largely left me to it. With her – I don't say I never 'looked' at another woman, but when I did it was a whim, nothing more. Malena no man could ever tire of. For all my regrets in life, loving her was the one thing that floated free and clear.

How *fine* that it was then Malena wrote me a letter, just as wise as its writer! How dearly I didn't care to know precisely what was on her mind, the complex little byways of her heart, the sound bases of her carefully weighed decision to leave me . . . Spare me, darling. Accept yourself as a quitter, deserter, traitor, shallow and self-serving. How I loathed her cruel-to-be-kind candour, her formidable emotional maturity, her warm wish that God would bless me and keep me. I can see the page still, and still I think: go fuck yourself, woman, get all your fist into your gob and stuff your pity back down your throat. If you don't choke, may it poison you, you and your little faggot boyfriend.

Thus my lover's tribute to her. Thus what love can do.

اه

A single man again, then. Still a 'catch'. But times had changed. I had used to devour a space with my eyes, such questing in my radar-appraisal of the talent in a room, so directed was I to the sexual-comestible, signs of good sport – a dirty laugh or an insolent look, didn't matter. Beauty, of course, was key: not merely the face, the whole structure, the integrity of line and the promise of some pleasing give— succulence, hidden and scented depth, delights to be made bare. But what now did I offer in return? With the best of my looks had gone a complementary portion of my charm, my ease. The mirror showed me blood in my eyes, drinker's wrinkles, grey in the hair and the creeping widow's peak, my now-habitual frown.

Not the worst-looking fellow, of course . . . but no more appealing than the sum of his social status plus your best guess at his bank balance. Which, in my case, was waning.

I soldiered on, of course, but had to endure rejection, and learning this lesson so late I learned it less well. I couldn't fail to notice the gazes of young girls flicking past my shoulder, however warm the lipstick-smile. I had been used to finding the limits of women, the soft cores of dependency and fear, before making my exit. (To wit: Eloise Keaton, whom I treated appallingly, once I'd lowered her protective shield of cheek, exposed the nervy girl who chattered to herself for reassurance.) Now, a majority of women appeared to think me just so disposable. Even where I got lucky – I could feel the women, in their *essences*, had begun to elude me. Intercourse now seemed a sort of gift for which I was meant to be truly grateful. I was paying for sex, whether or not I cared to see it that way. And like the client, I slept alone.

⚓

The rot, the infestation – as I recall, it began properly on what was Day #149 after Malena's departure.

The previous day I'd flicked idly through *Fine Art* magazine in my waiting room; seen the generous interview-profile of Killian MacCabe, accompanied by that languorous photo of him and Malena, her face pressed to his back, arms round his waist, eyes closed in the sun-warmth of love . . . That afternoon I cancelled Mrs Huffington's eyelift (cancelled also the subscription to

Fine Art), went to see Steven, and he wrote me a prescription for Remeron. '*I have to warn you, Robert,*' he said, with that Steven look, '*in your condition you might experience hallucinations . . .*'

I went to bed unusually early, not quite so benumbed by 12-year-old Balvenie as had become my crutch. My feeling on waking was so strange. I had slept for thirteen hours, and it seemed as though I'd been dreaming all that time – so vividly that for some moments I really struggled to remember who I was, what I'd done in this life.

Morning had crept into the room, swept the night shadows into corners, dispelled their grey hold – the light reviving all that was old and familiar. *Back to life*, the light said. *To the daily round, and burdens carried forward* . . . As I rolled about heavily under the covers, my regular aches and pains returned, as did the fragments of my biography. And yet I so badly wanted to revisit the dreams, in which I had been younger – a schoolboy, a student again. The eyes through which I had looked were those of a person half-formed but teeming with possibility.

The end of the dream, though, was disturbing: I was out in the city at night, walking darkened deserted streets, wanting to be bare as they were. I tore off my clothes, as if daring the night to confront me with some stranger. Then I had the sensation of rising, climbing, vaulting over rooftops, of being at large: an aura of predation, the tang of someone's fear, mine or someone else's, I couldn't say.

Resigned to wakefulness I got up, got dressed: formerly a hallowed rite in my day. From the day I started earning proper money I dressed well, always there was magic for me in throwing open the wardrobe door, revealing a costumier's wealth of hanging and folded apparel, accessories to be assumed. As if the wardrobe contained not merely the means of a transformation but even the doorway to another realm, akin to our own, yet strangely altered.

This game, though, had lost all its charm for me. My silent habitat, empty but for me (empty including me?), had come to feel like a stage-set bereft of an audience. It was too sparse, too neat, bizarrely untouched but by gathering dust, and defined by a very specific absence. Its stifling order was the cursed mark of myself. What it lacked was the creative chaos of my ex-wife.

So I stood there before the wardrobe, naked, heavily inert, thinking to myself: *Too much aloneness, it puts the head in bad places. As if one might do anything and it wouldn't matter.*

﷽

That day at the clinic was as dispiriting as any before. The morning with Lucinda Millard, discussing her labial tuck, dissuading her from any eye-watering foolishness around the clitoral hood. The lunch-hour rhinoplasty on Suraya Chakrabati, an entirely pointless finesse upon the facts. Then the post-lunch erasure of Eugenie Grainger's double-chin. For what these women pay me, I knew they expected more than my increasingly mordant and taciturn manners. Still, I saw myself behaving thus and there was nothing I could do about it. *Depression* . . .

With Mrs Grainger wheeled off to day-care, I made a decision to give myself a treat, bring home something old and beautiful. I cleaned up, drove south through Kensington down to Mayersburg's of Fulham, the great and sombre Victorian antiques warehouse. There I wandered down the long central aisle lit by globes, amid fellow collectors and refugees from the work ethic, each of us searching for gold. I spotted mine rising like an imperious ghost out of a cluster of dusty hanging mirrors stacked against crates. It was a tall ambiguous shape under a dust cover, blank as an installation by Christo. With no assistant nearby I took it on myself to tug away the heavy sheet. And there stood a huge, oval-shaped cheval glass, its frame carved from black walnut, crested by a garlanded cartouche with a relief of serpents, sinuously entwined. French, I decided, Empire style. Leaning closer, I found a pleasing wear and mottle to the plate glass, such that I could bear to see my own face. It was a fancy, no doubt, grotesque, perhaps – but a glorious piece. I had to have it. It seemed as though I'd been meant to free it from bondage. Delivery was arranged and I took receipt two days later, had the shifters lump it upstairs and into 'the closet'. The sheer dilettante-impracticality of the whole procedure had me laughing in wonder at myself, albeit not for long.

That evening I was expected to take up my patron's invite to the opening of the retrospective of French *fin de siècle* art, Odilon Redon, Gustave Moreau and other such horrors. I changed and had a dram of the Tyrconnell. Evening crept in but I kept the lights out, moving from unlit room to unlit room, beginning to feel incorporeal, observing my shadow from the corner of my eye as it watched me in turn.

At the exhibition I very soon, very wearily, felt my turning out had been an error. The main room was packed by private equity barons and tedious academicians; and the art, as I'd anticipated, was sickly: a profusion of crowded, opulent scenes, women routinely and luxuriously naked, men bent double with gross desire – in short, it dripped with sex, the painter's evident arousal barely masked by his brushwork. Still, the crowd had turned out for a highbrow turn-on, a spot of divine decadence. And wasn't I slipping about among them, sipping my tepid white wine? Still, I felt mocked by it all. Was man no more than this?

And then – I found myself following the movements of a young woman, a pearl among the swine, stepping lightly from canvas to canvas like a school pupil discovering 'the gallery' for the first time, instructed to take notes. A *belle dame*, without doubt, but the real genius was in how she'd attired herself. The dark chocolate of her hair was fastened up, her dress looked to me classic Yves Saint Laurent – black watered silk, bias cut on the bodice, with a voluminous skirt, bluish in its blackness where the light from the chandeliers rippled.

Could she feel the weight of my gaze? I wasn't concerned, for somehow it was as if I'd felt her eye on me first. I was intrigued, yes, for all my failing confidence of late – interested enough to keep looking, to see whose company she would join, whose arm she would take.

Instead she turned, smiling slightly to herself, stepped through the crowd and directly out into the evening. I was quite certain her exit had been for my benefit alone. I set down my glass on a plinth, and pursued her.

She was wandering alone down Bankside, swaying eloquently in the gloom, poised in such a way as to make her seem less vulnerable than a young woman otherwise would on a dim-lit and near-deserted riverside walkway. For a while I kept a cautious distance – I had no notion yet of what I would say to her, if I had the nerve. The longer I followed, the less I felt capable, yet I followed still.

Then, twenty yards ahead of me, she stopped, turned, her expression unreadable in the dark. My lips parted but no sound came – what I heard instead was the slap of soles on concrete behind me, then the blur of a man running past, directly at her. I saw her alarm, felt some kind of entreaty in my head. Then she, too, was running, but hopelessly, in heels, and the man – sturdy, Slavic-looking, vehement – was onto her, grabbing her, restraining her. She cried out, and in that moment I knew this was my deliverance from the role of shabby voyeur. I had instead been appointed rescuer.

I waded into the tussle, gave her attacker a hard shove then threw a punch at his jaw, the connection solid, numbing my fingers but knocking him down. I seized her hand, then we were running together, heading for the flight of stone steps that would bring us up onto London Bridge. I was already struggling for breath when I heard him bounding up the steps at our heels, so I turned and kicked out at his face. He fell again, harder, down a dozen steps to land on his head and shoulder. Then he didn't move. I turned, saw her wide-eyed face above me, took her arm again. And on we rushed.

Minutes later we were rattling past St Paul's in the back of a black taxi. Facing one another, still we hadn't exchanged one word I could remember. Her expression, which I had first taken for a kind of shell-shocked gratitude, now seemed rather cool and evaluating.

'That man back there?' I asked. 'Did you know him?'

She shook her head, then abruptly laughed – a tinkling, musical laugh. 'But happily for me, you came.'

I assumed then that I'd guessed correctly back at the gallery. At what stage she told me her name was 'Dijana Vukovara', at what point we agreed I should escort her all the way and up to her apartment on Cavendish . . . I simply can't say, for our journey there felt as if borne up on a kind of tide, and I was giddy – the adrenalin of the ruck, perhaps, but I felt my pulse was steady, even a little slowed. The world about me had become fogged and torpid too; and it was as though we were alone in it, two alone together.

The apartment was startlingly bare and semi-decrepit, as if vacant and awaiting renovation. Had she just moved in? I didn't ask. As a habitat it seemed to mimic my own, a mere rehearsal-space for a life. The first of the double reception rooms, at least, had heavy old red drapes and matching armchairs. I sat as I was bade. She lit candles over the fireplace, one, two, three, then turned with a demure look.

'Excuse me. I will retrieve what you need.'

She vanished through the partition doors. I rose and followed her. And the sight that met my eyes made me laugh aloud – for there was nothing whatsoever in the next room save for, centre-stage, my cheval glass. I say 'mine' since I couldn't believe it was anything but one of a kind. So the 'logical' explanation was that some form of sorcery had transported it. Suddenly she was standing there before the mirror, holding a decanter of sea-dark wine. But nothing came out of my fish-like mouth save for *'You know, it's the damnedest thing . . .'*

We resumed our seats. She loosened her hair and it fell down as a braid, while she tilted her chin at me, girlish, haughty but amused. Now, in this setting, her dress for the night struck me more as a hired costume than a piece from her own wardrobe. Still, I sat there wholly pleased with myself, 'the hero'. And this strange, slight-smiling girl seemed to find me worthy of her whole attention, as though she'd been waiting for me. We talked – rather, I talked, rambled, even – about the exhibition and its tackiness, London and its shortcomings, my life and its recent dysfunction, Malena's leaving me, my sexual loneliness, my sexual preferences . . . She sat, never moved, yet my glass was never empty. Her eyes seemed to draw more light as darkness engulfed the room. But seeing her smile at me, I was so sure we would be in bed before midnight – if bed she had, somewhere in this shell of a dwelling. And so I minded not a great deal once the fog crept in.

Then I was home again, like I'd never left – waking blearily to morning shadows, heavy-headed and trapped in a nagging, goading state of semi-arousal. I admit I could have happily fucked a hole in a toilet-stall wall. But there was something else at work, another feeling, in the vicinity of my heart, some charm working on me. I got up, went to my closet, saw my cheval glass standing there, imponderable.

For what I think were some weeks thereafter, I visited her every night, my work-days slipping by in an agreeable daze, for I knew that within a few short hours I would be stepping over her threshold, back into her world, taking my chair, the wine poured, her perfect face before me – a sense of suspension so ripe it had the feeling of reverie. And yet when I think about how and why I paid her these calls – nothing occurs to me. Darkness seemed to billow outward, wrap itself round me, engulf me, then I was gone.

Even when we were apart, she seemed to be beside me, albeit in peculiar fugues I can't recall. For sure I saw her continually, was good for little else. One night, at least, I broke the habit by accepting an invite to Grey's, and over a succession of brandies I found I had to share with him some of my wonder. 'There's no fool like an old fool,' said he, not unkindly, puffing amusedly on his Montecristo Robusto. Still, I had to see her, had to have her company. And when we were together I couldn't imagine us apart, for all that each night ended in the same fashion, my return alone to the chilly envelope of my bed.

Then, one night, she came to call on me.

I was sitting in my living room, browsing the *New England Journal* under the standing lamp, curtains open to the night. The room was, as ever, full of recesses and shadows that no light could fully shift. I grew aware of a draught, but not from the window behind me – no, this came from before – from the armchair by the recess, out of the light, where, it now appeared, someone sat.

'Dijana . . . ? Is that you?'

'Doctor. Please. You're not so sick. You expected me.'

'But, how did you get in?'

She didn't answer, only stood up and twirled. 'How do I look?'

Her 'look' was well heeled and yet somehow second-hand, picked from a pawn shop or some vintage outfitter. She wore a black velvet Russian coat with folded cuffs and half-belt, a tad shabby. Glaring from the middle finger of her right hand was a gold ring set with a fat fake ruby.

'Exquisite,' I murmured.

'Yes? Yes, I've decided – I chose well. It wasn't my ideal, rather more necessity, mother of invention. But, it seems to have worked.'

I got up and lurched toward the tantalus. 'Let me fix us both a drink.'

'But why?'

'Listen, I need a fresh drink.'

'Doctor. You need a fresh liver. A fresh "look" altogether. To slip inside of something altogether new. Wouldn't you say?'

I stood there and by her slight smile I knew – yes, it was past time for me to lay hands on her. The challenge of her eye, if nothing else, surely invited me.

'I'm sorry, did you want to examine me, doctor?'

She unbuttoned the coat, under which, remarkably, she was naked, then shrugged the black velvet off her shoulders. As she walked toward the stairs I studied her sway, the serpent line of her notched spine, loose hair lustrous on her shoulder-blades. She half-turned her head, presumably to observe my progress, though all she saw was that I wasn't moving. It was almost too regnant a performance.

'Is this your party piece?' I managed to say.

'It has been known', she murmured, 'to have an effect.'

I drained my glass as I studied her, that European body drifting down the upstairs landing, through my bedroom door. At last I mounted those stairs, followed her footsteps, found her there, ready and waiting. With what languor she'd spread herself across my bed! I got down over her, kissed her mouth, feeling her hard teeth behind her lips. I touched her, the impress of her flesh chill, firm, waxen.

You will imagine, then, the sudden sickness I felt in the realisation that I wasn't functioning – would not, for whatever unearthly reason, be capable of the deed. I just couldn't understand it. She, however, grinned at me, a kind of gleeful pity. I sat up onto the edge of the bed, riled, humiliated. In the silence a cloud, blood-red, seemed to descend over my eyes. And then I heard her – as I would hear myself think. Was she whispering in my ear? Or was her voice inside my head?

'*Uroboros* . . .', she seemed to breathe, and I felt the sharp prod of a nail at the faded tattoo on my bicep.

'Such a fine mind is yours, doctor. Long and twisting, rich in turns and courses, pulsing with invention like venom. Your body, though . . . ah, already so close to a spent vessel. Shame, such a shame. Just a little more time, a little more surrender to gravity's pull, and you will be an old, old dog, all gone in the teeth. And then, sad to say, who could possibly care?'

Had I really believed for one moment this virago was the late, great love of my life? It now seemed she'd been sent to torment me. I could see her reflected behind me in the glass of the Schiele print on my wall – 'Girl, Semi-Nude, Reclining', and speaking to me still.

'No conquests left for you, doctor. Only shipwrecks. The past then more painful, as life bears you ever closer to nothing, or worse. While the creases in your forehead deepen, your skin turns sallow, eyes sodden and dull. A face cursed by "character", a body abandoned by Nature, bound for the bone-yard . . .'

She had sat up, curled herself round me from behind: her fingers entwined at my waist, her breasts on my back, her chin on my shoulder, her mouth at my ear.

'And you *are* your body, Robert. Nothing else. There is no person apart from a body. I know you know that.'

I nodded, seething. 'What am I supposed to do about it now?'

'Doctor!' Again she prodded me with one red finger-nail. 'You are "supposed" to die. Rotted from inside by your own poison. Autolysis, putrefaction—'

Hearing that I seized her hands and wrenched them from me, threw my weight against her, back down onto the bed. 'Are you even *here*, with me? Because I'm think-

329

ing you could *be* me, just in a woman's skin, saying back
to me all the stupidest things I ever thought—'

Through my spitting rage She grinned up at me. Then
Her eyes turned eight-ball black, Her cheeks and nose
collapsed into a pool of putrescence: instantaneous and
appalling liquefactive necrosis.

I suppose I must have jumped ten feet back from Her,
the fear of God in me, landing painfully on the floor. But
when She rose from the bed Her face was restored, Her
smile serene.

I made it to the bathroom on my hands and knees,
there to vomit into the bowl. When I dared return to
my bedroom it was deserted, but I glimpsed Her figure
through the door to the closet, and I followed Her in.
She was standing by the cheval glass, gazing at me evenly,
then She was gone.

The next morning I dressed and left the house, decided
to walk to the underground. But my steps were heavy, my
eyes dark, the crowded streets indistinct. I felt I'd aged
overnight. I returned home, sequestered myself. Come
the evening I was listening to Bartók's String Quartet #1,
staring out through my window at an orb of a moon in
all her high, mesmeric splendour. Then She was at my
shoulder, Her breath in my ear.

'Who are you?' I said.

In the glass I saw Her reflection put a finger to Her
lips. But I heard Her voice in my head, saying something

so absurd and awful, vertigo-inducing, I simply couldn't accept it. I faced Her.

'What do you want? Why are you taunting me?'

'My intention is to guide you. In midlife, through these woods. Because you wish for a *vita nuova*? Is that not so? You should say it. We have no secrets here.'

'It's what I would want if I could have it, yes. As would anyone. What of it?'

'Be *sure* of what you wish. Is it really the new? Or only the old that you had but lost? To be the great artist, in your physical prime, admired, sought after, loved by the woman you love . . . ?'

'What more is there to want than that?'

'But doctor, somebody else has that life now . . .'

She laid hands on my shoulders, pressed me back round as to face the darkened window – only now we stood side by side at the doorway of some strange bedroom, its features limned by merest moonlight, its atmosphere one of sensual post-coital sleepiness. Killian MacCabe lay across the bed, pale sheets ruched at his groin, something Roman about his sculpted torso and tight dark curls. Then it was as though a breeze rustled through me, and Malena, naked as he, joined him on the bed. They curled into one another, whispering so low I couldn't hear. She laid her head on his chest, he took her long hair in his hands, picked it up and let it pour down softly from his fingers. Were I an honest broker, I would have said they were beautiful together.

But the freezing I felt in my heart was so wretched, I couldn't speak, even though a plea to them to *cease*, *desist*, was pulsing in my head. I believe Vukovara could hear me, but She remained impassive at my side. If I could have got my hands around MacCabe's throat in that moment then, no question, it would have been the end of him.

But reality reclaimed us: a buzzing sound between my ears. It was my front-door intercom, and in the blink of an eye I was opening up to Grey. In my disoriented state I was quite sure Vukovara would disappear – fade into the walls, evaporate through the mirror. Nonetheless I was trying to semaphore to Grey that I needed to be alone when I heard Her trill over my shoulder, saw Grey's eyebrows lift. She had sat Herself down with a drink, ready to receive company. I could hardly contain my anxiety, afraid Her merest touch might prove lethal to my friend. And yet somehow we made it through the risible charade of 'a drink'. The moment I'd seen Grey out, I knew She was gone – leaving me to brood over why She had revealed Herself in this manner.

I did not see Her again for some days. Evidently I was being left to stew. Grey called, told me frankly that he felt I could do far better than my latest 'sweetheart'. I assured him She and I were through. And I wished that were so. But She had got claws into me – about the ruin of my life, the bad joke of my beaten-down dolour. Even with my headspace free of Her voice, nonetheless I felt Her insinuations probing and clinging like a tongue, insistent, irresistible. She had planted something in me – a hatred, an intolerable burning envy I hadn't cared to confess to myself, of the man who stepped into my shoes.

That stage of my harrowing came to a head without warning on a night that Calder paid me one of his little visits. I was sorry, in a way, for my dull, morose manner – hardly good company for a hormonal young buck – but he appeared blithe once I'd poured him a dram and listened to him itemise the delights of his latest squeeze. Then I saw his gaze lift off me and I followed it. Vukovara was descending the staircase – fully clothed at least, in a clinging, stretching black dress.

'Och I'm sorry, Rab,' Cal blurted. 'Didn't know you'd a friend.'

'Nor did I, Cal.'

She rounded my chaise longue and slid onto his, close beside him. 'This is the son of the great Grey . . . ?' Her eyes shone in the half-light, and I didn't care for how She looked at him – he alarmingly glad of the attention, figuratively flexing his young muscles.

'Leave the boy alone,' I snapped. 'He has enough female fans of his own age.' Cal, I saw, didn't care for that 'boy'. By the same token, perhaps, he chose not to dally. With the door shut on him, I confronted Her with a glare. But the contempt in Her eye was immovable.

'You should not waste another moment, doctor. You know, I'm sure, why I have come. Why I showed you what I showed you.'

'Yes,' I said. 'To goad me. Toward an act. Well, hear this. I've no interest in revenge.' In my vehemence I possibly convinced even myself. 'Revenge is fruitless, I'll still be down here in my hole, with my wound. Do you take me for a fool? Hurting *him* only admits what I've lost and can't have back.'

As my words faltered, She leapt into my head.

'What if, by "revenge", you could redeem it all, and more? What if this body, doctor, were not your death? And you could feel again the fire, the vigour, the animating spirit, inside another skin?'

'No, it's impossible, how could I . . . ?'

'I will show you.'

I gripped the sides of my seat, for it felt suddenly as though my head were about to be wrenched off my shoulders. In a trice, I was elsewhere – sat in some bone-hard rocking chair, immersed in darkness. But my surroundings very quickly found focus for me – from the pages of *Fine Art*, no less – as MacCabe's workspace, his 'studio'.

Vukovara stood over a shrouded figure laid flat on a long bench. I stood, hobbled over to Her, knowing the figure was human even before She whipped aside the dust sheet to reveal MacCabe, stretched out and unconscious. With mirth round Her lips She held out to me a chisel and a club hammer. I kept my eyes trained on Hers.

'Of course – as your mentor taught you – you are "forbidden to dissect living subjects". Perhaps some other means to penetrate . . . ?'

She grasped me by my wrists, forced my dumb hands down onto MacCabe's sternum. And there beneath my fingers it was as if his skin were suddenly transparent to the eye. Just as I had been trained to 'visualise', only in three phantastic dimensions, I was seeing past epidermis to muscle, arteries, nerves, bones, viscera, lymph nodes. It was as if incision, the shining genius of surgery – that first fine shock of learning what lies behind the veil of the flesh – had only ever been a clumsy third-rate redundancy. Under my hands, glaringly apparent in the engine-room of Killian's abdominal cavity, was the aorta carrying blood from his heart, and the vena cava, bulging and blue, bearing it back.

'Wondrous, wondrous machine,' She whispered. *'Walls so strong, thick, elastic. Turgid with the health of rich red blood, coursing with every heartbeat. Life, doctor. Years of life . . .'*

She slid a hand onto my shirtfront, Her fingers trespassing between the buttons – and I seized that hand, for fear She intended to slash me open just like MacCabe, unveil to me the pocked, corroded branches of my own aorta, the plodding beat of my own stony heart.

'You see now? What I offer? Flight, from your body. Ownership of his. Do you comprehend? I speak of possession.'

Yes, I understood. And I laughed, bitterly, quite prepared to incur her wrath.

'I see. I am to— kill him? And by killing him, become him?'

'You will end his lease on life and inherit it. This will cause you no pain. You despise him, we know this. You and I, we have no secrets.'

'And how can I kill a body I'm meant to— "inherit"?'

'Fear not, I will know before it falls, the blow of yours that has force to kill. I will recognise your intent. You have heard, of course, the wives' tale of the virgin who was got

*with child? One ray of potent sunlight, that crossed her mu-
cous membrane as if through glass . . . Your great change will
be just like so.'*

The lunacy was so livid, I pushed Her away from me
with every fibre. *'Stop this, leave me alone, let me be.'*

*'Oh, if that is your wish – it will be done as you decide
. . .'*

And I was back standing before my cheval mirror –
gazing at a dying man, or so it seemed. Red-eyed, slack-
skinned, beaten down and haunted by failure. I pressed
my forehead against the cold glass, could feel it mist with
my breath. Cold, then colder still. She was there, at my
side.

'But you must decide now, doctor. I will be with you,
or gone for all time. As you wish it.'

'I can't. Can't do it . . .'

'Can't do what? Say what you mean. In this moment
of all, don't deceive yourself.'

She was right. My true choice was already made. I
could not walk away from it – this offer to stop the clock,
invert the world on its axis, turn day into night and night
into day.

'What you propose . . . I have to leave everything behind?'

'Leave what?'

'The life I've had. Everything that is me will die, yes?'

'No. What was you will live again. Your death a second birth. Is that so strange? We have agreed your body
is yourself – that has been the way of things. But I offer
to break the chain. What makes you believe you are you?

Think back on your life. Have you been One, or Many? Not, indeed, a succession of selves? You have changed before, you can change again.'

'Your offer— is more radical.'

'Radical, yes. A radical flowering of possibility . . .'

'It's a fantasy. A fool's paradise, you're fooling me.'

'Oh, no paradise, no, be assured. I will not lie. You will make payment, in pains. To which all flesh is prey, but in your case, more so. We will have what is ours, doctor, such is our bargain. For you, new life, a new lease, a gift of time. For us, in turn, your submission.'

I credit her this much, she gave me that chance, to step back from the vortex. But I was already lost, had crossed a line, however deep the fog into which I had drifted. If Her designs were malign, it seemed nonetheless a malignity that had long been present inside me. She knew as much, and so She had come. Her very presence had shown me that this life, after all, was not all – She was proof made flesh of a theomorphic power beyond my ken. In the face of that, as a learned man reduced to backward awe – I could only submit.

I saw myself falling and I fell. And – I do say *'Before I knew what I was doing'* – I was sinking arthritically to my knees, raking the floor with fingers splayed, bowing my wretched head before Her.

⁂

In that same instant – I had been sleeping, but now I was awake, albeit in gloom. I stood before the cheval glass, but not mine – rather, that in the rear room of Vukovara's apartment. Nested in the palm of my hand was a scalpel blade. I heard myself breathing, heard voices – saw light – carrying through the bowed doors of the partition. I pushed them apart, and was met by the sight of Her and a tired, scruffily clad, put-out-of-patience Killian MacCabe.

'Aw come on now . . .', he groaned to see me. 'What's *this*?'

'This is my associate, Mr MacCabe,' She purred. 'Doctor Forrest and I are in league and business . . .'

And with that She retreated, stood before the darkling surface of the cheval glass, reflective, as though She were made of the mirror. Clearly She awaited my decision, as if She didn't know, as if She didn't infest every thought in my mind. And MacCabe, my enemy – the apex of the triangle we formed in the space – he looked from Her to me – perplexedly, some veil of concern on his face. I saw his lips move: 'Robert,' he uttered, 'this is all wrong, man . . .' Nothing but wrong, indeed. I knew it, though. His fate was sealed. His, and mine. There was a din in my head and a blazing under my skin, commanding me – *now!* – to turn the tables, take as he had taken – cut him down, be done with him and claim his forfeit.

The scalpel was snug in my hand. I stepped in front of him, saw only the pulsing veins of his throat as he stared back. Then I flung out my arm in a fine rising arc, and barely saw him flinch before blackness fell on me. An after-image, though, stayed seared on my retina – his head thrown back, that blackness behind my eyes an arterial gout.

I experienced a vertiginous tipping and plummeting, the floor collapsing beneath me, and truly I plunged, falling helter-skelter and headlong into black, gathering speed, certain what came next would be the crushing of my skull, the utter pulverisation of my mind. Then it seemed as if I were travelling down a tunnel, a canal – rocketing, seeking a tiny aperture of light, breaching it – and I emerged.

It had taken scant seconds, and now I looked out through alien eyes, swimming back to consciousness, as if reviving from general anaesthetic for the gravest surgery. There at my feet was Robert Forrest . . . my poor self, laid out on the floorboards like one pole-axed by a blow, inert and waxen as a mannequin, fallen to one side, one arm outstretched, its fingers stiff and claw-like as if trying to escape drowning or stop the fall of the coffin lid. I stood over what I knew to be the last resting place of myself, and the vantage was dizzying. I got to my knees, rolled myself over – and something gripped my gullet, the breath forced from me – tears squeezed out too. My old eyes wide and exophthalmic, my mouth torn open and twisted, as though the life-force had made its exit there . . .

I looked up and there She stood, black eyes shining in triumph, teeth bared in delight, a mien of high, vicious amusement. I clambered to my feet, thinking I would lunge at Her . . .

And in that moment, coursing through my new body was a torrent of sensory data. I roiled and I flexed, I knew straight away, I was shorter, fitter, younger, without a doubt, and in that youth was a lightness, a readiness, a capacity.

She gestured to the mirror with a flourish, and I stumbled past Her, peered into its murk – confronting the impossible, at first afraid to touch, then putting fingertips to my soft, bristly cheek. I felt each wonder as I scrutinised it. The strong cheekbones. The fleshy lips. My fingers probing thick black coils of hair.

It was as if a deathly sickness had suddenly and gloriously flowered. The depraved sensation was so strong I wanted to cram a fist into my mouth – that it had been done like so, the sheer violation of it, the wanton exercise of power, that daemonic gift.

I turned back to Her and Her mouth was a line.

'Leave now. The rest is mine.'

Did Her lips move or was Her voice in my head? I knelt once more, reached into 'my' coat pockets – a cold pickpocketing – felt and found my keys, wallet . . . She, though, heard my thoughts.

'No. Hear me. Get out. You are finished here.'

'What'll you do?' This I heard myself blurting out in a South Dublin brogue. She merely bared those incisors, and in an instant I imagined a host of obscenities. But our business was done, I had made my bed, crossed my river, and so I did as I was commanded. I stole away.

Out the door, down the stairs, into the cloudless night and the streets glimmering by moonlight . . . my steps felt at first unsteady, then on air – the sheer outrage of the larceny was rushing through me like a narcotic. I was suffused with sensory newness, pressed onward as if by unseen hands. I'd felt this before only in the princely high of illegal drugs, but as moments passed I found a lucidity that was vital, clear, clean. I had taken on fuel, was holding a charge. It seemed as if I had powers in me over any passer-by, as if I could swat them aside or lift them over my head. (I swerved to miss crashing into a small girl and her grandma.)

I knew if I tried to reason through what I'd undergone then I would be insane. In any case my renewed appetite was such, there was nothing in my head or body that didn't swarm with evil impulse. The disease had reached its full fruition, the corruption complete. There were sins, I knew, that were triumphs, that gifted a quickened sense of joy. I felt the spirit of revolt in me, and I believed my mistress would approve. What could I do now but revel in my fortune? New life was what I had wished for, and it was beginning.

My steps carried me unerringly to where I knew I'd find 'my' car, a green Alfa Romeo Spider. The keys bulged where 'I' kept them always: left jeans pocket. Climbing in, I knocked detritus from the bucket seat, pledged to clear it out, knew I never would. My feet nestled on the pedals, I saw my dark eyes in the rear-view, three-quarter profile in the wings. I pulled out.

And I knew just where I was headed – my home of four years, the home I'd opened to Malena – my love, surely waiting there for me. My old mother disliked her, I knew this suddenly. Ma reckoned her aloof as Lady Muck. But I thought my old mother a meddlesome hypocrite.

The taps were open, the vessel of self filling up in flood-like torrents. Two of us in here, but I much the dominant dog . . . I laughed, punched the tape player, from which a bar-room racket erupted.

'Call me a feckless sinner and I'll tell you 'Go to Hell' for I've taken all my sorrows and I've drowned them down –'

I swapped the tape, found something dulcet.

'In the evening, under the moonlight, my spirits rise for you . . .'

Driving through Maida Vale I rushed a red light and a white van honked at me: 'Aw get on with ye, ye ballox,' was my involuntary response. It seemed an excellent riposte, only a version of what 'I' would normally come out with.

Up the garden path, the façade all climbing ivy, doorway set back under a stone porch, I turned the key, stepped into the hallway – felt the space breathe, inhaled it. To my left hung all my old coats, my old boots stacked below on some incongruous tubular Swedish rack. Then she was there in shadow at the top of the stairs – stairway to heaven! – then descending to me, and a wealth of care was in her lovely face even before she put her hands on my chest, brushed my lips.

342

'You're later than I thought, I was waiting for you. Did it go well? Will you come up and talk to me?'

I stole a long look in her eyes – so open, with her hair tied back – before saying what I knew I had to. 'Aw, didn't happen, babe. Didn't work. What she's after, I couldn't do it, even if I wanted . . .'

She frowned. Instinctively I crooked a finger fondly under her chin. The frown deepened, I realised the gesture was too much 'Robert'. I took her hand, she led me up. She was dressed like a dancer, choice items from her clingy, minimal Dane wardrobe, black leggings and top with crossover neckline. The bedroom was un-aired yet perfumed, sheets crumpled, clothes on the floor, ransacked glossy magazines by the bedside – piles of letters, tubs of hand-cream and neglected hand-tools strewn over the dresser. God, I had missed this mess.

As she turned to me I only smiled (as to say 'Why ever not, my dear?') and kissed her mouth, once, twice, soft kisses – found her hungry for them. Desire's creeping vine was rising like my spirits – for me, a long moribund force resurrected. I wrenched off my jumper, felt a sensual surge just in baring my chest, then lay back on the bed and pulled her onto me. She tugged the black jersey over her head, her face disappeared, and when it returned the cherries in her cheeks and the purse of her lips were joy to my eyes: the rosy flush of carnality. She unhooked her bra and flowed onto me, my hand went down her belly into her waistband, found her good groove, warm and wet as a wound. Her sweet breath was in my face as she freed me from my jeans,

343

I found her face with my hand, she took my fingers in her mouth.

What ensued was a powerful tussle – I couldn't help it, I wanted to bite her, devour her – yet it was well matched. Her on top of me was something of a twist, I confess, never my preference, nor had I thought her much fussed. But she responded fervently, 'Oh kill, oh kill . . .' and for some hallucinatory moments I believed we were partners in crime, before I realised she was calling 'my' name. It could have crushed my fledgling spirit, except that something in me was sure it was my intensity – *mine* – that was transporting her. *Can't you see me?* my mind was shouting as we stared at one another in passion's close grip.

Was I in a trance? Could I truly suppose this was Paradise? Even as our peaks neared, for one flashing moment I saw again the shell of my old self, ghastly, broken and lifeless on Vukovara's floor. And yet the powerful pleasure was driving out all else. So was that, indeed, all it took? The sensations were so strong, my sense of the thief's delight so sweet and suffusing . . . I should have felt the evil in it, yet I was sure what was pouring out of me was love for her, all of my love. Had any man loved woman more? And that love was much too great, my crime far too passionate and flagrant, for remorse.

❧

I woke in bed the next day as never before – or, at least, unlike anything I could remember. No stagger, no hangover's sour trace, the heaviness of limb and pangs of the gut banished. Strength was replenished through my organs. I flexed and stretched like a rowdy bantamweight newborn, finding myself pleasingly semi-erect. If I was proportionally a little reduced, nonetheless I felt entirely virile in this tight-packed frame.

Malena was moving around the room, still undressed, turning to ask me something, hand on hip. I drank her in. All was now open to me, just as it had been slammed shut by her disapproving postures in our bleak final months – her eyes uninterested, cloudy with other concerns.

She wanted me to say honestly if I thought So-and-So was talented. Those vestiges in my stolen head instantly told me So-and-So was the painter-turned-filmmaker whose upcoming movie, about Mexican anti-capitalist guerrillas, was a project she was minded to document in photographs from start to finish.

'Aw, you know, darlin',' I told her confidently, 'it's not the talent you've got but the way you use it. The whole package, if you like.' I laughed. 'I don't mind, you decide, it'll be for the best.' She scowled, but not really, and I kissed her. 'On my mother's life, I don't mind,' I cried, thinking this the lightest vow I'd ever laid down.

I didn't try to stop her heading into town. A day's privacy felt luxurious. First she brought me tea in a chipped mug celebrating Dun Laoghaire rugby; then I had the curious experience of sitting alone in the jacks over another man's stink. I dressed – no wardrobe to speak of, all my gear deposited unruly on a rickety chair. But MacCabe's scruffy wardrobe proved a delight to me, everything worn soft but clinging, the denims, the stretched and faded rugger shirts and tees, cardigans and coats that hung off the shoulders with punched-out pockets, the stained and spattered dungaree trousers baggy and full of intriguing small items. I pushed my feet into battered leather moccasins, hardly believing they would fit until all was snug. Then I climbed up to my studio, found it just as Vukovara had revealed it to me.

Soon I was booting up anew, grasping and holding and comprehending his world. My eyes saw what his hands did, and the hands contained an alien intelligence – I knew as soon as I picked up his tools. (Less facile – yet I couldn't resist – was his pneumatic air hammer, a marvellous toy.) And yet in my new housing behind his eyes, MacCabe's art simply didn't interest me. How odd was his eye, how primitive his taste! I knew as sure as the smell of my old self that artworks should be finicked and finessed, not left so coarse and half-finished.

Two blocks of stone were mounted on worktops – one of granite, one I took to be alabaster, both mean lumps, dauntingly large and with an imperfect, fallen-off-a-lorry look to them. A mischievous urge gripped me: if Killian was so 'respectful' of his raw materials, then I would do violence to them. I dragged over the air hammer and cylinder, opened the taps, hefted the tool and attacked the granite lump. It was innocent fun as I stabbed about abstractly for a while. Soon I felt the edge crack through, smelt fresh-ground silica. Then something whizzed past my left eye, nicking the cheek near the jaw-line. I touched blood, stood myself down, chastened. *Take care, always, with another man's tools.*

I rooted round, found and donned goggles, a dust mask, some distressed and fingerless leather gloves. I took up an angle grinder, fitted a diamond blade and began my assault anew. Within minutes I'd hunted out a long hooked pole, prised open the skylights so the clogging dust-clouds could escape. I broke away stone swiftly, intuitively, my head and hands harmoniously focused. A block of maybe seventy, eighty kilo-weight, this granite was surely meant to be a human figure, a trunk, a torso. Even in the roughest-hewn form there seemed a figurative logic, an assertion in the stone that drove me – even as I grew aware of a numbness in my fingers. But once I understood, belatedly, that the proportion wouldn't permit me a head, I stood back, pondered, and quit. A body without a face did not interest me. I didn't care for the direction in which my hands had tacked.

Wondering what would be my next trick, I turned to the alabaster, a two-hundred-pound hunk of delicate pale-white. I stroked its coolness, appreciatively, understanding how easily it could scratch and mark, was not to be assaulted – wanted delicacy, my stock-in-trade. Instantly I had a miniature in mind: I fancied I could make a face.

A mounted pin-board held a tacked-up Polaroid of Malena. I sat down at an old school desk with inkwell, found a large piece of paper, sketched her likeness swiftly in charcoal, concentrating on the elegant bones, fussing the lines here and there until I had a proper approxima-

tion of the flow of her glorious features. My schoolboy-
ish absorption filled me with glee.

Then Malena was at my shoulder, silently returned
from her morning's messages. And the disdain on her face
for my creation was . . . interesting. Not to say familiar.

Since I felt no special need to do anything other than
enjoy her once again, it seemed a simple matter to tell her
in earnest tones that I needed some 'downtime', didn't
wish to push myself in the short term, we were okay for
money and I had vague plans that needed some days or
weeks to percolate. A routine grew up whereby she came
home and told me by her knit eyebrows that she knew
I wasn't working my usual days. (Quite – for I'd been
out running, swimming, pumping iron, feeling tightness
all over my body, propulsion in my legs, heavy-lifting
strength in my arms.) I told her I was too busy thinking about her. It didn't always wash. But in the evenings,
without fail, we drank red wine, laughed, made love. In
truth I found it hard not to want her in the middle of
the day, if she was about. I was sweetness personified, a
voracious little boy; she let me have my way and I don't
think regretted it. I slept soundly, though I had ceased to
dream, a loss over which I felt mildly wistful. But there
was no doubt in my mind I could live on like this; nothing about it seemed beyond my reach.

Then came that contentedly lonesome afternoon when I wandered out to the garden with the petrol-fuelled hedge-cutter I'd found in a cupboard . . . I yawned, scratched, lifted the tool aloft over my head – and felt pain, sharp and hot as a soldering iron, in my shoulder. Instantly I turned clinician, palpated my neck. But the examination flagged behind what my inherited memory was telling me. This was a torn rotator cuff, a rugby injury of several years' vintage, imperfectly healed. I could nearly see in my head, a film of my life, a memory like a physical object – me as he, on a frostbitten pitch, falling hard with all my weight onto an outstretched hand. He should have seen to this properly years ago: cortisone and anti-inflammatory regimens, stepped physical therapy. Instead he'd sucked it up in silence. And in a flash his – my – apparent vigour seemed to me a sham, founded on sand, the structure fallible.

Grimly I knew, I had sleepless nights ahead, my prescribing rights burnt up along with my old identity. I lumbered through to the kitchen, upended a tray of ice into a plastic bag. As I cursed my luck, I was startled by a shadow fleeting across the pale walls. For the first time in what seemed a long while – I wondered where She had taken herself.

The list of what I hadn't known was to lengthen in the following days. I wanted to romance Malena, do things for her, proposed we take a jaunt overseas. But she cautioned me with her list of commitments. I began my renewed courtship with dinner at 'our place', the St John. I wanted to drink, she was all prudish 'Better not'. But by God she wanted to talk.

Shouldn't I have better anticipated and respected the shared emotional history of which I was now part? Or did I think it such a trifle next to 'ours'? At any rate, when Malena referred fondly to 'how we met' my blood seemed to chill. Taking my hand, she told me how she'd had to chivvy and prod herself to 'make the first move'. How could my good mood survive that? *You were so eager to be rid of me?*

Had I my choice I would have spoken of that day she sallied in on assignment to record the light bouncing off the sleek new surfaces of the Forrest Clinic. How she dallied in my office, asked me charmingly accented, impressively specific questions, then seemed to stop listening to my answers. Had it been the same with MacCabe? More or less? No, I felt it as it flooded me – that had been swifter, irresistible, more physical, the man impressed her before his milieu. They met in a quiet room at a house party, both wanting a moment's peace – he could have been anybody, in fact he was The One.

For the rest of that wretched dinner only strange and affectless lies fell from my lips, save for my account of the pain in my shoulder, and the need I felt for a bellyful of wine to relieve it. What else can it be but a vain quest for authenticity, when I laugh another man's laugh and swear on another man's mother and fuck with another man's cock? My mood turned sullen, truculent, upset her. That night she slept with her back to me while I brooded. How deep had been my self-hatred, to go out and erase myself? How deep my delusion that I could accept her love in this counterfeit manner?

In the morning I felt a hangover of psychic proportions, the delayed reaction to this insane transmigration. My temper had a new strange edge to it. My head wasn't right – headspace seemingly teeming with illegals, aliens, remnants of the host consciousness that had always resented my invasion and had now turned insurgent. My hands suddenly looked all wrong for my body. On the toilet, under the showerhead – I felt now that I was mourning my old odour. Because an acute, unpleasant sharpening had occurred, all of a sudden I could smell whole moods and auras in a room.

Before Malena returned home I'd taken the hair of the dog. I cajoled her into bed, only to find myself incapable. As she lifted herself from recumbent, sighing, there seemed to me a sheet of ice formed anew between us. 'You need to get back to work, Kill,' she muttered. 'A project. For your own sake.'

It took me longer than it should have, no doubt the gut-sickness distracted me, but having sought refuge in the studio there was a moment when I contemplated the alabaster and knew what I would do, even as I denied it to myself. I made a new sketch swiftly, from memory.

Then I studied the block for its grain, its fault lines, trusting myself entirely. I took up pitcher and hammer, knocked out what I knew to be a right-sized piece, a shallow square of thirty pounds or so, large and yet workable. I rinsed it, marked it. As I set it on a sandbag and retrieved my sketch, she wandered in, frowning quite implacably.

'Don't worry, it's not you,' I said with what I feared was a smirk. In fact her fleeting appearance seemed to foul my concentration, and in the inertia I developed a headache that seemed to wheedle its way needle-like through the corner of my eye. I drank most of a bottle of Nuits-Saints-Georges that failed to shift it. Malena returned, gave me the same grief, I snapped and told her I wasn't having it, and she stood there like a suffering icon of a faith that was foreign and galling to me.

'Why are you acting so strange? Making us so miserable?'

'I am your lover who loves you,' I told her in forbearance. 'I've always loved you.'

She flounced out. It was evening by now. I wondered if she would be seeking comfort elsewhere for the night. But soon I fell asleep in my bone-hard rocking chair. The next day I was showered, changed and at the coalface before nine, albeit no more active than sat in the chair, nursing my mug of tea. But slowly I dragged myself in front of the stone, resuscitated what had been yesterday's intention. With the point chisel I began to mark features, nose, lips, eyes – clearing stone from the low areas, leaving the highs of brow, nose, cheekbone, chin. Then the chisel mined into a small lump of quartz. Hateful imperfection! Furious, I abandoned it, lurched over and cut out another thirty-pound piece, resolved to begin anew.

At which point, enter Malena, shy-smiling, thrusting out the little blue-capped plastic wand – proof of life. The anxiety and hopefulness she'd felt – 'I' had felt – arose in me sickeningly, had been concealed from me, I knew, only because she had refused diligently to 'talk up' those hopes. But now she was radiant.

I looked at the test through clouded eyes. It wasn't the clearest, but on the side of positive. 'Faint,' I said finally.

'I've done two, the first was the same,' she gushed. 'Negative is sometimes positive, positive can't be negative . . .'

'And when d'you suppose . . . the magic worked?'

'Ten days ago, I'm sure, that's what I waited for. She was conceived on your birthday, Kill.'

No birthday of mine . . . Ten days ago my name was still Robert. A cold flush went through me, from scalp to crotch. I knew, suddenly, how long this had been planned, how dearly wished for – even while they were cuckolding me. His wish to be a family man, dovetailing into her yearning broodiness. Would I love this child? Never. What had I been dreaming of? The devastation of what I had done struck me anew, the desperate evil sham of it, to have thieved and padded out another man's skin, ignorant of the fullness, the plenitude of the life I stole.

She was visibly stiffening as I looked back at her and saw only someone else's little misfortune. 'Well . . . I need to work here,' I murmured. Tears were coming to her eyes now. She said many things to my back, among them: 'How could I have misunderstood you so much?' It seemed then to be her fate.

Early the next morning she packed up and headed off for two days' work on some film set in Belfast. Stood at the end of the bed she told me we would have to talk. I agreed to whatever I had to. Once she was gone I hurdled the stairs up to the studio.

I carved one chip at a time, my arms wearied, found

353

myself wiping dust off the stone onto myself, and yet liking it, my dirty, sweaty state. The rudiments done, I used a claw and my hand as a vice to clean up and carve the rudimentary shape of the face. Then with toothed chisels I smoothed the faceting left by the chisel, and made the curves pronounced: the streamlined cheekbones, the rounded tip of the nose, the bow and swell of the lips – those defining details. For sure there was a surgeon's assurance in my process, I knew where to cut and how the stone would respond, what would yield to the edge and how.

Close to completion, content to rest, I felt an urge to treat myself. With night fallen I walked out to a local bar: a youngsters' joint, big as a barn, thudding with music, beer pumps and a mountain of spirits glowing through the murk. Various girls had formed their own little circles to jiggle about, various blokes forming a wolfish perimeter. One girl with her midriff bared brushed by me, and I fought the urge to strike her. A girl with a cross tattooed on her shoulder asked my name.

'Robert,' I whispered in her ear under the din.

She whispered back that she thought me 'a bit of a sort'. She knocked back a shot with me. I grabbed the back of her head, pulled her in for a kiss. Then some thunder-faced skinhead was shoving me and bawling me out for 'fucking about' with 'his' girl. I was happy to step outside, liking my odds in this scrap, and I settled it in one with a head-butt that caught the eejit entirely and remarkably by surprise.

Thereafter I drank several more shots, eventually led that girl out back near to where the bins were shuttered.

As I pressed her against the wall, pain shot through me – irradiated me. The heart raced, the vital organs clenched in agony. I was bent double, could feel a loathsome inner quickening, as if I were being eaten, internally necrotised.

I vomited. The girl straightened her string underwear, re-housed her left breast, sashayed away, left me behind. I had to wait some minutes before I had strength in my limbs to get off the ground, but the pain remained. I had filled another man's skin, now it felt as though I were leaking out of it again, draining away. Paying the toll.

༄ঌ

Alone still, I returned to 'my work' with a new, frantic urgency, trying to ignore my discomfort, a headache that was a stony throb in my temples and back teeth. I used a rasp file to perfect the face's complexion, re-move all marks. With a riffler I made the back of the thing a concave hollow, and then, impulsively, decided to remove the carved eyes, leaving blank sockets. Then I sanded, working my way delicately down to the finest grades, cleansing away the scratches, clouding the air with talcum – my lady in make-up. Once it was dry I took a soft cloth, waxed it to a sheen, made a bed for it on the black velvet of an old jewel case. My work filled me with a strange, grim pride. Having admired it in three dimensions, I fell into the rocking chair and there slept.

I awoke to darkness all around save for a rectangle of bluish white marked on the floor by the moon through the skylight. From ten feet the mask stared sightlessly at me. At first I thought its voice was in my head. Then the lips of the mask moved. There was life behind the void of those sockets.

'*Doctor. Why do you summon me?*'

'I'd begun to think I was . . . abandoned. Left to my devices.'

'*No. In our business with man no account is ever closed.*'

'I'm sick – if you didn't know. Nothing's right any more . . . It's come over me, the wrongness of what I am, has taken hold, is what I feel.'

'*The flesh is unstable. Yes. I believe, then . . . your hold on this form is not tenable.*'

'Meaning what?'

'*The body itself rejects you, is allergic to you somehow. Your tenancy is being revoked. A chronic rejection.*'

'No, I don't understand that.'

'*Of course you do, doctor. As your immune system rejects alien cells that are ill-matched. This was the risk. Our bargain could never have been thought free of it.*'

'No risk you ever warned me of.'

'*We were concerned only with your need. And it was great. Come, if I could offer you now – the push of a button? Could you bear to be Robert Forrest again?*'

'Oh Christ yes, so gladly . . .'

The voice cut through. '*That was not our bargain. But, time I have sold you, time you will have. It is time, I think, for you to move on. Gone from here.*'

'What are you talking about?'

'*You know this already, doctor. There is no immunosup-*'

pressant for what ails you. But another donor may make you the match you require. You must take flight again, take possession of another vessel.'

'You mean kill again, die again, go through it all again . . .'

'Yes. And waste no time about it either. Understand, if you die in this body, doctor, then you are lost. Your debt is realised. I will collect.'

The taunting, the treachery was so foul I needed a hand on my belly to quell my gut. In the other I nursed my head, groaned. 'No, no, I can't stand it.'

'You have no choice. Only one means to minister to yourself. Take another life. And choose with care. Perhaps this time the choice will be apt.'

'Who am I supposed to prey on now?'

She laughed. *'Must I do everything for you? Think, doctor. Whom else do you despise? What else do you covet? Or might it be a kinder form of murder if you stole the life of someone you loved? Think on it, think hard. But fast. The hourglass is upended and set.'*

I heard noises below stairs. My love, returned at last, to save me from doom?

'I would add only this. Set your sights on an individual you can . . . overpower, conquer? With ease. Perhaps also one who has few ties to the world, one whose withdrawal from life would not be much lamented. I do believe you may find such people anywhere. They litter the streets. Little waifs and strays . . .'

Her voice faded. The mask was once more inert. I got to my feet, felt impotent rage throbbing through me. I

357

snatched up the heavy hammer, attacked the hateful face, annihilated it with a flurry of pounding blows. Some filthy Irish whiskey had been skulking on a shelf, now I opened it and drank, felt its heat to be good, encouraging of my instinct to smash up this prison of mine. At some stage Malena snuck in, fearful, realised at once she should not have. But I was done with the rage and the whiskey, drained of strength and frightened as a child, when the door creaked open once more and, to my horror, Grey stepped warily inside. I remember nothing of what got said between us – only that his concerned face, his dependable shoulder, were anguish to me, reminded me anew of everything I'd lost.

๛

In the days that followed, my condition still atrocious if no worse, I weighed Her 'advice', which seemed to me wholly malicious, a further joke at my expense. The notion She appeared to float of my climbing into the skin of some rough sleeper was loathsome. I saw, however, Her base logic.

If I was to plan a murder, then privacy, anonymity seemed essential. I would need to lure someone to a secure, unseen place, do them to death, find a way to destroy the old carcass . . . Some wretch with no address, uncared for, liable to do anything for money – yes, one could see the ease. But, my aesthetic sense aside, could I afford to inhabit a body in which I would be penni-

358

less, sickly, vulnerable, liable at any time to run out of road? No, I knew I had to take a bigger risk, seek out a personage inside whom I could sit easily – a man I could impersonate.

It struck me then that some of the richest citizens among us could meet Her criteria just as readily as the very poorest – essentially private people, detached, aloof, without dependents. Mentally I ransacked the small but not insignificant sample of men on whom I'd operated, whose intimate records I held. One jostled to forefront in my head: Tim Judson, mid-30s, bachelor, independently wealthy, bequeathed a huge property portfolio that he had only made larger. A little older than I would wish, ideally, and a little too much sought after by *Tatler*, albeit for his perpetual squiring of young girls reared on the royal estates. But in our discussions prior to my sharpening his cheekbones he'd casually boasted to me of his huge estate outside Stevenage, the quiet luxury annexe apart from the main house where he worked. Now, quite suddenly, I saw myself digging Timothy's grave within his own grounds.

His details were in my database, at the clinic but copied at home. I considered the ways of badging myself back into Artemis Park, the neighbours and the porter each holding spare keys. Otherwise I would have to make a raid. But as I shifted into attack mode I impressed myself with the speed of my resolution, felt something predestined in it.

At first it seemed I was mistaken: the following day I drove the Spider to Artemis, rehearsing various yarns – I was Forrest's nephew? His mechanic, plumber, gardener? – and I had parked, entered, got as far as my old front door – when I heard voices within, one of them unmistakably Grey's, suddenly my nemesis now – and I turned heel, my heart beating hard.

Relations with Malena, I could see, were near-unsalvageable, yet I knew she was bound to this man, albeit by ties from which he was most radically freed. Now I was fighting an insolent wish, an urge to be caught, to tell Malena precisely whom she was dealing with, to ask her how she liked her blue-eyed boy. Instead I kept myself to myself, drank heavier still, even on one occasion – according to evidence I've seen – called Steven. But the dark was coming down. I was feeling sicker and shakier by the minute, clammy-handed, double-vision, drastically unsteady on my feet. I was clutching my stomach as if to hold it together when Malena crept through my door with a tale of some footling dinner arrangement for her idiot Buddhist friend.

I followed her to the bedroom, thinking only that I would crawl under the covers awhile. She dressed in silence, asked me to put on a necklace for her. And then I saw my seeming redemption – in a drawer of her jewellery box, the keys to Artemis Park, unmistakable by the key-fob we chose as our small memento of Vienna's Leopold Museum. I knew how to stage the row, fake my stomping out in high dudgeon. Once she was gone I raced back down, snatched my prize.

I will say I do regret the manner with which I handled my final departure from the house. I had to use force,

force Malena from my path. It was, in retrospect, a bitter farewell, and if I'd had time to brood on it the sadness might have sunk me. All I can say is that as I left I heard her breathing. But I fully expected that on waking she would summon the police. My sands were running. I made for my old lair at high speed, sensing low-frequency tremors of Her voice in my head – as if warding me away. But I didn't see how or why She would stop me as I fulfilled what was Her bidding. Certainly there seemed enough evil in my plan to please Her.

Then at last, my illusory homecoming, a synthetic sensation of relief, restored to that uterine darkness where I'd lain low for so long. Probably I dallied longer than was sensible – but my old familiar habitat was consoling me a little. I went to my study, noting my therapy mask and #15 scalpel laid out on the dining table as if for some Apache rite. So I snatched them up, and in my study I took the J–L box file from the shelf, grabbed a box of latex gloves, started to cram all into the soft black leather satchel that was my usual carry-on – had begun, even, to feel some upsurge of spirit – when I heard the front door, and my hopes crumpled up inside me. Delicately as I dared, I detached pages from the file, pushed these into the bag, crept with breath bated into the dining room and behind the door, where I fixed the mask onto my face and took the scalpel in hand – a puny sword and armour. By now a torch-beam was darting round the walls. I waited, waited, only looking, only listening, not a thought in my head but escape.

I achieved it, finally, by violence, this having become

my crutch. I can only say that my assailant was larger and fiercer than me, and, again, when I struck him I required that he stay down. With this accomplished I was on my way, cutting and running, gone, gone, gone.

ક

A fugitive now – doubly so, triply – I abandoned the Spider near the station and made it by a hair's breadth onto a northbound train. When I recovered my breath, returned in my head to the business of what I planned to do to Timothy Judson – my spirits were instantly and heavily sunk by the grisly lunacy of it. I was miserable as I stared out of the window, discerning through the dark the fleeting grass-banks and backs of houses, my alien face superimposed in the glass, crossed by shadow. Now and then I glanced down the aisle to the other occupant of my carriage. He was sleeping soundly if hoarsely, a pitiful sight, a scarecrow of a man: 30-ish maybe, in a rancid black hooded waterproof and jeans, the left side of his face and scalp scarred by third-degree burns. His left hand, lolling on his lap, was also lividly burnt, and part-mutilated.

As I gazed, despite myself, he stirred, looked about him in terror, leapt up to the window. My eyes went to my boots, but I sensed his coming directly for me. His speech was impeded.

'Eh, fella, fella. Will you wake me in three stops? If I drop off, yeah? Three stops, will ya?'

I nodded. He leaned in, close enough that I could nose

him, and grasped my knee. 'Good boy, ya.' Then he released me, staggered back to his seat, and within a minute he was snoring again.

His pain was not my concern. I had to get myself
in hand, force myself back round to the scalpel in my
pocket, the mission I'd set myself. Behind me was ruin, a
hiding place razed. Ahead, so I believed, lay Tim Judson.
But what would I do, how long would I, *could* I afford
to lie in wait, if and when I found him? What if late summer saw him in the Hamptons, Barbados, St-Tropez . . .?
Could I lie low in long grass, on damp leaves? For how
many days, hours?

The train shuddered on past depots and sidings,
cooling towers and gas burners. Then the view opened:
fenced fields, farmhouses, enclaves glimpsed at the end
of unapproved roads. Woodland had a new appeal to me:
somewhere to lose oneself, cool dark depths from which
one might not emerge. A reverie of sorts crept over me
in spite of my plight. To think that I could daydream,
still – imagine I was headed somewhere, awaited by some
friend and ally.

We plunged into the darkness under a bridge. I felt
a tingling sensation in my palms, realised how clammy
were my hands. The sensation turned to ants all across
my skin – then agony through my innards, like a poison
injected in the shape of a questing parasite, through my
gut and up into my thorax. My gorge rose up, I needed
to breathe but couldn't, I was gulping hard, head roiling.

Not halfway through my journey, all of a sudden I was
sickeningly sure I had run out of road. I writhed back in

my seat, the darkness hurtling by on both sides of the near-empty carriage, and it seemed to me now I was being fired like a rocket straight into onrushing oblivion. I lurched from my seat, wanting a hole to be sick in.

And there I saw Her – through the glass of the inter-carriage doors. She stood squarely to me, perfectly poised, Her face a terrible pitying smirk. I grasped and rattled the door handle, was unable to budge it. With a slow shaking of Her head She lifted an index finger and wagged it slowly to and fro before Her face – the universal symbol of refusal – also the ticking of a clock. And in my head I saw Her turned hourglass, its running sands, understood that in the insolence of my self-pity I had dallied too long, so forfeiting my choice.

Then She was gone and I had no feeling but nausea, no thought but that nausea, save for the wishful fast-fading image of being safe and well in some parallel world. As I groped uselessly at the door my heart thundered, my throat pulled tight as a garrotte, and I fell. My eyes were up in my head, the strip-lights of the carriage like tracer bullets firing over me. Then the Burnt Man's face swam into my field of vision. But I was going, going . . . The face stooped nearer – that scorched landscape, bewilderment in its eyes, its breath toxic – yet driven by a pulse, holding a charge, no question. Life!

Going, going . . . and with all I had left my fingers found my scalpel, pulled it free, and I swung.

Then, once again, the headlong deathless plunge into black.

⠒

And there I stood, over the outstretched figure of the late MacCabe – alone with the dead man, my wake for Killian. His stricken beauty, the instantaneous ethereal cruelty of his demise, nearly stole my own breath – my hard, sour breath. Already I was aware of great muscular activity, 'shakes', about my new person: a very obvious debility of constitution. My clothes were uncomfortably adhered to me. I raised a hand – my 'good' hand – before my eyes in the hard light. It was grubby, knuckly, coarse. But mine. And gingerly I dared to touch the crust of my ruined face, knowing now my name – Darren – Darren Carver.

Away, away! was the thought in Darren's head. And so I resumed this 'new life' to which I'd been condemned.

Everything about my new misshape, my hideous predicament, was wrong, wrong, wrong. Back in the heat of the bargain with Her I believed I'd envisaged every conceivable danger and death-trap. Never had I imagined this – that I would be caged up for sport, locked inside a hideous wreck of a human form.

And yet, still, my wits were keen, my mind kept its cunning, whatever the volume of grey matter in the new head I'd invaded. I grabbed up my leather bag, crouched down by MacCabe and, carefully as I could, prised my scalpel from his fingers, tugged his wallet from his jeans, conducting now the fastidious corpse-robbing Vukovara had previously forbidden me. I glanced up in time to see a conductor galumphing down the aisle of the next carriage, and I ducked. But luck, magic luck, seemed to favour me: the train was easing down into a station. For all that, I was beside myself. As the brakes shuddered through the carriage I lurched to the exit, hammered at the console until the doors hissed apart. The platform was deserted but I felt eyes on me, broke into a run, even as the train rushed away at my back. *The guilty flee, though none pursue.*

To my right, beyond the station, was nothing but rows of grim sodium-lit semis. But beyond the opposing platform to my left I could see woodland, fields, the glint of a river. I felt innately familiar with this terrain . . . And I greatly desired the cover of darkness. I jumped from the platform, dropped to the stony trackside, picked across the lines. The stones were treacherous underfoot, jarring my ankles as I pounded along, under a masonry bridge, then clambered up a grassy rise and hauled myself over a spiked fence – landing badly. Still I ran on, ran for cover, to cover my face – into and over the fields, fast as my hampered legs could carry me, feeling a painful war within my ribcage. Then I stumbled, fell headlong, into some sludgy mire.

For some time I lay there, winded, on the sodden grass, as if the earth might rise on all sides and swallow me. Could I persuade it to strip me of every human trace, all identifying marks? My fingers scooped grass and mud. A return to clay no longer seemed so frightful. I felt the wetness seep into my clothes, a slowly loathsome sensation – like cold blood, a spreading stain as though a hole were blown through me, some gaping exit wound. And yet I didn't stir: that sensation of being mired, of sinking thus, offered a queer consolation.

As it could not last, so, finally, I got to my feet – myself as ever, and so radically not, alive still, but in what sense? I set to walking, unsteadily, hacked my way over a wire fence into the open plain of a grazing field. Beyond the next perimeter I could see the bleary lights of a squat pub, lights that drew me on through the dark.

I crept round the tables of the pub's silent garden, my driving thought to find sanctuary behind a locked door. Deeper than that, though, I had a hard need to face myself, acquaint myself fully with how I now looked to the world.

I ducked in the pub's back door, my hood up and chin to chest, clocked the familiar pictogram and pushed through into the men's toilet, wincingly sure that I'd been seen by a pair of wary eyes from the bar-room. But then I was stood before a soap-smeared mirror and the pitiless glare of a bare bulb, conscious of rank odour rising not from the stalls but, rather, the loose neck of my tee-shirt. Unfathomable to me, in that moment, that I'd ever found the smell of MacCabe so disagreeable.

At some point in his young life this 'Darren Carver' had suffered third-degree facial burns, the skin on the left side charred to hard eschars, much lost epidermis, nerve endings destroyed, hair follicles and sweat glands gone. Worse, some muscle underneath had burnt also – irreversible damage, lost sensation, probably a couple of forlorn grafts to limited effect. As for the rest of his – my – face, it had the haunting gauntness that comes when a body is reduced to feeding on itself for want of other sustenance. For what it was worth, the surgeon had made a decent job of the stumps of the two lost fingers, both gone at the proximal joint yet unscarred and tactile.

As I surveyed this devastation and my inheritance of it, some mental vestiges of the host were returning to me, in now-familiar fashion, yet far more ferocious, toothed and jagged than those that had struck me while I was housed inside MacCabe. The fierce force of the blast that torched Carver's face and blew off those fingers – I felt that anew – could even feel the miserly mercy that it had missed my eyes. I understood I'd lit that lethal little stove not to cook – since I had no provisions – but to keep warm in the arctic squat I then called home.

Shaken, I groped my way back and down onto the seat of a toilet head. Needing to piss, I found my crotch and rectum predictably disgraceful. Fumbling both hands into the anorak's pockets I located a square of card – my train ticket – and that touch brought another shard of self-knowledge. Tonight I had been travelling homeward – not in hope, indeed to a place I'd long ceased to consider home. Yet I was trying my luck, the last dregs of it. Carver's life-story had bled back into my head, versions of which, I knew, he had sworn out before many insensible audiences, over cans of drink frothy with spit, ratty little joints with barely any draw and hardly more tobacco. Slowly but steadily I was assailed by awful memories of a doormat mum and a bullying stepdad – a slob, a yob, *a mean fucking cunt.* Feelings of fear and rage, of rock-bottom self-esteem, rolled in like the tide.

I'd left rather than be kicked out – found building-site work, roofing and general humping. One day one of my oppos fell and broke his back – no safety net, I hadn't taken the time to fix it. An unconscionable error. I was finished in that game. I drowned my sorrows, far too long. The girl I bunked with told me to go. I lurched from sofa to living-room floor until I'd used up my favours, worn out my few mates. Still I had no way home. For a while, since it was summer, I slept in parks, washed in library toilets, mine-swept drinks off pub trestles. Then autumn gusted in. The hostels were essential, but it seemed me and the hostels didn't get on – me and the clientele tended to have 'issues', though no one could tell me I was as shit-house mad as some of them loons.

Nonetheless: barred here and barred there, stigmatised for 'aggressive behaviour', I had felt a growing need to exhibit my stigmata. I hardened up, coarsened for sure; found brief respite in drugs that gave me visions. The mob who turned me onto all that also got me into their squat. But the drugs messed me up, screwed my head on wrong, as it was that night I set myself ablaze. I could see myself in theatre as they worked on me . . .

And in that moment, from within Carver's skin, I saw this poor devil as his mother must have seen him years before – the bairn, the boy who surely made his parents fond at least once. And my narrow chest was jammed up with bland, gummy sentiment, my eyes began to stream at the miserable, pitiful shame of it. I could hear that I was muttering to myself – Carver's habit, never mine – but it just couldn't be helped.

Then the door before me was hammered and rattled, a voice cursing me blindly. I opened the door a crack and it was shoved wide by a burly shaven-headed man in a sweat-shirt as red as his face.

'Oi. Toilets for customers only, right? So sling it, you.'

Evicted, from such a palace . . . Shambling past him I felt my shame burn fiercer, transforming by heat into an anger, worsened yet when I saw the smug, scurvy faces eyeing me from the scant bar-room. I chose, then, to be a customer. I had MacCabe's wallet, after all. I ordered a large whisky – Grouse, their meagre best – tossed a ten-pound note on the bar. The landlord only glared, until one of those regulars cackled that 'Bob' could hardly afford to turn away custom. In silence my glass was filled.

Head high, I carried my prize back out into the darkened garden, sat at a trestle, whispered into the rim of the glass until I sensed I had company – a trio of stocky gents, regulars who, clearly, hadn't supported my case back there.

'*Oi*. Gimp. *Can't yew take a fackin 'int?*'

Was it the ungovernable in me, or the nothing-left-to-lose? In any case I tossed back my dram, stood and made my way round them, as if for seconds. Whereupon I was hit hard under the right ear, struck violently in the back too, and I went reeling. I tried to get square-on to my attackers, swung a counter into fresh air, but was punched again, right on the nose, and went down on the grass. Instantly a kneecap was squeezing on my diaphragm. I was hammered in the mouth, kicked on the crown of my head, '*Get his feet, his feet!*' was the last I heard.

I stirred probably within an hour or so, finding myself dumped like rubbish in long grass beyond the back fence, nothing broken, though my aches and pains were lancing, and Killian's wallet was gone from my pocket. The pub lights were out now, but I forced myself to limp back, make a search for my leather bag. I nearly shed tears at the triumph of finding it still nestled in the dark under my table.

Then I picked a way back out into the overgrown grasses, the cover of trees and the profound dark; came to a riverbank, and by a willow I found a boat covered by tarpaulin, hauled off the sheet and covered myself, stretched out on the ground. There I slept.

The sun rose hatefully early. I wanted no part of daylight. In my state I believed I'd be as well to roll my bones down the bank into the river and be done. And yet, something hard and insistent inside me, a beaten yet resilient core of ego, told me I had been tricked, assaulted, unfairly bested in the game. And I had to strike back, somehow.

I understood, under the warped rules governing the air I breathed, that another killing – my third! – ought surely to bring about a third 'transference' of myself; moreover, that opportunities might well present themselves in this remote environment. But my spirit was rock-bottom at the thought of yet another contaminating act. It seemed just as likely it would prove one more terrible self-deception – the deceiver's secret wish. Her amusement at my plight was abundantly clear. I distrusted most thoughts in my head, for fear She had planted them. And I could so easily see myself stood over another outstretched body, yet still in Carver's tortured form; running again, but this time apprehended . . . Bars and grey walls round the prison where I already languished.

Thus I saw no course of action but to seek an audience – a confrontation – with Her, in Her lair. And so, bone-weary, damp and cold, inexpressibly wretched, I started the hike back to London.

I must have trudged ten miles that day, through woods and by streams, into miles of fields of wheat and rapeseed, across construction dumps and timber yards, skirting new-build cul-de-sacs and cement factories. My boots, slathered in riverbank muck, let in all the while, a loathsome feeling. And yet, there were consolations. For a mile or so I idled through the lambent cover of trees shading a golf course; got on my belly and drank from a stream; spooked some horses in a sun-dried paddock, content at least to be shunning human eyes.

With light still in the sky I reached the London outskirts and a 1930s tube station. Now my challenge, over which I'd obsessed for some miles, was the price of a ticket. Though it pained me, I knew what I had to do. I dumped my backside on the cold paving, put my back to the brickwork, hung my head like a proper penitent; and, watching feet go by, I could just about bear to mutter under my breath, *'Spare some change please, sir, madam . . .'* It was a necessary rite: I had found my place in life. Still I had the strength to believe this was not how things were meant to end for me. Here, at least, my face was my fortune, earned me enough donations before I was moved along. I had money over for a bacon roll, which I slathered in sauce and devoured. An hour later I stepped out of Warren Street, headed for Fitzrovia, slouched awhile in the recess of a door before Her mansion block. But the porter busying round the foyer seemed an insuperable barrier. In one clear stretch I risked a dash over the road to ring at the bell of 6F, but the intercom speaker-box stayed silent.

With night coming on I sought shelter in an underground car park, stealing as far down as I could into the gloomy petrol-stinking depths of its subterranean circles. Mindful of CCTV I hunkered down under cars, scrabbled intermittently from spot to spot, alert to voices or footsteps. On one such run, I was 'made'. From forty feet a small girl in a red coat, grave-faced, Alice band in her

blonde hair, stared at me, with an unalloyed look of –
what? Not disgust, not pity nor fear – but, on reflection,
perhaps a compound of all three. Then her smart-suited
father was shielding her from me, lifting her up into his
BMW's child-seat. I was still trying to name the look
on her face when the strangest voice crackled through
my head: not mine, but not Hers, nor Darren Carver's
neither:

*What you think you see out there is not real. Little chil-
dren can see that. I told you, I knew when I was four. You see
it in people, their eyes, doesn't matter how old they are. They
know. They just know.*

Stunned where I stood, for some moments I could
hear only the rattle in my catarrh-ridden chest. Then a
hard Bangladeshi voice behind me, telling me to fuck off
out of his car park *yaar*. But he didn't need to lay a hand
on me, I shuffled away, dumbfounded still.

ﷺ

It rained that night. I'd have welcomed a flood to carry me
off, at least douse me clean – instead I felt cladded in my
own filth. As I skulked about central London the crowded
pseudo-civilised city seemed to mock me. Whenever I
heard bright laughter I took it for scorn. I was, of course,
invisible to a degree: most people couldn't bear to meet
my eye. But they saw me coming fast enough. I sat and
begged in any dry doorway until sent packing. Knowing
from Carver's bitter experience that no hostel would have
me, I further knew enough to avoid *the homeless*, so many

of them fucking nuts, in need of anaesthetising, even if it be by booze or pills. I wanted none of that. I rode a night bus, fellow travellers giving me a wide berth. Time crawled, seemed limitless, as it will when no one waits or cares for you.

I woke under a park bench in Kilburn, tortured anew by daylight and hunger. And so, finally, my feet took me to where my kind gathered: a day centre, where I shuffled through processing, was assigned a bowl of soup and settled into a plastic chair amid the open-prison ambience. Only a man sat with me, began to enquire gently after my 'situation'. I told him nothing. Still, he spoke of Jesus Christ. I couldn't stomach that, had to get free of the room.

They often say of my profession that the theatre and the pathology lab, the sight and smell of life and death so raw, endow us with a lofty notion of humanity as so much privileged meat. And I agree – from the heights of invasive procedure, life can at times seem a toy, a mere vehicle for eating and shitting and fucking – activities that are, at one remove, deeply ludicrous. And yet how dear and lost to me these functions now seemed, from inside my famished, filthy, effectively sexless body.

I was sheltering by rubbish bins behind a kebab shop, turning the leaves of a discarded *Irish Gazette*, when I came on the small plain notice of Killian MacCabe's funeral that very day. Witless, I made the decision this was where I was fated to be, if only from a respectful distance . . . And so, from across the gulf of a street I gave myself the grief of seeing Malena enter the church, the marks I'd left on her in another life still apparent. I hung my head, only then to see Grey, so stalwart and sombre . . . Again I longed for his company, mourned the loss of our bond, my severance of it. That night I burrowed myself into a copse on Hampstead Heath, and come daybreak I foraged out, determined to confront Grey on what I knew would be his morning run. Instead, he hobbled up the incline on a cane. A world of things I should have said to him . . . But, really, how could he have been expected to respond? Instead I behaved rashly, intemperately – I daresay aggressively.

Seeing no other course, then, I gave myself up to base instincts, what Dr Hartford used to call 'the hierarchy of needs'. What I had on Steven, our shabby shared business with that hopeless head-case Dole, I decided I would now cash in, albeit cheaply. In my bag I had note-cards: I scribbled out something I knew would freeze his blood, named my price, delivered it personally through his letterbox in Primrose Hill. But by the time I'd trudged back to my lair on the Heath my zeal had subsided. The whole shaming, hare-brained scheme seemed only further evidence – as if it were needed – of my degeneration.

The day was fine, cloudless, cheerless. I slashed my way into a shrouded place between bushes of Solomon's seal, overhung by horse chestnuts. There I lay down, clasped my bag to my chest – and felt with my fingers a small something that I'd neglected until now, deep within the lining of the inner pocket. There I found the token Eloise Keaton had gifted me in what I suppose were, for her, the hopeful days of our little dalliance: a bracelet, a black leather strap bearing a silver Asclepius, the snake coiled round the staff. Idly I fastened it round my wrist, admired its incongruous elegance. I took a notion, and from the bag I retrieved the page from my files summarising Tim Judson's medical record. Flipping said page I found, as expected, similar details for Eloise.

Her personal/family history I remembered well: no cancer, general good health, previous operations/hospitalisations all elective – likewise her medications, for better or worse. Eloise's seemed to me a gilded existence, for all that she cut a self-pitying figure – her trust fund matured, her Holland Park pied-à-terre, work for her hardly more than play, her beauty finessed by my own diligent hand . . .

Pensive, I found myself spying out through the drooping branches overhead at two kids hand-in-hand, boy and girl in dark school uniform, bright-eyed and glossy-haired and dawdling off deeper into the shade. *Where are you going?*, I wanted to demand. *To lie down together? By what right?* I felt a sharp urge to rise, lurch off after them. *Not without me! No way but through me! I will bless or curse your union, as I see fit . . .*

It took some moments for this fit to pass, like a shudder right through me. Becalmed at last, my gaze fell on a young proletarian mother sat on a bench, nursing her baby – banal, this image, a babyish aspect even to the mother with her scraped-back hair and soft pink clothes. Then, within an igniting instant, I was drastically groggy and brain-fogged – had to be hallucinating – for it was as though I'd been transported, fired out of my head and behind the woman's eyes, decanted into her skin.

Now I was the wet-nurse – and experiencing an extraordinary sensation of plenitude, 'my' breast pale but plump, coursing with life, the babe avid for me. I felt weakened at my core – chastened, even – and yet inexpressibly alive. I had full awareness, too, of how long had been the days until the baby came, my sluggish compacted innards, my slow-inculcated tenderness in that time of inaction, only waiting, nesting, girding myself to be oh-so-powerfully acted upon . . .

Then with lightning rapidity I was back in my old Carver-head, woozy, unnerved – also oddly saddened by a lingering emptiness as I watched the mother rise, stretch, roll her pram off down the hill.

I slipped into a doze, for how long I don't know, before I felt a kick in my ribs as if I were a mangy hound. I peered up into sunlight, still dazzling through trees, a dark shape over me. 'Please, brother,' I groaned, 'just let me lie a bit, I'll move on, I swear.'

I heard the tinkling laugh, shielded my eyes so as to properly make out Her, in Her Russian coat. If She was naked underneath, I cared not. 'What a waste,' She murmured, then was so calmly inscrutable and silent that I feared this was all She'd come to pronounce.

I wiped my mouth on my sleeve. Still, as I spoke my diction was tortured. 'Come to torment me, have you? Pleases you, does it, to see me like this?'

I could read nothing in Her eyes, for in the shade they seemed the purest black orbs. I glanced away, through the trees, saw children playing ball, then back at Her – but still the same horrid sight.

'*Humani nihil a me alienum puto*,' She enunciated. 'In human form I too am a poor relation on this earth. Incarnated thus' – She gestured down Her figure – 'I assume a certain risk, am prey to certain exigencies. Not so unlike yourself, *mi frater*.'

'Then don't waste your breath. I know what you want me for. And I want you to take me down.'

'"Down"? From your cross?'

'To whatever you've intended for me, from the start. I'm tired, I've no fight left – I want this to be done.'

She tilted Her scorning face at me. 'Such an insect you are. I see, your pride has been gored, your precious *aesthetic* sense violated. And you wonder, however did some *doxy* bring one like you so low?'

'I said, save your gloating—'

'Have you no mind of your own, doctor? To imagine what you could yet be capable of? Our bargain was that you be changed, translated. It appears wasted on you. You are making a mediocre, ingrate, third-rate fist of my *extraordinary* gift.'

'Lies. You've toyed with me, all along, thwarted me deliberately.'

'By no means. I warned you – brook no delay. Did you hear me?'

'You're in my head, aren't you? You knew what I had planned . . .'

'Not so. It was easier when you were "you", doctor. Your head was more settled, our frequency clearer. I have far less power than you imagine. And ours is a . . . volatile process. But you cannot convince me you are "done".

Truly, do you want to be dead? To be ours, and ours alone? Shall I take you now?'

I hung my head and, after some moments, shook it, slowly.

'No. "Life clings to life." The hourglass is turned, yes. But not yet run. In this body? I do believe you could serve quite some time – it has endured so much already, yet survived. But that is . . . not tolerable for you, surely?'

I exhaled bitterly. 'Of course not.'

'Then cast the die again. Take a life and live again. You know this.'

'What do you want to reduce me to?'

'Nothing other than the form that fits you truly. We will be in league until then. Be assured, I will honour our business, doctor.'

Perhaps She saw hope in my eyes. Perhaps I found something in Hers other than malice. She appeared to ponder.

'Possibly . . . you would be wisest to enter a headspace you know well. A life where the daily round inherited comes more easily to you. Someone who thinks fondly of you, trusts you – who might be persuaded to meet you, unsuspecting, on ground of your choice. Possibly, doctor, an old friend might do you one more service?'

Her fraudulent wide-eyed 'enquiring' mien made my skin crawl. 'Forgive me', I muttered finally, 'if I take no more lessons from you.'

'Oh, then do as you have done. Among the sub-humans, the living dead, despised and uncared for. Try your luck as a spider or fly. Did I warn you, doctor, to stay your hand in that way? Or did I not? Since you are still on two legs, let us say it was . . . no matter.'

She was herself arachnid to me in that moment, a vicious bag of venom. I grabbed Her throat. She didn't flinch, and for a split second I feared my offending arm would, by magic, be ripped from its socket. Instead She screamed – shrieked, so piercingly my teeth hurt. Beyond Her black shoulder I could see the fathers of those playing children now making tracks toward my hiding place at a concerned canter. I turned and stumbled off and away, did not look back.

She had got Her hooks in me again, yes. I understood the logic of stealing a life with which I was more closely acquainted. I confess, in the hours that followed – once I'd found peace and concealment hunkered in by the Hampstead Tunnel – I did contemplate what it might mean to despatch my old friend Steven. An attack on Grey I couldn't contemplate: for all my transgressions, the thought of this one filled me with near-Oedipal terror. In any case, that fracas we'd had persuaded me I'd never 'overpower' him in a million years, even were he on one leg. His hardihood was a huge part of why I loved him. I honoured it still. Steven, though, posed a lesser challenge. Whatever warm or plaintive memories I had of my old classmate, there was longstanding mutual grievance there too. Moreover, though sturdy enough on his feet, Steven simply didn't cut the same imposing figure as Grey. Usurping him in Professor Tessa's bed proposed a test. But more vitally, in my heart, I felt the whole notion . . . unpalatable.

Within the hour, though, I was exploring an alternative solution, one that crept over me as a waking dream. Crouched down in that darkened tunnel, my head had already begun to swim. But then something came at me – only from within, not without . . .

And I was surrounded by brightest daylight, a tableau of English summer, seen from a fragrant terrace overlooking landscaped grounds. Within moments I had my bearings from memory – this was Blakedene Hall, no doubt. But there was no sound for this picture, save for the blood beating between my ears. I was gazing out through foreign eyes.

I was not alone. Five paces from me Eloise was lightly asleep, her legs curled under her in a wicker chair. She wore the blue silk dress I'd bought her – tunic-style, kimono sleeves, cut on the lower thigh. Though her head had slumped a little, her flaxen hair kept a perfect frame round those elfin features. I was rapt in admiration of my handiwork when Steven Hartford shuffled into my view, his back to me, oblivious.

My lips parted – but I was silenced by a voice in my head, recognised it, the same voice I'd heard in that subterranean car park. It was masculine, low, fervent, and it spoke whirling, vehement words.

. . . *Hear me, I invoke thee, whom no man sees, master, lord of multitudes, I bow my head before thee, nameless, headless, feared by wind and rain, master, command me, I will do thy bidding, my shell has been emptied, my head blown open, my hands are yours to move, my throat yours to speak through, breathe your peace into me, master, rip*

clean through me if it be your will, this is my devotion,
submissive to you, mine not to question, let me only bring
you near us . . .

By then I believed I understood – my confederate, my
psychic ally was summoning me – whomsoever he believed 'me' to be. Given my wretched state, his fanaticism
struck me as demented. And yet we appeared to be of one
mind, he and I, my presence most impressive to him,
since he was offering me his body.

I, though, in common with my old friend Steven, was
staring anew at Eloise – at her golden head and elegant
throat, exquisite jugular venous pulse, the slow rise and
fall of her breath, the well-tended languor about her –
'the health of rich red blood, coursing with each heartbeat
– life, doctor, years of life . . .' And yet a life she knew not
what to do with. I knew every inch of her, inside and out,
knew just to look at her again that her melancholy sat so
deep – I could nearly see how deliverance from it might
be a kind of blessing.

And then I saw no more – was alone again in my tunnel, alone with an infamous idea.

I reconsidered Eloise's enviable material circumstances;
even that luxury-hotel aura of Blakedene, a five-star
bolthole, premium hiding place, three meals a day, movie
at nine, capped by a king-size slumber . . . Laughter rose
in my chest as the notion seemed to bloom before me.

I felt fate to be speaking, urging me to break with the
given – a radical departure, depraved, even. But hadn't
I always asserted, even in the toughest male company,
the part of me that is female, however deeply concealed?

And it suddenly seemed to me that a conversion of this order could conceivably serve as my redemption – its irony not necessarily at my expense, if I chose freely to recant my stormy masculinity, convert from swordsman to damsel, Don Giovanni to Donna Elvira. This was a penalty, a plea-bargain, I was prepared to accept. I was resolved – somehow, I would get to Blakedene – another trek, yes, but with an ingeniously shining goal in sight. A shadow, half-glimpsed within a reverie, had proved a revelation . . .

I mean, such was my insanity, you understand, since hallucination had become my guiding light. Because whatever the method in it, the possession of Eloise remained a mad idea, and the maddest part of all was that I truly believed it was my own.

ﻌﻠ

I escaped London before dawn. Requiring funds for my exit, after midnight I staked out an ill-lit cashpoint off the Harrow Road, gripping an empty vodka bottle I'd found under a lamp post. A single female would have been ideal, but custom was sluggish, time fleeting. Finally I knew, it would have to be that man . . . Light-footed, as he made his transaction I stole up behind and struck him very hard, then repeatedly. I couldn't risk his being fit to give a description. My spirits were dangerously high. It seemed to me amazing what one could carry off, alone and unnoticed and malevolent, to be without fear or care, to take what one wanted and run. I hastened to Paddington, got aboard the 0330 and rode out into Berkshire, limped the mile or so from the station into countryside, finding the wooded lanes that wound a leafy way round to Steven's upscale asylum.

Within sight of the gatehouse I was disconcerted to find a beefy guardsman – the loyal Goran, as I would come to know him – playing sentry. I ducked off the road, beat a path into the surrounding woods, but soon lost my bearings and realised I would have to find my way to the rear of Blakedene through the outlying fields of a nearby farm. In the act of same I was nearly 'made' by a curious little girl playing on her own in a bean-field. I stood motionless, glowering at her from beneath my raised black hood, until she paled, turned and ran – whereupon I blundered down into the woods, emerging before the sheer face of Blakedene's stone-wall rear, its solid wood door determinedly shut and locked. Precisely how I would invade the perimeter had never been fully clear to me – I had hoped merely for a chink in the defences somewhere, but none such was readily observable.

Then I heard the turn of an aged key, my heart jumped and I made a clumsy dash back to the shelter of the woods, hearing the door creak open behind me . . . Stretched on my stomach under a crop of hazel-bush, I watched a gloomy-eyed gardener shuffle a wheelbarrow backward out of Blakedene, then turn and head down the beaten track close by where I lay. I inched further into cover, watched him disappear between the trees – was silent on my belly still when he returned, barrow loaded with fallen branches. I had weighed up the urge to attack him and discounted it, conscious I had to proceed with maximum guile, leaving the minimal trace behind.

But with the door barred to me once more, as I lurked in the cool shelter I felt a powerful need of the confederate who'd lured me out here in the first place. I sensed I had to revive communications with my 'psychic ally'. I wondered if I could summon him as he had summoned me. My mouth was parched, I was hugely enervated, mentally beside myself. It seemed imperative to clear my head.

I found a mature willow tree, its low-hanging branches a veil, the tangle of gnarly roots at its foot a natural berth. And there I sat, drew my legs crossed under me. I quieted my mind, felt myself slacken physically, breathed in and out until those breaths were guttural. Whereupon a cool peace came down. I seemed to see the world about me even through the black of my eyelids, the sense of my physical housing falling away until I was pure thought, and yet in motion, surging up and out of my shell.

Then I was in his head – his room – his eyes were mine as we sat at the foot of his bed, in the clean white splendour of his room. But I felt him alerted to me, panicked, prickling, ill at ease all over.

Don't fear me. I am the one who walks always beside you. With that, at least, I felt his heartbeat ease. *Come, outside, unlock your door, open to me . . .*

His – my – eyes darted across to his work-desk under the window. On it sat a sculpture, a clay bust, its Grecian severity impressing me until the blankness of its eyes looked into me and I took fright. What power was I accessing here? Some measure of what She possessed?

In that shocked moment I was restored to my cold seat under the willow.

Night drew in. I held my hiding place, could do no other. The wait was torture, with no notion of whether our telepathy had persuaded him. In the dark and the hush, broken only by the trills and ululations of the birds, I tried and failed to meditate my way to calm, against my growing hunger and thirst.

Then came the sound of a familiar disturbance by the Blakedene wall, the door pushed open. Impulsively I retrieved my mask from my leather bag, strapped it to my face, set my back hard upright against the tree-trunk, my hands gripped my knees. And in the gloom I watched Tregaskis sneak his way down the beaten track, stealthy, snatching glances behind him. He came through the dense overhanging foliage, until he saw me, paused, his steps tentative. Even in the dark his eyes had seemed to gleam. Now they were narrow, troubled. The gardener's ring of keys clinked in his hand. I knew I had chosen my accomplice well. But he, clearly, had expected more than the grim sight of me. Face to face I couldn't delve inside his head. Still, by some means he would have to be brought to heel.

'*Don't look at me,*' I hissed, drawing out the threat. He started, visibly, did indeed – to my delight – avert his eyes.

'Who are you?'

'You know. There is enough between us, David.' He looked up to hear his name, I softened my address accordingly. '*Humani nihil a me alienum puto.* In human form I, too, am a poor relation on this earth – incarnated thus. We are brothers that way.'

I had him now. There was a dawning rapture in his face.

'Your sun is rising, David. Do as I ask, you will see your reward.' I tossed the bracelet to the ground between us. 'Give this to her. You know who I mean. A token. Tell her someone waits in the woods, waits for her, needs her. She will know. Lead her out here to me.'

I leaned back, held myself still as a lizard, watched him watch me – my mask between us but my nerves running as high as his. At last he nodded, stooped to retrieve the bracelet, his eyes never leaving mine. Then he was loping back in the direction of Blakedene's walls.

The day that followed was another condemned to a long and intolerable wait. And I waited, waited, all day long – edged nearer and nearer to outright dementia. This time, though, nothing of the agonies I'd felt in MacCabe, no physical discomfort drove me. But the need in myself to be free of my physical cage felt like a terrible craving – blood throbbing in my temples, an unfulfilled ache bound up with the ravening hunger in my gut. Frustration turned to rage – whereupon, or so it seemed, I summoned a storm.

For sure my foul mood became contiguous with the sky as it changed from white to black, gale-force winds blew up and shook the very woods, chased by pelting rain. I dug into my willow shelter for the hours it took to blow over – even slept awhile, after the rains were spent. Then, with darkness, calm was restored, both in the elements and my head. Even soaked and near-starved, I believed my hour had come. And so he brought her to me.

I heard the key, the creak – glimpsed the startling white of her nightdress, he also framed in the door, then pushing it to – she turning, uncertain, then stepping uneasily down the track and under the broadleaf canopy. I rose and darted behind the great trunk of a grey beech, scalpel in hand, tried to control my ragged breath. But she wandered right past my hiding place, only to pause before the willow. My bag sat there at its foot. I heard her call my name – low, stricken.

'Robert? Where are you? Robert . . .'

I studied the nape of her neck, her forlorn posture – truly a lost girl. Then I surged from cover. She heard me in time to turn, but had no chance to react before I struck – the speed my poor excuse for mercy, my unwanted apology. With the same speed came the abysmal pitch-black, the sense of being ripped from my corporeal moorings, violently displaced. And with that stroke, that single bound, I was once more delivered.

⚘

Darren Carver lay outstretched, and I stood, revived, instantly alive to my diminished stature, aware I ought to have been chilled to the marrow – and yet there was heat in me. I plucked up my belongings, abandoned the unfortunate Carver to the elements, and stepped out of the woods on exquisitely unsteady feet. Tregaskis swung the door to admit me to Blakedene . . . But on seeing me I saw his surprise, his wariness. I leaned to his ear, whispered bona fides to him.

389

'Your sun is rising, David . . .'

'My' voice now hers, just as grainy as I'd known it, nonetheless lifted from bass to contralto – that same voice that once questioned me keenly about possible scarring, the voice that urged me hotly when we were in bed, the voice that railed at me with four-lettered rage when I told her we were done. Now mine.

In the grounds of Blakedene Hall I could smell summer blooms, still fragrant, where the woods had been all autumnal dankness. This, my enchanted garden . . . But this settling of myself inside her was shattered as I saw Steven and his watchman marching up the lawn, combing the grass with flashlights. Swiftly I stashed my bag in a lilac bush, sat myself heavily on an iron bench, feigned uneasy sleep. Tregaskis, cottoning slowly but surely, fell at my feet. As such it was he who took most of Steven's ire once we were 'discovered' – this clear resentment of Tregaskis's status as my defender telling me all I needed to know of Steven's suppressed cares for Eloise. Still he led us, the naughty children, back indoors by the light of his torch. I marvelled a little at the grass under my toes, the fallen vines and trees strewn about – the chaos I remained sure I had wrought. Outside my bedroom Steven cautioned me. I apologised, solemnly promised I'd sin no more. Behind my closed door the room was indeed a delight, extravagant comforts, cut flowers – even the musk-orange scent of the Narcisse Noir I bought her, detectable in the air. I lay down, hugged myself, content in this confinement.

~

My eyes opened, to light creeping under the curtain's hem. I was in a strange bed, there was hair in my mouth – lying on my back I could feel my muffled heartbeat. I shielded my eyes, sat up, the covers slipped away and, looking down, it all came rushing back. With that agreeably fuzzy just-wakened feeling, I stretched my new limbs. This was a considerable novelty; and yet surprisingly familiar.

I flicked on the plasma TV by remote, half-listened to the radio news. It was World Suicide Prevention Day, Marc Jacobs was showing in New York, a strident young woman had a theory about 'killer capitalism'. Meantime in my opulent lodging I explored Eloise's belongings, inventoried the dresser – her Lulu Guinness vanity case, compact mirror and strewn cosmetics, pocked sheets of Nicorette gum. Throwing open her wardrobe I met a wash of familiar colour and texture.

During our affair I had tried somewhat to fashion her, draw out the gamine in her as opposed to The Girl from Ibiza-via-Goa. It hadn't taken, as proven by this riot of sun-dresses, faded denim, cotton skirts, peasant blouses . . . But the pricy *sous-vêtements* heaped in her drawers poured down between my fingers like silver. As I dressed, I was reminded again of the truth in this life that we all put our pants on the same way – one leg at a time. I understood I was late for breakfast, and would have to write myself a sick-note.

In truth I felt younger, lighter, happier in form, the sensations all strikingly sweet. This body I knew as well as any, in minute detail, and knew to be good, having assessed much of it professionally, its small deficiencies all balanced out by strengths. Eloise was never 'vain', only suffering exquisite points of self-doubt. I might have worked more on her, but she didn't care and I didn't push it, her body the one thing in her life she was mostly untroubled by.

She had taken no great care of herself, but even now I was struck by the bloom across 'my' skin. The little dark-brown mole to the left of the navel seemed, as ever, an agreeable punctuation. I palpated the left breast with the pads of my fingers – this a new perspective for me, the alleged 'expert' – and got a newly peculiar sense of an accumulation of smaller lumps, like a good bunch of grapes on the vine, but still milk-soft in my hand. I bent this way and that, inspected the course up inner thigh, little cerulean veins vanishing into auburn and hazel. Following up round the curve of hipbone I found myself pondering her belly, its slight roundedness – only natural and yet, to this particular eye, more than usually redolent of fecundity; whereupon a strong diagnostic instinct took hold of me.

Of course I had seen inside many people, the deepest recesses of their abdomens and peritoneal cavities, the brain within the skull. I reckoned my knowledge of female anatomy peerless. But this was a new dispensation for me: I felt I had to be sure of my condition. It was time to make use of that compact mirror.

I daresay Steven was surprised by my request, possibly

it stirred something in him he didn't care to acknowledge. But he gave his blessing, no doubt thinking it commendable, not least after I suggested it was something I did for 'self-empowerment'. And still I felt his care for Eloise, his gaze on my shoulders like a cloak.

Thus I was supplied with speculum kit, KY jelly and pocket torch. I warmed the speculum in my bathroom sink, urinated, wiped and settled myself on the bed – knees up, thighs wide, pillows under my rump and head, endeavouring to 'relax'. With the jelly I lubricated the bills and my index and middle fingers, burrowed one finger in to locate the cervix and judge the angle for the speculum. Satisfied, I made as unguinous an entrance as was possible, then – hearing my old self ('*We always ask our patients to take a deep breath . . .*') – I introduced the speculum, locked its bills, framed my view, positioned my mirror, and, hands free, clicked on the flashlight.

The sense of fathoming virgin territory was profound. I concede mild surprise that my fingers could delve so deep. Palpating gently, I assessed vulva and pelvic floor muscles. My fingertips brushed cervix, and I pressed on my belly over the uterus, gauging size, next locating and sizing the ovaries. Finally, by mirror and torchlight I was able to make out the little bulb of the cervix, the external os glistening, pinkish, cyst-free – a perfect circle. I adjudged myself to be right in the middle of my menstrual cycle – thus fertile. It was an absorbing process and, if I am honest, a beautiful sight to behold – however surpassingly strange it was to now find myself physically defined like so.

I did little else with my 'first day' other than retrieve my bag from the back of the gardens at a suitable moment. But never again would I flout the Blakedene house routine, the 7am alarm, the 8am communal breakfast . . . Thereafter I trooped down like a good soldier, albeit careful to bring along for my defence something from Eloise's rack of Gallimards and Flammarions. Genet's *Un captif amoureux* made a shield for me from one stocky bespectacled man, clearly a nerd who pumped iron, and insisted each day on telling me how complete was his recovery, how I had to hook up with him for drinks 'on the outside' as soon as he was back in charge of emergent markets at BarCap.

In general I was no better than semi-conscious through the morning's three-hour Cognitive Behavioural group. I preferred to admire the grounds through the open window, feel the sun on my face, exercise my new-sharpened sense of smell. The 'art pavilion' I adored, and there befriended poor anorexic Sara, who made very striking colour-fields but was continually supervised post-mealtimes to ensure No Purging. I felt invigilated myself, since Art was the domain of my confederate Tregaskis, and I was wary that he display no overpowering weirdness in relation to me. Mercifully he seemed silently proud of our secret compact, went about his own business even if his eyes followed me. It was only that I felt him dogging my steps, wishing further instruction, enlightenment as to when our 'bargain' would be fulfilled. I warded him away with meaningful stares. I suppose he couldn't be sure what I might do to him, had I the inclination.

I had enough in my own headspace to be contending with – had made the now-familiar encounter with all the stored sense-memory of the host body. Inhabiting Eloise's mind brought its share of unwelcome, even disturbing discoveries, but none quite so disturbing as those wrought by the inner life of the wretched Carver. Still, I sensed how great had been her recent mental tumult, and the instinct led me to her curio-like violet-coloured diary. Just by laying fingers on it I learned a stunning amount, unhappily so. And yet this nightmare past of hers was one from which I felt I had newly awakened. I felt some share of Eloise's peace, of knowing she was cared for. A significant part of that, I saw, was courtesy of Steven: I had to grant him his clinical success. And yet it seemed to me he had done little more than be a sympathetic ear, an undertaking that had cost him extravagantly, in time and much else. And still he seemed to want to keep me around, a few more days of 'aftercare'. But by any account I was done there.

The vigour I felt was considerable, yet held in reserve. There seemed no need to exert myself, only to tend my garden. I was going nowhere, but felt a curious pleasure in busily doing nothing – watching music videos in tee-shirt and track-pants, dipping into *Elle* and *Marie Claire* between sessions with Radiguet and Lautréamont. My old Forrest-impetus, the former knife-sharpness in my head, had been traded for a curiously diffuse sensation: the world felt turned inside out – melancholy had a new face and a new name – but I experienced a new interest too in the things around me – concepts, behaviours. It seemed I could better make out the light falling on the edges of things. And this began to feel like the true prize for which I'd sold myself, a means by which I could forget the recent ordeals, reap the grace I had bargained for, before whatever reckoning fell due.

One morning I threw open the window and a light freshening air pervaded the room. Until then I'd paid only cursory attention, a man's disregard, to the flowers in the clear vase on the sill: heavily fragrant honeysuckle, violet, tuberose, lilies a perfect white with perfect yellow pistils, not perfectly fresh but unwilted yet on their tall stalks. At the touch of one petal, though, my sense of Eloise's relationship with Leon Worrell became precise and vivid. (My sense of 'Robert Forrest', how I had treated her, came bundled in the same, and made a sour reproach.) But the flowers directed me to hunt out a letter kept folded in her bedside. Here, then, was my protector. And for the first time in my bargained-for out-of-body state, I felt a pull that was not quite voluntary – a proper residual instinct or urging of the former host. I hadn't thought Eloise contained such strength of will. But I had the strangest conviction now that this was a door to which I had been led.

Watching and waiting from the seat by my window, it occurred to me that Eloise might need glasses. Maybe it was the Indian-summer heat that made a haze before my eyes, but then as I saw Leon's hip-rolling stroll up the Blakedene drive – visibly not quite at ease yet focused, expectant – I felt an unaccountable cloggy drowsiness come over me, a sort of sensuous inanition. I had to steel myself for this meeting I'd requested, since it seemed to me that whether I could function in his presence would determine whether I had any hold over – any stake in – this life I'd so presumptuously robbed.

Seated in the wainscoted library I knew we were being watched, but Leon's eyes were fixed on me, possibly the most solicitous gaze I'd felt in years. I heard myself asking after Clyde, his son, how things were for him at school. Leon sighed, meaningfully.

'Ah he's bright, so bright. But it's a problem, see. My boy's got a sweet way, sweet manners – I'd like him to keep 'em – but I just don't think they're gonna let him.' ('They', I discerned, were the rough boys, the bane of Leon's life, males like his brother.) 'I was done with all that bad-boy shit time I was fourteen, man. Lynval, he still thinks he's the *bwai*, and I'm the broke-joke, coconut boy. Good job he's not so tough.'

I enquired after the state of his business: he sounded a little defensive, for all that his order-book was full. He asked how my treatment had gone, eyes a tad clouded by suspicion. I gathered he found the Blakedene techniques (and tariff) outlandish. I had to agree, but also felt bound to persuade him my cure had taken. 'My shrink, he's a sound man, Leon. He's shown me I've only got one life to live, can't let it be defined by somebody else – what happened in the past . . .'

He wasn't wholly mollified. So what was I going to do now? What did he *want* me to do? He shook his head, said that was 'typical me', happy-go-lucky, not to be trusted, my time with him just an optional accessory. His face was only rueful as he chided me: I intuited that his tongue could get a good deal closer to sandpaper. But in truth I was more involved in the sense of how beautiful this man was, how much bigger than me he now seemed. Something shifted me nearer to him, urged me to tell him I would like for 'us' to try a new start, a proper be-ing-together. He absorbed this, rubbed his chin, weighed me in the balance.

'I got to be who I am, Elle, got to speak my mind. Don't want to have to brush off the life I already got. Can't shed my skin, y'know?'

I assured him that nor could I – that such integrity was vital.

'And Clyde, he's gotta to have structure round him, Ellie, that means more than just being his buddy in the playground.'

I told him I knew as much. His smile remained on the edge. He looked aside, shaking his head mildly. 'Well, you know how it is . . . We both got troubles enough, now we're gonna get shit off people all day.'

'Fuck 'em,' I said, smiled, laced his fingers in mine.

He laughed, properly, heartily, truly amused by me. 'Hey, this is good, Elle. Straight talking. How come we never talk properly?'

'*De quoi voulez-vous parler, mon chéri?*'

'*Uh, la poésie . . . ?*' he deadpanned. Now my turn to

laugh. He came over earnest. 'Means a lot to me you wore my earrings, girl. And that dress – does mad things for your eyes.'

No such intent to please had been in my head at the time I put my clothes on; but, clearly, a charm had been over me. In the easy hush between us I suggested we could have a furlough out in the grounds, unsupervised. Behind our smiles was a clear seriousness. I was a little light-headed, in the pit of my stomach a tremble, within my hips a distinct hollowness – familiar and yet radically new.

We walked between the beds, hand in hand, very purposely to the outer limit of the estate, under cover of those copious lilacs. By now I knew what I would do. He kissed me, my lips slightly parted, and he took the invitation. Blood was shooting through my body now, the warmth radiating to my face. He murmured that he had 'no protection', I professed I was myself unprotected, but wanted him to know this was simply no hindrance to the abandon I was feeling; and this he seemed to appreciate.

I helped him free of his jeans, braced myself against a pine trunk and took him in my arms – he most concerned, most touchingly, for my comfort. I helped him inside, the crown of him first insistent and then pressing home – before the novel sense of hosting him, a startlingly alien invasion under my skin. It felt an indignity of sorts, but one I had to get past; and, indeed, other feelings were taking me over. I got my thighs round his hips, I was internally pliant, his motions were considerate and careful not to hurt me. I was surprised by a few words that fell from my mouth in urgent, exhortative whispers – 'passion words', industrial strength. If I decided it was right, this was because there was a voice in my head, probing like a tongue, light and whispery, telling me so. And for all that the new sensation was consuming me quite brainlessly, I should have listened more closely, since the voice was no longer mine.

In our post-coital erotic banality – as he courteously produced tissue paper so that I might wipe myself – something settled me in my resolve: I was going to leave here, go free, with him.

It was not, you understand, a passing fancy – not that my brains were screwed loose, I wasn't fooled by an afterglow, for I'd known higher ecstasies. No, rather, it was a wholly unprecedented form of gravity's pull I felt acting upon me. As a man – at best – I only ever toyed with the notion of assuming the onus of fatherhood. On occasions when tough decisions had arisen, each time I closed the book mentally, had three children aborted in the womb – and 'children', I must culpably admit, they surely were. Now, in Eloise's body, I had begun to want to feel bonds, ties to ground, the true weight and seriousness of the world. I believed I had some inkling of 'the biological clock'. I was entertaining what it would mean to be so profoundly, parturiently heavy.

That said . . . conscious of the wild-mercury element in my mental state, my volatile physical being, I opened two sets of accounts on the matter. With Leon we made plans as lovers do – the broad essentials agreed, the traps and vagaries all to come. Steven folded into my scheme when I shared it with him, as I had known he would. I told neither of them it was my intention to keep the terrible Sir James on board somehow, win him round on the far shore of this indiscretion. There were material needs to consider. I would emerge, I believed, as a more dutiful daughter, ditch the clubs and the bang-bang music, do something with my life that befitted my brain. I wondered suddenly about opportunities in surgery. The aptitude was alive in my hands. And that world would scarcely have seen the like of 'me'.

Tregaskis posed me a minor inconvenience the night before my departure. After all, I'd kept him sweet with pledges that the hour was nigh. These he now, understandably, ceased to accept. I visited his room intending to calm him. He got hold of my wrist very tightly. But I got my nails to his throat, made him painfully aware of my intimate knowledge of the major veins of the neck. That proved the end of his rebellion. Before I swept out, I shoved his awful clay bust off his desk and to the floor, where it broke – a careless revolt of my own.

He got his revenge, of course, put his evil eye on Leon's and my escape by taking a lunatic leap from the Blakedene veranda. Leon was inevitably thrown by the gruesome sight of the open fracture. For me there was only fury – fury I was forced to fight down. But as we drove away and out toward Oxfordshire, our first night *à deux*, I saw a different sort of clenched grimness in Leon's features. It was jealousy, simply. He had decided, some-how, that there had been 'something between' Tregaskis and me.

The hotel proved to have been a false inspiration, a chimera. In the corridors of that place were ghosts for me, ghosts of myself and Malena. Leon and I dressed smartly for dinner but in silence. Inevitably, once we were seated and the wine poured, he brushed aside my toast, since he had an urgent question: *'Who've you been here with before?'*

I heard myself arguing, in the lowest, most decorous possible voice, that Robert Forrest was nothing to me now, that he had no reason to be envious or insecure. This only riled him further.

'That's not it, Elle. I know it's him was envious of me, everything about me intimidates him . . .'

I could not tell him that this had never occurred to me, that Dr Forrest had barely registered his existence. What I knew, heart sinking, was that I had undone much 'good' work. And this only the least of it, as we endured the meal. I knew, too, how much finer a part-ner, a lover he could have been to her. I understood truly now – that hope, that wellbeing I had been feel-ing, it was Eloise's by right: at a point where she had begun to contemplate living again, living fully, I had destroyed her life.

That night we slept coldly beside one another. He, I knew, was only turning over old doubts, prodding some poorly healed wounds to his pride. For me, the dream, the illusion, was over. I was in mounting dread – dread of

Her, Her hated reappearance, grinning like the harbinger of the end, 'the host unstable', time to move on . . .

‿℮‿

We were out on the motorway back to London before noon. Our relations remained arctic. I was counting the miles. Some music on the radio seemed to abate the tension. I was tapping my fingers idly on the window when I looked up and glimpsed Her behind me – reflected in his driver's mirror.

She was there and then was not, still I heard Her behind my eyes.

Where are you running to now, doctor . . . ?

No, no, you say – why are you with me?

To witness for myself. Your stunning departure? You have been most inventive. Sadly for you, this cannot continue.

Why? What business is it of yours?

All mine, doctor, entirely mine. And this, I will not accept. It is disreputable. Aberrant. By any standard. What made you think you could carry out a violation of this order?

You— you let me do it.

Fool. You are beyond my control. You are responsible.

No, I felt you there, always.

You wished it so. But I had no part of it. And now I require that you move on . . .

Leon was watching me as I muttered to myself – riled, at first, like a lover in a mood, then baffled, then actively alarmed. He grasped my arm, I reeled from him, suddenly fighting for my breath, demanding that he get us off the road, seek help. As he protested, I was gripped once again by parasitic pain all over and right through me – those abysmal sensations that seemed to signal my end. And as before, there was nothing in my head but the need to save my life, prolong the nightmare-cycle, by any means necessary.

The lie came quickly to me – that we were being followed. My distress Leon could only have read as authentic. Manfully he bossed the crisis, sought an exit from the motorway, tried to calm me though I was climbing up the seat in agony, at one point quite recklessly grabbing the wheel. He got us off-road, down country lanes, headed deep into autumnal forest. I was ebbing away, I knew, even as I urged him deeper, deeper, and we rattled down a rutted track adjacent to a ridge, a steep drop off to the left, down a bank to a ravine.

There he stopped. I begged him to go to the car boot: did he have a weapon, anything to defend us? He was dumbfounded, clearly, but as fast as he ducked out, I was ransacking Eloise's luggage, found my leather bag, located my scalpel. He hauled himself back in beside me, crook-lock in hand, his face was pure and frantic 'care'. I saw the pulse in his strong left carotid artery and I thrust the blade – made my sightless dive into the tunnel.

۞

I emerged shaken, swooning, seated, my hands – black-skinned hands – grasping the air before me like Lazarus. I was he, and she quite prone in the passenger seat, head slumped. The sight of her, lifeless, knifed me to the heart in a way I couldn't have anticipated. Gently as I could, I touched her face, lifted her chin with a finger – and saw that her throat was a bloody rift, lacerated, a slash there mapping the wound I would have left on Leon were I not now within his skin.

Devilry. In an instant my heart was hammering, I forced my way out of the vehicle – the daylight all around was a horror to me, the seclusion couldn't shield me for long but I had to fight an impulse to shout at the sky, protest this new punishment, this latest treachery.

I thought fast, reckless. No right solution came – the bulk of the car and what it held was the size of my predicament, rising by the second. All I could think to do was to try to eradicate it, burn it down.

I removed my bag from within her luggage. Seeing Leon's nestled by it, I chose in a stroke to swap my crisp shirt and jeans – my 'country wear' – for khaki combats and a bruise-blue hooded top. I could feel power in my new trunk and legs, in the grasp of my hands, and yet I knew I was fundamentally helpless.

I freed the car's handbrake, got out and shoved, slipping and staggering, but succeeded in pushing it over the crest of the slope. Once it had struck a tree and halted, I made my stumbling descent, unscrewed the petrol cap, tore a strip of shirt-cloth and soaked it, then tied it to the driver's seat and set it alight. I jammed another strip into the cap-hole, ignited that for good measure. Then I crashed my way on down through the trees, grabbing branches for support en route to the ravine floor, my footing hazardous. At my back I heard the crackle of fire, smelled smoke, then heard bangs resonant as gunfire. Within moments I knew, behind me was an inferno.

Pounding through the clinging tangle of the wood, adrenalin driving me forward, I was sure – at last – that the scales were gone from my eyes. She was willing me to fail, I was sport for Her, there was no bargain, no rules, only ever-deepening, widening torment. Had I really imagined it could be otherwise? Yes – for a span of days I'd let myself believe I had, as part of our business, been loaned some share of Her powers. The word is hubris; it has special and forceful application to those so foolish as to solicit the devil.

There would be no easy escape from the artfully made fall-out of my latest outrage. Hell to pay, I knew – this was news, the world would know of it, though never know the half of it – the ruination I'd already caused, the madness I'd set in train. Police would soon be attending, an exclusion zone thrown out, how swiftly I could only guess, but for sure I was now a fugitive with a face, name and number. Once again I would have to hide my face. First among the frantic notions flaring in my head, I thought about burrowing myself down somewhere in this very wood – lodging in the hollow of a trunk like some parasite. But to sit in the dirt, trembling, awaiting capture? No, I had to get back to the city, lose myself, diffuse myself there, in that sprawl. London was not so far away.

There was money in Leon's wallet. I broke out of the woods into a stretch of meek grey suburb, dashed across a motorway, boarded a commuter train at Denham – mine the lowest head in the carriage. At Northolt I switched underground. By now I was devising the story I would tell, improving on what I-as-Eloise had babbled to Leon while gripped by the convulsions of oncoming death. Half-satisfied, I allowed myself to slump back in my seat awhile, near to sleep, under my clothes my various scrapes and bruises stinging sorely. What kept me awake was the whiff of gasoline off my hands. I was on dangerous ground.

Worse, I was feeling sick, physically sick – in no way renewed by fresh, younger flesh as I'd been previously. But this was not the all-consuming nausea of The End; rather, a flat, dull wretchedness that leached right through me. How long, I wondered, would be my lease on this body? It felt inherently 'unstable'. Would I be running forever now, in permanent flux, a succession of temporary, vulnerable physical shells?

The train hammered its way in and out of central London, carried me out east to Bethnal Green. Hackney was my turf, my hood – in the parlance I knew Leon disdained. My dilemma had been whose door I would knock up, whom I could rely on, given what was liable to fall on my head and, by association, theirs. My default choice would have been my car-dealer pal Curtis, but then it was his pride and joy I'd abandoned in flames on a woodland slope, a woman's body inside it. I could count on Alvin, Rufus, Spike – my subcontractors – to buy my story, give me shelter. Police were not widely reckoned a force for good round Dalston and Stoke Newington. But tracking any of these men down in the time I had felt impossible. Conceivably my ex-partner Sheanna could give me an hour or so's grace. Yet at this notion, an image of 'my' son surged into my mind . . . and I felt some immovable piety there – a powerful residual refusal to bring my contamination into that house.

In the end I made my choice on, I suppose, the same basis as Steven once chose to drag me into a black hole of his own making, believing Robert Forrest the least judgemental soul of his acquaintance, the friend closest to a pure amoral state. There, he chose well. Here, I chose badly, as it turned out. I chose 'my' brother Lynval.

Down the drabness of Kingsland Road, a journey I'd never liked even from behind the wheel of my van; turning off to the square of new-build low-rise in Holly Street, up the stairs to his door, his den. Lynval was showing two sullen boys out, and they sneered at me in concert. My rag-tag dragged-through-a-hedge demeanour seemed to bring Lynval some amusement, and he bade me enter, offered me a can of lager and a toke on a small fragrant pipe, both of which I declined.

Studying Lynval from the opposing sofa as I told him my tale was like peering into a distorting mirror. He was I, only shorter, leaner, more gaunt in the face, his hair and beard razored with odd oriental zigzags, his eyes a little reddish and opaque, his smile much thinner than mine. The clothes he wore were only a box-fresh, more fancily embroidered version of the street-wear I had on me, but he carried himself as if they were the finest threads. And he appeared genuinely rapt, thoughtful, even tickled by my story – not surprised, by any part. Still, my request for money, clearly, gave him a valuable chance to levy judgement on me, for the sad folly of my acting so 'white', trying to be chocolate to that rich girl's milk. I sat there and took my licks – staring fixedly at my big hands, calloused by long work with bradawl and chisel – tamping down the urge I felt to wring my brother's neck. Lynval told me he would see what he could do; first I should oblige him by hitting his bathroom, showering my broke-joke self, perhaps availing myself of his wardrobe.

Behind a locked door, the shower hissing ignored, I looked hard at my eyeballs in the mirror. What had I done to Leon's face? The sheer starkness of my hunted, haunted desperation was so clear, so disfiguring of him – this considerate mother's son, this diligent if troubled father, this complicated but essentially honourable man whose life I'd traduced. The alienation from self that I felt was vertigo-like, I could smell my own corruption, the manner in which I'd made myself irredeemable.

In my head was a fragment of a book that I – and Leon, to my snobbish surprise – both knew: that the only true journey was not to a foreign country but behind foreign eyes, to perceive the world *avec les yeux d'un autre, de cent autres* . . . A hundred, though, seemed to me an interminable punishment, standing there alone with my pointless physical prowess, my redundant self-education, my broken heart.

No, I didn't want no shower, no change . . . I wanted to be running again. I stepped quietly from the bathroom, to the threshold of the living space. No Lynval did I see. But peering round a corner I saw him on his

410

cramped veranda, pacing slowly, muttering into a phone.

'Well he here now, man. Decision be yours. Could be your business, could be, if what he say happen happen, oddawise . . . Naw man, mi just concerned citizen, mi tell you what mi know, if it be mi brethren or whatevah . . .'

My brother, my 'brethren', this bad *bwai* was, I now understood, also a *nark*, an *infarma* . . . I didn't hesitate, moved, dropped the latch, was gone, directly to the stairwell and back onto those grey streets.

I headed north, out of Dalston through Canonbury, taking the backstreets, past terraces and estates, wincing in heatless autumn sunlight that nonetheless gave the windows of houses a blank, white-hot glow. I badly needed to turn the day dark before sundown. At Finsbury Park I tramped onto a disused railway line made into a rambler's path, strode along this grassy embankment until it led down onto the old track bed, sombre and shaded by oak, beech and ash. I trudged some miles. A pair of joggers passed me at pace, a hapless father with pushchair rather slower yet more hasty. Otherwise I saw not a soul: this, clearly, a place where one went not much wishing to be seen, with its odour of dead leaves, dog shit, cheap stimulants. At Highgate I made reconnaissance of a masonry train tunnel, found it suitably dark and dank, rated it a hideout. I pressed onward, though, through the mournful Highgate Wood and into another maze of backstreets, before I chanced on a truly promising bolthole.

It was a cemetery north of Muswell Hill, evidently abandoned to the wild, densely tree-lined. I hopped a wall and found myself in a relic of the nineteenth century. Graves were overgrown, stone crosses protruding from tall grasses as though some essence of decay had condensed in them. Certain tombs were adorned by carved figures, spider-webbed by creeping vines. Others were reduced to piles of rock. I passed a decapitated angel with calmly crossed hands; a gravestone with a carved skull atop it. This, the land of the spider and the beetle, deadness laying claim to all matter.

Shrouded by trees at the rear of these grounds was a stone chapel, its roof bashed in by a fallen yew. Within, everything was in pieces, though the area around the font seemed miraculously unharmed. I shifted some broken pews into the rudiments of a lean-to shelter, and I lay down and found sleep.

When I woke, in profound darkness, even I could feel a chill in my blood. I decided to forage out. With the change in my pocket I bought provisions, an evening newspaper at a shop on the Broadway. I didn't have to ransack the paper to find my face staring out at me from Page 5: a holiday snap, me and Sheanna in Corfu, cropped – if I remembered right – to exclude baby Clyde crawling under the table. The zoom-in accentuated my proud chin and red eyes, induced by some alcohol and the camera flash.

I felt it now, some deep-lying vestige of the anger and frustration of this man; also his conflicted feeling for Eloise – there had been a crushing tenderness there, but also a veiled desire of attainment, an undigested resentment of unearned money. Leon was modest, 'humble', yet proud of himself, keen to impress. As a youth he had learned the art of staring right back at girls who stared at him. Eloise he had certainly wanted to touch, from first sight. I knew for sure, as no one else could, that when their skins met they felt the same wonder. He shuddered, though, always shuddered, whenever and wherever she introduced him clumsily to 'friends'.

Those two lives, those twin hopes were buried now, thanks to me, and the gravestone I'd erected was this news story, this gift to all the sensational papers, the revived myth of the psychopathic black man at large. My umbrage, I knew, was a waste, too little too late. But it struck me very suddenly who would be feeling similarly, even more acutely, seeing this same travesty. My reptile mind went to work.

I waited until morning, passed the night on the chapel floor, then dialled Steven's number from a call-box: a simpler blackmail, a better version, played with more pronounced distress, of the fiction I as Eloise spun to Leon, I as Leon spun to Lynval: the killing of Eloise a job ordered by hired goons of Sir James Keaton. I heard the misery in Steven's voice. Yet his solicitude for me was great, urgent, affecting. Without question he would meet me – clean clothes, money, a friend's ear, all of these I could have. That same night he came to my lair. When I found him, when he took hold of me, embraced me, I was surprised to feel myself moved. The hateful tears that sprang to my eyes were not wholly feigned. It pained me that I then had to go through with my performance. It pained me worse, though, that Steven had brought me no assistance other than a plan to deliver me to the police. The brute hopelessness of my predicament pressed down on me again. I meant him no real harm, but I certainly intended to take from him something I could use. I knew I had sufficient force in me.

Shouldn't I have anticipated that Grey would step from the shadows, the dependable presence, the loyal wingman, the rock? Yes, and it ruined immediately any chance I had of 'working on' Steven – since Grey is the man for whom no useful ends permit errant means, for whom no crooked road can come to any good. Thus our pointless face-off, my ungovernable urge to taunt him – taunt both of them. I hadn't even determined how to make my exit when I felt crushing pain in my head, and Grey jumped at my disadvantage to rush me. I hit him very hard, in my fury I stomped on him, might have injured him very badly had Steven not rugby-tackled me. For all that I had enough in the tank to best them both, I felt in horrible shape by the time I was clear. I tracked back through Highgate Wood, bedded down in that old tunnel, the floor carpeted with damp leaves. I longed for sleep, yet felt so brutally head-sore I wasn't certain I would wake.

But once sleep had claimed me I suffered an appalling dream – my first since I'd left Robert Forrest behind. I was being trailed, taunted by some woman in the street; in the next instant I was stabbing her with some pointed instrument, piercing her throat repeatedly, she not quite dead, life in her eyes though her head was near-severed, bobbing, ghastly. Then the ground shook, godlike intervention, and my bones were being ripped out through my flesh as if by some great invisible barb, spine and rib-cage wrenched gorily from my chest . . .

Daylight found me in physical inertia but slow-growing mental certainty. I remained a capable man, if nothing else. And I saw nothing left for me but one last stand against my tormentor.

ઢ

Once night fell I threw up my hood and picked my way through the wood to Highgate station, rode the train to Warren Street, emerged into rain and wet mist, pressed on into Fitzrovia. I was sodden as I mounted the stone steps up to the double doors of that Edwardian mansion block. But no door was going to bar me, I intended to have my confrontation by any means. As it happened, the entrance clicked and swung open for me. I was awaited, it seemed.

I mounted the stairs to the sixth floor, slipped down the corridor, outside the door to apartment 6F. Turning the doorknob, I found it unlatched. I trod on tiptoe into the gloom of the entrance hall. All within was silent, shadowy – a novice in these matters would have thought it deserted. A small white card lay on the parquet. It is-sued from Dr Grey Lochran FRCS(Ed), and requested that a Mrs Ragnari call him.

I stepped left into the darkened reception room. And there She stood, in Her Russian coat and cowl, before a trio of lit candles on the mantelpiece.

'Good evening, doctor.'

'Dijana. Is that still . . . the best name we have for you?'

She was impassive. 'This is what you came to ask me? Why do you waste your precious time? There is nothing for you here. In that new skin of yours you are a badly wanted man. You must keep moving.'

'Where? Where does this end? Am I meant to do this forever?'

'Of your physical being, there will be an end, I am sure. It ends when I am done with you, or when you surrender. But a-ways to reach that yet, I suspect. Promises to keep, miles to go before you sleep. Above all, you must remember, you are ours for eternity, doctor. I appreciate you struggle to grasp the concept. And I fear I can't explain it to you. Beyond the petty hourglass I have, myself, no true cognisance of time . . .'

It was then I asked Her to tell me what was Hell. Her answer left me alone in the ruins. Her triumph was complete in Her appalling smile.

'But for all that, tell me,' She said, 'do you still regret our business?'

Then She stepped lightly across the floor and slipped between the double-doors. I recovered myself, followed Her into that room which was the double of the one we'd left – the same parquet, the same great damask curtains torn and frayed – save for 'my' cheval glass lording over all. She stood apart from it, motionless, Her back to me. I was recovering the ferocity I'd brought with me, the desire for violence that had carried me here.

'Before we're "done" – I don't know how, but I will make you regret our "business" too.'

416

My words were hollow. I stared at Her dark and narrow shoulders, the glossy mane of Her hair, waited to see what haemorrhaged eyes, what putrescent face She would turn on me. But silence reigned still, eerily. I stepped in front of the mirror. And there at its depths was myself – in full length, the body and face of Dr Robert Forrest.

I wore the dark suit in which I had met my demise. I seemed a little startled, yes, but soon free of that surprise, for what was more familiar and dearly beloved than my own countenance? The look in my eye was so affecting, meek, chastened. I touched my cheek, my brow, with a tenderness I thought I'd lost long ago, as if I were a father to myself. *Where have you been to, my prodigal one?* With what a bursting heart was I ready to forgive the flaws and failings in myself I'd once held to be insurmountable! If the years had not been entirely kind, there were enduring qualities in myself I had overlooked, distracted by the merest vanity, overbearing pride, truly hideous folly . . .

And then the surface of the glass shirred and warped, distorted, as if vomiting forth the illusion it had held like water, and the mirror showed me I was Leon once more, that hunted sickness restored to my face.

'Goodbye, Doctor Forrest . . .'

I heard the words in my head, nowhere else; felt the affront of a door shut hard in my face; and was seized by a frenzy. Her back to me still, She was shaking like a dog. A blast of freezing air crossed the room to me. And I lunged at Her, spun Her round, held Her wrist and slapped Her across the face just as hard as I'd strike a man. Her head whiplashed violently, Her hand shot to Her face – and when Her eyes found mine again the look was unmistakably one of shock, mingled with real, naked fear – with horror. Oh, but I drank that in.

I was insane, lost, the impulse was irresistible, such a dominant part of me in that moment. I seized Her, forced Her to the floor, found the scalpel in my pocket and stabbed down into the heart of Her face. I had not thought for one moment of what would surely follow . . . but then came the throes of the change, the plummet, the revived surety that the shift had occurred.

ى

A dead weight lay half-across me, I heaved myself free of Leon, hair across my eyes, my pulse racing, my arms painfully thin.

I found my unsteady feet, looked into the glass – saw a ghost, a girl with no memory of where she came from or where she had been, no sense even of her own name. The room was frigid. I knew I had to be gone. Leon's body – was it best left abandoned here? In my new and consuming fear of what forces would be after me, I decided in an instant on the act that might conceivably cover my tracks. Without another thought, I stooped, moulded the scalpel into Leon's palm and slashed open his throat.

As I watched the blood flow, I heard the front door creak in the dark somewhere behind me.

Sick, I darted aside into shadow with a practised stealth – made my way deftly through the cover of blackness, the unseen route back to the door – didn't dare look behind me, found the light and ran. From on high above me I heard 'Dijana!' shouted with awful force. But I was not She, that was not my name.

~

What I had seen in the mirror was a terrified female –
quite stripped, for sure, of whatever powers 'Dijana
Vukovara' had possessed. And that fear stayed with me,
cold in my bones, as I dashed blindly through darkened
West End streets – skittering on heels, threading clumsily past strangers, avoiding eye contact – too scared to
stop, but clueless, purposeless, as to where I should go.
Nothing beckoned. I was homeless and penniless, physically shaken, vulnerable and yet too traumatised to contemplate the enormity of hunting out a safe place where
I might lay my head down. So I kept pacing the streets,
for all of the night, hiding in recesses and alleys when the
soles of my feet were too raw. I stole fruit from an all-
night store, drank from a fountain, ghosted from point
to point until dawn. I believed I was by nature a hard
woman to find. But who was I anyhow? Still, in my headspace, I was receiving no data, no input whatsoever from
whomever had been the last occupant.

Rather, my head was in a hellish, boiling state. More
than ever before I felt I had filled up a previously empty
vessel. And yet there was something there, a sonic trace
– a sort of drone, a muted cacophony between my ears, a
babble. At intervals, a stinging sensation shot through me
from head to toe, excruciating, sciatic-like pain through
bone and muscle to the tips of my fingers. It was as if the
flesh had been infected, poisoned, by the pure malignity
of its old inhabitant. I started to wonder in what insidi-

ous ways this new sense of evil might creep across me; or whether, in my degenerate state, I could even distinguish what was Hers and what mine.

Then, with the dawn, I found a growing sense that my stumbling feet were leading me, drawn by some sense memory to pound a familiar route. Up Baker Street and down the Euston Road I drifted on some implacable tide, until I was gazing up from street-level at a huge, long, sombre brownstone apartment block, adorned here and there by Art Deco detail, somehow anonymous in its hulking prestige, but ghostly in the pearl-light of dawn, the sea of blank windows suggestive of many hundreds of flats within. I climbed the path to the main entrance: 'Keppel House' the lettering on the awning. Before me a grid of door-buzzers, and in that moment I was altogether certain which to push: #371. I was answered by a crackle, an accented female 'Hello?', heard my voice, newly husky, asking to be admitted.

'Mund të më ndihmoni mua?'

A buzzer sounded, I pushed on the heavy main door and was admitted, rode a gated elevator to the fourth floor, and was standing for some long moments, perplexed, before #371 – when a stout 40-ish woman with small features, a bowl of dark hair and a faint moustache came out of the neighbouring door.

'Senka, gde si bio? Mi smo bili u potrazi za vas . . .'

Her name, I knew, was Bojana. She gestured me hurriedly, concernedly into her sparse flat. A humming computer and scribbled workbooks occupied a cheap plywood desk; the gallery kitchen was quietly spotless.

A double bed took up most of the living space, and I longed to lie down on it, but it was clearly in use as one more worktop rather than somewhere to sleep. On it sat stacks of washed and pressed bedsheets, plastic buckets full of squirting detergents, two hundred paper sheets for toilet seats, a job-lot box of prophylactics ... the mingled odour of hotel and hospital stores. And shapes of a buried reality were starting to emerge in my head.

Bojana was boiling a kettle to my right, asking me if I'd come back to work? Miras would be glad to see me. But had I made things right with Tamerlan? Was that all settled? She was addressing me in Serbian because she was from Sarajevo and I was a Kosovan Serb from Novo Brdo.

She pressed a mug into my hand and then led me next door into #371, the room I used to work, where the chairs were comfier. Polina, she muttered, was out getting her breakfast at McDonald's.

She had directed me to sit, like a child, and I did feel some benefit from the armchair's soft support – until a rap at the door, whereupon she hastened outside, and low muttering crept in from the hallway. I craned my neck from seated, saw a pale, balding man staring at me, most directly and charmlessly. Bojana was telling him I was her 'friend', not available, not for him.

I squirmed in the chair, out of his sight, so caught sight of my reflection in a full-length mirror stood in the corner of the room. In my inky, crumpled clothes, alarmingly whey-faced, I saw all my desperation still. Then the revived memories were erupting in my head, like a physical sensation, a blow falling down on my head with each.

I was Senka Boskovic, yes, daughter of Luka, farmer from Novo Brdo. I left from Pristina wanting a life beyond the fourteenth century, beyond the blighted everyday. London was my goal, my ambition to find work as a manicurist. But I do believe I knew full well in due course I would work as a prostitute.

My boyfriend Dragan was my accomplice for the journey, and Dragan did love me, we suffered together our awful shared lodging, tried to carry out plans we'd made together. But London is nothing but money, and the plain fact was that we owed three thousand pounds to the smuggler, the fixer. When all else failed, Dragan pimped me. His first efforts in this line, done in pubs and clubs, were miserable for both of us. A couple of 'successes', my leading strangers back to our shared mattress, sordid humiliation for £40 and £50. Then we tried a pitch in Soho. I was picked up for soliciting, but given a second chance. Dragan believed we needed a partner, tried to sell an 'interest' in me – a terrible error. I suffered more, he suffered worse. I never saw him again.

Bojana was back, reaching awkwardly up to a locked cupboard over the fitted wardrobes, bringing down a cardboard box and hefting it into my lap. I picked up the items strewn therein, pathetic things – a cloth scarf, black plastic sandals, tangled hairbrush and hair-bands, No 7 lipstick, pay-as-you-go phone. I held them and turned them, one by one, as my old life ebbed back into me. Bojana pressed a thick, grubby roll of banknotes into my hand, £300, my last day's wages, that day I disappeared . . . I was too stunned to show gratitude.

Tamerlan the Kazakh, master of whores, told me Dragan

had crossed him, accrued a heavy debt, and now that debt was on me: Dragan was history, like the fourteenth century, and now I worked for Tamerlan — was installed in his Berwick Street walk-up. That first day I simply refused to work. Indeed no man cared to touch me, since I couldn't stop crying. Tamerlan came round personally to resolve that situation, 'break me in', in the manner I knew was his hallmark. I was told briskly and in detail how my family would be made to pay, after I was done paying. He put the fear of God in me. I had no resort to the law, Tamerlan revelled in my helpless illegality.

My 'dates' were made through the internet. I received summons by text. Bojana ushered callers in and out. I was Aneta, I was Lucia, Natasha or Valera, Douschka or Veronika, Eva or Maria — like all the other girls I had a hundred names, multiple ages, numerous countries of origin. Our operations moved house more than once to avoid detection. But Keppel House came to seem solid, anonymous, 'high-end' . . .

Bojana, her crumpled face all superstitious fret, was extending to me two ibuprofen tablets and a beaker of water. Another rap at the door and there was Miras, burly in his black leather windbreaker, hardly 'pleased to see me'. Bojana waddled over to intercept him, an argument in antic tones began. Miras believed I was trouble, that Tamerlan would be having strong words. All this had redounded on him too, for he had been my guard, twenty-four hours a day.

Sexually, in myself, I had always been demure, reserved. Now my work was so fetid I wanted to scrub out my skull. Some men resisted paying, others demanded what they hadn't

paid for, violent and unsafe practices, of a piece with what
they thought fitting from a whore. I got familiar with male
sexual failure, male infantilism, the casual and pathetic
brutality that commonly accompanied these. My working
day started at 11am, my hourly rate £150, of which I kept
two twenties and a ten. I did seven or eight dates daily, and
there wasn't a day went by when I didn't either wish myself
dead or feel myself already buried, under rocks.

Miras was on the phone now, and making it his job to
obstruct my path to the door. I was impotently aware of
just how dreadful things were looking for me. I contemplated trampling a way over the bed, stood and walked
to the mirror. At closer quarters I saw the slap I as Leon
had given this face was still discernibly ruddy on my
left cheekbone. And then I saw my dark eyes, widening starkly, as a sense-memory as sharp as a jagged shard
sliced right into me . . .

. . . *standing before this mirror, I had waited for a man*
to come, hoping he'd never show – a man who came when I
didn't expect him, noiselessly and fast, behind my back like
a shadow falling over me . . . A blur of darkness, an evil va-
pour, filled with malediction. And then I fell, into the black.

Dizzily I felt a sensation of draining from my face,
staggered a little, toppled backward into the armchair.
My heart was pounding as if down to the last, an odious
sickness rising.

Miras had seen the money in my hand, was stood over
me now, barking at me, grasping my hand and shaking
it. I loosed some notes onto the floor, he cursed me, bent
down, and I knew there'd be no other chance – I lashed

out a foot, knocked him over, leapt up and stamped on his chest and head with all the force I had in me. Bojana's mouth hung open slack, in horror, as if I were her errant child. I dashed clear and into the corridor, thumped the elevator buttons, got it just as I saw Miras dragging himself out of the door, bloodied, a gun in his hand.

In the foyer, running for the double doors, I could see out into the daylight, see striding up the path the squat jowly man I knew as Tamerlan, flanked by two lieutenants. I turned tail down the corridor, concealed myself as I heard Miras and Tamerlan in heated exchanges, then edged my way out of this 'respectable place' through a fire door. I didn't stop until I was riding an underground train out of Baker Street. I stumbled off at Waterloo, vomited my guts onto the platform, wiped my mouth and dragged myself onward.

This because I was animated, felt myself febrile, by an idea, a vision of a place of greater safety – the Hartford family cottage, where Steven had once encouraged me to hole up and knock out my original paper on immuno-suppressants in facial transplant. The place had seemed to me then just as austere as Steven himself, but I was certain it would be currently unoccupied; more certain still that I remembered where Steven secreted his spare key; certain beyond doubt that no one would look for me there. I headed up to the Waterloo overground station, bought a ticket to Sawford, and from there connected with the small line from Hythe out to Dungeness.

ول

My business with Steven over those days – my conduct, the lengths to which I was forced – even now stir up a perishing sense of disgrace in me even now. Having trekked so far only to find the clapboard cottage evidently occupied, I changed my plan in haste – had now to engineer a meeting with Steven, carry off some sort of convincing role-play. He proved harder to track down than one would have imagined, yet I found him by loitering round the local watering hole, for all that I narrowly escaped a sort of molestation out of which Steven, implausibly, emerged as my white knight.

I found him changed, though – deeply changed, fundamentally unstable – my handiwork, I'm sure, the poisoning of his life and prospects. Will it be believed if I say I felt some sympathy for him still? I did wish to offer him some comfort. But I was myself struggling to function, had to hide myself away for hours while loathsome sensations wormed their way through me. Under the skin I felt myself to be decaying matter, food for maggots and moths. My 'impersonation' was hard to keep to. And when I sensed Steven had begun to think fondly of some kind of extended domesticity for the two of us, the warning sounds in my head became a clamour once more. For a moment, as we walked in some shaded woodland, I contemplated an invasion of him . . . but baulked at the last. Instead I resolved only to buy time. I used what I had to hand – I took him to bed. And I think in that moment I became conscious of a rot that was irreversible.

When we were done . . . he lifted himself off of me,

off of the bed, with the haunted look of one whose core had been cracked beyond repair. He belted himself into a robe, stumbled out of the room, I heard him moving around. I tried to succumb to sleep but couldn't. There were sounds in my head, the flitting and twitching of moths, bellicose croaking of frogs, the odour of the marsh in my nose. But after a while I didn't know any more what was sleep and what was waking.

Then I was conscious, sat up in the gloom of dawn. My face was alive with pain, lips twitching, my tongue a parched worm incapable of forming words. I thrust my hand up in front of me and found it a ghastly stone-grey, the fingertips blackened and striated. Spidery black lines crept down my nails like cracks in a frozen river.

I groped out of bed toward the wardrobe, pushed away the clothes that hung over the mirror, knowing what I would see – something dreadful – those same spidery lines webbing the left side of my face, like intimations of gangrenous decay, my wild eyes in the glass drawn to them like a magnet to iron filings. At my shoulders, between my breasts, on my thighs – patchy purplish stains mottled the skin.

In sheer derangement I pulled on the clothes I'd discarded, snatched at whatever I thought I could use from any surface, focused wholly on immediate flight. Until I grew conscious of the silence that had seemed to have settled beyond the bedroom threshold – and my momentum slowed.

I tiptoed through the door to the living space, detecting instantly a dry, stale, rancid feel to the air. Underneath the living room table, on which Steven's laptop glowed still, he was lying on the floor, beneath a thick woollen rug, in a foetal curl. Uneasily I trod nearer – whereupon the completeness of that silence sent a shudder through me. I knew it, then – before I laid a hand on his head, turned him to me, saw his sightless eyes, tongue semi-protruded through bluish lips. The pill-jar stood by a mug on the table-top. I knew he would have measured and imbibed his dose meticulously, with small sips of water.

I pressed fingers to my brow to stop the images coming to me unbidden, of the boy, 'the brave Stevie', with whom I'd laughed and cavorted and chattered excitedly of all the grand things we'd do out in the big world. Disgraced far beyond tears, I held his head to my chest, sat with him in a pitiful dog-like observance of mourning for my old classmate – until finally the cold in the room, the stinging pains inside me and all they portended, were intolerable.

I erased his computer files, emptied his wallet, ransacked Tessa's wardrobe and drawers for accessories that could cover me more completely than my long coat and scarf. I found gloves, boots, outsized black sunglasses, a wide-brimmed floppy hat in black straw. Fully swathed, I had a sick sense of looking much more conspicuous than invisible. But there was no more time. I scuttled out and away, left Steven and the cottage behind me in grey light and morning mist.

It was not until a pair of women sat down opposite me in the train carriage, both clad in full, enveloping burqas, that I felt I had at least adequate protection from prying eyes as I retraced my journey back to London. But in my hard seat, the brim of my hat pulled low, hugging myself as if that might make me smaller, I was wondering all the way if it wasn't sheer moral hideousness that had begun to rot this body.

I holed up in the cheapest lodging I knew of, a guesthouse on a Victorian terrace in Crouch End. There, with the door locked and curtains closed, I passed a night stretched out like grim death and trying to suppress my groans, until I was insensible. Still I awoke, my blood still pumping, pain still acute, my skin's disease visibly worse.

The more that death seemed to own me, the harder I fought, unready to lie down and be done. But I wish . . . I truly wish instead I'd found a hole down which to throw myself, put an end on it all as I deserved. What happened next I never, ever intended or wished for – but should, after all, have foreseen.

⁓

The palliative I had in mind seemed obtainable in this body, for as long as something of it remained. I wanted access to hydromorphone, the strongest possible pain-killing injection. And I knew of a place that held a co-pious supply, albeit behind glass, under lock and key – the renowned Forrest Clinic of St John's Wood. I knew, moreover, that a full replica set of keys and security fobs lay in a drawer in the home office of my ex-friend Dr Grey Lochran. Burglary, though, was not an option, not in my wracked state. And yet it seemed to me I might still call on one ally within the Lochran household – someone who had kept faith in me, in whose eyes I was surely still untarnished. My plan was immediately clear, obvious, irrevocable. With Senka Boskovic's phone I dialled the number of my godson.

Calder remembered me well – 'Dijana', that is – I could hear excitement kindle in his voice. My own was low, controlled only with difficulty, yet I tried to replicate the come-hither she had worked on him once at my place. I knew within moments that he was convinced, willing to believe all I was saying – that Robert and I had endeavoured to vanish, 'go underground' together, but that Rab now had urgent need of some resources from his workplace, and no means to achieve entry without arousing suspicion.

'He's relying on you, Cal, I don't think there's anyone else he has the same regard for. So you must, must keep our secret, tell no one, above all not your father, he could never understand as you do . . .'

I heard the pull in my throat, my urgency wholly unfeigned – indeed I had to temper it. But I heard in return the boy's keenness, his sense of being called, the staunch readiness to do what was needful for 'Rab'. My instructions were precise as to where in his father's office he would have to forage. I warned him, though, to step with care.

Come the evening I stood in the shade of the tall, shimmering Scotch pines hemming the driveway of the Forrest Clinic – that so elegantly landscaped site, set back from its smugly prosperous residential street. In the

431

London dusk my Clinic looked like a fortress of forbidding panels in glass and burnt-sienna concrete. But I had to penetrate those defences: every nerve in me was alive with pain.

Gazing heavy-heartedly at the familiar façade, it seemed to me fated that I should be seeing the old place, surely for the last time, in fading light. Its design and construction had meant the world to me. Kuwabara, my architect, a genius of sorts, enlightened me to the theory of how a structure's façade ought, like a 'smooth skin', to wrap round its steel skeleton of pillars and beams. Nonetheless I had directed him sternly in turn: my Clinic was to be monastic, a place of privacy, a sanctuary in the city. Hence those glass panels were opaque – veils, not windows – and each one etched with an abstract pattern of entwined snakes that Kuwabara thought utterly vile, but in which I had exulted.

Meaningless now, as nothing, those prissy, aesthetic cares . . . The whole structure, which I'd planned as some dynamic mirror of self, was already a mausoleum, its flawlessness mournful. And this had been so, I understood, long before I made my 'bargain'. Whenever the courts ruled finally that Robert Forrest was dead then it would be sold, probably razed or gutted and re-converted by some property developer just as rapacious as my father, the proceeds of the sale minus death duties duly conveyed to my brave godson . . .

I heard Grey's powerful black Audi A8 growling up the street at speed before I saw it, and I hastened to hide myself between the pines. But I observed Cal climbing out, lean and robust in leather jacket and faded jeans, that angular imperious tilt to his head, eyes watchful. I had told him to follow the course of the moat-like water trough that flowed round the front of the Clinic to the back. And as he went I followed, ten wary yards between us, to the courtyard where the water burbled into boxed ponds between wooden decks, overlooked by the blank windows of the day-care suites.

I watched Cal unlock the rear door and enter, keeping the lights out as we'd agreed, swiping the wand that disabled the blinking alarm. At which point I hastened across the deck to join him within. Instantly I read his disquiet in the face of my outlandish black-clad state.

'Dijana . . . ?' he said uneasily. 'Where's Rab?'

'I will take you to him, Cal, but please, first, what we need . . .'

Passing him, I punched in the code that released the inner door. Poor Cal followed my steps faithfully through the darkened interior, past the warm-shaded leather-upholstered comfort of reception and consulting, into the immaculate clean-lined white world of Theatre. My steps were shambling, sickness coursing through me – my whole presence palpably fraudulent, I was sure. But I staggered onward, however stricken, because, now, once more, I had hope against hope.

I found the hydromorphone on the shelves in stores, but my trembling fingers caused me to drop and smash two ampoules onto the floor. I was forced to ask Cal if he would administer the injection, by no means sure of his consent as the laden hands I held out to him shook like an addict's, my eyes unreadable behind those black glasses. Possibly, in that moment, he was persuaded by the severity of the groan that issued involuntarily from my chest, and the fearsome dosage I was requesting, as would tranquillise a panther.

I ushered him to the operating room, nearly collapsed onto the mattress of the Eschmann table, and watched from recumbent as Cal scrubbed his hands, sunk a needle in the ampoule, withdrew it then flicked the spike deftly. Lolling back, I hiked up the skirt of my dress, bared my thighs and pressed with fingertips to locate a vein. As I did so, the hat fell from my head. And then, I believe – under the unflinching angle-poised light of the theatre, in what Cal could now make out of the ruined landscape of my face and thighs – he felt the enormity of what we were engaged in, the true horror of my person. He bent his troubled face down to mine, as if to identify me finally as an impostor.

And there, so close up, I recognised anew the faint purplish scarring on his left cheekbone and by the left eyebrow, the warrant of my cares for him, the protective impulse I'd always had for this bold, venturesome boy. His breath was sweet, however hard his eyes. I put my hand on his chest, as if to withstand the attack . . .

And, with a lightning surge through my diseased fingers, I could feel him – feel as if to see all the good life inside him. Life! *Strong, thick walls, elastic, turgid with the health of rich red blood* . . .

My own pulse was sinking to sludge, my breaths hoarse and heavy, vision blurring, of a piece with the crushing

434

pain in my head. I understood I was going, being sucked and torn out of the world, torn into pieces, this the near-death moment I knew better than a friend.

'Your— rash,' I heard Cal, as if from a great distance. 'It's spreading.'

It ought to have completed its work, eaten me whole. But what was inside me, that which had demanded more, was once again impossible to suppress or withstand. I had fallen before, was falling still – but the spirit's uprising couldn't be stopped.

The tremors in my fingers were resolving, not to calm but, rather, a morbid rigidity. I groped to the instrument trolley at my side, felt for the tray of sterile carbon-edged steel, my claw-fingers found and closed round a right-sized blade. Cal's eye had followed my hand, his brow creasing. With my left hand I reached and touched his face – my goodbye, my *pentimento*. He flinched, and I flung up the scalpel in my right, let the blow fall down on his neck sufficient to bury it.

ॐ

I revived to find I had toppled backward and a few yards clear of the operating table. The crown of my head was tender, had sustained quite a crack – conceivably I'd been unconscious for a while. When I stood, newly tall and rangy, seemingly full of force, all I could see on the table before me was a foul black stain-like matter, as if burnt down to powder by the fiercest furnace-like heat. A vague, acrid vapour seemed still to linger in the air.

But when I leaned close to read the runes of that stain I believed I could make out what had once been finger-nails, hair, teeth . . .

Her life-cycle appeared complete – also my own. I could glimpse my shadowy reflection in the glass sur-round of the theatre doors, and so had confirmation I was masculine and vigorous once again – renewed, re-fined, finally and irrevocably condemned.

I did not hide, but hung my head, accepted my pun-ishment, as had been decreed. I drove that fast car all the way back to its berth, stepped across the threshold of hearth and home, saw in the drawn faces of my parents how deeply and dearly I'd been awaited. And from those loving, forgiving looks I had to turn my face, since every inch of my skin felt on fire, burnt as if by the nuclear furies of the sun.

Pointless to prolong my account – attempt contrition, seek redemption, when I've played that hand and lost. The way back was shut to me at the same instant I crossed over, to the other side of the mirror. I failed to acknowledge it, I now believe, because for so much time it seemed as though my eyes merely studied the terrible things my hands did. In that way I could see myself not as malefactor but victim. Now I am moved to awe at the evil I've done; moved to wonder if it was always in me; to fear how much more I'll be made to pay for it.

I deserve to burn – ought to burn myself. I did attempt that form of atonement, since I didn't believe I could live out another day in the body of a child – a child beside whom I'd sworn always to walk, to watch over, shield from deceit and the corruption of evil. I let myself dream – a dream is all it was – that by self-destruction I could still, somehow, be saved. But my 'father', with every fibre in his being, wrenched me back onto the side of life. He would always do so, such is his virtue, blind to my wickedness. And he will always be too late. No one can be saved, not now.

But I sense I have done as She always intended – I have found 'the form that fits me'. My business with Her is closed, albeit not yet concluded. So, once again, I will take to my heels and run. If the death-pains come again, will I let them finish their work? No, I haven't got the guts for the noble Roman way, the honourable *seppuku*.

I am alive, and afraid, and in that fear I will live on until the life is torn from me.

The password, Grey, is *selvaoscura*. This and much more you must know. *'Midway upon the journey of our life I found myself within a forest dark.'* I have abandoned all hope. And yet, still, I exist.

Glossary

the criminal', Baudelaire, 'Le Crépuscule du
soir', *Les Fleurs du mal*

p. 379   '*Humani nihil a me alienum puto*' – Latin,
'Nothing human is alien to me', Terence,
Heauton Timorumenos, Act 1 Scene 1

p. 379   *mi frater* – Latin, 'my brother'

p. 410   '*avec les yeux d'un autre, de cent autres . . .*' –
French, 'with the eyes of another, a hundred
others . . .', Marcel Proust, *La Prisonnière*

p. 421   *Mund të më ndihmoni mua?* – Albanian, 'Can
you help me?'

p. 421   *gde si bio? Mi smo bili u potrazi za vas* – Serbian,
'Where have you been? We've been looking for
you'

p. 437   *seppuku* – Japanese, 'stomach-cutting, self-
disembowelment'

p. 438   *selva oscura* – Italian, 'dark forest', cf. Dante,
Inferno, Canto I, line 2

Acknowledgements

This novel has been cast within the Gothic genre, and here and there pays homage to some of the most famous novels of that style – some of these among the best-loved novels ever written. So I very much hope my various small thefts will strike the reader as respectful/affectionate, that being the intention, rather than merely larcenous/outrageous.

The actual landscape of London, north London in particular, has been used and slightly abused for the story's purpose, with the changing of some names and slight topographical modifications.

Dr Jonathan Lohn, Dr David Briess and Professor Charles Brook responded very kindly and helpfully to various research enquiries of mine. Obviously they bear no responsibility whatsoever for the fanciful uses I made of information given.

The therapeutic technique used by Steven Hartford on Eloise Keaton is an incompetent variation on Dr Francine Shapiro's renowned Eye Movement Desensitisation & Reprocessing (EMDR). It is not identified thus because Hartford's deployment of it is, as he admits, half-understood, 'improvised' and unprofessional. I'd wish no imputation whatsoever to be drawn from this fiction as to the actual effectiveness of authentic EMDR.

The cold-therapy surgical recovery mask supposedly 'invented' by Robert Forrest is a product actually invented by others, and widely available in the market, though not in black leather.

At Faber and Faber I owe a huge thanks to Lee Brackstone, the most patient, incisive and altogether canny of editors; also to Walter Donohue, Lisa Baker, Kate Ward, Kate Burton, Eleanor Crow and Rachel Alexander. I'm grateful also to Neil Titman for his careful copyediting and to my agents Kevin Conroy Scott at Tibor Jones and Christine Glover at A. P. Watt for their support and advice.

Also by Richard T. Kelly

ff

Crusaders

In 1996, just before the rise of New Labour, Reverend Gore returns to his native Newcastle charged with planting a new church in one of the city's rougher estates. As he settles into the local community, he becomes involved with Stevie, a local 'security consultant', Lindy, a street-wise single mother, and Martin, an ambitious local Labour MP. But these relationships draw Gore into a moral crisis in this extraordinary debut novel, driven by sharp social observation, darkly desperate humour and an undercurrent of impending violence.

'Kelly's seriousness of intent and direct moral interrogation call to mind contemporary American giants Roth and Mailer.' Joel Rickett, INDEPENDENT ON SUNDAY

'I can't remember a modern British debut that offers a more convincing portrait of so many different walks of life, or that paints its portrait of an era and a region with greater credibility.' Andrew Holgate, SUNDAY TIMES